GROANING
SHADOWS

GROANING SHADOWS

PAUL FINCH

GROANING SHADOWS

First published in 2009 by Gray Friar Press.
9 Abbey Terrace, Whitby,
North Yorkshire, YO21 3HQ, England.

Email: gary.fry@virgin.net
www.grayfriarpress.com

Typesetting by Gary Fry

ISBN: 978-1-906331-11-5
Trade paperback

CONTENTS

For my mum, Margaret,
and my sisters, Katie, Caroline and Charlotte,
who've encouraged me all the way.

THE SUNDERED FLESH

Ben ...

John is much better now.

This is a great relief to me as I still count myself one of his closest friends. The last time I saw him, he was capable of going outdoors on his own, even at dusk, and, according to his mother, he's now able to stand and look on the frontal façade of a church without turning hysterical and running madly in the opposite direction. She is hopeful that he'll soon be reintroduced to the world properly. He might even, one day, be able to get himself a job and some lodgings, and start to make his own way in life again. If this is true, it's great progress. But I shouldn't be too surprised. John has always been intelligent, and, like me, he's now in early middle-age, a period in life when one tends to take stock, to consider the many lessons one has learned and to apply them to one's present circumstances. It may be, therefore, that at some point in the not-too-distant future, John Price – largely through his own efforts – will re-emerge from the darkness and be as normal and rational as the next person.

I've long been close to him, unlikely though this acquaintanceship must initially have seemed. He was the first student I spoke to on my first day at university. We just happened to be in the bar together in our hall of residence, and only began to chat out of politeness. On the surface at least, we were 'chalk and cheese'. I'd always been thought of, in my Lancashire home town, as a bookworm. My appearance underlined this: I was bespectacled, nerdish, permanently dressed in out-of-date fashions, and with no physical attributes. I'd arrived at Goldsmiths College, University of London, to study History & Religion, a scholarly course that would require I spend most of my time in the library or my room, buried in books. John, on the other hand, was a student of Sports Science, and he fitted the bill for that admirably. A big, robust, southern counties lad, with a shock of golden hair, a cleft chin and sparkling blue eyes, he was personable and charismatic, and very fit. Almost everything he did bespoke virility and athleticism; he moved with a lithe, pantherish grace, which drew every female eye to him as soon as he came into a room.

It seemed unlikely to the point of implausibility that we two would hit it off together, but such is the melting-pot of university life that normal patterns of behaviour are often distorted. As a result, John and I struck up a lively relationship almost straight away. We discovered a mutual interest in movies and fantasy fiction. We found that we shared the same sense of humour, and in addition – and perhaps this the most important thing – at

1

nineteen years old, we, neither of us, had ever lived away from our parents' homes and were already, after only one day, finding London overwhelming in its noise, its brashness and its confusing cosmopolitan culture.

The sheer drabness of the place also came as a shock to us.

Goldsmiths was located close to the border between two of London's south-east boroughs, Lewisham and Southwark, and in the early 1980s both of these were in a depressed and neglected state. Crime was rife, and living conditions varied from the derelict to the nearly-derelict. It struck the two of us hard; in John's case, because he hailed from an entirely rural backwater, and in mine because, though I knew about poverty, cobbled streets and terraced houses, I'd never before seen so many tramps and diseased prostitutes, or as many back-alleys filled with discarded syringes and condoms. On top of this, the urban sprawl seemed to go on forever, extending in all directions. Our hall of residence was only five miles from the glamorous West End, but betwixt us and those lively, neon-lit streets lay a dismal concrete jungle that even the most intrepid explorer might have been loathe to challenge. This sense of embattlement drew John and I even closer together.

I mention all this as an introduction – to who we were, and to the world we suddenly found ourselves living in. Of course, in time that world was to prove far from unpleasant. The average university – even a non-campus university such as ours – has a serene ambience about it. In England, colleges tend to be ornate, ivy-clad buildings, rabbit-warrens of rooms, passages and lecture theatres; bewildering places on one's first day, but always reassuring in their aura of bookish tradition and age-old academe. Even at Goldsmiths, sandwiched between notoriously villainous housing-estates, you felt relaxed, almost coddled, as though you'd suddenly stumbled upon an oasis of peace in the midst of mayhem. But even without that, life was to treat us well. Man can attune to any environment. Within months we were cheerfully settled in that run-down corner of inner London. We had a happy circle of friends and were well advanced in our studies. Day-to-day life was hardly comfortable, but we were satisfied within ourselves, and hopes were high that good things lay ahead.

Inevitably, as the terms rolled by, and we progressed through the respective modules of our courses, the reality of thesis and examination began to descend, and by the commencement of our third year, John and I were seeing much less of each other. Geography also played its part. During our second year, John had taken a house with a bunch of other friends, while for ease of study I chose to remain in hall, so we no longer bumped into each other as often. Of course, we still met for drink-and-chat sessions, exchanged ribaldries if we spotted each other in the library, left joking messages in each other's pigeon-holes. But by the time that final third of our university tenure arrived, education was seriously weighing on us. We were loaded with work and came to lead almost solitary existences, only occasionally emerging from our rooms to stumble towards the nearest cafe or kebab shop.

It's therefore all the more remarkable that, in the February of 1985, with our 'Finals' less than four months away, I received a very curious communication from John. He left a phone message with the receptionist in my hall, asking me to contact him on an urgent matter. He even went so far as to beg me not to let him down – and those were his exact words; I must "not let him down"; "vital though I doubtless considered my studies to be, it was imperative for the sake of sanity that I break from them and go to see him".

I was still living in Lewisham at this time, though John had now taken a bed-sit flat in Camberwell, which was about two miles away and foreign territory to me. I called him back, and found myself talking to a terse, nervous individual who I barely recognised. He wouldn't give details over the phone, but insisted that we meet, so we made arrangements to see each other that evening in a pub called *The Thirsty Scholar*, situated just off the Old Kent Road, about half way between our two residences.

Thus far, I've assembled this record from my first-hand recollections. However, out of necessity, much of it will need to be heard in John's own words. I visited him several times in 1986, during his period of recuperation at the Mile End Hospital for the Seriously Disturbed, and was able to glean some notes from his tortured ramblings. I've now edited and re-ordered these, and am able to proceed with this narrative as though, at certain points in it, John himself is giving a personal account.

John ...

I got the first letter in mid-December, and the second one shortly after I'd returned from my Christmas holidays. The envelopes were grubby, thumbed and dog-eared, the handwriting on them done in blotchy red ink, and spidery almost to the point of being illegible. Neither was signed, but both requested that I attend a certain address – 79, Bermondsey Wall – at my earliest convenience, as it would be of "great interest and benefit" to me.

For those who don't realise it, college life is filled with this sort of oddity – anonymous contacts, notes from people you've never heard of before, in-house mail that has been misdirected. Even then, the missives concerned are usually a jape, or they're seeking to recruit you (perhaps to some pointless society that you expressed an interest in while you were drunk at the Freshers' Ball). Either that or they want to evangelise you:

3

universities are packed with sects and cults and even mainstream religious groups who view themselves as missionaries in a godless world. In any case, I scrunched the notes up, tossed them in the trash and got on with my life. There were other things on my mind that were of far greater interest: primarily my growing affection for Josie Wilkes, who was now, I finally realised, much more than just a girl I'd taken to bed after a party. We'd had five dates by that December, and were getting on really well. I know that blokes like Ben Carter called me superficial for it, but I'd always gone for girls who were what you'd describe as 'lookers'; usually blonde, usually pretty, and usually stacked. And Josie, being a trainee-dancer at the Laban Centre – an arts institute associated with the college – was all these things and more. In addition, she was lively, talkative and fun to be with, and by the Christmas of 1984 I was definitely starting to think that she might be 'the one'.

In that respect, it surely isn't surprising that I gave the two letters from Bermondsey only minimal attention. Josie was taking up most of my time, while my build-up to the Finals, then only six months away, was coming in a close second. I had what you might call a full calendar.

The third letter, however, was less easy to ignore.

To begin with, it had been written in large, jagged, spiky characters – as though the correspondent had been extremely angry at the time. Secondly, it no longer promised dividends if I responded, but was openly threatening if I didn't, and I quote:

Your continued disregard of my invitation could be deemed one of two things: pig-ignorance, or rank bad manners. Either way, I suggest you reverse this attitude of yours promptly, and attend me, as I have requested.

Thirdly, it ended in some kind of religious quotation, which I found vaguely ominous:

Oh wretched man that I am! Who shall deliver me from the body of this death?

Fourthly, and perhaps most worryingly of all, there was neither a postmark nor a stamp upon it, which suggested that it had been delivered to my residence by hand.

My first reaction to this was, again, that it was a joke. But as I read and re-read it, I wondered if I might have offended someone. Could it be a jilted ex-boyfriend of Josie's? If so, she'd never mentioned one. In fact, I'd had no trouble with anyone that I was aware of. The address I was

4

being asked to attend was the same as before: 79 Bermondsey Wall. I consulted my London A-Z, and only found it after some considerable leafing back and forth. It was on the south bank of the River Thames, just across the water from Wapping. At the time, this was a warehouse district, much of it derelict or in redevelopment as part of the ever-expanding 'Docklands' scheme.

I considered taking the letter to my personal-tutor, maybe even the police. But eventually I relented on that. As a criminal offence, 'stalking' was unrecognised back in the mid-1980s, and even if it hadn't been, it wasn't the sort of thing that grown young men reported. Of course, I wasn't stupid enough to just go up there and knock on the front door. Instead, I opted to check the address out from a distance. The following Saturday, I would catch a bus to Bermondsey and view the place from the anonymity of a nearby street-corner. Josie was performing that afternoon, as the Laban Centre was involved in a local arts festival, so I'd have the whole day to myself.

London's Docklands has become a byword for successful urban redevelopment.

Mention the word 'Docklands' now and most folks will picture the glittering glass towers around Canary Wharf, the slick new overland railway on the Isle of Dogs, the swish wine-bars, the purpose-built hotels and business venues, the many quays, pier-heads and jetties all adapted into attractive, landscaped features. But it wasn't always so. When I was at college in south-east London, the Docklands was somewhere you didn't go unless you had to, and even if you had to, you didn't go there at night.

Of course, it wasn't night when I finally answered that third letter, it was mid-afternoon. But it was a bitterly cold January day – the thin covering of snow had turned to sheet-ice, while the droning wind had a knife-like edge – and a part of London where nobody lived and nobody worked any more, so I expected to find it deserted. I wasn't wrong; the moment I got off the bus, the sense of loneliness was tangible.

The bus-top was close to a row of houses, though all of these now stood empty and were blocked off at their doors with sheets of corrugated iron. The dismal plots that had once been their front gardens were deep in frozen weeds and the frosted-over detritus of drink and drug abuse. When I set off northwards, even this sad remnant of community gave out to the vast but silent structures of what had once been the East India Company warehouses. These great, cavernous buildings occupied the riverfront for miles. They were ranked against the water's edge three or four deep, creating a city within a city – an eerie place of silence and solitude. When I ventured among them, it was like entering a labyrinth. There was an

5

uncanny stillness. My footfalls clicked loudly in the frigid air. I glanced upwards and saw rusted girders criss-crossing the sky, pieces of guttering hanging loose, birds' nests stuffed into the recesses where bricks or ventilation grilles had fallen away.

According to my A-Z, *this* was Bermondsey Wall.

I began to check around for numbers, and found many of them still legible, painted on the various doors that I passed – 72, 73, 74, 75. They even alternated from left to right, the way they would in a normal residential district, though these doors were all made of steel or heavy timber, and had mostly been locked and chained. It was a surprise, therefore, to reach the point where 79 should be, and find a hive of activity. I rounded a corner, expecting another warehouse door, and was confronted by a busy demolition site. It was strewn with brick-rubble, and thronging with workmen all gloved and helmeted, and packaged against the cold in donkey-jackets or thick plaid shirts. Trucks and earth-movers were also present, alongside piles of building materials, and several deep trenches, which looked as though they'd been dug for the purpose of laying pipes or foundations.

Close to me, a hydraulic lifter was shuffling back and forth, tank-like, on gigantic caterpillar tracks. Its engine-pipe pumped out noxious fumes, and a yellow beacon-light spun on top of its driving-cab. Its motors made a deafening roar. In addition to lifting-forks at the front, which were currently laden with massive, squared-off sections of concrete, the lifter was also equipped with a huge jib, which projected maybe thirty feet into the air. A winch was fixed at the top of this and heavy chains descended from it. They swung dangerously as the metal mastodon pirouetted around on the pulverised earth. The instant its driver saw me, he shut the machine down and leaned out of the cab. He was a burly guy in his thirties, with scars on his cheeks and hanks of black hair hanging from under his hardhat.

"Oy!" he shouted in broad Cockney. "What's your game?"

"Sorry," I said, approaching. "I don't mean to trespass, but I'm supposed to be meeting someone."

He looked puzzled. "One of the crew?"

"No ... well, truth is I don't know. Is this 79 Bermondsey Wall?"

He stuck a gloved thumb over his shoulder. "*That* is. But there's no-one there."

I gazed past him, at the side of an old church.

I hadn't noticed it amid the general dereliction because it so was disused. Planks were fastened across its broken windows; its brick walls were black with soot. I thanked the guy and trudged off across the rubble.

"I said there's nobody in there," he shouted after me.

6

"I know." I glanced back. "But I might as well check now I've come."

"You shouldn't be here at all."

"I'll not be long."

He said nothing else, but continued to lean out of the cab, watching me, until at last I'd rounded the corner of the church. I was now in front of its main doors, of which there were two pairs, spaced about twenty feet apart. Both were chained up, but between them, fixed to the stonework, was an old message-board. A sheet of glass had once protected this from the elements, but only teeth of it now remained, so the hardboard beneath had mildewed badly. Not that it was completely unreadable. Along the top, I was able to make out the vague words:

79 Bermondsey Wall

and beneath that,

St. Wulfstan's C of E

I took the pad and pen from my bomber-jacket and noted it down. I also checked the rest of the wording, though from what I could gather this was nothing more than a schedule for services, community group meetings and such.

Someone then came round the corner and confronted me. This time, I suspect, it was the foreman of the site. He was a big black guy who looked like a boxer. He had a shaved head under his hardhat, and a square, sturdy body sheathed in fluorescent waterproofs.

"This is private property," he said sternly.

"Yeah, I'm sorry. I'm going now. Someone was supposed to be meeting me here, but I think it's a wind-up."

"Nobody comes here," he said, adding rather unnecessarily: "This church is closed."

"Any idea how long it's been closed for?"

"Good few years I reckon. Are you going to hop it, or what?"

"Yeah." I shoved my notebook away. Then something else occurred to me; an odd kind of thought but one that was maybe worth investigating. "I don't suppose there's a vicarage attached to it? Or a presbytery? I mean … that would have the same address, wouldn't it?"

He eyed me suspiciously. "What're you up to? Don't you know this whole neighbourhood's condemned?"

"Yeah, I know that, but well … it's quite important."

There was a brief silence as he weighed me up. Almost certainly he was contemplating the best and most legal way to eject me from the premises without having to go to the trouble of getting the police to do it for him. Someone called him from the other side of the site. Irritably, he glanced over his shoulder.

"I'll be out of the way as soon as I've checked it," I said.

The foreman was called again, and now it became apparent that his presence was needed urgently. He glanced back at me, and reluctantly nodded. "Okay ... there's a house on the other side. You can get to it through that ginnel." He indicated a narrow passage, the entrance to which lay beyond the right-hand set of doors. "But listen," and he started backing away, "when you've finished there, I don't want you coming here again. We can't stop work just for sightseers, yeah?"

"Yeah," I agreed.

"Clear off when you're done. We have enough trouble with Skid Row types hanging about." And he was gone, walking back around the corner.

I took the ginnel he'd told me about, and followed it down to the far end of the church, where I turned right onto a small access-road. And came to an abrupt halt.

I gazed up at what must once have been a grand Victorian townhouse. The porch was arched in archetypical ecclesiastical fashion, as were the windows to either side of it, though both of these were broken and boarded with planks. When I pushed at the rusted iron gate, it fell from its hinges. I walked through, and, finding no possible access via the front door, sidled around the building, passing through a garden that was now just frozen twigs, and finally discovering one smashed window that hadn't yet been blocked off, or if it had, the blockade had since been removed, probably by junkies.

I peered through it into a dank recess that stank of decay.

I was tempted to call out, to announce my arrival, even to eff and blind – to finally get vexed about the intrusion on my life that this nameless correspondent was making. But for some reason now, I didn't want to. I didn't want anyone to even know that I was here. But now that I *was* here, it would seem like cowardice not to at least explore.

Very warily, I climbed through – into an old closet or scullery. It was a tiny room, completely bare of décor, but an open door connected it to the rest of the house.

I paused, took a deep breath, zipped my jacket tightly and commenced a slow, stealthy investigation. It struck me straight away that the vicarage hadn't been abandoned for very long. It was damp throughout; everywhere the wallpaper hung off in strips, the skirting-boards were green with mould, but nowhere was it dripping, nowhere had the floors rotted through. There was even the odd item of furniture; an old bureau in what once might have been the study, a gutted armchair in a spacious, lounge-type room. There was also evidence of vandalism. In the central hall, on the wall facing the bottom of the stairs, in an explosion of blood-red spray-paint, I read another of those bizarre quasi-religious quotations:

Wheresoever the carcass is, there will be eagles gathered together

In the kitchen area, a second one read:

Turn you to the stronghold, ye prisoners of hope

The kitchen was the most furnished room that I'd so far seen. Many of its fittings were still in place, albeit thick with grime. But in the pale winter's light it made for a melancholy scene. A gust of icy wind set its shutters tapping and hinges creaking. From the outside, I could still hear the sounds of the workmen, though they were muffled and distant. Aside from these, I knew there wasn't another human being in miles. This place was as bleak and soulless as anywhere I'd ever been. Suddenly I just wanted to go, to head straight for home. There was nothing for me here. I'd been duped. But of course, one other thing remained. One thing that would nag me endlessly if I didn't at least take a look at it.

The upper floor.

Don't get me wrong, I didn't *want* to go up there. Not at all. This scabrous ruin of a house was oppressing me with its dinginess, its dankness, its aura of neglect. Yet I was acutely aware that I still hadn't fully inspected it. I could go back to Camberwell if I wanted to, relieved that I'd been here and had found nothing, but I knew that if I went back without having looked over the *entirety* of the house, and then those letters started arriving again, I'd only have to return. And that was something I was absolutely sure I didn't want to do.

So – yes, the upstairs.

On the way up, every stair-tread groaned. At the top, positioned so as to immediately strike anyone who'd ascended, was yet more graffiti, again in shocking, blood-red paint:

Put thy shoes from off thy feet, for the place whereon thou standest is holy ground

I gazed at it for several moments before moving on, prowling from room to room. Again, every window was broken, though often there were shreds of curtains still attached, their ratty, dust-thick material rustling in the breeze. Finally, at the very rear of the house, I found evidence of *recent* habitation.

An odious mattress, black with soaked-in filth, lay in the middle of the room, surrounded by torn-open tins, empty milk-cartons and the scraps of discarded food. There was even a bucket in one corner, filled with what looked like toilet slops. If the thermometer hadn't been hovering just below zero, I suspect the stench would have been intolerable. Not that it wasn't bad enough. I still had to wrinkle my nose.

I stood in the doorway, surveying the disgusting scene and now getting the distinct impression that I was being watched. It was deeply discomforting, but at least it meant that I was onto something. I picked my way around the mattress to the other side – where I made a find that stopped me in my tracks.

A pile of grubby envelopes and folded sheets of letter-paper lay next to the mattress, all bound together with elastic bands. Inserted under the bands was a red biro.

Only with trembling hands was I able to reach down and pick these items up. But before I could pocket them as evidence, I noticed something else underneath them. It was flat and squarish, and, though faded, covered with what had once been colourful if arcane illustrations – suns, moons, shooting stars, symbols of the zodiac. Arranged around its edges, in symmetrical patterns, were the ten digits and the letters of the alphabet.

I didn't have to be an expert on the occult to recognise a Ouija board.

And that was when I heard the faint shuffle overhead.

I looked slowly up.

I don't know how long he'd been there, in the loft trapdoor, watching me. I couldn't see too much of him. Owing to a shaft of watery light slanting across the loft behind him, he was little more than a silhouette, albeit a hideously thin and ragged one, though in this case his thinness didn't necessarily equate with frailty. He seemed to be hunched, half-coiled, like some predatory beast about to drop down and attack. I saw hands gripping the edges of the trapdoor that were grey with filth, and though narrow and wizened, bearing long, yellow fingernails that were more like talons. Amid the frenzied, mop-like hair, which hung over his face, I imagined two crimson slits for eyes.

I ran for my life.

I don't mind admitting it.

After everything else, to find an apparition like that not three feet above my head was too much. I bolted through the door and along the landing towards the top of the stairs. From somewhere behind me, I heard a shrill, bird-like screech, followed immediately by a loud *thump*. Then feet were coming in pursuit. It made me run all the harder; I hurtled down the stairs regardless of how rickety they were. Once I got to the ground floor, all manner of rubbish hampered me – I slipped and tripped on just about everything, but the next thing I knew I had kicked my way outside via the kitchen's loosely-boarded back door. Soon I was on the river-front itself, dashing eastwards along a muddy walkway. To my right, there were more sealed entrances to abandoned warehouses; to my left, the waters of the Thames slapped on the silted embankment. I still felt trapped, hemmed in. This entire stretch of the river was deserted; on its far bank I saw only more gaunt relics of Victorian industry. Nobody was around. So I ran even faster. And it must have been for miles, the heart jack-hammering in my chest, the sweat pumping out of me. I glanced back once, half-expecting to see a lunatic shape on my tail, but thankfully there was nobody there.

A relatively short time after this – though it seemed like an eternity to me – I cut back inland, following a railed path to a disused kiddies' playground. On the other side of that, I managed to jump on a bus just as it was pulling away.

It's a difficult thing, fear.

Healthy young men aren't supposed to feel it. They certainly aren't supposed to run from it like headless chickens. But that evening, as I sat there in my room, the darkness of winter having fallen outside, only a dull black-and-white glow emanating from my crackly old portable TV, I felt no shame. If anything, I was still in shock, still amazed that I'd managed to get away at all. The sweat that coated me like grease was ice-cold; I was still breathing hard, still trembling.

Of course, in one respect all this seemed ridiculous. I'd been living for two and a half years in one of London's toughest neighbourhoods. In that time I'd had several close-calls, only just avoiding confrontations with drunken vagrants or student-hunting Millwall fans. Yet on all those occasions, afterwards, once safe and sound again, I'd been able to laugh it off, to mark it as another thread in the rich tapestry of life that was south-east London. But this incident had been *too* unnerving. I felt like a mouse who'd just spent ten minutes trying to get a piece of cheese off a trap, and had finally given up and wandered away a split-second before the trap sprung; or like some fly, who'd toddled all over a spider's web and, by some miracle, had not adhered to it, while all the time the loathsome, multi-eyed predator was watching from a close but shadowed corner.

All I could do was sit there and ponder. When I'd first got home, I'd found a note from Josie to the effect that the arts festival had been a success, and that she and various friends were going to celebrate in *The Rosemary Branch*, the pub next door to college. I unhesitatingly dismissed her request that I meet her there. Apart from anything else, she'd be with her dancer mates, nearly all of the male ones being gay. (Remember, this was 1985, and in those days twenty-one-year-old straights didn't willingly associate with 'queers'). Additionally, the majority of them – both girls and boys – were pretentious arseholes who I couldn't stand on principle.

But of course, these were nothing more than excuses. In reality, I was too nervous to go outside; though even staying indoors I didn't feel one hundred-per-cent safe.

And with good reason.

I was disturbed at about two o'clock in the morning by sounds of movement. I sat up in bed, instantly wide-awake. I'd been dreaming about snow-filled ruins along the Thames river-front, about icy winds and bizarre, sacrilegious texts scrawled on the walls, so I was already primed for an alarmed response.

I heard the sound again – a faint *scratch*, followed by a distinct rustling, as of paper. I knew immediately what it was; somebody was pushing a note under my door.

There could be a perfectly legitimate reason for this. But I doubted it.

Once again, my heart started slamming my ribs; the sweat ran so cold on my body that my teeth began to chatter. Fear. All over again, though this time with a difference. Because now there was nowhere to run to. All of a sudden the fight-or-flight response was on me, and this time *fight* was the only option. I leaped from the bed, grabbing out for my bed-side lamp and snapping it on. Yes, a scruffy letter had indeed just been shoved under the door, and even from this distance I could see that it bore the usual red ink scribbles on its cover.

My blood up, I bounded across the room, turned the lock and yanked the door open.

The house I was living in was typical of the terraced Edwardian townhouses now gone badly to seed that make up so much of London's inner suburbs. It had long ago been divided into apartments, though 'apartments' is perhaps the wrong word; it creates an impression of well-heeled comfort, whereas in fact these apartments were nothing more than an extension of student bed-sit land. Outside in the passage, the carpet was embedded with the crumbs of decades. The window at the top of the stairs had been broken ages back, and was still covered with a polythene sheet, now greenish and liberally streaked with bird-droppings. At least three bicycles were always in attendance, padlocked to the upper banisters. It was cold and dark even during the day, and smelled permanently of damp.

I charged out into it, just in time to see a spry figure darting down the stairs.

"Hey!" I shouted. "Hey … *you bastard!*"

Despite my terror, I gave chase, but he reached the ground floor before I did, clearly intending to go out of the house the way he had come in. A single-panelled window to the right of the main front door had been jemmied open, and he lurched towards it, coming briefly into view in the pale moonlight. He seemed to be wearing a single garment, which hung as far as his feet. It was like a woman's dress, but of heavy, dark material. As before, his hair was a tangled mop, lank, hanging in all directions. He was carrying some kind of large tool, which I fancied might be a chisel.

"You bastard!" I shouted again. "Who the hell do you think you are?"

And that was a fortuitous call, because this time he glanced around at me – and tripped, going sprawling to the floor right in front of the window.

I jumped down the last few stairs, and was on him. Though he'd frightened me earlier, I now had the righteous wrath of the enraged citizen. Before I knew what I was doing, I was hitting him with both fists, though that was a mistake. What I *should* have done was try to restrain him and call for help from one of the other residents. The intruder, who was strong and wiry, was therefore able to wriggle free and clamber back to his feet. I tried to get up as well, but now he smashed his chisel down on my right shoulder. Pain lanced through me. I gasped, twisted to one side. He turned to continue his escape, but I grappled with him again, this time going for his throat and managing to catch him in a choke-hold. He resisted furiously, throwing himself about like an eel. My hands slipped loose, so I grasped at his clothing, snatching hold of his collar and hanging onto it for dear life.

And that was when he stabbed me.

I was clearly stronger and fitter than he was. I guess he felt he had no option.

He thrust the chisel point-first at my already battered shoulder. The blade ploughed through the upper muscle, hacking out a great chunk of flesh. The pain was searing, blinding; I felt hot slime gush down over my naked chest.

I tottered away, clutching at the wound, while the intruder, with lithe athleticism, vaulted out through the tiny window. I was only wearing under-shorts and, even if he hadn't been armed, it would have been foolish to pursue him, but I was too angered to just sit there in the darkness and mope. So I turned the key to the inside door, tramped over the heap of bills and free newspapers in the porch, and drew back the bolt on the outer door.

The five steps leading down through what our landlord laughably described as 'a front garden' were deserted. I descended them to the pavement, looking left and right. But the frosty street was bare of life. The only sign that anyone had been there was the piece of torn clothing I still had in my hand.

13

I peered down at it, dumbfounded.

Ben ...

It was midweek, so even a popular haunt like *The Thirsty Scholar* was relatively quiet. Not that I'd easily have noticed anyone else in the pub that night. Quite frankly, I couldn't believe the state John was in.

He was seated opposite me in a corner of the snug. We were both nursing pints of bitter, but whereas I was half way through mine, John's sat untouched, even though we'd been in there ten minutes. We were always fairly casual – jeans, sweat-tops, sneakers, that sort of thing – but John's gear was mussed, rumpled, even dirty. He looked exhausted; he was blotchy, sallow-cheeked, bleary-eyed. And he evidently hadn't shaved for days. Not that any of this was surprising after the story he'd just told me. Even under his loose running-top, I could see that his left shoulder was misshapen. I put that down to the extensive dressing that they'd applied at Lewisham Casualty.

"How's the wound now?" I asked him.

He shrugged, as if the wound was scarcely important.

I looked down at the letter he'd handed me. This was apparently the most recent one, the one that had actually sparked his clash with the intruder. It was everything he'd said the others had been – grubby, dog-eared, written in garish red ink, though phrased with sufficient eloquence to suggest that the perpetrator was an educated man. It read:

I appreciate that you have finally responded to my missives. However, I do not appreciate that you entered my house uninvited. Thus, I am returning the favour. The next time, I trust that you will do as I ask, and meet me in St. Wulfstan's Church.

Below that, was another of those flowery quotations:

My father hath chastised you with whips, but I will chastise you with scorpions

John was correct in his assumption that it was biblical in origin. I recognised it immediately. It came from the *Book of Kings.*

"And you've absolutely no idea what this is all about?" I asked him.

He shook his head. "None at all, I swear it."

"In which case, you've got to go to the cops."

"But he hasn't really done anything wrong, has he?"

"He stabbed you!"

"Yeah, he could claim self-defence."

14

"John, he broke into the house."

John shook his head. "Into the communal area. He didn't try to enter any of the private apartments."

"I'm sure the police will still be interested in talking to him."

He watched me steadily, seemingly more confused than frightened. He was pale, incredibly haggard. "What I really don't understand is *this*."

And he indicated the second object that he'd brought into the pub. It sat on the table between us. It was a hard circlet of stiff material, filmy with grime; almost brown whereas once it had been white. I could see dried blood-spots on it, but it wasn't difficult to recognise a clerical collar.

"Does anyone else apart from priests wear these things?" John wondered.

"Not unless it's for fancy dress."

"And then there're those religious passages."

He'd made copies of the ones he'd seen in the house. A couple, I'd recognised instantly. The one about standing on holy ground came from *Exodus*. The one about the carcass and the eagles was from St. Matthew.

"And that church?" John added. "St. Wulfstan's ... I mean, what's all that about?"

"I can check *that* out for you, at least," I said. "One of my course-tutors has got contacts at Lambeth Palace. There are bound to be records of all the churches in London, and the stories behind them."

He nodded and sat back.

"You're a wreck, pal," I told him. "How soon do you start your Finals?"

He gave a contemptuous snort. "Jesus ... I haven't even thought about those."

"You're going to have to soon. You don't want to throw three years of college away."

"Tell me about it. Not easy, though ... with this thing hanging round my neck."

"I still think it's a police job."

He sighed. "If all else fails, it will be. But I don't fancy that. I mean, I broke into *his* house first, didn't I."

"You broke into a derelict house. There's a difference."

He shook his head. "I don't know what the hell I broke into. I'll tell you, Ben ..." and he visibly shuddered, "that's the weirdest set-up I've ever seen."

We left the pub side-by-side, chatting idly.

I tried to steer the conversation onto other subjects, but it was impossible. John made several brave attempts to go along with me, but

15

invariably would fall silent and gloomily survey the pavement as we strode along.

I wasn't sure exactly what I was able to do for him, but I knew that I *could* look into the matter of the derelict church. Therefore, my first port of call the next day was the college library, though, only after several hours spent wading through a variety of old documentation, did I find anything referring to a St. Wulfstan; St Wulfstan of Haselbury, an English hermit of the twelfth century, who had reputedly enjoyed the gift of prophecy. Of course, this didn't help me much. As I'd suspected, I was going to have to go all the way to Lambeth Palace, where detailed records were kept, to find anything about the church building.

As it transpired, this wasn't as difficult to arrange as I'd feared. Initially, I had to tell my tutor the truth about my mission. He was startled and, as I'd done, advocated police involvement. I pointed out that for some reason not yet clear John sought to avoid this, and added that, for the moment at least, I was purely interested in the background of St. Wulfstan's. After expressing some reservations, my tutor acquiesced and made a phone-call on my behalf. As a result, the following Monday, at ten o'clock in the morning, I was admitted to the Palace – the central offices of the Church of England and indeed the Anglican Communion worldwide – located in Archbishop's Park, just across the Thames from Westminster. I was shown through to one of its many reception chambers, a small oak-panelled reading-room, complete with ornate stone cornices, a leather topped desk and a well-stocked wood-fire. I sat and waited, and was presently greeted by one of the Palace librarians, an elderly white-haired cleric, who told me to call him Barry. He shook my hand, sat across the desk from me and laid out a variety of dusty tomes.

"I understand you wanted some information about the archdiocese's various deconsecrated churches?" he said.

I took out my pen and notebook. "Well … one of them."

"One of them?"

"St Wulfstan's, Southwark."

Barry's snowy eyebrows arched, and, rather comically, his mouth made a perfect O.

"St Wulfstan's?" he finally said. His demeanour had rapidly changed from one of casual friendliness to one of cautious uncertainty. I didn't need to be a detective to sense that I was on the trail of something.

Barry pursed his lips as he considered, and, with a distinct lack of enthusiasm, began to pick his way through an especially large volume, finally settling on a page half way in.

"St. Wulfstan's, Southwark," he said, pausing to clear his throat. "Well … it ceased to function as a church in 1969."

"Why would that be?"

"The usual reasons." He eyed me. "May I ask why you're interested in St. Wulfstan's? I was led to believe you had a wider remit."

"Oh, it's just part of my course?"

"St. Wulfstan's is?"

I nodded brightly.

"Have you been there?"

"No, but I plan to."

"I shouldn't!" And he said that very quickly, almost as though alarmed. Then he smiled again. "What I mean is, well ... it's not the most salubrious part of London. In fact, it's rather dangerous. That whole area's being redeveloped. St Wulfstan's itself is due to go under the demolisher's hammer some time soon."

And that *did* interest me. St. Wulfstan's was clearly the centre of John's problem, and now I learned that it only had a short time to live. There could easily be a connection there. Interesting though it was to ponder this, it hadn't gone unnoticed by me that Barry had subtly altered the direction of the conversation.

I decided to alter it back.

"With regard to St. Wulfstan's being closed," I said "I know the area's derelict now. But it wasn't in 1969. Most of the dock-yards were still working then, weren't they?"

"Yes they were," he admitted. "But as a residential district, Bermondsey Wall was ... well, dying. There was virtually no congregation there at all by the end of the '60s."

"I don't suppose you'd know who the last incumbent was?"

He nodded, but, again, didn't seem especially eager to part with this information.

"It would be helpful," I said.

"Yes ... er, that would've been Reverend Lassiter."

"You sound as though you know him?"

"I know *of* him."

"And ... just out of interest, what happened to him? After the church was closed, I mean."

Barry thought about this, then, rather firmly, closed the book. "Reverend Lassiter retired to the country, I believe. He has a sister who lives at a place called Ringwood. I think he went to live with her."

"Is he still alive, do you know?"

"I don't know," Barry said, standing.

"I don't suppose you have a contact number for his sister?"

"Even if I did," and he moved to the door, pointedly opening it for me, "I wouldn't be able to give out that sort of personal information."

17

"Of course not," I said.

I thanked him politely, gathered my gear and left.

My interview at Lambeth Palace hadn't been all I'd hoped it would be, though I *had* learned something; namely, that discussions about St. Wulfstan's, Southwark, and more importantly, Reverend Lassiter, the last vicar there, were off-limits. But the librarian's attitude, rather than dissuading me, had made me even more suspicious, and his ill-advised mentioning of Reverend Lassiter's sister had provided another lead.

Once again, I made progress more quickly than I'd hoped. The only Ringwood I could find in the atlas was a small country town in Hampshire, and I promptly found a phone book for it. It occurred to me, of course, that the retired cleric's sister might no longer be contactable under her maiden name, or that she might not even be living. But I was determined to try, so I scanned through the directory, found half a page of Lassiters, and rang them one after another. This was the era before mobile phones, so it cost me more ten-pence pieces than I wanted to spend, and more time in a tobacco-imbued payphone than was probably good for me, but, after drawing ten blanks, I finally struck gold.

"Er ... Mrs. Lassiter?" I said.

"Miss." She was an elderly lady, shrill of tone. "Who's speaking please?"

"Hello, Miss Lassiter ... my name is Benjamin Carter. You don't know me, but I'm a student at Goldsmiths College, London. I was wondering if I might speak to you about something."

There was a suspicious silence at the other end.

"I received your name from Lambeth Palace," I added.

"Oh, from the Palace." Now she sounded interested, even flattered. More to the point, she *didn't* sound surprised. I mean, how many people will get an enquiry via Lambeth Palace, and *not* be surprised? I was suddenly sure this was the person I was looking for.

"Miss Lassiter," I said, "I'm trying to make contact with your brother."

"I have three brothers," she replied. "Well ... *had*. Two of them are dead."

"Oh, I'm sorry. The one I was thinking about was a man of the cloth. Vicar at St. Wulfstan's in Southwark, I believe?"

"Yes," she said. "That would be Roland. *He's* still alive."

"Oh good ..."

"But I don't know where he is."

"Ah ... I was under the impression that he'd retired to live with you back in 1969?"

18

"Oh no, not at all." She paused, as if again wondering exactly who I was and what my business might be. "No, 1969 was the year in which he was defrocked."

"Defrocked?"

"Yes. He was quite opposed to them closing his church, you see. He wrote many letters, led campaigns to keep the place open."

"To keep the place open ... right." Again, I felt I was making ground. "Well, that puzzles me a little bit, Miss Lassiter. St. Wulfstan's was in an empty part of London, wasn't it? They *had* to close it down."

"Not at all. At least not in 1969. There was a thriving community there then."

"I see. And your brother made this point?"

"Indeed he did. Most forcefully." A hint of regret came into her voice. "Rather too forcefully, I'm afraid. He went to Lambeth Palace personally. Made a sit-down protest outside its doors, and when he was invited inside, got into an argument with the archbishop, finally becoming aggressive. Even violent."

I wasn't sure how to respond. The idea of a vicar getting violent with his own archbishop was something quite novel even in an irreverent age like the 1980s.

Miss Lassiter seemed to sense this. She added: "My brother was ex-military, you see. During the war in Korea, he was a chaplain in the Commonwealth Brigade. He was quite young then, of course, but like most soldiers, very fit and well trained. He was involved in the fighting on Hill 355, and even though he wore the clerical collar, he still picked up a rifle and joined in."

I thought of the blood-stained collar on the pub table in *The Thirsty Scholar.*

"So what happened after he was defrocked?" I asked.

"I'd have to say, I don't know. I've never spoken to him since. I receive occasional letters from him, telling me how he is, how he feels life in Britain is deteriorating. He's quite 'High Church' in his views, you see ... staunchly Anglican. Very old-fashioned."

"Miss Lassiter ... do you mind me asking you, are these letters rather untidy?"

"Excuse me?"

"Written in red ink perhaps?"

"Red ink? Well, yes. But, I don't really see how ..."

"Please Miss Lassiter, this is very important. I know someone else who's been receiving letters from your brother, but these are unpleasant letters. Threatening letters."

For several seconds there was complete silence, just dead air. I half-expected the old lady to hang up indignantly, but she didn't. Instead she gave a long, heart-felt sigh, before saying: "I'm afraid Roland's temper was always his Achilles heel. That was probably the soldier in him. He was always a good preacher, a determined leader of men. But on a one-to-one basis he could be quite difficult. And this got worse after the Korean War. He was taken prisoner by the communists, you see. And I'm afraid they rather mistreated him."

"How terrible."

"Of course, none of this had anything to do with the closure of St. Wulfstan's," she added. "After my brother was dismissed, the church was still deconsecrated and shut down. Personally, I think it was because of the disturbances there."

"Sorry ... the disturbances?"

"St. Wulfstan's was a very disturbed building, Mr. Carter. It long had been."

"In what sense?"

"In the sense that it was haunted. I think the term for it now is ... polter ...?"

"Poltergeist?" I suggested, feeling a chill down my back.

"That's it. Poltergeist activity. Things were thrown, broken. There were strange noises ... cries, groans. It got so that people living and working nearby became wary of going near the place."

"And that's why it was eventually closed?"

"Well ... an investigation was held. I think an attempt was even made to exorcise the building, though my brother objected most strongly to this." The old lady's tone seemed to sadden. "He felt that he could contact the spirit and reason with it."

"Reason with it?"

"I'm not sure whether he was in the right mind at this time," she said. "It was in the final run-up to his expulsion. He must've been very distracted. But he felt sure the spirit was trying to pass on a message, and that he, as someone who'd been close to death several times, was the ideal person to interpret that message."

"I don't suppose he ever worked out what it was?"

"Not as he ever told me." But she seemed to stop and ponder. "He *did* mention that it was from someone called Scott. I think he said ... yes, James Scott. Someone called James Scott."

"James Scott?" I repeated slowly.

"Yes. But shortly after this, Roland was defrocked. And, as I said, I've never had a conversation with him since. There are no return addresses on

20

any of his letters. Excuse me, you *did* say you were calling from Lambeth Palace?"

But I was hardly listening. Thus far, I'd been trying to solve John's problem with the wrong half of my personal expertise. I'd been looking for the solution in religion. Maybe I should have been looking in history.

John ...

It was a relief to have Ben on the case. The plain fact that I'd been able to talk to someone about it had relieved the pressure a little. But in my heart of hearts I knew I couldn't leave it at that. I mean, at the end of the day, what was Ben apart from a college friend whose nerdish intellect might cast a modicum of light on the problem?

For my own part, I was well aware that I was letting everything else slip. I hadn't done any work in several weeks. A number of essays were over-due, and I hadn't even started the prep-work on my thesis. It was madness to continue ignoring these things, but the necessary concentration was out of reach. I wasn't eating or sleeping properly, and felt constantly strained and tired. I couldn't go out of the house without glancing over my shoulder, and on at least two occasions – once late evening in the changing-rooms attached to the college gym, and another time, while walking back through the subway from New Cross Station – I'd become convinced that I was being followed, and had ended up running as if every devil in Hell was after me.

Another part of my life that I was neglecting was my relationship with Josie. She'd left several messages by this time, and I hadn't responded to any, the reason being that I didn't know what to say to her. Pretending everything was okay and behaving as normal, was simply not on. I was being stalked by a potentially dangerous enemy, and to bring a girlfriend along under those circumstances would have been reckless in the extreme. Of course, I couldn't tell her this. She'd do as Ben first had, and insist I inform the law.

Which, again, was totally out of the question.

There were good reasons why I didn't want to go to the police, though they weren't reasons I was comfortable admitting, even to my girlfriend or my best mate. It's not something I even like putting down in writing. Basically, some three years earlier, back home in St Albans, I'd been convicted of burglary and, as a result, had drawn a six-month suspended sentence. I should hastily add that my crime hadn't been burglary in the traditional sense. I was coming home after a drunken night out, and suddenly passed a newsagents shop, which, as a schoolboy, I'd been banned from by an over-zealous proprietor. In a fit of intoxicated pique, I picked up a brick and threw it at the window, which duly shattered. The next thing I knew, a range of quality goods were suddenly available to me – and this included fireworks. It was the final week in October when this happened. A friend's bonfire party wasn't too far in the future, and, in my semi-inebriated state, it now occurred to me how heroic I'd appear if I turned up there with armfuls of extra rockets. I thus reached in and began to cherry-pick the best items. At that same moment, the proprietor, who I'd forgotten lived over the shop, came out and tried to grab me. I ran, but he still recognised me, and the following day I was arrested.

In court, I blamed my drunkenness, but also pleaded guilty and expressed deep remorse. For these reasons, the magistrates were inclined to be lenient. The theft had been a relatively minor one; nevertheless, technically, I *had* committed burglary, and that was a serious matter. I thus received my suspended sentence and earned myself a criminal record. And this was the chief reason for my reluctance to go to the law now. If I walked into a cop-shop and admitted to breaking into houses up in Bermondsey, I wasn't at all sure I'd be walking out again.

We were well into February by this time. It was a rainy lunchtime, and I was brooding on the whole problem as I sloped into the college canteen. My thoughts were disturbed by Josie cheerfully calling my name. I glanced up. She was seated in a corner with several of her dancer buddies. On this occasion they were all girls, and they looked truly gorgeous; lithe, feline creatures, clad in spandex leotards and fluffy leg-warmers, their hair tied up in ribbons. Despite this, I only acknowledged them with a half-hearted wave, then slouched to the service-counter, where I joined the back of the queue.

Josie came over to speak to me – in that delightful, prim, tip-toeing way that all ballerinas have. But when she saw me up close, she stopped short.

"John ... you look awful."

I shrugged. "Not been feeling well, that's all."

She put a hand to my forehead. "Why didn't you tell me?"

"I thought you had better things to do. The arts festival, for instance."

I was trying to sound surly, even insolent. It was a horrible predicament, but involving Josie in this affair was the last thing I should do. If being cruel to her was the only way to make her back off, so be it. But it wasn't easy; I genuinely cared for her.

"I don't understand," she said.

"I don't think this is working out."

"What do you mean?"

I shrugged again. "I've got loads of exam work to do ... and, well, you move in different circles from me."

"Are you serious?"

22

I nodded, attempting to be indifferent to her growing dismay.

"You've never talked like this before." A tear now glistened in the corner of her eye.

"I know, but it's probably for the best."

"It isn't, and you know it isn't."

"Josie," I said harshly, "look at that shower over there." I indicated her dancer chums. "Do I fit in with that lot?"

"I won't be with them for ever. But me and you, I thought, well ..."

The queue moved up a little, me along with it.

"Hold on to that dream, Jose," I said dismissively.

"John ... why are you treating me like this?"

"It's nothing *you've* done. It's not ... well, it's just not possible, okay. Now go back to your mates. Chuck a couple of *pas-de-deux* in while you're crossing the canteen. Let's see if it gets a laugh."

That was a really unnecessary comment. Extravagant dance-floor manoeuvres, performed on the spur of the moment in the corners of common rooms, or on the college lawn out back, were something the more pretentious members of the Laban crowd were frequently given to. But Josie certainly wasn't, and mocking her like that wasn't just heartless, it was totally unjustified.

Little wonder she retreated, staring at me as if I was someone she no longer knew. I couldn't meet her tearful gaze, so I turned my back on her. A second later, she'd gone.

Ben ...

I homed in on the Duke of Monmouth for two reasons: firstly, because his name was James Scott; secondly, because he died in 1685, exactly three-hundred years ago that year. As it transpired, the concurrence of the two dates – 1685 and 1985 – was a coincidence, but it still put me on the right track.

I didn't have to delve too far into the history section of the college library to find out more about Monmouth. Thanks to my studies, I already knew plenty. His story is a grim one, even when written out in brief, as it must be here.

The roots of Monmouth's rebellion against the misanthropic King James II were planted in the previous reign. After the English Civil War and Oliver Cromwell's brief dictatorship, kingship was restored to England in the shape of Charles II. But Parliament was still powerful, and, though he was popular with the people, the new ruler had to play a constant and astute political game to maintain his position. Of course, this couldn't last. When Charles died, he had no legitimate heir, and the throne passed to his hot-headed younger brother, James Stuart. Where Charles had engaged in subtle diplomacy, James issued belligerent edicts; where Charles had been judicious and conciliatory, James was bullish, pig-headed and vengeful. But there was another, even bigger problem. Charles had been a Protestant, whereas James was a Catholic. As Parliament was still heavily swayed by the Puritan movement, this made it exceptionally suspicious of its new king, to such an extent that, not long before James's coronation, certain MPs considered the feasibility of offering the crown to Charles's eldest illegitimate son, James Scott, Duke of Monmouth – and the touch-paper was lit to open revolt.

Monmouth was a confirmed Protestant, but he was also a malcontent. From earliest youth he had been groomed by his father's enemies, who had filled his head with all sorts of nonsensical fantasies about his one day becoming king. In truth, it was simply not possible for an illegitimate to be crowned: it would have tarnished the divine status of the monarchy, and at a time when Parliament was seeking any reason it could to reduce the king's influence, that would have been catastrophic for the royalist cause. But the young duke remained stubbornly unappreciative of this. Convinced he was being gravely wronged, Monmouth had persistently and vociferously opposed the planned succession of his uncle James, involving himself in various treasonous plots along the way, and finally being banished from the kingdom by his aged father, which only served to alienate him all the more. When James was eventually installed as James II, Monmouth's rage became all-consuming. Believing he had the tacit support of Parliament, he returned to England less than two months after his uncle's coronation, landing at Lyme Regis and raising the banner of insurrection. He quickly amassed a force of five-thousand men, but unwittingly was playing straight into King James's hands. The new sovereign might have been an ineffectual politician, but he was a capable military man, and he had a real yearning to strike a clear and crushing blow against his normally intangible foes.

Monmouth, no small soldier in his own right, won some initial skirmishes, but once his imported weapons were seized by agents of the king, his cause was doomed. On June 11th 1685, the royal army, under the Earl of Feversham, finally brought him to battle at Sedgemoor in Somerset. The would-be usurper, lacking the ordinance to match his opponents, his rag-tag followers armed largely with pitchforks, was completely defeated. But his humiliation did not end there. King James, determined to take exemplary action against the rebels, handed those captured to Lord Chief Justice Jeffreys, the infamous 'Hanging Judge', and the so-called Bloody Assizes followed. At least a thousand prisoners were brutally punished for their involvement in the debacle, many transported to the colonies, others imprisoned for life, and over three-hundred sentenced to be hanged. Monmouth himself, who fled the battlefield, only to be taken a month later, was beheaded on Tower Hill, though fate had a grisly twist in store for him. The headsman, who was allegedly drunk at the time, bungled the execution, and after eight blows of the axe, the gasping, shuddering duke's head was still attached to his body. It was only finally removed when the executioner's assistants sawed it loose with their knives.

Of course, as evidence of what John and I were looking into, this gruesome tale was entirely circumstantial. There could have been any number of James Scotts connected with St. Wulfstan's church, Southwark. But I couldn't help drawing obvious analogies between the Duke of Monmouth and Roland Lassiter, both committed and idealistic Protestants, both warriors, both taken prisoner and savagely punished.

I felt certain there'd be some kind of link but I couldn't be sure, and I was in no real position to look further into it. It was late evening by then, and the library was due to close. I checked out the biographical book that I'd gleaned most of my information from, *The Pitchfork King*, and headed back to hall, determined to pursue the enquiry at some time when I was less tired.

John ...

It was a miserable day when the real horror at St. Wulfstan's began.

Sunday mornings in the inner city are usually pretty desolate, but this one was awful, being overcast and rain-drenched. I'd been out to get a newspaper and a Mars bar for my breakfast. I still felt weary and ill. When I got back to the house, I was soaked and bedraggled. It was early in the day – half past nine is very early for a student, especially on a Sunday – so I wasn't expecting to find anyone up and about when I got back to the house. But Jules was there, a friend of Josie's. When I arrived, she was on the step, waiting for someone to answer the doorbell. She was huddled under a waterproof and carrying a stuffed haversack, which suggested that she'd probably spent the night at her boyfriend's and had popped by here on the way back to her flat.

If she was surprised at the state I'd slipped into, she didn't show it. She addressed me curtly and without preamble: "Josie got your message last night. She's already gone. I must say, I thought you'd have set off too by now."

I stared at her. "What're you talking about?"

"That church. Up in Bermondsey."

I was wet to the bone, but now a chill went through me like I'd never known.

"You left her a message last night," Jules added. "Said you wanted an urgent chat with her, but you'd only be able to see her today, at ten o'clock, over at ... what's the place called?"

"St. Wulfstan's," I said slowly.

"That's it." She looked at me strangely. "You *did* send that message?"

Of course I hadn't sent any kind of message to Josie since I'd seen her in the canteen the previous week As I ran blindly down the street, I heard Jules call something after me, but I lacked the time or inclination to reply.

Seconds later I was on a bus, heading north towards Southwark. It wasn't a short ride, and all the way I sat and peered out through the grimy window, so white-faced that the conductor avoided me, probably assuming I was an addict. When we reached Bermondsey Wall, I leaped out and pounded off like a mad thing. A canyon-like entrance loomed between the two nearest warehouses. I entered it at speed. All my previous terror of this place had evaporated in the light of the danger Josie was now facing. I followed the passages between those black, monolithic structures without a thought for myself. If this sounds heroic, I don't mean it to. It was the idea of Josie, so sweet, so gentle – *here*.

I turned the corner onto the open space beside the church, and two things struck me immediately: Firstly, the workmen were not present; I'd hoped to enlist their help if there were real problems, but I should've realised that on a Sunday they'd be absent. Secondly, the huge front doors to St. Wulfstan's were still chained shut, so nobody – neither Josie nor my stalker – could actually have got in there. I slithered to a confused halt. A second passed, the rain beating down on me. I looked across the demolition site. Materials were still piled here and there, pits were fenced off, earth-movers and JCBs stood half sunk in the oozing morass.

Then I spotted an oilskin canopy: fluorescent yellow, and set up in the very middle of the site. A watchman's hut, I realised as I plodded towards it.

"Hello! Anyone here?"

It was a comforting thought that Josie might be inside, possibly sharing a mug of a tea with some gregarious construction guy. But there was no reply.

I drew the flap aside – and found a macabre scene.

The watchman was still present. He wore a cagoule-type cape, the hood of which had been drawn back, and sat on a stool in front of a portable stove. He'd clearly been leaning over this, warming his hands, when the assailant had struck.

The back of his head was now a mass of bloodied rat-tails, a grisly tangle of torn flesh and matted, crimson hair. Lying beside him on the dirt floor was a large spanner. This too was bloodied; bits of flesh and hair were stuck to it. I stared at the casualty, numbed. Was he alive or dead? I reached out, touched his arm, tried to shake him – only for his head to loll lifeless onto his broad shoulder. He slumped to the ground. I stood there frozen, the rain pattering on the tent-roof. Then I backed out again, and turned – and that was when I spied the side-door to the church. It was narrow, inconspicuous; I hadn't paid attention to it previously because, like the main entrance, it had been firmly closed.

Now it stood ajar.

I scrambled towards it, but halted before I actually reached it. Some brief, primal instinct prevented me from blundering into what was almost certainly a trap. But I knew that I couldn't just stand and do nothing. Josie's life might depend on me.

When I finally *did* enter, I was surprised.

Given the bleak exterior of the church, it was as though I'd stepped from one world into another. The place had not been empty for very long, so I hadn't expected a massive amount of decay, but the large numbers of candles that had been lit and now stood glowing in the various alcoves, made it look almost pristine. Much of the church was still handsomely painted. Its vaulted ceiling was blue and covered with stars; against every support-pillar there were statues of saints, all smiling benignly down. Of course, first appearances can be deceptive. It soon struck me that most of this décor was coated with fine, grey dust. The foot-spaces between the pews were scattered with torn, muddy hymnals. There was a strong odour of damp.

Warily, I began to explore, turning first along the southern aisle towards the altar, very little of which actually remained. Doubtless, all the valuable accoutrements had been removed when St. Wulfstan's was deconsecrated, for there was no table or tabernacle. No linens hung over the communion rail, while the towering arched window at the rear, once an impressive mural of stained-glass, was filled with holes and held together by two long planks, nailed in the shape of an X. Spacious transepts stood one to either side of the altar; when I checked the southern one I saw that its floor was a mosaic depicting St. Wulfstan himself – an archetypical hermit, bearded, tonsured, wearing monastic robes, and seated at a lectern, quill in hand. The mosaic was now dirty and in many places broken. At the far side of it, what looked like a sacristy door stood open on a shadowy recess. I didn't fancy traipsing into there, but was resolved to investigate every nook and cranny if necessary, and would probably have gone in boldly had I not suddenly heard the moan – the long, drawn-out, *female* moan.

I whirled around, stepping up onto the altar platform, and gazing down the length of the church. There was no movement, but despite the candlelight, the farthest reach of the building was now in dim shadow and my eyes had to strain to penetrate it. Another moan followed. I hurried down the central aisle. Along the way, I glanced upwards by pure chance – and that was when I saw her. Or rather, saw her arm, which protruded through the bars of the railing on the upper gallery.

I stopped dead. For a moment I was too appalled to move.

Then I broke into a sprint. In the far right corner, I spotted the foot of a spiral stair. Taking it at reckless speed, I emerged into the upper gallery. Its central podium had once served as the mount for an organ. Upright pipes were ranked behind it, while to either side there were foot-wells, probably where choristers had used to stand. In the furthest of these, Josie lay curled, one arm hanging down through the railing.

Dropping to my knees beside her, I had the desperate urge to grab and hug her, but first I checked for injuries. There was nothing obvious, but she was still insensible, sweating and muttering something inaudible. I did everything I could to revive her: listened to her heart, massaged her hands, tried to make her comfortable by inserting my jacket, in a bundle, under her head.

Whatever I did, it made no difference.

Only when I bent forwards and kissed her on the lips – an action born of sheer anguish – did I note the faint chemical odour.

I straightened up, aghast. I'm no expert, but I felt certain it was chloroform.

Ben ...

It was a bit of a shock to my system, on a wet, cold Sunday morning in February, to suddenly find myself on a bus bound for Southwark. But the information I'd discovered the night before had left me no choice.

After putting in a heavy Saturday afternoon in the library, I'd been determined when I got back to hall to let the whole thing lie – possibly until the following Monday, when I could pick it up afresh. But I hadn't been able to sleep, so had sat up in bed that night and continued to read *The Pitchfork King*. What I'd then found, at the very end of the book – in fact buried in a half-forgotten postscript – had woken me up completely.

I'd been planning to speak to John anyway, regarding the various bits of data I'd uncovered, but *this*! When I saw *this*, everything else fell into place with chilling clarity.

As a result, I went round to his house early that Sunday morning, and, when I got there, found a full-on commotion. Several of the residents had been disturbed by a repeated ringing on the doorbell. When they'd finally answered, they'd found Jules McAvoy, an acquaintance of John's through his latest girlfriend, Josie Wilkes. Jules was in a real state, and, when I arrived, immediately latched onto me. We didn't know each other well, but she recognised me as a pal of John's, and promptly poured out a tearful story of how she'd arrived with a message about Josie planning to meet him at this old church up in Southwark. John had promptly gone green and raced off. As a result, Jules was now wildly panicking, convinced that Josie was in danger. I tried to calm her, not telling her that I thought exactly the same thing.

I only managed to extricate myself from her about five minutes later, when a post-grad student took her in for a cup of tea. I climbed onto the first bus I could find, and here I was, en route.

I didn't really know where Bermondsey Wall was, but thankfully had my A-Z, and was already flicking through it. For further reference, I'd also brought *The Pitchfork King*, which was probably a mistake, as it was too fat a volume to fit into my anorak pocket. Furthermore, I doubted that John – being a modern man – would believe what it said in there, even if I shoved it into his face.

John ...

I was still struggling to wake Josie, when a sound tore through St. Wulfstan's that almost burst my eardrums.

It was a grinding mechanical roar, and at first it was so loud that it seemed to reverberate through the entire structure. Plumes of dust fell around me. I felt the timbers under my feet start to quake. I stood up, and gazed out over the nave – and saw, to my disbelief, that a great steel arm, jointed in the middle and packed all the way down its underside with thick cables, had come smashing in through the window of the south transept. It was the jib of the hydraulic lifter that I'd seen on my previous visit here. There was a change in tone of the engine outside, the *squeals* and *crunches* of gears being shifted, and then a series of *clanks*. And now, from the winch at the top of the jib, the heavy chain descended, thudding down into the transept, completely shattering the mosaic floor.

At first I was so amazed by what I was seeing that I forgot all about Josie. But then a ghastly thought struck me. Was the church about to be demolished? Had this been the plan all along – to lure us into this place so that my intended and I might die in a deluge of wood and masonry?

It couldn't be.

No crew had been present outside, and even if they had been, they'd have found their watchman by now and would have called a halt.

So what was it? What in God's name was happening?

Half a moment later I had my answer. For a figure appeared in the open side-door. A spindly, tattered figure – like a scarecrow or beggar, or perhaps a combination of the two. It was clad in skirts and a cloak, which even in the dingy half-light I was able to identify as a clerical cassock.

It was *him*, my persecutor.

He came slowly forwards into the building, peering up in my direction. He had a shock of grey-white, frizzy hair, which hung about his head like the leafy part of a bush.

And he was armed with a pick-axe.

I felt faint when I saw that. Though he was gaunt, rail-thin even, I knew how strong he was. But after staring up at me, he turned and went in the opposite direction, along the southern aisle towards the altar and the south transept. When he entered that part of the church, he commenced a furious attack on the floor, raining smashing blows on its surface. Within seconds he was through the already fractured mosaic; he bent down and starting chucking pieces of it to either side. After this, he took hold of the chain hanging from the intruding jib.

That was when I noticed that it had a large hook attached to the end of it.

Clearly this maniac had something worse on his mind that plain murder. Something much, much worse.

"You bloody lunatic!" I bellowed. "What the hell are you playing at?"

He gave no answer. He didn't even look at me, just fixed the chain to something on the floor that I couldn't see, turned and hurried back down the aisle towards the exit-door, dragging the pick-axe behind him. When he left the building, he closed the side-door behind him with an echoing *bang* that at last roused me from my shock. Whatever was going on here, I had to try and stop it. I ought to go dashing straight down there – but Josie? Shouldn't I look to her first? Before I could decide, there was another change in tone from that mechanised mastodon outside. Its roar rose rapidly to a terrible new crescendo. I saw that the chain was being cranked up towards the winch, though now it was burdened with something. When the chain pulled taut, the crane-arm itself began to shudder as though over-faced with weight. Outside, the engine howled; there came a series of *clunks* as more gears were adjusted, and from beneath the shattered tiles of the south transept, I realised that something like a giant lid was being lifted up – a colossal slab of granite, maybe eight feet by four in size.

What he was doing this for, I couldn't imagine, but I knew that I mustn't wait any longer. I hurried down the spiral stair, crossing the back of the church and running up the southern aisle, where wafts of dust came swirling towards me. Some sixth sense advised me to stay back, but no – for both mine and Josie's sakes, I was impelled to discover what this was about.

30

And then, silence.

So intense, so ear-splitting that I almost stumbled and fell.

The machine outside had been shut down.

I now heard new sounds: a *scrape* and a *thump* from beyond the side-door. I pictured the iron ring of the door handle being turned sideways, and some object – probably the handle of the pick-axe – being thrust through it and jammed it into place. Enraged, I hurled myself at the door. But it wouldn't budge. There wasn't an inch of give in it.

And, right on cue, I heard something else, something I won't forget for as long as I live. It was a *rustling* sound, like the crackle of old newspapers or bundled autumn leaves. I glanced around and upwards, half expecting the demented vicar to have appeared in one of the windows overhead, ready to launch another mindless attack on me.

However, these new sounds did not come from up there, but from somewhere else, somewhere much closer to hand.

Ben ...

In keeping with what can only be described as my acute nerdishness, I'd come from Lewisham equipped with two textbooks but with no money for bus-fare.

The result was that I found myself turfed off the bus several stops early, in Rotherhithe, and had to go the rest of the way on foot, which meant getting thoroughly soaked as sheet after sheet of rain fell over me. If this wasn't bad enough, I was in unfamiliar territory, and, though I had my map-book, I tried to take what I thought might be short-cuts, only to find myself weaving through mazes of drear back-streets, past endless boarded-up properties, and over empty lots that didn't look as though they'd been touched by a developer since before World War Two.

To make things worse, I wasn't concentrating properly, but was still mulling over the additional detail that I'd discovered in the postscript of *The Pitchfork King*. It would have been nice to dismiss it as unimportant, as fantasy, as an author's amusing and trivial anecdote at the end of his work. But something told me it was none of these things.

According to the postscript, after the Duke of Monmouth was executed, King James ordered that his already mutilated remains be quartered and displayed on different entrance gates to the city. Fears were expressed by royal advisers that this additional act of revenge might be one too many for the largely Protestant population. The king wavered, and in the meantime Monmouth's supporters took the opportunity to steal his truncated body away, and remove it to a secret sanctuary. The Crown was angered when it found out, but it still had possession of the traitor's head, which it was content to inter in an unmarked grave somewhere inside the chapel of St. Peter ad Vincula, in the Tower of London.

As for the body, that was never found. Its whereabouts remained a mystery even into modern times, though rumours persisted that it had been secretly buried in an unnamed chapel somewhere on the south bank of the River Thames – in Southwark.

John ...

I turned wildly, scanning every avenue of the candle-lit church. Nothing moved. Even the choking clouds of dust were slowly settling again.

And then my eyes fell on the south transept.

The central piece of its flooring had been torn up of course, and still hung swaying about twelve feet overhead. But it wasn't this that had drawn my attention. It was the noisome, black pit that had been revealed beneath it. Even as I stood there, goggling, from out of this pit something indescribable was climbing slowly into view.

Ben ...

One warehouse district is much like another. And all share the same attribute of not being mapped out in detail in the A-Zs of their respective cities. I knew that I was in the Bermondsey Wall area by now, as evidenced by the hulking, empty buildings on all sides of me. But with regard to street-names, the A-Z was no help.

I shoved it into the back pocket of my jeans, and continued to run, exhausted though I was. Under normal circumstances I'd have given up by now. Even if I'd been running like this because I was late for an exam, I'd have given up. Nature would have necessitated it. I'm no weakling, but I'm no athlete either; I haven't got great reserves of strength and stamina. On this occasion, however, after what I'd read and learned about the 'Pitchfork King' – not the book, the original man – stopping and going home was not even an option.

John ...

It's the most unmanly thing in the world, to scream. Yet I'm not afraid to admit it, I screamed. Over and over again in the minutes that followed. Until my throat was raw, my voice hoarse. Until the sounds coming out of me were more like inhuman screeches.

The figure that processed slowly towards me through the swirls of dust moved in awkward fashion. It was unsteady, uncoordinated, it tilted from side to side – though none of this was really puzzling given the grotesque mutilations that had been wrought upon it.

32

Again I tried to scream, but now my voice was a choked rasp. I continued to stumble backwards, so transfixed that only when I partially tripped over a loose stone was I able to turn and flee. My eyes half-blinded with sweat and dirt, I went hand over hand between two wooden-backed pews, barking my shins and ankles – yet always those lumbering, dragging feet were close behind.

A statue of the Virgin Mary came up on my left. She gazed down serenely, and a mad idea struck me; perhaps I could reach up and drag her from her shelf, throw her heavy plaster shape into the path of my pursuer? But I was too panicked to stop and try; I could only gibber and sob and totter on. By now I had retreated across the entire breadth of the church, and was stumbling down the northern aisle, the shambling shadow still in my wake. But no escape route was open. In fact, I was approaching the rear of the church, which meant I'd be hemming myself in. The entrance-doors were still securely fastened, and the only other exit from there led up to the organ gallery – and Josie.

Dear God, I could not lead this horror to Josie.

So thinking, I lurched back across the nave and started up the southern aisle again, having almost completely circled the interior. Still it pursued me, that thing, that swaying, indistinct *thing*; filthied, covered with moss and soil, hung with the tatters of mouldy clothes and wads of spider-web. I reached the side-door. I wanted to put my shoulder against it as hard as I could, but there wasn't time. Instead I kept going, at last passing into the south transept, stumbling on the rubble there, and coming to a horrified standstill as a black pit yawned before me – an oblong pit, some eight feet in length. From where I stood, it looked bottomless.

I teetered there on the brink, knowing that such a thing could never be, insisting that the dust and darkness was again confusing my eyes, that all pits – no matter how loathsome – have a bottom. Not that I could bring myself to even attempt to jump over this one. I was too weak, too exhausted. And once again those relentless feet came stumping up from behind.

With my last vestige of strength, I turned wildly, a final hysterical shriek on my lips: *"All right ... all right! But why me? For Jesus's sake, why me!"*

Ben ...

It was the last thing I expected to see when I came sliding around that final corner.

Not that the long-promised Docklands redevelopment had actually started, not that huge pieces of mud-spattered machinery – earth-movers and JCBs – were scattered all over it, not that the teeming rain was turning the whole place into a swamp; but the fact that, in the very midst of it all, kneeling against the side of a hydraulic lifter, his elbows resting on its caterpillar tracks, his head bowed in prayer, there was a clergyman.

I spotted him straight away, and briefly was oblivious to everything else: to the fact that the lifter's jib was thrust like a spear through a window in the southern wall of St. Wulfstan's church; to the fact that, from somewhere inside that venerable structure, I could hear a succession of shrill shrieks. The clergyman sensed that I was there. He jumped to his feet. He was filthy, his cassock torn and threadbare, his hair wild and thick with grease. But his face was *feral*.

That's the only way I can describe it. It seems inconceivable for a man of the cloth to have a feral face, yet this is what he was like, a human hyena: cheek-bones like blades; eyes narrowed to blood-red slits; a jutting, pointed chin; brown teeth clamped together between shrivelled blue lips; and all of it ingrained with the dirt of decades. And despite the horror of this, or maybe because of it, I finally noticed the screams from inside the church. I glanced towards it and spotted that its side-door had been barred from the outside by having a heavy pick-axe shoved through its ring-handle.

Still in a daze, I looked back at the vicar and saw that he'd picked up a spade; it was long-handled with a huge, steel blade.

"You're … gonna be in serious trouble!" I warned him in a voice that I hoped sounded confident and authoritative.

It did not have the desired effect.

He came lolloping silently through the mud. I was fixed to the spot; only at the last minute, when he swung the spade back over his shoulder like some Dark Age warrior with a battle-axe, was I able to move.

I was completely unused to combat. I'd never played any physical sport, and the last fight I'd been involved in had been at nursery school, but ancient instincts kicked in. I darted to one side, just managing to avoid a blow that would probably have split me down the middle, only to slip and fall over and have to scramble away on all-fours. I risked a backwards glance: the deranged vicar had swept the spade down with such force that it had sunk into the sodden ground, and now he was struggling to retrieve it. I jumped up again, feeling that I'd been given breathing-space, that this was a chance to get away – but hesitating. Because something inside told me that I shouldn't just desert this place while my friend was in desperate need.

And that, thankfully, was when a third party intervened.

About twenty yards behind the vicar, a figure came lumbering out of a yellow, rainproof tent: a broad, heavy-set man in a cape-like cagoule. His hair was mussed and dirty, his face streaked with blood. He seemed

34

uncertain where he was, until he spotted the vicar and realisation clearly dawned on him.

"You!" he shouted. "Hey you ... you grizzled old skeleton!"

The vicar turned wildly, and immediately his body-language changed. All at once he went from being the hunter to the hunted. He glanced back at me, the reddish eyes wide. He looked round at the big man again. We stood to either side of him. He was trapped.

"I think there're some people stuck in the church!" I called to the newcomer, who I assumed was a watchman of some sort. "This nutter's trapped them there. I think he's trying to kill them."

The watchman was still unsteady on his feet, but now came forwards. "You old git!" he snarled. "You've bloody had it, mate."

Abandoning his spade, the vicar turned, and, picking his ragged skirts up, fled back across the site towards the hydraulic lifter. Only then did I notice that its upper crane-arm had been driven in through the church window, something the vicar himself must have been responsible for. An image came to me: of this strange, forgotten man watching patiently from the ruins as these great mechanical leviathans were operated, all the time absorbing information, learning how they might be controlled.

I staggered after him, still frightened but realising now that only desperate, reckless action might prevent an even greater disaster.

"He's going to attack us with that thing," I cried.

"Don't worry," the watchman said, stumbling alongside me. "He can't drive it."

But the vicar had now climbed into the machine's cabin, where he sat down and began a complex rearrangement of the gears.

"I think he already has," I replied.

When the watchman also saw that the jib had been forced through the church's window, his mouth dropped open. "Jesus ... *the keys!* That's what he hit me for. I keep all the keys back in the hut!"

With an ear-shattering roar, the lifter rumbled to life. Only the fact that it was deeply embedded in the mire prevented it lurching into full movement. Diesel fumes funnelled into the air. The entire machine began to violently shake as the cleric/driver throttled it. It was only a matter of time before it tore itself loose.

"Go round the other side, cut him off," the watchman instructed me.

Obediently, I circled around the hydraulic mammoth, at any moment expecting it to come shuddering towards me. The mud was churning to slurry; chunks of rent earth flew through the air.

The vicar saw what we were doing – that we intended to catch him in a pincer-move, and his manipulation of the controls became frantic. The lifter shifted slightly on its axis, pivoted round maybe ten degrees. There was a *crash* as the jib struck hard on the side of the window, sending fissures racing through the brickwork. This seemed to spur the watchman into action. He ran forwards, and, with a single bound, leaped over the caterpillar tracks, catching hold of the ladder leading up to the cabin. The vicar abandoned the controls and spun around. He kicked hard at his assailant, but the watchman was bigger than him, younger and much stronger. He took every blow on the chest and face, ignoring it even when a gout of fresh blood burst from his nose. He lunged forwards with a ham-like fist, catching the vicar in the abdomen and driving him backwards into the cab, where he fell over the controls, knocking them askew.

The lifter responded. With a grinding of steel, its upper section rotated, and the jib was again forced into the church wall, but now with maximum force. It ploughed through the wood and bricks, crushing everything in its path, casting down tons of rubble inside. Dust erupted upwards in volcanic clouds. The church roof – no longer supported – sagged inwards and then partially collapsed, beams falling, followed by showers of plaster and broken slates.

The vicar still lay across the gears, but as the watchman climbed into the cab alongside him, he jumped up and tried to exit the other way – only to find *me* there. I was still down on the ground, probably the most unthreatening figure he'd ever seen: thin, bespectacled, clad in a dripping anorak. Absurdly, I was still clasping my copy of *The Pitchfork King*. But the fact that I was *there*, a potential hindrance if nothing else, caused him to hesitate. He stood in the open door, eyes wide, froth hanging from his clenched mouth.

I launched the only weapon I had at him – the book.

It opened in mid-air, losing momentum, flopping over and over, presenting no danger whatsoever. All the same, the vicar tried to avoid it. He stepped down and to one side, and inadvertently placed his foot on the caterpillar track just as the vehicle finally began to lurch free. The next thing, his feet had gone from under him. He landed heavily on top of the steel treads, and was dragged remorselessly forwards. It only took a second for him to realise the terrible danger he was in. He gave a hysterical squawk before being hurled down onto the ground, directly in the path of the advancing machine.

I had to avert my eyes. Up in the cabin, the watchman did everything he could, grabbing at the controls. But it was too late. The vicar's frenzied squawk became a shrill squeal – and then, with a *crunch* of flesh and bone, it was abruptly silenced.

John ...
I have a vague memory of lying in debris.

36

A fog of dust hung over me. I think I was in pain, for I had been struck repeatedly by falling objects. I might even have suffered broken bones, but I have no exact recollection. One thing I *do* remember: two men clambering towards me through the filtered daylight. One of them was calling my name.

At first I couldn't reply. I didn't dare. Because I was sure the unspeakable terror I had just lived through was not yet over. Just to one side of me, albeit swallowed under a mountainous pile of rubble, I could sense the presence of my enemy. In fact, I could do *more* than sense him; I could feel him. Because protruding from under those bricks and planks and shattered lumps of masonry, a leathery claw was visible – stiff now, rigid as though long dead – yet resolutely hooked upon the collar of my shirt.

Ben ...

It's difficult to gauge exactly what happened in St. Wulfstan's Church, Southwark, on that wet February day in 1985. As I said earlier, I've done little more here than condense the delirious rantings of a man who spent the next few months in such severe shock that at one point he almost became catatonic. So, no real conclusions are possible.

I did everything in my power to try and convince John that he was mistaken. That the thing he thought he saw was nothing more than shadows and dust; that, thanks to his persecution at the hands of the deranged Roland Lassiter, he was at the end of his emotional tether and easy prey to hideous fantasies. But he was insistent. He refuted every one of my reasoned arguments. When I told him that the headless body found in the rubble was nothing more than bones and rags, and was centuries old, he foamed at the mouth, tore his hair. When I agreed that the presence of so foul a thing in the church was a mystery, but advised him that police experts had pored over it and now suspected it had probably been embedded in the wall several hundred years earlier, he howled about the opened tomb in the south transept. Apparently, later on, police excavations *did* reveal the presence of an oblong pit in that area, but so much damage had been done to the fabric of that part of the building that it was difficult to work out its exact depth or dimensions, or whether anything had ever been stored inside it.

Naturally, John lost Josie. In some cases, the sharing of a ghastly experience can strengthen a couple's relationship. It might have done in this instance had John not been so mentally scarred. Josie visited him in hospital, but found only a railing wreck of a man, who accused her of complicity in the crime, saying that, if it hadn't been for her, he would never have been lured to that dreadful place. Later on he relented, but by then the harm was done.

I too was on the receiving end of his accusations. When I told him the things I thought I'd found in the textbook, he castigated me for not acting on them sooner; blamed me for letting him walk into danger without any kind of warning. What could I say? In some respects he was right. I'd first come to suspect that something was amiss at St. Wulfstan's during my interview at Lambeth Palace. But once that was over, I'd allowed several days to pass before I'd pursued my enquiries. In my defence, I'd been shooting in the dark. I hadn't actually been aware of what I was looking for, and had only got as close to the truth as I did through several strokes of fortune. But what exactly was the truth?

Even at the end of that rainy Sunday morning, when I saw the dusty form of John Price being loaded into the ambulance and gibbering that "they'd run out of time", that the church was "coming down and they'd had to act" – even then I refused to believe that anything supernatural had occurred, assuring myself that this had all been the result of a madman's spite. I would remain fully convinced of that to this day, if it hadn't been for one thing. A final item in that postscript at the back of *The Pitchfork King*, which I never mentioned to John, and probably never will for fear it could drive him back over the edge. It was a small detail, nothing peculiar, in fact something that I'd come across several times previously in my historical studies and had actually been lax in not associating with this business from the outset.

It was the matter of the headsman – the famously inept headsman, who so savagely butchered the Duke of Monmouth on Tower Hill. That horrific incident was neither the first nor last occasion on which this particular civil servant would display his callous incompetence. In fact, his very name would soon come to serve as a by-word for negligence and brutality in the business of taking lives. We remember him as 'Jack Ketch', though in fact that name is a soubriquet derived from Sir Richard Jaquett, who held the office in earlier days.

Monmouth's executioner's real name was Price. John Price.

WE ARE THE SHADOWS

Dawn-Marie knew she wasn't drunk because she'd only had nine Bacardi-breezers. And she knew she'd only had nine because she'd counted them all as they'd gone down.

It might have occurred to her, as she went hurrying out of the bar on that icy January night wearing only a mini-dress and strappy, high-heel sandals, with no tights or stockings on and a thong instead of knickers, that she *should* be feeling the cold and maybe the fact that she wasn't was something to do with her having imbued her body with more alcohol than was good for her. But things like this rarely occurred to Dawn-Marie when she was out on the town to get wrecked.

The main problem at the moment was catching up with the rest of the girls. They'd left a few minutes ahead of her, presumably because she'd been chatting to that handsome young bloke at the bar and they'd assumed that she was 'in'. Well, she wasn't 'in' yet. No sir. At ten-thirty pm it was far too early for that.

She shouldered her handbag and walked as prettily but demurely as she could down the neon-lit alley. She also tried to walk in a straight line. It was important to make sure the blokes knew you weren't tiddly, otherwise they'd be all over you like flies. Not that there was much chance of this at present. The bitter chill, which, now that she'd been outside for a few seconds, she was finally starting to notice, meant that the majority of the Friday night boozers were all indoors instead of cluttering up the pavements like they tended to in summer. It also meant that every establishment she came to was packed.

Bar 13 had a mock-Tudor façade, but inside it was very glitzy, all mirrors and polished surfaces. Dawn-Marie pushed her way in through the noisy, jostling throng, but there was no sign of her girlfriends. She popped into the Ladies to touch up her lipstick and eye-liner, then went back outside and continued along the row. The next place was *The Cattle Market*, a larger premises which she'd always thought very appropriately named. Its barn-like interior, though vastly more spacious than *Bar 13*, was equally crammed with revellers. It stank of beer, sweat and vomit. The music was being played at deafening volume, and a stroboscopic lightshow flickered crazily. Once again she fought her way inside, but there was no-one in there she knew. In fact it was awful, the last place she personally would have chosen. Every bloke she now pushed past tried to hit on her, while the floor was littered with bottles and cans. She cornered one of the bouncers and tried to describe her friends. But his only reply was: "How old are you, love?"

When she indignantly told him that she was nearly twenty, his cynical smile suggested that this was just the sort of lie he'd expect from a silly little underage tart. However, he didn't turn her out. She left the bar of her own volition.

Now she was annoyed as well as puzzled. What the hell did they think they were playing at, leaving her behind like this? When she was out with the girls, they all stuck together – at least until they tapped; that was the normal rule. Okay, now and then they got separated – Friday nights could be pretty riotous in Kelgarth. But you didn't just abandon people. She fished her mobile from her bag, but in her drunken annoyance, fumbled and dropped it. It landed on the pavement and burst apart, circuits and batteries skittering in all directions. Swearing, she sank to her knees, but as she gathered the bits together, a lad came up, stood in front of her and unzipped his fly. She told him to piss off, which he and his mates seemed to think hilarious. None of them offered to help her as they stumbled away into the night, hooting with laughter. She got back to her feet, and only then did it strike her that she may have drunk a little more than was beneficial – the mere act of standing upright made her dizzy.

The next port of call was an older, more traditional pub called *The Cromwell*. This was about a hundred yards further on, and to get to it Dawn-Marie had to walk down a steep flight of steps. She was now facing the harbour, and the North Sea wind that enveloped her was edged with ice. At the bottom, a man was standing in an alcove, smoking a cigarette. He surprised her, because it was dark down there and the first she saw of him was the ember eye of his fag-end as he materialised seemingly from nowhere. Instinctively, she stepped away from him.

Despite the weather, like most lads about town he wasn't wearing a coat. His white silk shirt was open at the collar, its flaps hanging down over the front of his pants. He had short black hair, razored-off sideburns, and a sly, wolf-like countenance. He appraised her with interest. Ordinarily Dawn-Marie would be flattered. She was only just eighteen, and her figure slight and girlish, but she was developing all the right curves and her legs were to die for. Her hair, which hung well past her shoulders, was naturally blonde and a glimmering honey-blonde at that. However, tonight she was starting to find the constant male attention tiresome, and in this situation rather spooky. She walked quickly up a narrow passage towards the next street, glancing back once; the man had made no effort to follow. Already she could see only the tiny red speck of his cigarette. Relieved, she strolled into *The Cromwell*, suddenly feeling

40

confident that a bunch of familiar faces would be gathered at the bar waiting for her.

But they weren't.

Nor were they at the bar in *The Jolly Roger,* nor in *Flanagan's.*

She pressed on resolutely, trying one watering-hole after another, but painfully aware that time was no longer on her side. She was feeling a tad headachey. It was the stress, she told herself, the aggravation – when she should be shacked up with all her mates, sinking more alco-pops, she was alone and wandering the desolate streets. Talk about wasting the best night of the week.

She tried yet another bar, and another. In one she treated herself to a drink. Though almost inevitably, the fact that she was on her own gave guys in there the wrong idea. One old boy – a real odd creature, with longish white hair, pale eyes and a cat-like smile – had the cheek to swivel round on his bar stool and ask her "how much?" She sent that one off with a flea in his ear, though in truth it indicated how far she'd strayed from her normal beat. In fact, now that she considered it, she'd drifted right out of the nightclub district, and had intruded into a less fashionable and rather run-down corner of town. Okay, she was still on the harbour, but Kelgarth's was a very big harbour – one of the largest in South Shields – and much of it was derelict.

She strode quickly along, turning corner after corner, no longer even sure where she was, and at last emerging onto the seafront. The harbour wall was to her left; this meant that she was headed back in the right direction for the night life, though she'd already decided that her next port of call would be a taxi-rank.

After the thumping music and raucous voices that had invaded her ears all evening, the only thing she could hear now was the click-click of her heels on the pavement. To her right, Kelgarth's dark, industrial buildings rose into the murk, their crumbling, gothic facades black with soot and streaked with seagull feces. There were still patches of snow in this district. Great lumps of it lay frozen in the gutters, and by the feel of the wind coming off the sea, there might be more to follow. Dawn-Marie's exposed arms and legs were numb, her upper body rigid. She was sobering up, which meant that her headache was getting worse. This infuriated her even more; she'd definitely be having it out with the rest of the girls – the night had turned into a disaster.

She glanced over her shoulder, hoping to catch sight of approaching headlights. There was nothing. Except a black, flitting shape, which might or might not have been a man ducking out of sight.

It was about thirty yards behind her.

Dawn-Marie stopped in her tracks. Suddenly the chill up her spine had nothing to do with the sub-zero temperatures.

She walked on fast, trying to tell herself that it was nothing, and that she was over-reacting. All she'd seen was a bloke walking along the seafront. She glanced over her shoulder again. There was no sign of him. On one hand this was a good thing; highly likely it meant she'd been mistaken. But on the other it could be bad; it could mean that the man, if he really *had* been jumping out of sight, had nipped through one of those occasional breaks in the harbour wall, beyond which flights of steps led down to the beach. This in turn might mean that he'd not just been stepping out of sight, but that he might actually be using the beach to get ahead of her. Dawn-Marie glanced up, just as another of those breaks in the wall approached.

It wasn't much of a beach down there – a narrow margin of sand and shingle, covered with litter and sewage, and, even though the pits had stopped working years ago, still the colour of coal-dust. But someone could easily use it as a short-cut. The man might be waiting in this approaching gateway right now.

Dawn-Marie slowed down nervously.

Was she serious?

Did she really consider this a possibility?

No, of course she didn't. In forty minutes she'd be home, trying not to wake her mam as she made a cup of tea, and counting the cost of a crap evening, which would really only be measured in how much cash she'd unwisely spent.

She almost laughed. She was getting paranoid in her old age. Boldly, she decided that she wouldn't even take the precaution of crossing to the other side of the road. She'd walk past the break in the wall, and, glancing through it, would spy what she'd spied through all the others: the dark emptiness of the benighted sea. All she'd feel would be another blast of bitter wind. But in actual fact, she didn't see or feel any of this.

What she saw was the tall, stocky figure of a man in a donkey jacket. What she felt was the ferocious blow that he landed on the side of her head with a stone.

Dawn-Marie had never been struck before in her life, and was stunned by it. What sounded like a hollow explosion went off in her head, and then her knees buckled, and her tall, slim heels gave way beneath her. The next thing, she was lying on the pavement and the man's talon-like fingers had knotted in her hair. She gave a terrified squeal as he dragged her through the break onto the top of the beach-steps, where he looked down at her and raised the stone again.

She peered helplessly up. Initially she couldn't see anything, just the outline of a bushy head. But then he stepped into a beam of sodium-yellow light from one of the street-lamps and his face was fully illuminated.

Dawn-Marie was so horrified by that visage that she gave a single, prolonged screech – which continued without stopping even after he'd smashed her in the mouth and knocked out several of her teeth, even as he hauled her down the steps into the waiting darkness.

To say that Les Cannock looked exactly the way Bob Blackwood had expected him to would be an understatement.

Bob got most of his leads from cops who were more interested in feathering their nests than in doing their jobs, and they came in all shapes and sizes: young and old, male and female; some looked nervous, while others seemed completely unconcerned by what they were doing. Yet almost invariably there was something seedy about them, something vaguely untrustworthy. Or perhaps that was just the way Bob viewed them. Cops who took money to provide tip-offs to freelance journalists were nowhere near as low on the scale as cops who took money to turn a blind eye to crime. But it was difficult to regard them as upright pillars of law-enforcement. Even those who gave off an aura of efficient professionalism, or those whom he knew for a fact were ace thief-takers – if they deigned to take his money, they'd be forever marked in his eyes as slippery customers.

That's why he wasn't surprised when he finally met Les Cannock, who up until now he'd only spoken to on the phone. Cannock, a detective-constable in Kelgarth's divisional CID office, was a walking cliché. He was squat and podgy, thinning on top and with a red, piggy face. His tie-knot was loose, his shirt stained. He even wore a grubby raincoat.

They met in a country pub three miles outside town. Bob was at a table by the window, finishing off a ploughman's lunch and a pint of lager. He was dressed as he'd said he'd be – white training shoes, jeans and a brown leather jacket. Being tall and lean, with grey hair which he always wore cut very short, his appearance was already distinctive enough. As was Cannock's of course. The cop had refused to describe what he'd be wearing for the meeting – he'd said he wanted to scope out the plot before deciding whether or not it was a goer. But as soon as he walked into the pub, Bob knew it was him. A few seconds passed before Cannock pulled up a chair and sat down, having bought himself what looked like a treble whiskey. They shook hands and got straight to business.

"I get fifteen percent of whatever you make from the story, yeah?" Cannock asked.

"Those are my usual terms," Bob said.

"How do I know you won't be pulling a fast one?"

"You don't. But as a courtesy, I'll let you see all the paperwork, including my pay-slips."

"Who are you planning to sell the story to?"

"Depends how good it is." Bob sipped his lager. "If it's sensational and it stands up, any one of the dailies will take it. If it's better than that, I might hang onto it and write a book. And yes, you'll get fifteen percent of that as well."

"You'll obviously keep my name out of it?"

"Obviously."

"But the top brass will know that someone's informed."

Bob was surprised by that statement. Cannock was evidently newer at this than he'd expected, and he wasn't sure if that boded well.

"They always know someone's informed. It won't bother them too much. People inform all the time."

"I'm not bent," Cannock said, looking troubled. "I want you to know that."

"It wouldn't make any difference to me if you were."

"But I'm not."

"I'm only interested in the story."

Cannock sniffed, swilled some Scotch. "In giving you this, I'm blowing a major confidence. My boss would have my guts for garters."

Bob shrugged, as if this was par for the course.

"It might even interfere with what's turning into a major enquiry," Cannock said, staring at him hard. "That doesn't worry you?"

"If you mean does it prick my conscience, no. Not at this stage. First I need to hear the story, then I'll have to make a decision. I'll be running it by your bosses anyway."

Cannock shuddered at the very thought. "They'll not be pleased."

"They never are," Bob said. "But they'll then be in a position where they have to confirm or deny. Either way, it won't stop me digging. But if they're prepared to play ball, I might be willing to sit on things for a little while. That's the way it normally works."

Cannock appeared to consider this as he took another shot of Scotch. His already reddish face reddened even more. Finally, he put his glass down.

"In a nutshell, we've got a series of assaults in town. We haven't made it public yet, but the whole thing's starting to turn weird."

He reached under his coat and pushed a handful of documents across the table-top.

44

Bob perused them. They were photo-copies of standard divisional crime-reports. No doubt the originals would have photos, witness statements and such attached. These were merely top-sheets, but there was plenty of information in them. They referred to three separate indecent assaults; in each case, a female in her teens, whilst out alone after dark, had been beaten around the head, then forced face-down to the floor, where she'd been denuded of her underwear and assaulted from behind.

"DC Cannock," Bob eventually said, "you may not have made it public, but anyone in your local press who's got half a brain will soon realise that these cases are connected. Likewise, anyone with half a brain will know they're not the sort of thing I'd be interested in."

"Come again?" Cannock looked genuinely surprised.

"You brought me all the way down from Newcastle to look at a series of sex assaults? This sort of thing's ten-a-penny."

"How would you react if I told you that in each case it's a different perp?"

Bob was slightly more interested in that. "But the MOs are virtually identical?"

"Yeah, but that's part of the mystery. Look at the descriptions of the assailants."

Bob scanned the crime-reports again, in particular paying attention to the descriptions given by the victims. "Okay, they're all different, but that's not uncommon."

"Wrong again. Check these out."

Cannock slid more paperwork across the table: three sheets to be precise, each one containing a police photo-fit. Evidently they'd been compiled on the basis of the aforementioned descriptions, but there were huge discrepancies between them. This clearly wasn't a case of one perpetrator and the witnesses' memories playing tricks. The first one portrayed a man in late middle-age, bald on top, with a round, saggy face and pebble-thick glasses. The second was a much younger fellow, with a mop of fair hair and lean, aquiline features; even through the impressionistic device of a photo-fit, he looked rather handsome.

"What do you see?" Cannock asked.

Bob shrugged, half-sniggered. He fingered the one depicting the man in glasses. "I know it sounds daft, but that one looks like John Christie."

Cannock smiled. "Funny you should say that. The girl in this case, Ginnie Walker, had seen the film *10 Rillington Place* about four nights earlier. And that's just what she said – he looked like that bloke Christie. What about the others?"

Bob looked at the second picture again. "I don't know, could be anyone."

"Neville Heath?"

Bob eyed the cop curiously. "Neville Heath was hanged in 1946."

"You don't say. Wasn't Christie hanged too?"

"Yes. 1953."

Cannock leaned over and tapped the third photo-fit. "Here's one that wasn't hanged."

Bob stared at it for several seconds, before saying: "This is a joke, right?"

"No. This is the photo-fit provided on the testimony of the most recent victim, Dawn-Marie Wilkinson, who suffered a severe assault last week and is still in hospital."

Despite all the ghastly things he'd covered in his long years as a crime reporter, Bob felt a prickle on his scalp as he regarded the third picture. On it was the face of a man perhaps in his mid to late thirties. His most striking feature was his hair, of which there was a lot – it was dark, thick and curly. It sat high on his head almost like a hat, but then grew down either side of his face, forming a dense beard and moustache. It was an absurdly dated style, but it was also chillingly distinctive.

"Obviously this looks like Peter Sutcliffe."

Cannock grinned. "Just what the victim said. Her exact words: 'It was Peter Sutcliffe'."

"Who's still banged up in Broadmoor?"

"We've checked, yes. And yes, before you ask it, the other two are still dead."

"Okay, okay ..." Bob pondered. "Some nutter's going around disguising himself as famous serial killers. It's a good story, but ..."

"Look at the physical characteristics."

Bob checked the reports again, and it was true. In physical terms, all the assailants were noticeably different: different heights, different builds, different body shapes.

"What have we got here?" he said, half to himself. "Some kind of crazy club?"

"I can see you're getting interested."

"I am," Bob agreed. And there was no doubt about it, he was.

Bob took a room in one of Kelgarth's town centre pubs, but pretty soon wished he hadn't.

The pub, which this year called itself *Mike's Bar*, looked okay from the outside. It was part of a terrace sloping down towards the harbour, and had a red brick exterior with mullioned front windows. Inside however, its main feature was a gigantic flat-screen TV, which was deafeningly loud and seemed to be permanently tuned to one of the football channels.

46

Furnishing was sparse – in fact there were only a handful of tables and chairs arranged around the perimeter of a vast central area, which comprised little more than a beaten wooden floor. The walls were plastered with photographs depicting scenes of drunken mayhem occurring right here on this spot. By the background tinsel in some, they'd been snapped during Christmas parties, but the rest could have been taken at any time of year. Whatever the occasion, there was a basic unity of content: girls dancing on the bar, men lying on the floor, a general absence of clothing, and copious quantities of beer being poured down throats or over heads.

Whoever the owner of the pub was – whether his name was Mike or not – he clearly regarded this type of behaviour as a unique selling-aspect of his establishment, because alongside the pictures there were also long lists of spirits, each one of which was apparently available for a generous discount at its own particular time of the week; the idea seemed to be that you could drink very cheaply right around the clock in *Mike's Bar*.

Upstairs, it was equally less than Bob had hoped for.

There were only three guest-rooms. Two were on the first floor, though, according to the young bar-maid who showed him up, one was no longer useable due to damp, while the other was being used as a lumber-room. The 'family room', as the bar-maid called it, was on the second floor, at the very back of the building. The stair that led up to this was dark, narrow and musty, with brownish stains streaked down its walls. The room was clean enough, but had the atmosphere of long disuse. At least a year's worth of dead flies was strewn along the bottom of its single narrow window, while in the en suite bathroom the plastic shower door had broken off and was held on by sticky tape. The bed was a double, and the quilt and pillows on top of it fresh, but the bed itself had a large hole in the upholstery on one side, through which Bob could peer into its cavernous and rather grimy belly.

None of this really surprised him. It was Kelgarth after all.

Dumping his bag, he went back to the window and gazed across a glum panorama of chimney stacks and crooked TV aerials. At one time cranes and the funnels of ships would have been in view from here. Instead, the skyline was bleak, empty, white with winter cold. The only building he could see of any significance was the towering stone edifice of Kelgarth Secure Hospital on the distant South Shore; its miserable inmates were the only people who these days came to the town for the purpose of staying here. Once an epicentre of heavy industry, famed for its shipyards, coal mines and salt pans, Kelgarth was a shell of its former self. The last of the shipbuilders had pulled out in the mid 1980s, while the only remaining pit closed a couple of years after that, though, needless to say, much of the muck and debris they'd generated was left behind. The main industries here now were the retail and service sectors, though these only employed a fraction of the population, while a fraction more commuted to Sunderland, Newcastle or South Shields to work. The majority of the town's inhabitants were still unemployed, many of its properties abandoned. The air of depression was tangible even to someone who'd only been here half a day, like Bob.

It was almost a relief at that moment to hear a knock at the door. It was even more of a relief to open it and find Ellen standing there. She gave him that old sexy smile, then sauntered in without being invited.

"I heard you were in town, and I just couldn't believe it," she said. "I thought no-one would be dumb enough to try and interfere with one of *my* investigations – again."

She'd changed her hair since Bob had last seen her. Instead of being shoulder-length with highlights, it had returned to its normal brunette and had been cut very short. She was wearing a black roll-neck sweater, black trousers and a beige mac – a routine ensemble, yet, as always with Ellen, it somehow accentuated her trim but shapely figure.

"Nice digs," she commented. "You realise every dickhead in Kelgarth comes here in the evening?"

"Meaning that I won't be out of place?"

"Meaning that a gentleman of your advancing years needs his sleep, and isn't going to get much in this establishment."

"Compassion. That was always your strong point. I'd offer you a cuppa by the way, but I seem to lack the facilities."

"Don't worry about it. You won't be around long enough to make one."

"You mean you're running me out of town, sheriff?"

She appraised him, pursing her lips – probably deciding that he'd lost weight, that his clothes were looking old and worn again. "Bob, what exactly are you doing here?"

"My job."

"If that job's concerned with a certain series of indecent assaults that have occurred over the last few weeks, it isn't going to pay you very much."

"My instinct says different," he replied, and that wasn't just bravado.

After twenty years in the game, Bob now relied almost entirely on instinct. Last year it had led him to uncover a massive financial scam among City types in London. The year before, it had helped him connect a series of murders in southern Scotland – he'd got a book-deal out of that one.

48

"Since when does something as mundane as a creep who likes to wear different Halloween masks merit *your* attention?" Ellen asked.

"Since I learned the facts and decided that this case is anything but mundane."

He began to unpack, shoving his few toiletries and bits of spare underwear into the cupboard. Ellen sat on the bed and watched him.

"What have I done to deserve this," she wondered, not really posing it as a question.

"I know," he agreed. "First decent case you've had since you transferred in last year, and then I show up to spoil the party."

"There's really nothing in it, you know."

"In which case you can share with me what you've got."

"I didn't share with you even when we were married."

"I know. So why should you start now?"

"Seriously Bob, the last thing we want is this thing turning into a three-ring circus."

"Ahh … you mean the public don't have a right to know?"

She stood up. "Can you imagine what their reaction would be if this story got out? We'd be swamped."

"Not my problem."

"Do you have to be such a bloody mercenary?"

"Anything that puts bread on the table."

She walked around, looking exasperated. He imagined that she very rarely got exasperated during her normal working day, but with that archetypical knack that ex-husbands have, it always seemed to be different when he was around.

"The local hacks have agreed to keep the details of this case under their hats," she said. "Why can't you?"

"I may do," he said, smiling.

"Don't give me that look. I'm not here to make some kind of deal with you."

"You're not here to rekindle our love-life either."

"Bob, this is intended as friendly advice. But if you want to take it as a warning, that's up to you. Our chief-super is not an understanding man. They don't call him 'Robocop' around here for nothing."

"No," Bob chuckled. "I bet the streets of this fair town are absolutely crime-free."

"What I'm saying is that he has all kinds of ways to lean on undesirables. And if he thinks you're causing us a problem …"

"He'll lean on me. Fair enough. And I'll lean back. I'm not a rookie, Ellen, you should know that. I don't respond to threats."

"Well, I've spoken to you." She shrugged, was suddenly tired of the conversation. "That's all I was sent here for."

"Hell of a job to give to a DI."

She walked towards the door. "I guess the boss thought *I* was more likely to get through to you than some office junior."

"He's not of totally limited intellect then. No, I'm sorry, love. I'm hanging around for a few days. This is my living, you know."

She nodded resignedly, but, before exiting, said: "Just out of interest, is he one of ours?"

"Who?"

"Your source. I don't expect you to name him. But at least tell me if he's one of ours."

"You know my lips are sealed on that."

"It's just that if he was, say, in one of the victims' families, or someone in the local press, at least I'd know I could trust my own team."

He smiled again. "Sorry."

"Not even if I offer you *my* source in exchange – the guy who tipped us off that you were here?"

Bob had been wondering about that, but resisted the temptation. "Sorry."

She gave the room another once-over. "You know Bob, you really can do better than this place."

"The spare room at your house perhaps?"

"Still got the cheek of the devil, I see."

"Would you have me any other way?"

"You won't break this case before us, I promise you."

"Is that a challenge?"

"We may already be half way there. You haven't the first clue what we've got."

He laughed. "Come on Ellen, you know you're not going trick me into divulging anything."

She pursed her lips again – it was such a turn-on when she did that. He'd thought it the day they first met, fifteen years ago, and he'd still thought it the day they divorced, twelve years later.

"No doubt we'll be running into each other again," she said.

"I hope so."

And then she was gone, out onto the landing and down the stair.

Bob watched her. As always on the few occasions they'd met since the divorce, he felt a pang of self-pity about the way things had turned out, and then a pang of self-loathing.

They'd been a good match, even professionally. In the early days their jobs had been complimentary to each other rather than incompatible. It

50

had seemed perfectly acceptable that a police detective and a crime reporter should be married and living together. But then, whilst covering a gang-rape in a local hotel, he'd heard from a grass that the police suspected players from a visiting Premiership football team – including several prominent names – and he subsequently broke the story in one of the tabloids. He hadn't got the information from his wife, but as she was one of the investigating officers, tongues inevitably began to wag and she found herself under intense pressure. It had been a huge miscalculation on his part; he'd assumed that he and she had respected each other's independence of profession to the point where, if there ever was a clash of interests, there'd be no hard feelings. What he hadn't understood was that, deep down, Ellen had been tolerating his occupation rather than accepting it. As far as she was concerned, her work was essential, whereas his was distasteful and parasitic; because she loved him, she'd been putting up with it – but she could only put up with it so far.

It had been amazingly short sighted of him not to recognise that, he now realised. While the story about the football players didn't exactly destroy their marriage, that was definitely the day the rot set in. He could still hear her hurtful but perceptive response to his awkward apology: "You're a selfish prat, Bob. Just because writing hot copy's the only thing you're good at, that doesn't mean it's the only thing that matters." They'd both learned truths about each other that day that were frankly too uncomfortable to live with for long.

Whenever his thoughts strayed into areas of regret like this, Bob always tried to laugh it off. Okay, so he was selfish – so what? He was a man of the world, he'd remind himself; earning a living was the bottom line. And if idealistic little prigs couldn't deal with it, that was their problem. But of course occasions would arise – like just now – when he'd be forced to remember how much this approach to life had cost him compared to how much it had gained him, and he'd have to admit that it was his problem too.

He glanced around at the bare room, with its tiny turret window. How similar it was to all the other rooms he'd lodged in during his so-called career. Ellen had been right – he could do an awful lot better.

It soon became apparent that interviewing any of the victims at this stage was a non-starter.

Cannock had said that they were being guarded twenty four-seven by members of Ellen's team – no doubt press enquiries would be dissuaded in the strongest possible way. Besides, there were other problems, and Dawn-Marie Wilkinson, the most recent victim, exemplified them. She'd suffered a severe concussion during the attack, which almost inevitably would render her recollection of events hazy. Add to that her emotional trauma, and you'd have a witness statement that at the very best could be described as 'unreliable'.

Bob pondered the big pile of paperwork that Cannock had supplied him with.

It could be a coincidence that two of the victims had named known serial murderers while trying to describe their assailants. Dawn-Marie Wilkinson had said that she'd been attacked by Peter Sutcliffe (in her first statement, she'd used his more famous moniker, 'the Yorkshire Ripper'), but was this as far-fetched as it sounded? Sutcliffe was one of the most famous British killers of modern times, and had a very distinctive look. The chances were that anyone, if shown a picture, would recognise him. Was it possible that Dawn-Marie, in the terror of being brutalised by a bearded man with thick, fuzzy hair, had jumped to the immediate and horrible conclusion that it was Sutcliffe who'd somehow escaped from prison? Ginnie Walker had claimed that her attacker "looked like that bloke Christie". But by her own admission, she'd been influenced by the movie *10, Rillington Place*, which recreated the Christie murders with macabre realism. The third person, Neville Heath, in all honesty could be discounted entirely. It was only Cannock who'd mentioned him by name (though it was discomforting to remember that Heath was probably the least well-known of this devilish trio, and no-one but crime historians would probably recognise him now, which might explain why his victim hadn't).

It was a big mystery; there was no doubt about that.

Detailed profiles of the three girls would be nice. Bob wondered if maybe they were connected to each other, if perhaps, by some remote chance, this was a bizarre game they were playing, which had gone badly wrong. He could poke around to see if they actually knew one another, though Ellen's team would already have done that and Cannock would have told him, so he doubted it would be a profitable line of investigation. In fact, it might prove to be highly *non*-profitable. If this became a major story, at some point he'd have to interview the victims or their families, and if he'd already got on the wrong side of them by asking questions that implied they themselves were somehow culpable, it would be all the more difficult.

Instead of sitting around all day puzzling over aspects of the case he could only guess at, he decided to concentrate on those aspects for which he had hard facts.

He plugged his lap-top in and booted it up. From his bag, he retrieved a four-gigabyte memory stick, which contained his own unique version of CrimInt – a gigantic database of the most active and violent offenders in the UK, which he'd built up himself, illegally, over the last twenty years. There were thousands upon thousands of names and personal details on there. It wasn't by any means complete, but for his 'academic' purposes it was pretty comprehensive.

The first basis he opted to search on was *modus-operandi*. A clear pattern had emerged: the victims were all young women aged between eighteen and twenty-three. They didn't share any particular characteristics – they weren't exclusively blonde for example, or especially bosomy – but they'd all been stalked and assaulted whilst out alone at night. In each case they'd been subjected to what psychologists referred to as a "blitz attack", being struck frenziedly around the head with a blunt object. Yet despite this, there was a suggestion that their assailant was 'organised' – in other words fully in control of himself. He'd clearly trawled for his victims rather than stumbled out of a pub drunk and bumped into them, and in each case he'd only launched his ambush when close to a 'lair', where he could work on them undisturbed. The same routine had always then been followed: the victim had been made to life face-down with her bottom raised; her skirt had been lifted and her underwear forcibly removed. All had then been penetrated with some hard, unyielding object – not a penis, not even a finger. One had thought it was the neck of a bottle; another said it was a piece of wood, though medical examination had revealed no telltale splinters.

None of this was particularly edifying of course. As always with sex crimes, Bob felt that he was being intrusive, even voyeuristic. Okay it was his career, his interest was purely professional – yet these were real human beings who'd been badly damaged, whose dignity had been shattered in the most intimate way, and he was prying into it because he hoped to make a quick buck. Ellen had once said something like this to him: "I always feel bad when I'm interrogating rape victims, yet I'm only doing it to try and prevent the same thing happening to someone else. I can't imagine how *you* must feel, Bob."

Bob took a mouthful of the coffee he'd brought up from the bar. It was tepid and vile. He swallowed it in a gulp and tried to shake the guilt from his mind. He was doing his job, that was all. Distasteful as it might be, he had to cover every base. And it wasn't as if he was personally confronting the girls with the sordid, humiliating details; this was a private investigation – just him and his glowing computer screen in this dingy little upstairs room, which, now that he thought about it, made the whole thing seem even shabbier.

"Fuck it," he muttered to himself.

He commenced his first search; he'd considered going straight for those offenders who had a penchant for wearing masks or disguises, but

53

now decided that this was still the most unquantifiable feature of the case. So initially it would be a straightforward search-and-elimination based purely on the details of the *MO*. However, to his disquiet (he'd been doing this job for two decades now, yet he never ceased to uncover things that disquieted him), when he hit the 'locate' command, the names of nearly five-hundred suspects appeared on screen. He refined the search, knocking it down to men aged under sixty. But that still left over three-hundred. He refined it again, this time asking only for repeat-offenders. It sheared off less than forty.

He pondered. It was time to divide the data in two.

Sex offenders, particularly serial sex offenders, often committed their crimes while travelling. This was usually because, owing to the nature of what they were, they tended to be loners and drifters rather than settled family men. But there were others who were quite comfortable in a static location. To them, their hometown was their hunting ground, and they would sit like spiders in the middle of a hideous, ever-widening web. He opted to target this latter group first, simply because Kelgarth was such an out-of-the-way place that he doubted it would figure on anyone's map if they didn't already live here. His next move therefore was to refine the list of suspects to those who were natives of north-east England.

In one fell swoop, it was reduced to three.

Pleased, he examined them one by one. The first was Kevin Nulty, a fifty-five year old mechanic from Sunderland, though it soon became apparent that he couldn't be involved; during his last prison-term he'd developed severe diabetes and had to have one of his legs amputated. In any case, he'd always tied his female victims' wrists, and there was no evidence of that here. The next one was John O'Donald, a man in his late-thirties who hailed from Durham. Eighteen years ago, he'd attacked two students at the university in two consecutive weeks. His *MO* had been almost identical to this one, though he'd masturbated at the scene of each crime, and it was this DNA – completely lacking in the Kelgarth series – that had finally snared him. Since his release from prison six years ago, he'd been covertly observed by the North East Regional Crime Squad, but had stayed clean; in fact he'd married, fathered two children and was now considered to be inactive.

This left only one possibility: James Van Ruthers, a chap now in his late-forties, in whose case there were both pluses and minuses.

On the plus side, his *MO* had been startlingly similar to this one. In Newcastle, between 1991 and 1996, he'd attacked eight women – several of these were prostitutes, but others had been victims of opportunity: young girls on their way home from nights out, a nurse leaving a late shift, and so on. All had been beaten over the head with a stone, then dragged to a pre-prepared 'lair', where they'd been thrown face-down and had their underwear torn off. On the minus side, Van Ruthers had assaulted each one of them with his fingers rather than an implement. Also on the minus side, he was now institutionalised for life, having been deemed unfit to plead through diminished responsibility. Bob would have dismissed the entry there and then had some odd instinct not kept him reading right through to the end.

It was a sobering shock when he saw the place where Van Ruthers was currently incarcerated – Kelgarth Secure Hospital.

Angeline felt like hell.

She had a severe cold, possibly even flu. And she was also in desperate need of a fix. It was a toss-up between the two, which she owed her current state of suffering to the most. Her belly was aching with withdrawal cramps, her head swimming with fever. Her skin was hot and prickly – it felt tight over her thin, weak bone structure. At the same time she was sniffling and sneezing, constantly coughing up catarrh.

January was never a good time of year to be on the game. It wasn't just the long nights and the bitter cold, it was as if the johns were all spent-up after the Christmas rush. She'd walk her patch for hours and never see any of them. In fact, tonight she wasn't seeing anyone at all. She shuddered with agony as she strutted up and down the stretch of darkened pavement. Stockings, heels, a thin blouse and flimsy skirt, and beneath that naked ass and pussy to allow quick, easy access, were hardly the best protection against the gnawing chill. She only owned one coat, a windbreaker, but that was old and tatty, and the stuffing was hanging out of it. It didn't make her look very alluring when she wore it. Not that she was much of a sight without it, if she was honest with herself. Her hair was ratty, her make-up smudged. She didn't remember the last time she'd eaten a proper meal, and that was almost certainly showing by now.

She'd woken up that afternoon to discover that she'd been burgled. Almost certainly it was someone she knew, because not only had her handbag been rifled, and the purse and bottle of vodka inside it taken; whoever it was, they'd also been behind the cistern in the toilet, where she kept her stash of junk. It was only a single condom's worth, but it was all she had, and now it was gone, along with the three clean syringes she'd recently got from the needle-exchange.

She'd spent the next hour causing a ruckus, which hadn't gone down well. None of the losers in the adjoining bed-sits said they knew what she was talking about. A few just told her to fuck off. She'd liked to have gone to see Mr. Corns, the building's owner, who lived downstairs. But his response would have been the same as always: she was a couple of weeks behind on the rent, and that was all he was interested in. To make things worse, she now couldn't pay next week's rent either, so there'd be no option – she'd have to blow him.

She wouldn't normally balk at such things. In fact, it was an arrangement they'd come to several times in the past, but recently she'd been finding it difficult. Mr. Corns – a greasy, overweight blob of a man – had a slimy, misshaped cock, which was a cheese factory at the best of times, but on the last two occasions it had been swollen and red, and emitting green goo. At a push, she could probably get through it, but on the last occasion Mr. Corns himself hadn't seemed too keen – and Angeline knew why. Her needle-tracks were now openly visible on her pipe-stem arms, she was worryingly emaciated and the scabs around her lips were definitely not cold sores.

So here she was, on the coldest night of the year so far, tottering up and down on her spike heels, her head like a lump of iron, feeling frail enough to snap in half should the wind get any stronger. And that was when she suddenly saw the car lights approaching.

Quick as she could, she tried to smarten herself up. She slung her bag over one shoulder, and adjusted her skirt so that a stocking-top was visible through the slit in the side. As an afterthought, she loosened another button at the front of her blouse, hoping, probably in vain, that it would show more cleavage than breastbone.

The car prowled past and didn't stop. But at least it *prowled*; in other words it went slowly. Whoever the driver was, he was looking.

Immediately Angeline felt better. Even if he didn't come back, it was a john. That was a big relief and meant that she'd made the right decision choosing this particular patch. There were two that she normally worked. Her preferred one was closer to the seafront, a sleazy alleyway running between the backdoor of a kebab house and the neon-lit front of a sex shop. Business was never massively good there, but you were out of sight of the main road network and rarely bothered by the police. Where she was now, her second-choice spot, which was under one of the viaduct arches close to the old museum, was more open and therefore more risky, but at least you could put the goods on show.

More headlights came spearing through the darkness, this time from the other direction. Angeline moved to the edge of the pavement. Some instinct told her it was the car that had just passed. He'd made a U-turn and was taking a second look. She loosened another button on her blouse.

The car pulled up on the other side of the road and stopped. Angeline stayed where she was. You had to let them come to you, then, if it was an undercover cop, you could always claim you were an innocent pedestrian. However, the thought of undercover cops was not a pleasant one, and now that she was looking more closely and could see that there were two people in the car, she felt a pang of unease. Not that she was concerned about being arrested and charged. Fuck – she already had a sheet as long as her daddy's dong (with which she'd once been intimately acquainted). But the whole procedure would take hours. It could be mid-morning tomorrow before she was back on the street, and how strung-out would she be then?

The car's front passenger-door opened, and a man climbed out. He was tall and lean, with slicked-back dark hair, wearing a heavy overcoat and scarf. He stood watching her over the roof of his vehicle. Angeline returned the stare boldly. He looked rather fanciable – though that didn't really matter. All she wanted at present was his cash.

The car's engine was now switched off, and the driver got out. Angeline was surprised to see that it was a woman: she was shapely, had platinum blonde hair, which was cut short, and wore a beige mac and woolly mittens. She closed the car door with a *bang*.

If they were cops, this was very unorthodox. Maybe they weren't vice. Maybe they were CID, come to ask her a few questions about a real crime. Maybe they were Drugs Squad – Angeline almost snickered; boy had they picked the wrong night.

The twosome approached, crossing the road very slowly.

Of course they might not be cops; they might just be a pair of freaks. That didn't worry Angeline at all. She'd sooner eat snatch than dick. It wouldn't be the first time some guy had paid her to put on a show with his wife. But they were now half way across the road, and for the first time she noticed how curiously they were walking: unsteady yet stiff, advancing with awkward, heavy steps. What was more, their facial expressions hadn't changed – they were stern, distinctly unfriendly, and damn it, weren't they also familiar?

Soon they were only a couple of yards away and she was able to focus on them properly.

After the life she'd lived, Angeline had often thought that nothing could ever make her scream. With a body as wasted as hers, surely it was beyond imagining that anything could make her run. But she did both those things now. She screamed, in fact she *shrieked*. Then she turned, kicked her heels off and tried to stagger away along the pavement that led beneath the railway arch. The loud footsteps of the duo followed her.

It couldn't be *them*. How could it possibly be *them*?

She glanced back over her shoulder. They were darkened silhouettes as they too came under the arch.

"Get away!" she screeched. "Get away!"

She continued to retreat, but now backwards, oblivious to the broken glass piercing her stocking-clad feet, regardless of the rats chittering irritably as they scuttled away from her. She turned around and started stumbling forwards again. She re-emerged into the light, but now her knees were threatening to buckle beneath her. Swaying sideways, she tottered against a set of cast-iron railings. She glanced up. The façade of the old museum soared into the night. She'd been here as a little girl, she remembered vaguely, but now it was dusty and silent, its walls covered with the rags of fly-posters. And then those footfalls again, coming out from under the bridge.

Whimpering, she worked her way along the railings, clinging to each bar for support. Her nose was running freely, her head pounding as though someone inside was trying to knock his way out. She looked back. Through blurred vision, she saw them approaching. Surely she'd been mistaken? Perhaps she was hallucinating? But no – no she wasn't. They were coming right towards her and she could see them quite clearly.

Ian Brady and Myra Hindley, 'the Moors Murderers'.

But as they *had* been: young, virile, handsome, bizarrely seductive despite the hideous cruelty everyone now knew they were capable of.

"You're d-dead!" Angeline stammered at the woman. "You died in jail! I saw it on the telly!" She looked at the man. "And y-you …" She couldn't put it into words, but she'd seen recent photographs of him: sickly and decrepit, terminally ill in some prison hospital somewhere.

"Oh my God," Angeline choked.

A few moments previously it would have been inconceivable for her to think about anything other than injecting heroin into her bloodstream. Now that was the last thing on her mind. Horrified and bewildered, she scrabbled up the steps to the museum's front door, only to find a sheet of corrugated metal there instead.

"No, n-no," she gasped, beating futilely on it.

She pried her fingers around its edges and tried to yank it loose, but was too weak.

And then a shadow fell over her. Helpless, unable to breathe, Angeline sank down to her knees. She glanced fearfully around. The man was at the bottom of the steps, his hands in his pockets, his expression unchanged. But the woman had ascended and was standing very close. In her mitten-clad right hand, she held a half-brick.

Kelgarth Secure Hospital looked escape-proof even from a distance.

It stood on a high headland jutting out into the North Sea. The cliffs surrounding it rose two-hundred feet above the rocks and crashing waves, so there were three sides to it from which egress was completely impossible. The fourth side, the landward side, was only approachable via a number of checkpoints, all manned by uniformed security guards who had the look and bearing of the ex-military. The fencing was exclusively twenty feet tall, each section mounted either with cameras or coils of razor wire.

The final drive to the front entrance was made along a single-lane road hemmed in from either side by high walls over the tops of which watchtowers were visible. As Bob approached it, it looked less and less like a medical facility and more like something from a dystopian nightmare. It still retained its original 1930s exterior and was therefore monolithic in structure, utterly faceless – it could have been a power station or warehouse. There were no windows in it; its once redbrick façade was now black and green with weathering and salt-erosion. Framed on the grey winter sky, it was a drear and dismal monument to an age-old problem that even the most modern thinkers had failed to resolve: the fate of the criminally insane.

The director of the institution was a Doctor Harold Hawkins, and he'd agreed to Bob's request for a visitor's pass with surprising speed. He received Bob in a side-office, just off the asylum's central reception area. He was a tight-mouthed, narrow-eyed man, with thin sandy hair; he looked alarmingly like a young Patrick McGoohan but without the charisma. Throughout their conversation, he showed almost no emotion, but sat behind his desk, fingers steepled together, barely moving.

"It's unusual for journalists to come here and request to interview our inmates," he said in a clipped tone. "But it's particularly unusual that a journalist should seek to interview a nonentity like James Van Ruthers."

"Eight serious assaults hardly makes him a nonentity," Bob replied.

"Nevertheless, it's not as if he murdered his victims. The physical damage he inflicted on them was in some cases relatively minor."

"As I mentioned on the phone, my new book is concerned with the *development* of the typical psychopath. Not necessarily the consequences of his actions."

"The 'typical psychopath'? What an amusing notion."

"Just a turn of phrase."

"I wonder, are you qualified to write such a book?"

"Well …" Bob was starting to feel awkward under the doctor's lidded gaze.

"I myself have authored twelve books on the subject of psychopathology," Hawkins said. "Yet I doubt that, if you put them all together, their total sales would amount to half the figure that you probably achieved with your last book."

Bob was surprised that Hawkins even knew about his last book. *The Lowland Wolf*, in which he'd connected the murders in southern Scotland and thus kick-started an enquiry that finally netted a highly proficient sex killer, had sold pretty well – it had flown off the shelves for the first few months. But surely something like that didn't irritate an academic like Hawkins?

"Obviously I'm writing for the same audience of laymen that I was writing for last time," Bob replied. "I'm not trying to pass myself off as a mental health professional. But until recently, true crime books have been concerned with the details of the crime and the investigation. There's been very little from the perpetrators' point of view."

"Why should there be?" the doctor asked. "The perpetrators are, as you succinctly put it, psychopaths. Can their opinions or views be worth anything at all?"

"I won't know unless I get to speak to one or two of them."

"Which brings me back to my previous confusion – you've only requested to interview James Van Ruthers."

"And you replied that it would be okay to do that, Doctor Hawkins. I hope I've not wasted my time coming here."

"Well that rather depends on what you hope to gain from it. There's nothing to stop you interviewing him. Our patients regularly receive visitors. There are no rules against it, so long as the visits are authorised by me and the patients are willing."

"Is this your way of getting round to telling me that James Van Ruthers is unwilling?"

"On the contrary. He seemed rather pleased at the prospect."

Bob considered this. Hawkins was clearly dragging things out to try and elicit information. It wasn't entirely surprising: this was his domain, and it would almost certainly be an affront to him if anything occurred here to which he wasn't privy.

"May I ask what Van Ruthers's diagnosis was?" Bob said.

"That information would normally be confidential, but I suppose it's important you understand what you're dealing with. James Van Ruthers is a paranoid schizophrenic, Mr. Blackwood. That means he suffers disordered thought processes and lacks any form of structured psychological identity."

"Is he violent?"

"You mean will you be in danger while you're speaking to him?"

"Well, yes."

"We have several categories of patient here in Kelgarth: A, B and C. A, as you would imagine, are our high security inmates. They are characterised by extreme deviousness and a willingness to commit any

60

act, no matter how atrocious, if they think it will serve their purpose. Needless to say, they are kept in isolation. Category B inmates are also violent, but are more predictable; they are deemed to be controllable in a restricted population environment. Category C inmates are non-volatile and make up the bulk of our general population. They may pose a risk – they wouldn't be here otherwise, would they?" For the first time, Hawkins allowed himself a brief, thin smile. "But for the most part they are compliant with our rules, they socialise harmlessly with other patients and, as a result, enjoy considerable freedoms."

"And James Van Ruthers is … ?"

"Category C. Which means that you can sit with him unsupervised, and chatter away to your heart's content."

Bob couldn't help wondering why they hadn't reached this point in the conversation a few minutes earlier.

They walked upstairs initially in silence. The hospital was very basic and functional. The passages and stairwells were all of bare, whitewashed brick. There were regular checkpoints: barred slide-gates, which again were operated by uniformed guards sitting in security booths. They passed countless closed steel doors. Whether these led to storage chambers, wards or even cells, Bob didn't know, but none of them had handles on them or viewing ports. Only after ascending to the top floor by a lift with a control keypad in it, the combination of which – according to Doctor Hawkins – was altered every day, did the atmosphere change. Up here, they walked through open recreation areas: there were facilities for pool and table-tennis, there was even a television room and a library area with racks of books and magazines. Staff were constantly on view: burly men with crew-cuts, who in truth were only distinguishable from the security guards by their white t-shirts, white trousers and white training shoes. But there were also patients around, some in pyjamas, some in ordinary clothes. For the most part they were lounging, reading or sleeping. No-one was doing anything that a novice like Bob might deem to be 'psychopathic'. The doctor now took him into a residential corridor. Doors led off it, though most of these stood open, revealing small rooms containing beds, writing desks and such. They were almost like student quarters. However, the one they stopped at was closed. All the doors they'd seen on this top floor had plaques on them, each one bearing a different name. This one read: *Van Ruthers*.

"I thought you said he wasn't kept locked up?" Bob said.

"He's in here voluntarily," Hawkins replied. "He has no real interests you see. He goes through his everyday motions in normal fashion. But he doesn't read, doesn't write, doesn't watch television. He mixes with the other patients when he has to … during meal times, during exercise. He partakes in group therapy because we insist on it. But usually he'd rather be alone in his room, where he meditates."

"Meditates?"

"That's the impression we get. But whether anything's actually going on inside his head is another matter."

"I don't understand."

"Neither do I," Hawkins said with another thin smile. And he pushed the door open.

There was nothing menacing about James Van Ruthers – far from it.

When Bob entered the room, the patient, who was wearing a t-shirt and shorts, was seated on his bed, legs crossed, hands folded in his lap. His eyes were closed, though he clearly wasn't asleep. He was in early middle-age and somewhat portly, with a mop of red-gold hair. When he opened his eyes, they were startlingly blue. With his pinkish expression and plump cheeks, they gave him a kind of 'toy-pig' look.

He smiled. "Robert Blackwood, I believe. What an unexpected pleasure." His accent was Geordie, though milder than most blue-collar Tynesiders'. "Take a seat." He indicated the chair next to his writing table. "Will you be joining us, Doctor Hawkins? Only, if you are, you'll have to stand."

Hawkins was about to reply, but Bob got in first: "I'd rather you didn't stay, if you don't mind, doctor. You said it'd be okay for us to chat unsupervised, and that's the way I'd prefer it."

Hawkins stared at him for a second, then withdrew and closed the door.

"You're not in any danger," Van Ruthers immediately said.

"I realise that." Bob took the seat, and filched a notebook and pen from his pocket. He also produced his Dictaphone. "Okay if I use this to record our conversation?"

"Be my guest. Of course, if that fails, you can always ask Doctor Hawkins for a copy of *his* tape." He pointed to a high corner, where a small video camera was located. "He'll be watching us throughout, listening to every word."

Bob gazed up at it.

"He feigns a lack of interest in my case," Van Ruthers added. "Claims to be unimpressed by me. But really he's dying to know why you're here."

"I'm amazed he hasn't already worked it out."

"I'm afraid his natural arrogance often prevents him from seeing the wood for the trees. But let's get to it – you want to know if I can get in and out of this place?"

Bob had trouble keeping the expression of surprise from his face.

"You look shocked." Van Ruthers sounded disappointed. "You thought Doctor Hawkins would know why you were here, but didn't think I would? Not very flattering."

"Can you get in and out of this place?"

"It's hardly likely. Even we Category Cs are watched twenty-four hours a day."

Bob couldn't help thinking that they'd 'got to it' rather quickly, but while the iron was hot, he decided to strike. "Does someone help you? One of the staff maybe?"

"Why would they do that?"

Bob was aware of Van Ruthers watching him intently, as though to try and discomfort him. He'd interviewed psychopaths before, and this wasn't a-typical. Nor was their habit of replying to questions with questions of their own. Everything was a game to these people, a contest. But Van Ruthers had startled him with his knowledge that something was going on outside, and the journalist already felt as if he was on the back-foot.

"Perhaps *you* can tell me why they'd do it?" Bob said.

"And perhaps I can't. But let's not pussyfoot around, Mr. Blackwood. This series of attacks on the young women of Kelgarth have got my fingerprints all over them, haven't they – metaphorically speaking. Ah, I see I've surprised you again. You're thinking: 'Even if he bothered to watch television, he couldn't possibly know about this latest series because it hasn't been made public yet'."

For the first time in a long time, Bob was lost for words.

Van Ruthers smiled again. "I'm sorry to say that there's no magic trickery involved. The police have already been here to discuss the very same thing with me."

"I see." Bob could have kicked himself.

"A rather pleasant officer, in fact. Detective Inspector Ellen Blackwood. Relative of yours?"

Again Bob was caught off-guard. It would be sensible to say 'no', but in that brief moment of hesitation the truth became obvious.

"How interesting," Van Ruthers said. "So ... sister, cousin? There's no obvious resemblance. Wife?"

"Try ex-wife."

"Better and better."

"Ellen and I haven't seen each other for years, and there's nothing between us. So, though having this information may please you, it's unlikely to give you any leverage."

"Why would I need leverage?"

"Quite," Bob said, feeling as though he'd scored a minor point.

He pondered his next move quickly. Thus far, Van Ruthers had leaked what he knew about the recent attacks in order to gain the upper hand. What he specifically *hadn't* mentioned was that there might be more than one assailant, and that they'd been wearing odd and scary disguises. This might be because he didn't know about that, and if so, it could prove the key to whether or not he was involved.

"Okay, Mr. Van Ruthers, so you're aware why I'm here. Surely it's in your best interests to dismiss yourself from suspicion?"

"Why should I need to? There are cameras all over this building. Whatever time it was when these young women were being attacked, you'll find me on film somewhere within these walls. Oh, unless you're still thinking I have an accomplice on staff – someone who might have messed around with the tapes." His smile broadened. "There are other explanations too."

"Such as?"

"Maybe the assailant is a copycat."

"I've considered that."

"Maybe it's *more* than one copycat?"

"More than one?"

"You suspect there may be more than one of us on the inside, Mr. Blackwood. Could there not, just as easily, be more than one on the outside?"

Van Ruthers was an archetypical psychopath; that much was plain. The relevant tidbits he offered were mixed in with all sorts of other rubbish.

"Do you perhaps know who these copycats are?" Bob asked.

"How could I? All my letters, emails and phone-calls are carefully monitored. I have no unsupervised contact with the outside world. Oh – unless I'm getting help from an accomplice on staff."

"How do these people get in touch with you?"

"You seem quite sure that it's 'people' rather than 'a person'. I thought we were talking hypothetically?"

"I *know* it's people rather than a person."

Van Ruthers laughed. "In which case you should ask them."

"I will." Bob put his notebook and pen away. It was a bluff, and in that respect a risky strategy, but he had to draw Van Ruthers out more; the guy clearly wanted to talk, but was enjoying the run-around too much. "Because *you* evidently know nothing."

Van Ruthers feigned shock. "You think it's just coincidence then that these attacks are happening here in Kelgarth, the place of my confinement?"

"It may not be coincidence. Whoever the perps are, they may be honouring you in some twisted way, but it's certainly none of your doing." Bob stood up. "As you say, you're confined here. You'll be confined here forever. Your life and influence are over."

"Maybe, maybe not."

Bob headed for the door.

"Just out of interest, Mr. Blackwood, how do you account for the fact that some of these assailants were wearing the faces of men who died for their crimes?"

Bob stopped, glanced around.

Van Ruthers grinned. "Oh dear, have I surprised you again?"

"Not really. The police could have let that slip while they were speaking to you. Though I'd be surprised if Ellen did. She only ever operates on a need-to-know basis."

"Ellen didn't."

"Doesn't matter." Bob moved back towards the door.

"Nor did she mention the incident last night."

Again Bob glanced around. "Last night?"

"How could she have done? She came to see me two days ago."

"What incident last night?"

Van Ruthers shook his head regretfully. "Another woman was attacked. This time the consequences may be severe. I'm afraid she was in poor physical condition. Oh, in case you're wondering, the assailants were Ian Brady and Myra Hindley – as the brutalised victim is no doubt telling your ex-wife's officers right at this moment."

"You're full of shit."

"I'm full of something, Mr. Blackwood, but it isn't shit."

Bob couldn't help himself; the news-hound in him suddenly had to know more. "Give me the details."

"I may."

"You're a sick bastard."

"And you're an investigative journalist. Why don't you go and investigate?"

"Like I say, you're full of it. No wonder you're a flyspeck under Hawkins's notice."

The patient's cocksure grin swiftly faded. Suddenly he was red in the cheek.

"Hawkins!" he spat. "Hawkins is a clown, a buffoon! His attempts to understand me have been lamentable, farcical!"

His rant continued, but now in low, intense monotone; his brow had furrowed, his eyes were narrowed to gimlet points: "Don't make the same mistake, Blackwood, and confuse me with some ordinary, everyday lunatic. I have a particular power. Do you understand that? A power I was born with, but which has matured as I myself have matured, and which, during the eleven years I've been imprisoned here, has been honed until now it's really quite exceptional ..."

At which point the door burst open and Doctor Hawkins was there, in company with two white t-shirted henchmen.

"This has gone on long enough," he said sternly. "We can't allow our patients to be getting excited like this."

"We're done anyway," Bob replied.

"If only we were," Van Ruthers said.

"Aren't you due for your medication?" Hawkins asked him coldly.

"If you say so, doctor."

Moments later, Hawkins was escorting Bob down towards the reception area. The doctor was taut, pale in the face. His hands were knotted behind his back as they walked.

"I have to say, Mr. Blackwood, if anything appears in print implying that patients here are being assisted to escape by members of my staff, or even *allowed* to escape, I will sue you until your finances cease to exist."

"Thanks for the quote." Bob held up his Dictaphone to show that it was still recording. "You're saying there's no way Van Ruthers could have left this hospital in the last few weeks?"

Hawkins looked flustered, but couldn't resist the opportunity to boast. "Escape from Kelgarth is out of the question. It would require all our security systems to malfunction simultaneously. It would also require a significant number of our staff to make career-ending mistakes, and *that* is inconceivable. I handpick my people personally, Mr. Blackwood. To even suggest they'd be so lax is scurrilous muck-raking. I'm amazed you listened to some of the things that man was telling you."

"It's all delusion, is it?"

"James Van Ruthers is an entire grab-bag of delusions. Surely that's obvious? But then maybe it isn't to someone as unqualified as you. Allow me to explain: Van Ruthers's problems are based on extreme sexual inadequacy. He suffered it all his life until it finally fractured his mind. Now it's become an essential part of one huge egocentric fantasy in which he believes that his inability to arouse himself in the normal way is because his body is storing up its maleness, rather like a living battery, and that at some point this latent energy or power will break out in destructive and alarming ways."

Bob said nothing. It was true. The patient had been quite vociferous about this 'power'.

Hawkins continued: "I'm firmly convinced that he was sincere in the explanation he offered for his crimes. Namely that his attacks on those women – always from behind, never face to face, and always with his index finger rather than with his permanently flaccid penis – were a

66

genuine attempt to drain this energy before it reached critical mass. He actually thought he was helping us. Of course he has a different attitude now, as you saw for yourself. Now he's become withdrawn and resentful. He's angry that he's being punished. Not that his anger manifests itself in any visible or even verbal way." The doctor's tone became contemptuous. "Van Ruthers likes to imagine that he's a pressure-cooker of masculinity just waiting to explode, but actually he has fewer masculine traits than any heterosexual man I've ever met."

"You feel really challenged by him, don't you?" Bob said. He stopped and turned to face the doctor. They'd now reached the reception area, where members of staff looked on with interest. "Why's that? Is it personal? Is it because he resists analysis? Because you can't break him? Or is it just general scientific snobbery – because he doesn't actually fit into you and your colleagues' ordered pattern of madness?"

Hawkins paled. He looked fazed that his professional ability was being called into question like this; or perhaps it was just that he didn't like being upbraided within earshot of his underlings. "So it's your belief that Van Ruthers may actually *have* a special power?"

"I don't know," Bob replied. "I came here to try and solve a very peculiar puzzle. And I don't feel any closer."

"He's playing a game with you, that's all."

"We'll see."

The front door had now been opened, and Bob strode towards it.

"Might I remind you, Blackwood, that you're a populist author – no more, no less. You have no qualifications, no respectable credentials, no professional discipline of any sort. You don't know what you're doing here, and are totally out of your depth. You're playing at this enquiry, and if you persist with it, you'll likely make a complete fool of yourself."

"Story of my life," Bob muttered as he walked out into the rain.

It was now falling in torrents from an ink-black sky, and, as he didn't have an overcoat, it quickly drenched him to the skin.

The comments that Hawkins had shouted from the hospital door were a painful reminder of the sorts of issues that tormented Bob all the time.

"You're out of your depth."

"You're playing at it."

Morality aside, he still liked to think of himself as a professional. But even on that simplistic level, his work was hit and miss. Okay, he had occasional successes like *The Lowland Wolf*, but generally there were long periods between cheques, and his conscience often asked him if his 'job' wasn't really a hobby that now and then earned him money? There were times when he even regretted quitting the *Newcastle Evening*

Chronicle, where he'd started out as a salaried journalist all those years ago. He'd left because of the office politics, which had driven him mad, but also because he'd been in a desperate hurry to be his own boss, perhaps naively desperate. It was at times like *this*, spent ploughing the wintry streets, following a vague story with no apparent beginning, middle or end, when he suffered these doubts most acutely.

That evening he opted to fathom out what he knew so far, and at the same time drown his sorrows. But it immediately became obvious that downstairs in *Mike's Bar* would not be ideal. The football on the big screen – at present an Italian match – was at deafening volume, while at the same time equally deafening music was being played from the juke box. Even though it was only midweek, various twenty-something boozers were already dotted around the establishment in groups, bawling to one another.

Instead, Bob went down to the seafront and found his way into the *The Rusty Anchor*. This was one of those curiosity pubs, which, if you got them all together on printed paper, would make an interesting tour-guide for visitors to the UK seeking eccentricity as well as alcohol. It was built into one of the stone piers that stuck out into the harbour. The upper section of it, which had a roof, bay-windows and such, looked normal enough, and in fact had once been the harbour-master's cottage. Now this was the part of the hostelry where the landlord and his family lived. However, the punter's entrance led you straight down a flight of stone steps into a basement-bar that was almost at sea-level. Its windows weren't portholes for nothing.

It was seven o'clock in the evening, so the place was still relatively quiet. Bob ordered himself a beer and a whiskey, and sat in one of the corners, where he planned to read through every scrap of information he'd accrued so far. In addition, for the fourth time since leaving the hospital that afternoon, he tried to call Les Cannock. The detective wasn't answering. In fact, this time there was no connection at all; it was as if Cannock's mobile had suddenly been taken out of service.

Frustrated, Bob checked through an evening paper. It contained no reference to the 'Brady and Hindley' attack that Van Ruthers had eluded to, so either the local press were keeping their bargain with the police, or it hadn't happened. Bob suspected the former. Van Ruthers wouldn't have come out with something like that if it wasn't true; what would be the point? Okay he was a maniac, but he was a maniac with an agenda – that much was evident. Bob was also wondering where Doctor Hawkins fitted into this. He hadn't expressed surprise at any of the things he'd overheard Van Ruthers saying. He might not believe it because he'd concluded that his patient was a habitual liar, but surely he'd have commented on the strangeness of it: attacks carried out by serial killers who were all either dead or in prison; it was hardly run-of-the-mill insanity.

Bob got himself another couple of drinks. Whatever the outcome now, this whole thing was well worth a write-up. Yet where to go with it next? It would probably make sense to peruse the crime scenes, and see if there were any potential witnesses living or working nearby who would speak to him.

He drank quickly, letting the warmth of the Scotch erupt inside him. The fact that he hadn't eaten since breakfast would probably help speed the alcohol to his brain. But he didn't care, and shortly he was back at the bar again. It was moving towards mid-evening, and the place was filling up; the clientele here were older and less raucous than those in *Mike's Bar*. The landlord, a short, bald man wearing a smart shirt and tie, chatted and exchanged quips as he pulled their pints. When the moment arose, Bob also had a word with him, showing his press card and claiming to be involved in a survey for the 'North East Enquirer', a name he'd plucked out of thin air.

"I'm wondering what the state of crime is in Kelgarth?" he asked, as the landlord served him. "I guess you must be pretty well in the middle of it down here on the docks."

The landlord shrugged. "It's the usual thing, you know. Binge drinkers, piss-heads. Saturday nights are the most bother."

"Violence against women?"

"You're joking, aren't you! Most of the time it's them who's causing it."

"I'm talking about sex offences," Bob said, a tad self-consciously. It was an awkward conversation to suddenly spring on someone. "I mean, statistically there's been a rise in violent crime, and in sex crime – as in unprovoked attacks by strangers. You get a lot of that in Kelgarth?"

The landlord eyed him curiously. "I'm not really the bloke to speak to, mate. Perhaps you'd better go to the police, eh."

Bob smiled and nodded, then ordered another beer and whiskey. It was probably an idea to forget about work for the time being. He didn't feel he was getting anywhere, and nothing bugged him more than 'relaxing' in the evening when there was still a lot to do. But he was clearly no longer in an adequate state. First thing in the morning, he decided, he'd try to track Cannock's home address through the phonebook. Failing that, he'd check the crime scenes. Pleased to have a plan, he closed his notebook – and saw someone at the far end of the bar whom he recognised.

It was a man standing alone. He was handsome in a slightly old-fashioned way: his dark-blonde hair was cut very short, parted and brushed to one side, and he sported a trim, clipped moustache. He was large in build, though that might have been down to the cashmere overcoat he was wearing. He looked right back at Bob with an unflinching stare that was quite unnerving, and as such, other details – odd ones – became noticeable. There was something curious about his complexion: 'clean-shaven' didn't really cover it – he virtually glinted in the bar-light. What looked liked a glass of red wine stood in front of him, yet he made no effort to touch it. In fact, his hands rested one to either side of it on the bar-top; inexplicably, given how warm it was in the pub, he was wearing brown leather gloves.

It slowly occurred to Bob who the man was – or at least, whom he looked like. Ronald Colman, the old film star of the 1940s. Whoever this guy was, he was the twin of Ronald Colman.

Or perhaps not.

Because wasn't there someone else quite famous, who'd they'd all said looked a lot like Ronald Colman?

Bob's pint was half way to his mouth. Now he almost dropped it, the beer frothing down the front of his shirt. Shakily, he tried to replace it on the bar, but was only partly successful – it tipped sideways, slopping down his clothes again. He managed to catch it in time. When he glanced up, the figure at the far end of the bar had gone.

"No," Bob said under his breath. "No!" He jostled his way through the crowd.

Suddenly there was no sign of the man. The glass of wine was still there, but then the landlord retrieved it and took a sip. Bob turned and looked around. Just behind where the man had been standing, a door connected to a passage. It was marked for the lavatories.

Bob opened it. At the far end, at the foot of another of flight of stone steps, an emergency exit stood ajar. An icy breeze gusted through it. He went straight down there and peeked outside. A narrow wooden catwalk ran along the side of the pub, a single steel barrier separating it from the sea, the black, foaming surface of which was only about four feet below. Bob glanced in both directions. Towards the shore, the catwalk ended at a stone stair, which led back up to the top of the pier. In the other direction, the seaward direction, it vanished into darkness. Bob chose the latter. He felt he was being lured; his quarry hadn't staged that piece of theatre in the pub merely to tantalise him. In that respect, perhaps it was a mistake coming out here, but what other choice was there?

The temperature had dropped again since that afternoon, and when another gust of wind ripped across the water, it was filled with sleet. Bob proceeded anyway, even though he could only see a few yards ahead. Under his feet, the catwalk timbers creaked. He reached the end of the pub, and found himself at a kind of landing area – a wooden extension to

70

the stone pier, where masses of empty barrels and crates filled with bottles had been stacked. He ventured forwards again. A motion-sensitive light came on, but it didn't reveal a great deal. Directly ahead, the catwalk – now just the edge of the landing area – continued right up to a point where the steel barrier turned inwards, signalling the end of the pier. However, there was another passage running along the back of the pub, and a couple of aisles leading through the stacks of barrels. Someone could still be lying in wait here.

"Hello?" he shouted, but his voice was lost in the wind.

The sleet pelted him, turning steadily to snow. It settled on the woodwork, which he'd previously thought slippery through being covered with mould, though now he realised that it was coated with ice. He moved on, passing one stack of empties after another. The next aisle appeared on his right. He glanced down it, seeing the barrier on the far side, snowflakes whipping over it. He shivered and rubbed at his eyes, which were watering with the cold. This was a fool's errand for sure; who'd be out here?

Then a figure stepped into view at the end of the aisle.

It was a featureless – a silhouette framed on the distant harbour lights. But it was of large build; either that or wearing an overcoat.

It stood stiffly, regarding Bob in silence.

"Okay," Bob said, advancing slowly. The passage between the crates and barrels offered respite from the wind and snow, but he was still shuddering. The intense cold had sobered him a little – suddenly he was as nervous as he was curious. "I don't know who you are, but you clearly want to talk to me and I definitely want to talk to you."

The figure didn't move until Bob was about six yards off, and then it stepped out of sight, this time to the left, as though heading for the end of the pier.

"Hey!" Bob hurried forwards as much as the treacherous footing would allow, and blundered around the corner.

The figure was about fifteen yards ahead. It had reached the end barrier, turned and now stood facing him again. He saw the clipped moustache, the deadpan expression.

"You want to tell me what this is about?" Bob said. "I know who you're supposed to be, but I want to know who you are really ..."

Before he could say more, he sensed movement behind him. He tried to spin around, but the slippery boards threw him off balance. He staggered, had to catch hold of the barrier. A second figure had been standing around the corner, just out of sight. It now lunged, and a blunt object struck Bob squarely on the right temple. There was a hollow *bang* in his head, and the next thing the catwalk had hit him in the back, knocking a cloud of breath out of him.

He lay there insensible, vaguely aware of snowflakes plastering the side of his face and a hot stickiness creeping through his hair – and of something circular and metallic being pressed under his chin. His mind reacted, wanted him to strike out, but his body wouldn't follow. A figure was crouching over him, though he couldn't really focus on it – his skull was full of crunching pain, like the worst hangover he'd ever had. However, slowly his senses began to clear. His hearing first: the muffled roaring became wind and waves. His vision second: there was indeed someone crouching over him; someone who wore a black knitted ski-mask with slots cut for the eyes, and in one hand wielded a shotgun, a sawn-off pump, which he held against Bob's throat.

Bob tried to speak, but was still too groggy.

The figure lowered itself until they were almost face-to-face. And then, with deliberate slowness, reached up and tugged its mask off. The features below were narrow and angular, with a tight clamped mouth and eyes that were slivers of evil. It was disturbingly familiar

"You … you're …" Bob mumbled, but he still couldn't speak properly and anyway, he now realised that he was being pushed.

It wasn't just the man hunkered over him, it was the big man with the moustache. He'd come back along the catwalk and was lending a foot. They were shoving Bob sideways – with ease, because he was sliding on the ice. Only at the last second, as he came back to full wakefulness, did he understand what they were doing.

"N-no!" he stammered. "No!"

He grabbed at the hunkered man, whose main bit of clothing looked like an old flak-jacket, managing to catch a handful of coarse material but losing hold of it with the cold. He grabbed next at the collar, plucking something free, though now it was too late and he was going over the edge.

Bob dropped like a stone, hitting the surface of the sea hard.

It closed over him with a thunderous *boom*.

The icy plunge revived Bob fully, but by then he was deep under.

Gagging, he fought his way back to the surface, where he only managed a couple of mouthfuls of air before foam crashed over his head again. The temperature was numbing; in his weakened state he was already losing control of his limbs. He tried to kick off his shoes, but couldn't; tried to breaststroke his way forwards, but the current was swirling and he'd lost all sense of direction. The lights of the pier – suddenly a considerable distance to his left – were tilting out of his vision.

Foul suds slopped down his throat, blinded his eyes. The weight of his waterlogged clothes dragged him beneath again – a foot, two feet, three feet. And only then did he strike the shingle bottom. He used this to try to push himself back upwards, but the water was so cold it was virtually gelid. His joints were locking, neuralgic pains shooting through his head.

With a colossal effort – the sort only a man facing certain death can summon – he projected himself back towards the surface. But then another wave crashed over him, the buffet to his head knocking him so senseless that he swallowed brine and snorted stinging bubbles. After this the backwash hit him, pulling him down again. His struggles grew weaker as his body literally refrigerated. The *suck* and *grind* of pebbles was at first deafening in his ears, though gradually now it began to fade and he wondered if he was finally drowning.

Then he heard something else – it sounded like someone calling his name.

Though his neck screamed in agony, he lifted his head up, and through blurred vision saw the outline of the shore in front of him. It didn't look half as far away as he'd expected, which gave him wild hope. He fought his way forwards desperately.

Lights appeared to be moving on the beach. He raised himself up and tried to wave his arms. It was a feeble effort. Nobody could have seen, but now nature gave him a helping hand. Another heavy wave caught him in the middle of the back, rolling him over and over. He tumbled in the surf for several yards, head over heels, bubbles again filling his nose, stinging the front of his brain like a swarm of wasps. The seabed dragged along his side, jagged and prickly with grit, but signifying that he was at last in the shallows.

"Bob!" the voice called again. It sounded like Ellen.

"I'm here," he choked, regaining his feet.

A few yards ahead, he saw figures wading out towards him, thigh-deep. It was deeper where he was – it came to just below his chin – and with the backwards and forwards swelling of the tide, it submerged him again and again, but now, with survival only a fingertip away, he barged his way headlong, coughs wracking his lungs.

"Bob?"

It *was* Ellen. In one hand, she wielded a strong electric torch.

"Ellen," he gasped.

She swung the beam onto him. He heard her intake of breath even over the roar of the sea. "Over here, he's over here!"

Other figures homed in.

Bob reached out for her, tripping and falling again. But her hand now clamped his wrist and yanked it with such strength that at first he thought she'd dislocated his shoulder. Then other hands got hold of him too, and he was being hauled forwards, his toes and knees trailing though rubble and clinker. Seconds later, he was lying facedown on the beach, coughing and retching, heaving up mouthfuls of salt-froth.

The detectives, two of who were young blokes, sank to their haunches around him, panting for breath.

"Good Lord," Ellen stuttered. "You're so lucky we were watching you."

Bob glanced up at her. "Does that mean you've got them?"

"Who?"

"The two guys who pushed me in."

She looked nonplussed. "Guys who …?" She indicated one of the younger officers. "Eric said you left the pub by its back door. When he got round there, you'd gone over the side."

Bob chuckled. "Then I'd suggest your team's surveillance training is not all it could be."

"Whatever, it's a miracle you're alive. Thank God the tide was coming in. You want to go to hospital?"

He climbed wearily to his feet. "Why would I want that?"

"Get that knock on your head seen to."

Bob felt at his temple, from which fresh, hot blood was still trickling. "Only a gash."

"You've also been half-drowned."

"I've been in the sea, that's all. People do it every summer."

"Not in *this* sea."

"I'm fine," he said, glancing around.

Driftwood, broken stones and the usual clutter of debris strewed this desolate corner of beach. Ahead, a flight of concrete steps led up to a gap in a high wall.

"Let's get you warm at least," Ellen said. "And you guys as well." She turned to her men. "Get back to the nick and get showered. Telephone debrief in forty."

Shivering, they traipsed in single file up the steps to the seafront road, where two vehicles were parked in the darkness. The first was a silver Lexus RX; Ellen unlocked it and pushed Bob into the passenger seat. She had a few more words with her team, then climbed in herself, starting the engine and switching the heater on. She sat looking at him.

"What am I going to do with you?" she wondered.

He shrugged, enjoying the sudden gush of warmth, though it soon had his toes and fingers tingling painfully.

"You should get checked out, you know," she said. "You probably need a whole range of shots."

"I doubt even germs could've lived in that sea."

"I ought to arrest you under the Mental Health Act, Bob."

"What's stopping you?"

"Believe it or not, I'm actually off duty. The lads called me in when they thought you'd drowned."

For the first time he noticed that she was in jeans, sweater and a quilted anorak, not her formal office garb.

"And you came running?" he said, touched.

She put the Lexus in gear, and pulled away from the kerb. "Don't read anything into it. It's difficult enough being a cop with you as my ex without you committing suicide as well – and on *my* watch."

"If I'd died out there, it wouldn't have been suicide. Those fellas tried to kill me. Which means I'm onto something."

"Whatever you say."

"You feel the same thing, or you wouldn't have been tailing me."

She glanced sidelong at him. "If you're talking about James Van Ruthers, did you honestly think that we wouldn't already have considered him?"

"I know you went to the asylum."

"But you thought we'd missed something?" She shook her head. "That place is totally escape-proof."

"Yeah, that's what they told me as well."

"Yeah, and that's all they did – they *told* you." She changed gear and turned the car off the main road. They were now moving away from the harbour area and through rows of residential housing. "We on the other hand tested every one of their security procedures to the limit. There's no way any patient could get out of there, so let's leave it at that."

Five minutes later, they arrived at Ellen's house. Bob hadn't seen it before, but it was much as he expected: a pleasant, three-bed detached in one of Kelgarth's few suburban neighbourhoods. The front garden was enclosed by privets; the drive, which was surfaced with ornamental brick, swept around it to a tall beech-wood door painted white.

"Any particular reason why you're bringing me here?" he asked.

"You got first-aid gear in that shitty little room of yours?"

"No."

"Shut up then."

Inside, the house was immaculately tidy, and furnished with exquisite taste. Again this was no surprise. There'd never been a moment during their married life when Bob hadn't felt that the spacious home they'd shared together wasn't so smartly presented that it wouldn't have passed for a show-home. The same couldn't be said for his current dwelling, a cramped bachelor pad centred around his work-station and strewn with papers and fast-food cartons.

Ellen led him straight upstairs, showing him first to the spare bedroom, then to the bathroom. She'd have her shower in her bedroom's en suite, she said. Soon Bob was soaking in a piping hot tub. On Ellen's instruction, he'd left his soiled and sodden clothing in a laundry basket in the corner. He'd also left the bathroom door open.

"For God's sake!" she said, passing by in a robe. She closed the door loudly.

"It's nothing you haven't seen before," he shouted.

"What makes you think I want to see it again?" came the muffled reply.

Shortly afterwards, he heard the sound of water running as she took her own shower. He relaxed into the bubbles. She'd supplied him with soap, shampoo, even body-lotion. But it took quite a while to scrub himself clean – black grit, like coal dust, had embedded in his fingernails and scalp. Once he'd finished, he wrapped a towel around his waist and stuck his head out of the door. A robe was waiting on the banister for him. He put it on, then carried the laundry basket downstairs. Ellen was already there, wearing a knee-length nightie, a cardigan and slippers. Her hair was in damp ringlets; she looked fresh-faced and pretty. She was in the process of hanging up the telephone.

"Debrief done?" he asked.

She nodded. "How's the head?"

He prodded the wound gingerly. "Seems to have stopped bleeding."

She ushered him into an armchair, then examined it up close. "You could do with stitches. In the meantime," she produced some Elastoplast and a jar of antiseptic cream, "this'll have to do."

"Ow!" he complained, as she anointed him.

"Don't be such a baby."

"How'd you feel if you'd been clobbered with a twelve-gauge?"

She stopped what she was doing and gave him a frank stare. "So our friends are now armed?"

"Not quite." He winced again as she applied the sticking plaster.

"What do you mean 'not quite'? Are they or aren't they?"

"I think it was for effect."

"I don't follow."

"Go back to what I said before. Somehow James Van Ruthers is involved in these attacks."

"Bob, I know you've got good instincts, but honestly, you are so far off-beam on …"

76

"I know about the incident last night," he interrupted. "Brady and Hindley."

She looked shocked. "Whoever you've got on my team is singing like a canary, isn't he."

"On the contrary. I've not been able to get in touch with him for two days."

"So there *is* someone?"

"You know there is. The point is it was Van Ruthers who told me about last night's attack. Now how is that possible?"

Ellen plainly didn't know. She seemed shaken as she moved to the drinks cabinet and poured them both a tumbler of Johnny Walker.

"And there's something else," Bob added. "I recognised the guys who dumped me in the drink."

"Go on."

"The one I followed out of the pub – he was John Haigh."

"As in 'the Acid Bath Murderer'?"

"Yeah. The one who was hanged in 1949. And I'm not mistaken. I got a good, clear look at him."

"And the other one?"

"I didn't see him at first because he had a ski-mask on. But just before they rolled me over the side, he looked me right in the face – and he took his mask off."

"Because he wanted you to recognise him?"

"Why else? And I did. It was Donald Neilson."

"'The Black Panther'?"

"Who, if I'm correct, is still serving a full-life tariff without possibility of parole?"

Ellen rubbed at her brow, troubled.

"That's what I meant about the shotgun?" Bob said. "The Panther always carried one. But on this occasion I think it was to complete the outfit – a sort of prop."

"This is getting more insane by minute."

"You don't believe me?"

"Of course I believe you. It's just the craziest thing I've ever known."

"It's also the crux of the case." He knelt down in front of her. "Ellen listen – these serial killers from the past, they're not just an irritating aspect of this. They're integral."

"What, the fact that the perp likes wearing masks?"

"The guy dressed as Haigh wasn't wearing a mask. I saw him full-on, and I'm telling you, he was the dead-spit."

"The dead-spit of what, old photos you may have seen?"

Bob stood up. "Ellen, you know this is more than just some weirdo playing games. At the very least there are two perps."

She shook her head. "We'll just have to add them to the list."

"And that's it?"

"What else do you want me to do?"

"To start with, you can give me everything you've got about the Brady and Hindley incident. The full details."

She stared at him. "You smoking dope, Bob? You want me to commit the very offence that I've been suspected of my whole career, even though I'm completely innocent of it?"

"Oh, so it's okay for you to follow me and see how my leads pan out, but I can't follow you?"

"Damn it Bob!" She jumped to her feet. "I'm a police officer. You're a …"

"A what?" he asked. "A hack? A parasite?"

She crossed the room to the drinks cabinet, where she topped her whisky up.

"Sorry that's how you feel about it," he said. "Here's me thinking young girls are being hurt in Kelgarth, and that me and you were on the same side trying to stop it."

"You know I can't divulge sensitive information."

"Not even if I give you something in return?"

She glanced round at him. "What are you talking about?"

He held something out. It was a small plastic tab with a piece of damp string attached. "I managed to hang onto this while I was in the sea."

"What is it?"

"A shipping tag. I yanked it off the Panther's flak-jacket."

Ellen examined it. Despite it having been immersed, lettering was still visible under its laminated surface.

"Look at the date," she said. "August 1987. Someone bought a coat in 1987 and they're still wearing it?"

"More to the point, someone bought a coat in 1987 and the shipping tag's still on it. Just out of interest, who are 'Quantock & Son'?"

"A costumers in town."

"A what?"

"They supply costumes to theatrical companies, fancy dress at New Year, stuff like that."

Bob was surprised. "And that pays? In a town like this?"

"They've always been one of those oddball little outfits you'd never imagine would make any money. These days, they probably take most of their orders on-line and make deliveries. Look at this …" She was still reading the tag. "'Item nine of fifty-one'. This was part of a bulk order."

"To where, I wonder?"

"We'll ask them in the morning."

"'We'?" he said. "Is that 'we' as in the 'royal we', or as in 'me and you'?"

She sighed. "I'm having no luck getting shot of you, am I? I suppose the next best thing is to keep a close eye on you."

"Your friends in the Northumbria Constabulary won't like it."

She shrugged.

"Or is blood still thicker than water?" he asked.

"Don't even go there, Bob. I have a different life now."

She sat in an armchair, crossed her legs, let one slipper dangle as she sipped.

"Thanks for looking after me," he said.

"Don't read anything into that, either. You were drowning, I rescued you. It's all part of the job."

He crouched alongside the laundry basket and picked through its contents. It wasn't just wet, but thick with sludge and oil. "I don't suppose you've got any man's clothing here? This lot's going to need to go to the dry-cleaners."

"You only brought *one* set of clothes?" she asked, not sounding surprised.

Now it was Bob's turn to shrug.

She got up and headed for the stairs. When she came down again, she was carrying an old tracksuit and a pair of trainers.

"Thanks," he said. "You always keep stuff like this handy?"

"It got left behind, that's all." She went into the kitchen and ran her empty tumbler under the tap.

He followed her in. "Just out of interest, who by?"

"Ask no questions, you'll be told no lies."

"So there's another bloke in your life?"

She checked the back door was locked, then flipped the kitchen lights off and went through into the lounge. "Not at present. But we've been divorced three years, Bob. You expect me to live like a nun?"

"No, it's just that … I mean, I always thought …"

She turned to face him. "Why don't we just keep this professional? You've already got to the inner circle of the investigation. You've got decent bed and board for the night for the princely sum of nothing at all. You ask for any more, Bob, and I'll wonder if you're trying to exploit my good nature."

He nodded. But when she headed past him for the stairs, he reached out and placed a hand on her left breast. She halted, froze.

"Take that away right now, or you'll get it back broken."

"I've missed you, Ellen."

"No-one's fault but your own." He withdrew his hand, and she continued to the stairs. "Turn out the lights when you come up."

"Look, just because I blew it once, that doesn't mean I'd blow it again."

"Don't compound that indecent assault by telling pathetic lies, Bob. You came to Kelgarth to write a saleable story. Not to romance me."

And then she was gone.

It was undeniably true. As her bedroom door closed upstairs, he could have kicked himself. It had seemed so natural just then, so familiar – being together with her, both undressed and relaxing after a hard day at work. And yet it was an illusion. Having seen her up close again, smelled her, touched her, bantered with her, he desperately wanted her back, but not so much that it was the reason for him originally coming here.

It was always the same, he thought ruefully: he'd got off his backside and made the trip from Newcastle for one reason only – to earn some cash. Even though he was sincere in his feelings for Ellen – and at this moment he'd defy anyone to prove otherwise – it was a side issue, a by-product of his work. And what kind of basis was that for a long-term relationship?

The following morning, Ellen drove them both back into Kelgarth. En route, she produced the shipping tag and placed it on the dashboard. It was now enclosed in a sterile slipcase.

"You thinking of taking this to the lab, or something?" Bob asked.

"They might be able to lift something from it."

"Sure they will – *our* prints. Anything else will have got washed off."

"You never know. In the meantime, have a look at this."

She fished a dog-eared paperback from her pocket. It was a self-proclaimed history of mass murder in the UK, entitled *Butchered Britain*. The author was one Edgar Allenby.

Bob was surprised. "You're a copper and you read books like this?"

"Why do the homework when I've got you guys to do it for me?"

"You'd better not have any of *my* books in your collection. Not after all the years I've been made to feel like a tosser for writing them."

"Check through it, will you?"

"He's not much of a writer, Allenby, you know."

"All I need is some stats."

"Walks around at conventions like he's God's gift."

"The stats, Bob."

He flipped the book open. "Stats for what?"

"I want to know how many official multiple murderers we've had in the UK. That means rampage killers, family killers, the lot – not just serial killers."

"How far back are we going?"

"The beginning. From when records were first kept."

"There are bound to be more than that."

"It'll do for a start."

Bob found what he was looking for in the intro. "According to this, between 1837, when our first official serial killer, Thomas Wainewright was transported to Tasmania, and 2001, when this book was published, we've had fifty-eight cases. If memory serves, there've been at least four more since 2001."

"How about between 1837 and 1987?"

"Why 1987 – oh, you mean the tag?"

She nodded.

He made another count. "Fifty-one … Christ!"

"Yeah," she said. "'Item nine of fifty-one'. Mind you, it probably doesn't mean anything."

"Hell of a coincidence if it doesn't."

They drove on in silence, pondering this, and reached *Quantock & Son* about ten minutes later. It was a cubby-hole of a shop, half hidden in a roofed side alley and sandwiched between two vacant units, the caged-off porches to which were crammed with litter and old newspapers. Inside, it was Victorian in its quaintness. Racks of gaudy clothing – everything from pantomime costumes to military uniforms – hung down either side, while on the shelves above there were innumerable hats: tricornes, toppers, Stetsons, even a frontier cap with a raccoon's tail. The serving area was more reminiscent of a pawnshop. It was a hatch rather than a proper counter, but no sooner had a jangling bell signalled their arrival than an avuncular-looking gentleman appeared behind it. He was short, plump, white-haired and dressed very smartly, with a pair of half-moon spectacles perched on the end of his nose and a tape measure draped around his neck.

He introduced himself as Mr. Quantock Junior, and, when they'd explained their purpose, said that he was happy to help. He told them that in 1987 none of the company's transactions had been computerised, though his late-father, who'd been running things in those days, had been meticulous about keeping records. He then withdrew into the shop's rear section, saying that he'd have a look in the filing cabinets; when he returned, he had a slip of yellowing paper with the look of a sales-docket.

He indicated the shipping tag. "That's indeed one of ours. It was part of a batch of costumes purchased by the Crime Museum."

"Crime Museum?" Bob said with interest.

"Kelgarth Crime Museum," Ellen replied. "It was on Jocelyn Street. It was a hokey thing, really. A kind of gimmick. For the tourists, you know."

"What tourists?"

"Exactly. That's probably why it only lasted a few years. Another fortune in tax payers' money flushed down the drain." She turned back to Mr. Quantock. "Am I right in thinking that this bulk order consisted mainly of costumes?"

"Solely of costumes. This particular one …" and he held up the docket, "comprised a camouflage jacket, black leather gloves and a black knitted ski-mask."

"Can you print out the full order for me?" she asked. "Would that be possible?"

"I'm afraid not. As I said, in 1987 we were still working on paper. It's all filed in our back room. You're welcome to come in and have a look."

"That's fine. I'll get one of my detectives to give you a call. Thanks for your time."

They made to leave, but, before exiting, Bob turned again. "Just out of interest, Mr. Quantock … these costumes. What would the Crime Museum have used them for?"

"Exhibits, I'd imagine."

"Did they have actors working there?"

"One or two, I believe. That sort of thing was quite popular in the 1980s. Didn't they used to call it 'living history'?"

They left and walked down the passage to the car park. The roof was glazed, but its leading had rotted in many places and the grimy panes hung loose. Cold rain, which again had replaced the snow, dripped steadily through.

"Well," Ellen said, "we tried."

Bob glanced at her. "And we got a result. Didn't we?"

"The Crime Museum's derelict. There's nothing there."

"It's a lead."

"I'll grant you that – it's a lead. Now we know where these people stole their costumes from. But it can't have been difficult. The place has been empty since 1993."

"You'll at least try to trace the actors who worked there?"

She looked amused. "You mean they went crazy because they lost their jobs, and now they're continuing to impersonate killers, only this time for purposes of revenge?"

"You don't discount that possibility, surely?"

"There's one main problem with it, Bob. If the museum closed in 1993, why wait fourteen years before you put your evil plan in motion?"

82

They'd now reached the car park. Ellen's Lexus was the only vehicle there. Rain lashed it, and they had to hurry over to avoid getting drenched.

"Let's at least check the place out," Bob said when they'd got into the car.

Ellen gave a deep sigh, then put her key into the ignition. They circled the harbour area, and headed out towards the South Shore, but, before they got there, they entered a particularly run-down district. Along its seafront, there was a row of what had once been Edwardian townhouses. Now they'd been converted into low-rent bed-sits. Their formerly whitewashed facades were flaking, their narrow front gardens cluttered with all types of rubbish: everything from tin cans to discarded mattresses. The streets behind them were equally desolate, filled with broken glass and litter. Many of the cars there had simply been abandoned, while others had been burnt. The few shops were boarded up.

"I can't believe the council located a museum here," Bob commented.

"It wasn't always so bad," Ellen replied. "Or so they tell me. But then I've only just moved here, so what do I know?"

"This whole bloody country's decaying."

They approached the museum by passing under the arch of a railway viaduct, and saw that a large section of pavement in front of it had been cordoned off with crime-scene tape. The steps themselves were concealed beneath a waterproof tent. A uniformed bobby, his helmet and slicker dripping with rainwater, was standing on guard.

"This is where the Brady and Hindley attack occurred?" Bob said, surprised.

Ellen nodded.

"It's right outside the place."

"Another coincidence."

"Another one?"

"The other attacks were nowhere near here," she pointed out.

"We should go through that place with a fine toothcomb."

"I will. But I'm going to do it legally. That means I have to get permission. We'll probably need a Health and Safety assessment first."

He groaned. "Why join the fuzz if you're worried about Health and Safety?"

"It's the law."

"It'll delay everything."

"The place could be a deathtrap, Bob. I'm not sending my guys in there blind."

They were now parked opposite, so they were able to look the building over properly. In a former life, it had been a factory warehouse. It was huge and square, towering to maybe sixty feet, and built from functional red brick, which had now blackened with smoke and dirt. Some changes had been affected in more recent times, presumably to make it look less like a fragment of declining industry and more like a visitors centre. Ornate iron railings had been erected along the front. The entrance door, of which they could see only the top above the rainproof tent, was arched and corniced. The windows looked newer than the rest of the building, though they were thick with grime, and even though fifteen feet off the ground, many had been broken and were now covered with boards which, in their turn, had been covered with fly-posters. It was a true eyesore.

"Okay," Bob said. "Get the permits. But what are we going to do in the meantime?"

"I'll tell you what *you're* going to do." She put her foot to the gas again. "You're going to Kelgarth Police Station, where you're going to ask for Detective Sergeant Biggins. You're then going to give him a witness statement about the incident at *The Rusty Anchor*. Tell him I sent you."

"And what are you going to do?"

"I'm going to re-interview Van Ruthers."

"I told you he was involved."

"I'm not convinced of that yet. But I need to find out how he knew about the Brady and Hindley attack."

"You're going to keep me in the loop though, yeah?"

Once again she looked exasperated. "Bob, why? Will you get it through your head – we're not working together, we're not partners. This is a very serious criminal enquiry and I'm already way out of line having involved you so much."

Bob didn't immediately respond. He was an outsider here, he knew. And the more argumentative he became, the more likely she was to keep him at arm's length, which, as he'd now suddenly remembered something else discomforting, could prove a real disaster. Every scrap of paperwork he'd collected on the case had been left in *The Rusty Anchor* the previous night. Anyone could have whipped them. If that had happened, and Ellen stopped talking to him, he'd have absolutely nothing.

"I'd rather you took me to *The Rusty Anchor*?" he said. "I can make my own way to the station afterwards."

"There's a canteen at the nick if you're hungry. It's probably cheaper too."

"No, there's something I have to do."

"Suit yourself."

They reached the pub and he opened the passenger door, but he didn't get out straight away. He turned to face her. "If I give you the name of the officer who tipped me off about these crimes, you've got to promise not to lift him on the strength of it."

Ellen regarded him wearily. "How on Earth can I promise that?"

"You've got to promise, Ellen. Keep an eye on him from now on, feed him stuff on a need-to-know, pull him the next time he does it ... but not this time or it's no deal."

"Why are you offering me this now?"

"I don't want to be shut out."

"You know I can't share intel with you."

"Anything you give me would be completely confidential. I don't want to prejudice this case anymore than you do. There's no way I'd break this story until the perps are all banged up."

"It won't be much of an exclusive then."

"It will if you give me the inside track. Anonymously of course, but with all the juicy detail – you know, the stuff the rest of the pack will have to gloss over."

She still looked wary, but perhaps realising that under these circumstances *she'd* be in charge of what he knew and what he didn't, she finally nodded. "All right. But I want the mole's name now."

"And you won't lift him yet ..."

"Just tell me who he is."

"Cannock."

"Who?"

"DC Les Cannock."

She nodded and pursed her lips, then said: "Cute, Bob. Hilarious in fact." And she pushed him from the car.

"Wait a minute, what are you doing?"

"Your jokes are in increasingly poor taste."

She leaned over to close the door, but he blocked it. "You welching on me, Ellen?"

She glared at him. "You know perfectly well that there are no officers on my team called Les Cannock. However, the chap who runs things at *Mike's Bar* is called Les Cannock. And he's the one who tipped us off about *you*."

And she slammed the door closed and gunned the Lexus away.

With it being mid-January, the sky was darkening to black by late afternoon. The rain continued to fall, the North Sea wind blasting it in frenzied swirls.

Bob, who only had an anorak over the tracksuit Ellen had loaned him, huddled in the damp telephone booth as he tried to place his call. He'd discovered two things on getting back to *The Rusty Anchor*: firstly, the bar staff had retrieved his missing paperwork and kept it for him; secondly, someone else had retrieved his mobile phone and presumably kept it for themselves.

"DI Blackwood," said the voice on the line.

"Ellen … it's Bob. Look, don't hang up!"

There was an irritated pause, then: "What do you want now?"

"First off, I've only got a handful of change, so I've got to make this snappy."

"Fine, I've no problem with that at all."

"Ellen, I think we're being set up."

"Have you given that statement to Sergeant Biggins yet?"

"No …"

"Jesus Christ, Bob!"

"Just listen. It's about this guy Cannock."

She said nothing. By the background noise – faint radio chatter, the dull thudding of windscreen wipers – she was on the road.

Bob continued: "I only had one meeting with him, Ellen, but he didn't just tip me off about your investigation. Before we left the pub where we hooked up, he took me out to his car and gave me a shed-load of paperwork. I mean stuff pertaining to the case. When we first met he chucked me a few morsels to draw me in. But once I was in he gave me the real meat – analysis reports, witness statements everything. I've got it here in my hand."

She paused before saying: "And it's legit?"

"I'm certain. So if he isn't a real cop, how did he get hold of it?"

"He probably is a real cop. He'll have given you a false name as a bit of extra insurance for himself."

"The same name that was given to you? And incidentally, the barkeep who contacted you from *Mike's Bar* – guess what, he doesn't exist either. I went there to check."

"Look, where are you going with this, Bob? I'm trying to work."

"Will you stop treating me as if I'm not on your side. Just listen to what I've got to say, it's important. When you saw Van Ruthers, did the interview take place in his room or in one of the rec areas?"

"In his room," she said. "He hardly comes out of it, apparently."

"Did you have a bagman with you?"

"Of course. DC Mulligan."

"And did either of you take any paperwork in there with you? Paperwork from the enquiry, I mean."

"I certainly didn't." The ludicrousness of such an idea was implicit in her tone.

"Can you say the same for Mulligan?"

Several telling seconds passed before she replied: "No."

"Is he likely to have done?"

"Terry Mulligan's a rookie. So I suppose he might have."

"Okay. Suppose Van Ruthers snaffled some of Mulligan's paperwork while he wasn't looking?"

"Oh Bob ..."

Bob waved his fistful of wet, crumpled documentation as if Ellen was in the phone booth with him. "All he'd have needed is one case-file. Just one. Mulligan leaves it on the floor, Van Ruthers kicks it under the bed, done."

"That didn't happen."

"You're one hundred percent sure?"

"One of the two of us would have noticed."

"Not necessarily."

"If not that, Mulligan would have reported it missing afterwards."

"Would he? If he knew it meant he'd get the bollocking of his life?"

She paused again, clearly wondering. "He'd have taken the bollocking rather than leave something important in the hands of a suspect, I'm certain of it."

"Suppose he thought he'd dropped it in the street somewhere?"

"That's a whole lot more likely than him letting Van Ruthers pinch it."

The conversation was briefly interrupted as Bob shoved more coins into the slot.

"Van Ruthers claims he has special powers," he said.

"I know."

"Unusual abilities."

"I know."

"Suppose he's not lying?"

"I can't believe I'm listening to this."

"I'm not talking about magic, Ellen. It doesn't have to be anything as dramatic as that. What about sleight of hand?"

"Even if that's true, how did this guy Cannock get hold of it? Who is he even?"

"I don't know. An actor maybe, someone Van Ruthers hired."

"You're telling me that a mental patient under twenty-four hour supervision is able to hire an actor to do a job for him without the consent, or at least the knowledge, of those in charge?"

"Well ..." Bob said awkwardly, "this is where it all gets a bit speculative. If you want my opinion, I'd look at Doctor Hawkins as well. He's an oddball, but it's not just that. Van Ruthers couldn't really pull any of this off without an accomplice."

"Hawkins an accomplice? Bob, this is nonsensical fantasy ..."

"Just bear it in mind, that's all I'm asking you to do."

"I won't even consider it."

"Then why are you going back to the hospital? Why are you going to see Van Ruthers again, if every single pointer we've got doesn't indicate that he's responsible for this?"

At the other end of the line, Ellen might have hung up there and then, infuriated by Bob's strident opinions and tiresome meddling, not to mention the soaring self-confidence he always seemed to possess that he knew her job better than she did. But ahead of her now, the towering form of Kelgarth Secure Hospital was emerging through the rain-soaked gloom, and there was no question about it – every instinct she had was telling her that James Van Ruthers was behind this spate of attacks. And because it was impossible for this to be true, there had to be *another* factor, and though she didn't want to admit it – as they'd already considered most of the probables, this other factor would have to be one of the improbables.

"Just go and give that statement to Sergeant Biggins," she said.

"I will," Bob promised.

He wasn't lying. He intended to give the statement. But there was something else he needed to do first. At that point his money ran out and the phone went dead.

Suddenly he felt very alone.

This was a forlorn corner of Kelgarth. The light in the booth was perhaps the only light in a quarter-mile or so. The rest was darkness, rain and dismal, decaying brickwork. He stepped outside and looked around. The Crime Museum lowered over him. But this was its unlit rear section. On all sides lay dereliction: to the left, an ex-parking area was covered with litter and last autumn's leaves; to the right stood similar buildings to the museum – gaunt, spectral ruins, boarded up, dark with soot. Directly in front of him there was a fence, broken in many places, and on the other side of that a flight of stone steps leading down to the museum's basement door.

Bob cautiously descended. The actual door, which lay to one side, looked to have been wrenched from its hinges, and, by the exposed metal and freshly splintered wood, this damage had been inflicted relatively recently – which was a worry. Did dropouts hang around here now, drug-addicts?

Bob hesitated to go further. Was this sensible? He had no mobile, and the police constable who earlier on had been posted at the front had now gone off duty and had not been replaced – that had been the first thing Bob had checked for on coming back here. At first it had pleased him, but not now. Of course, the alternative was returning to Mike's Bar and hoping that Ellen would deign to call round and give him an update when

88

she'd finished at the hospital. It was no contest. He took the electric torch from his anorak pocket, switched it on, and advanced into the interior.

The first room looked as if it had been used for storage. It contained rent-open boxes and old shelving, but everything in there now was green with mould. Beyond it, through another smashed door, he peeked into a second room. Clues to the building's industrial past were in evidence here: hanging cables, corroded stumps where machinery might once have been fixed. There was a third door on the far side of this, several feet from the ground and accessible by low, wooden stairs. In this case the door was still attached, though it sagged from rotted hinges, with only a sliver of darkness visible behind it.

Bob walked stealthily across. His first foot on the stair creaked loudly, as did his second – he imagined they could be heard in the farthest reaches of the building. At the top, he teased the door open with his torch. Its light struck the facing wall of a passage, which ran off to the right. Bob glanced down it – and froze.

An elderly woman was standing there, wearing old-fashioned clothes.

At first he didn't move, hardly dared breathe. She wore a dingy dress, the skirts of which came down to the floor, and over this a tatty shawl. On her head there was a coalscuttle bonnet. Though her face was turned towards him, her eyes wide open, she didn't react. Gradually Bob realised that he wasn't looking at a woman, but at an extremely lifelike effigy of one. Feeling braver, he advanced. The floorboards creaked again. There were draperies of dust-thick cobweb above his head. Only when he was close to the woman, did he see that she too was covered in dust; it was wadded in the folds of her clothing, ingrained into the rim of her bonnet.

"You're a waxwork," he said aloud.

The resemblance to a real human being was uncanny, but he only needed to touch the tip of her beak-like nose to confirm his suspicion. He walked slowly around her. Her garb was intended to be Victorian, but it looked distinctly second class, as if this was the facsimile of a working woman rather than a posh lady.

"So, what are you doing down here?" he wondered, this time more quietly because he didn't like the echo of his voice in the chambers above. "Some vandals pinch you and then decide you were too heavy?"

He moved on and reached another stair. This one led up to a narrow landing that was basically a T-junction, with two closed doors at either end. For no particular reason, he opted to go left. Just as he did, he heard a noise in the passage below – like the rustling of old cloth. He halted, listening intently. But the noise had ceased almost as soon as it had begun. He went back down the stair to the passage and shone his light along it.

The motionless shape of the woman stood as before. Bob waited and watched. Again he held his breath, but there was no further sound.

"It's quite irregular," Doctor Hawkins said, fidgeting behind his desk. "I mean, detectives come here all the time – that's something we have to live with. But mostly they've made appointments."

"Normally I would," Ellen replied. "But this enquiry's moving fast. I need to see Van Ruthers now."

"You realise my staff will shortly be changing shifts? It's an awkward time"

"It won't take long. A few things have come up since I last spoke to him, that's all."

The doctor looked oddly flustered, as he had from the moment she'd arrived.

"There's one other thing," she added. "Van Ruthers is watched continually on CCTV, correct?"

"Of course. All our patients are."

"Good. If you don't mind, I'd like to see the tape covering the meeting I had with him last week."

"I'm afraid I do mind."

"It's important, Doctor Hawkins. Something may have happened during that interview, and I'd like to see it again."

"It's quite impossible."

"I wouldn't like to have to insist."

He smiled another of those thin, wry smiles that he seemed to specialise in. "Insist away, it won't make any difference. The tapes here are re-used again and again. Quite likely, that one's been wiped several times since last week."

"You're not even prepared to check?" she asked.

"I don't need to check."

"You said the tape had 'likely' been wiped, not 'definitely'."

He was now leaning back in his chair, his arms folded, his legs crossed – a tautly defensive posture, which almost certainly meant that he was about to lie.

"Inspector Blackwood, I can assure you the tape you want does not exist."

Ellen didn't like any of this. The guy was literally squirming. She hadn't wanted to believe Bob, yet thus far his suspicions looked to be right on the money.

"Don't you even want to know why I d like to see it?" she wondered.

"I have no interest."

90

"You say that a lot, don't you … where James Van Ruthers is concerned. Rather like a suspect who protests his innocence too much."

"A suspect?" Hawkins jumped to his feet. He looked outraged, but managed to keep his temper in check. Instead, he came stiffly around his desk and opened the door. "Van Ruthers is in the gymnasium. At his own request, he's taking his exercise period alone. Feel free to make your way down there. It's clearly signposted. Unfortunately, I can't spare anyone to escort you."

This was clearly a breach of protocol. There were 'open' sections of the hospital that were perfectly safe for visitors, but the gym would be accessible to patients. Admittedly, they'd probably attend it under supervision, but to send a visitor down there alone – presumably unconcerned about whether he or she strayed from the path – had to be against regulations. Before she left the office, Ellen felt justified in enquiring: "Are you in on this, Doctor Hawkins?"

"I beg your pardon?"

"It would explain a lot." Deep inside, she could hardly believe what she was saying, but suddenly it was all adding up. "These special powers Van Ruthers boasts of – have you seen them maybe? Are you studying them? Is that what this is about?"

Hawkins's flushed face had now paled almost to white. His taut lips quivered. "As I say, DI Blackwood, the gymnasium is clearly signposted."

"I'm sorry if I've caused offence. But I can't think of anything else he'd have on you."

"If you'd like to leave now please. I'm far too busy to entertain this childish speculation." As she left, he added: "Make further accusations of this sort, and I won't hesitate to take legal action."

"I didn't make any accusations, Doctor Hawkins," she replied. "I asked you a simple question. And so far you haven't answered it."

Bob hadn't really been sure what he was going to do when he got into this place.

It crossed his mind that maybe he'd only intended to stick his head inside, have a quick sniff, and then go back to *Mike's Bar*, which, for all its faults suddenly seemed a much more desirable place to be. But now he was deep within, and it seemed pointless, having come so far, not to at least look around properly.

Because of the nature of its subject matter, the Crime Museum's curators might consciously have sought to retain an urban industrial aura, or maybe they'd just cut costs by utilising the building as they'd found it. Either way, its main exhibition halls still looked more like warehouse hangars than repositories of relics. There was bare brickwork everywhere.

Water dripped from overhead girders. Stairways leading to higher galleries were of basic steel. Occasionally there were remnants of its more recent life: his torch picked out empty display-cases, deserted podia. There were also images. In the back of one damp recess, he found what looked like a blown-up sketch of a public hanging: a hooded man, his legs and arms bound with belts, dangled over a wildly cheering crowd.

There were also more wax figures.

In fact the next one gave him a heart-stopping shock. He'd no sooner turned from the 'hanged man' recess, when a face seemed to leap at him out of the darkness. It was thin, pallid in complexion, in fact virtually white, which contrasted sharply with its bright red lips, black, greased-back hair and slanting, black eyebrows. The dark pits of its eyes and the sinister smile on its mouth gave it a genuinely malevolent aspect.

Its sudden appearance was only a trick of the torchlight – the ugly figure was standing just left of the recess, quite close to Bob's shoulder. But he was still surprised. He'd been sure there was no such form alongside him when he'd first stopped here. He looked it over more carefully: it was wearing a shabby 1960s suit, the jacket buttoned up rather nerdishly, both shoulders patterned with dust. However, its face was the most distinctive feature, and he'd seen it on photographs many times. It was Graham Young, the mass poisoner and self-styled Dracula look-alike.

Yet again, the effigy was so realistic that Bob couldn't help prodding it. It rocked rigidly back and forth. He shone his torch further afield, and saw other figures dotted around the vast interior. The moving patch of light played further tricks. It was difficult not to keep imagining that some of them were actually moving. Not by a lot – just the odd twitch, the occasional shift in posture. Realising that he was letting the atmosphere get to him, he moved swiftly on. Another few minutes poking around and then he'd be out of here.

On her way to the gym, Ellen wondered about Doctor Hawkins.

He'd looked defensive and guilty; his responses to her questions had been, at best, evasive. Even his anger had been faked – almost as if the real emotion he'd felt at that moment had been fear. It was hard to believe that an eminent psychiatrist could make these rudimentary errors, but maybe Hawkins suffered from that condition typical of so many high-ranking doctors and scientists: a failure to understand that those around them are not all micro-intellects.

The double-doors to the gymnasium now approached, one of them standing ajar. It struck her as strange that there was nobody on guard here. In fact, she'd passed a couple of checkpoints that had been oddly unmanned. She felt renewed uncertainty about Hawkins. It would only take a phone-call from him to stand his staff down.

She peeked through the double-doors rather than going straight in.

The gym was of standard design: a polished floor, wall-bars, a pile of foam-rubber mats in one corner. The only difference from a school gym was that the high windows here were barred and covered with coils of razor-wire. There was nobody present except Van Ruthers, who was in the very middle, sitting legs-crossed on top of a vaulting horse.

His eyes were closed, as if he'd been meditating. But now they snapped open. "DI Blackwood, what a pleasure. Not that it's any surprise."

"It isn't?" she said, advancing warily.

"Wasn't it the great Sherlock Holmes who said: 'When you have eliminated all which is impossible, then whatever remains, however improbable, must be the truth.'?"

"Meaning?"

"Meaning you've finally decided that, however unlikely it seems, I simply *must* have some involvement with these crimes in Kelgarth."

"Either that or you know someone who does."

"But even then you're confused, aren't you?" He smiled. "Because you know I have no contacts with the outside world that aren't carefully vetted."

"So how does he talk to you?" Ellen asked. "You got a mobile phone no-one knows about?"

He chuckled. "Do you know how often each corner of this building is searched? Do you know how thorough those searches are? Especially those of our personal quarters?"

"So it's a member of staff?"

"Who did what?"

"You know what?"

"Ah, you mean Brady and Hindley's attack on the prostitute?"

It was difficult for Ellen to conceal her surprise. So Van Ruthers also knew the latest victim was a prostitute – another well protected secret.

"The only person who could have told you that is a member of staff."

"And if he did, it stands to reason that he must have committed the crimes, because not only are you now bewildered that I know about the attack in the first place, but you're additionally bewildered that I know who the victim was. How would you feel if I also told you that she was wearing a black skirt, a green blouse, and no underwear at all, the saucy little trollop …"

"I'll get your friend," Ellen said. "If I have to tear this place down brick by brick, I'll find him. And I'll make sure he knows that you're the one who led us to him."

"I'm disappointed in you, DI Blackwood. You're a woman, yet you're also a high-ranking CID officer. That means you must have something about you. You can't have blagged your way into that position through positive discrimination, the way they do in the uniform branch. Yet thus far in this enquiry you've shown alarmingly little imagination. Your ex-husband is steps ahead of you, I'm afraid."

"My ex-husband's a writer. He can afford to be imaginative."

"And you're a detective. Can you afford him to crack the case before you do?"

"Why did you involve him?"

"Me?"

"Bob was deliberately brought into this case, and the way I see it, there can only be one reason for that – to sensationalise it."

"Interesting idea."

"But on this occasion I think that you – or whoever you've got on the outside – may have miscalculated. I've come to an agreement with Bob. For once in his life, he's decided to treat this series of crimes for exactly what it is. Not as a titillating story for the tabloids, not another chapter in some trashy, exploitative book. But as the lewd and depraved actions of someone hopelessly sick. From today onwards, his only interest is to help me solve it."

"And you believe that?"

"I know him better than you."

Van Ruthers smiled again. "But not as well as you should. Your ex-husband's a bloodhound. He enjoys the hunt as much as you do. But equally like you, he enjoys the kill more. The difference is, *unlike* you, who's satisfied to see another felon put behind bars, and then goes back to her cold, empty house with nothing more than a half-hearted clap on the back from her superiors and the usual instruction that she mustn't give interviews, he sees his name in print and his books on the shelves. He dines in triumph, drinks champagne and is surrounded by pretty little authoress wannabes who'll do *anything* so long as he reads their latest draft."

Ellen couldn't conceal a smirk. "Trust me, Bob wouldn't recognise that outcome."

"But he will this time." Van Ruthers's smile faded. "Good as his promise to you was, wait until he gets a load of *this* selling point."

He closed his eyes, squeezing them shut as if concentrating. She watched uncertainly. A few seconds passed before his posture relaxed. His hands went limp, his head slumped onto his chest.

Ellen stepped towards him. Then she heard the *clump* of approaching feet. She turned. They were still alone in the gym, but now she noticed a folding metal door a few yards behind her. It had concertinaed part way open; beyond it, a dim passage receded between two rows of lockers.

The outline of a man was advancing up that passage – slowly, clumsily.

Ellen's hair prickled. She knew she should drag her phone from her mac pocket, or make a dash for the exit. But for some reason, probably morbid fascination, she did none of those things. She stayed where she was, semi-hypnotised, as the figure came fully into view, shouldering its way past the partly open door.

It was dressed in swanky, late-Victorian fashions, wearing an elegant evening suit with a frilled white shirt and cuffs, a black topper and a black cape with a red silk lining. But none of this immediately struck her because she was too busy focusing on its face – or rather on its lack of face. There were no distinguishing features at all: no nose, eyes, mouth or ears. Neither had it any hair. Despite the topper perched on it at a jaunty angle, its head was nothing more than a pale, skin-toned ovoid.

The apparition didn't come any further, but remained next to the open doorway. Suddenly it was still again, perfectly still – like a dummy.

She heard a grunt behind her. Van Ruthers had woken up. He shook himself, took a deep breath and then smiled. "Recognise him?"

"How can I recognise him?" Ellen stammered. "He has no face."

"That's because no-one knows who he was."

"What're you talking about?"

"Work it out. You're a police officer aren't you, and this is one of the most famous murderers in British history. I admit the lack of face is a bit theatrical. But artistic types are often given to pretension. Well, have you guessed?"

She nodded slowly, bewildered as to what kind of game they were playing here, but fascinated nonetheless. "For what it's worth, whoever Jack the Ripper was, it's unlikely he prowled the streets of Whitechapel dressed like that. Firstly, he'd have been spotted as an outsider. Secondly, and more likely, he'd have been robbed."

"Valid points. But then I didn't make him."

"*Make* him?"

He nodded, grinned. "See for yourself. There's no-one inside there."

Unable to stop herself, Ellen went over and examined the figure more closely. She touched its arm, then its chest. Both were hard, unyielding. When she pushed it, it rocked stiffly.

"This is some kind of animatronic?" she said, incredulous.

"Far from it. It has articulated joints, but apart from that it's solid plastic. Aside from the head and hands of course, which are wax."

"Wax?" She put her fingers to the featureless face, and indeed it was wax: cool, smooth, lifeless. "But that's not possible, it was walking."

"Oh, they do a lot more than that. As you've now surely realised."

She turned slowly to face him, only to see that he was dropping into the same half-trance as before. There was a rustle of cloth. She spun back around – the effigy had changed position. Its head had turned to look directly at her. It raised and flexed its right hand, then pushed it inside its jacket. When it re-appeared, it clasped a long, thick-bladed knife.

Ellen started to backtrack, but the thing didn't immediately come after her. Instead, with a speed of movement that was truly shocking, it swung the blade sideways and chopped clean through an electric cable that ran from the locker room door to the ceiling. When Ellen glanced up to see what the cable connected to, her blood ran cold.

The surveillance camera for the gymnasium.

Now she realised why the faceless horror hadn't come straight into the room before.

Knife in hand, it advanced towards her.

Bob had never expected the Crime Museum to be so big that he would get lost in it, but suddenly he wasn't sure which way was forwards and which was back?

From what he could see, it was composed of four main exhibition halls, all with adjoining rooms and annexes, but arranged in a basic square. He'd now wandered through at least three of these, but having got turned round a number of times, could no longer tell which was which. He strode down a connecting passage. It had a steel grille for a floor, which *clanked* with every footfall. Half way along he came to an alcove on the left, where, when he shone his light into it, two more of the wax figures were standing. He'd seen a number of these by now; each one represented a famous mass murderer from Britain's past. In this case, the one on the right was Peter Sutcliffe.

Bob climbed up onto the low dais. With its thick beard and moustache, and dark, shaggy hair, the effigy might have stepped straight out of a police mug-shot. Like all the others, its lifelike eyes seemed to fix on him. He examined its clothes: a donkey jacket, jeans, scuffed boots. Bob wondered if requisitioning this *very* outfit and sending it to the forensics lab would yield results. Could it be that Dawn-Marie Wilkinson's attacker had worn these same clothes?

Then he spotted something else, and the breath caught in his throat.

He bent to look more closely, and there was no mistake. The figure's right hand was spattered with red-brown spots.

Suddenly Bob's pulse was racing; his mouth had gone dry.

He straightened up, stepped back down into the passage. Again his feet *clanked* on the steel floor. He shone his torch onto the other figure. It depicted a short, thin man with a narrow, rather peevish face. It had a shock of black hair and was wearing square-framed spectacles; its clothing was a sweatshirt and a pair of green, canvas pants. It looked completely unremarkable, could have been anyone you'd pass in the street without noticing. But Bob recognised it as an effigy of Dennis Nilsen, the necrophiliac slayer of fifteen men and boys in the early 1980s. The encircling darkness now felt extremely cold and empty; the journey back to the world of light seemed a long one. Again, Bob shone his torch on Sutcliffe's bloodstained hand.

It had to be a joke or trick. But no-one was laughing, least of all himself.

He hurried on, walking down the passage towards the next exhibition area. When he reached the entrance to it, he stopped to think. Moonlight glimmered down; again it was a vast, cavernous space. Was this the hall he'd come into on first entering? If so, all he had to do was circulate its outer wall and he'd find the cellar stair.

But then he heard a sound – a *clank* on the corridor floor.

He whirled round, shone his torch back down the passage.

Peter Sutcliffe had stepped from the alcove. As Bob watched, Dennis Nilsen did the same thing. Together, they turned slowly to face him. The lenses of Nilsen's glasses shone like fish-eyes in the torchlight.

"Enough!" Doctor Hawkins bellowed, barging into the gymnasium. "It's gone too far! For God's sake man, stop this!"

The faceless effigy was still advancing on Ellen, knife in hand, but now it froze – and Van Ruthers woke up. He glared at the intruder.

"Why Doctor Hawkins, what's the matter? Annoyed we turned your TV show off?"

"You think you can just do anything you want?" Hawkins said.

"I *know* I can."

"My God, you're a maniac."

"You're the maniac, Hawkins," Ellen retorted. "Allowing him to bring this monstrosity in here? And don't tell me you didn't – how else did it get past security?"

Hawkins stared at the effigy with revulsion. "I'd heard his boasts, his ludicrous claims that he could animate the inanimate, that he'd been honing his talent for years and now was manipulating mannequins to continue his crime wave. Of course I didn't believe him. When he first showed me examples of his ability, it was simple objects – books, cups, pens. I watched on the video monitor as a wad of paperwork slid out from your colleague's valise and crept across the floor of its own accord. But even then I doubted his wilder claims. He said he would prove it beyond doubt. Suggested I bring one of the effigies from the Crime Museum, saying that he would make it walk, jump, dance. I scoffed, but he assured me it would work, told me he had a particular psychokinetic link with that place. As a young man, it had obsessed him; he'd practically lived there in an effort to understand his condition. I needed to know more, so I complied. I entered the museum at night, and brought out the first one I found."

Hawkins shook his head, as if he couldn't believe what he'd been party to. He approached the silent figure with unwilling steps. "And then he demonstrated it for me."

"A demonstration," Van Ruthers said, "at the end of which you wept with joy."

Hawkins nodded, as if he couldn't believe that either.

"You should have wept with shame," Ellen said. "You knew about these attacks, yet you did nothing?"

Hawkins was still gazing at the effigy. He seemed vague, helpless. "They were guttersnipes, he said. Silly, drunken slatterns, whose unmarried, drug-abusing partners did the exact same thing to them every day. But enough's enough, Van Ruthers." He rounded on the patient, suddenly himself again. "I'm not aiding and abetting this mindlessness any more. You can take your amazing powers and your weird and wonderful dancing dummies ..."

His last word was a choked gasp; crimson foam burst from his lips.

Slowly and deliberately, the faceless effigy withdrew the long, steel blade from between his ribs. Hawkins made a helpless gesture, then dropped to his knees. Blood began throbbing from his side as if from a faucet. He turned a stricken face to Ellen, then toppled over.

"Poor Hawkins," Van Ruthers said, opening his eyes again. "If only he'd realised that he was being exploited too, that he was just another cog in my machine."

Ellen stared at him speechless.

He continued: "He was totally mesmerised. Completely taken in by the fantasy that, when the world knew me and was astounded by me, he'd be my keeper – that to get to me, they'd first have to go through him. He assumed it would save his career. All his books have failed, you see. He regarded this place as the end of the line – this town, this facility." Van Ruthers smiled. "And I'm afraid that's true for you too, DI Blackwood."

Ellen turned and ran. Behind her, cloth rustled as the ghastly thing came alive again. She vaulted over Hawkins's body, and dashed for the double doors. She'd almost reached them when they slammed closed. She grabbed frantically at the handle, but a metallic *thunk* signalled that a lock had fallen into place.

Bob didn't look back until he reached the top of the steel stair.

Below, the two figures came into view again, stopping side by side in a blot of moonlight. A third figure joined them. This one was much taller and broader at the shoulder and wearing a tight, dark uniform of some sort; it was also carrying an axe.

Bob's face prickled with sweat as he backed into the shadows. He clamped his mouth shut, feeling certain they'd hear it if he didn't hold his breath, though deep down he didn't know if these things could actually hear anything.

A door creaked open – it was somewhere up here with him.

He looked left, and saw rays of moonlight spilling onto the wide metal catwalk that comprised the first floor gallery. What looked like a woman in a long black dress and with a black lace veil over her head, shuffled into view. He turned and fled the other way, now regardless of any noise he might make. And he *did* make noise, plenty. Not only did his feet echo on the steel catwalk, but, as he'd switched his torch off earlier and still hadn't dared to put it back on, he blundered into an empty display-cabinet, sending it hurtling to the floor below, where it smashed deafeningly to pieces.

Panting, he halted at a point where the catwalk turned sharply right and crossed the exhibition hall as a bridge. Something was coming over it towards him. This figure was perhaps the most bizarre yet: it was a dapper chap, wearing a bowler hat and wielding a cane. It also had an absurd handlebar moustache, which stuck out several inches to either side of its face.

Again Bob retreated – until his back bumped against a door. He turned, opened it and slipped through into what looked like a small storage-room. Closing the door behind him, he switched his torch on. The room was draped in cobwebs and cluttered with boxes and crates, but there was a window on the far side of it. This had been boarded, but only with a couple of planks, which he was sure he could loosen. He jammed a chair under the door-handle, then advanced on the window and threw his shoulder in. The boards resisted, and now he heard fumbling on the other side of the door. Frantically, he increased his efforts. The boards broke outwards, and he pitched clean through, falling several feet before landing on a rusty iron platform. He was now on the outside of the building. It had stopped raining, but a hard, wet wind tugged at him. He glanced around – the platform was the upper section of a fire-escape; little more than a rusty lip hanging forty feet above a mass of demolition rubble. Ordinarily, just standing upright on this would have made him dizzy, but now, without thinking, he hurried down the ladder-stair, even though it was loose and rickety, and its rungs slippery. He shone his torch ahead – and only just avoided disaster. The rungs ran out some five feet down. The bottom three-quarters of the ladder had fallen off, leaving him suspended in mid-air.

Somewhere above, he heard a breaking sound – it was the storeroom door.

He shone his torch directly downwards: but still saw only twisted girders and shards of shattered stone. Even if he hung full-length by his fingertips and dropped, it would still be well over twenty feet. However, to his left there was another window. It would mean going back inside, but what choice was there? He switched his torch off, shoved it into an anorak pocket, then fitted his fingers around the planks and yanked them loose. Beyond those, only jagged teeth of glass remained. His slid between them, unconcerned that they plucked at his clothes and scored his flesh.

On the other side it was pitch-black. He crouched on bare floorboards, sobbing for breath. There were still noises overhead. He heard the rattling of the fire-escape as something alighted on it.

Rising to his feet, he hobbled forwards. A heavy black curtain hung in his path. He tried to feel his way through it, at last finding the edge and peeking around.

A figure was standing there with its back half-turned to him. He immediately recognised the cashmere overcoat and clipped moustache of the John Haigh facsimile. Slowly, robotically, it was turning its head from side to side, as if confused about where he was. At the sight of this, Bob felt intolerably weary; he was now sweat-soaked, his body wracked with pain. Then he went rigid – as the cold metal of a shotgun muzzle was pressed into the side of his neck.

A loud *clack-click* signalled the ratcheting of a shell into its breach.

As the knife-wielding monster paced Ellen around the gym, she watched it visibly strengthen and become steadily surer of its balance and footing. Van Ruthers, still perched cross-legged on the vaulting horse, was now in a deep trance. Evidently, the further in he went, the greater the control he had over his puppets.

This one had now lost its top-hat, yet somehow its featureless, egg-like head made it seem even more malign: it was the embodiment of namelessness, a walking anonymity. Not that it was *walking* any more. Wherever she ran, it darted in front of her. It leaped from side to side, clambered easily over every piece of apparatus she pushed into its path. And when it was close enough, it struck viciously with that butchering blade – hard enough to slice through a tackle-bag, to puncture a medicine ball. Thanks to her own keep-fit regime, Ellen had kept one step ahead of the thing; she'd even managed to use her mobile to place a call for back-up, though out here on the South Shore that could take ten minutes to arrive. Now however, the monstrosity was finally backing her into a corner. Only one avenue of escape remained: the wall-bars. Snatching off her shoes, she flung them at it one after another. The first missed, but the second knocked a chunk of wax out of its blank face. Something blue glinted underneath, but the monster didn't even flinch. Instead, it closed in for the kill. Ellen spun around and went scuttling up the bars, just getting out of reach before the blade swept down and sheared three of them in half.

When she reached the top, about fifteen feet up, she glanced down. It gazed at her, for the first time seeming unsure what move to make next. Only after apparent lengthy consideration did it slide the knife back under its jacket and commence to climb.

Ellen's heart sank. She'd hoped it would find this task impossible, but it ascended swiftly, staring up as if it had real eyes. Even the wax cracking and flaking off its hands caused no delay; what looked like blue plastic claws were visible underneath. She started to slide sideways; another idea had just occurred to her. The wall-bars were arranged around the gym in sections. Between this one and the next was what looked like a pulley – two lengths of chain attached to each other at the top and bottom. She reached it and, clinging to the bars one-handed, yanked one side of the chain downwards. As she'd hoped, a series of thick climbing-ropes swung out along a runner on the ceiling.

She glanced back. The effigy was now almost at the top of the bars.

"That's it, keep coming," she said. "But anyone can climb wall-bars."

She turned again. The six ropes had now slid out to the full extent of their runner. The nearest was perhaps four feet away. Her plan was simple: to jump out and catch it; then to jump to the next one, and the next one, until she'd reached the furthest, at which point she'd climb right to the top and pull what remained of the rope up behind her. She imagined that by then she'd be well out of reach, but, even if she wasn't, support units would almost certainly have arrived.

The faceless thing was now edging sideways towards her. With one blue claw, it drew the blade from under its jacket again.

"All the better," she shouted. "Let's see if you can do this one-handed."

And she dived out. She caught the first rope easily, swinging back and forth so that she was also able to catch the second one. She transferred herself over to it, then glanced back. The thing was watching her as though helpless.

"What's the matter, Van Ruthers?" she laughed. "Suddenly found the limit of your amazing capabilities?"

Patiently, it pushed the blade back under its jacket.

"Go on, follow me," she urged. "I'd love to see you."

But that wasn't its plan. It didn't reach for the ropes, but for the chain pulley, which it now began to work in the opposite direction. The next thing Ellen knew, she was travelling back along the runner towards the wall.

"Bastard," she breathed. "You bastard!"

She had less than a second to make a decision. She glanced down – fifteen feet! The effigy meanwhile had hooked one arm around the top bar so that, as well as hauling on the pulley, it could draw the knife. Another foot and it would be able to slash at her. She had no choice: she dropped, like a stone.

It struck anyway, leaning far out and down – and losing its grip on the topmost bar, which was still moist with Ellen's sweat.

Five feet down, the woman caught hold of the rope again, and, though it flayed the palms of both hands, managed to halt her descent. But the effigy plummeted past – all the way, striking the gym floor headfirst and with shocking force. Its ovoid skull burst apart like an overripe fruit, wax fragments flying in all directions.

Despite the pain in her hands, Ellen swung down after it as quickly as she could. When she landed, she saw that its entire head had vanished; only the upper portion of its plastic spine – a blue-tipped needle – remained. The rest of its body lay in a crumpled head, its broken limbs tangled in its cape. But it wasn't dead. It was twitching, trying to get up. It reached feebly out for the knife, but Ellen got there first, sweeping the weapon away. When the monster tried to rise, she pressed it back down with her foot.

"Time's up, Jack," she said. "You're well overdue your appointment with the hangman."

102

* * *

It was the biggest gamble of Bob's life.

The shotgun wasn't real – it was a prop, part of a costume. Or if it was real, it wouldn't be loaded. Or would it?

He took the chance, throwing himself forwards through the curtain, grabbing two handfuls and yanking the entire thing down. It was heavy material, again impregnated with dust, and it fell over the effigy on the other side of it like a barrowful of wet cement. There was no gunflash in response, no thump of lead into the back of Bob's skull, but he wasn't out of danger yet. He careered forwards, his own momentum propelling him, only to rebound from the John Haigh figure still struggling beneath the curtain, and crash into a wooden guard-rail, which broke beneath his weight. He fell a considerable distance before landing on his back on another of the empty display cases. It collapsed with the impact, winding him badly and piercing his flesh with innumerable slivers of glass and splinters of smashed wood.

He was groggy when he got back to his feet, but not so much that he wasn't aware he was still in the lions' den. On all sides he could hear movement. As his eyes attuned to the darkness, he spotted grotesque shapes winding towards him through the wreckage of former exhibits. He lurched away, sighting the foot of another metal stairway. He dashed for it, but then saw a figure descending: the woman in the black dress and widow's veil. There was suddenly no doubt who this was – Catherine Wilson, hanged in 1862 for burning seven people to death with sulphuric acid. Even now she carried a glass bottle with a stopper in it. As Bob veered away, she threw it. It just missed him, exploding on a steel stanchion.

He was now hobbling blindly, but spied a tall, wide passage filled with pale moonlight from a series of square, overhead windows. Again it reminded him that this place had formerly had industrial uses; he could imagine forklift trucks being driven up and down it. He started forwards, but half way along wondered it if might lead to an outside loading area, the doors to which could now be barred. Would he be trapped in a cul-de-sac? He slid to a halt, seized with indecision, but, glancing backwards, saw various figures advancing after him through the intermittent moonbeams. He ran on, the heart thumping in his chest. The passage turned in a right angle and he stumbled around it, finding himself in open space again. As he'd feared, there were two huge doors here, both closed and chained. But to their left there was a smaller, narrower door; this one stood open and more moonlight glowed on the other side of it. He scrambled through, closing the door behind him, then reaching for his torch – only to discover that he'd lost it, almost certainly when he'd fallen from the gantry. He wanted to curse, scream. But instead he listened.

Feet, of which there seemed to be a great many, came steadily closer. The sweat began to freeze on Bob's brow. He fumbled frantically to see if there was a lock on the door, and found a bolt. He thrust it home, then backed away a couple of steps, bumping into something; it was a low table, laden with all kinds of junk which, in the dim light, he couldn't make out. He glanced past it, to see where the light was coming from. There was a narrow window, again without glass but with boards nailed over its exterior; moonlight was creeping through its chinks. Surely he was now on the ground floor, which must mean that he could kick his way out this way.

But what if he wasn't on the ground floor?

All the noise he'd make breaking the window open would be for nothing, and would alert those things, which now sounded as if they were just on the other side of the door.

He could hear them shuffling around, their bodies colliding, their feet scuffing the floor. They were looking for him, he realised; they were confused, they couldn't understand where he'd gone. He backed up further, trying to slide around the table, and becoming wedged between that and a shelf arrayed with old bottles and cans that would *clatter* if he tried to force his way past. So again he halted and held his breath.

Oddly, the sounds beyond the door had now ceased. What did this signify? Had the mannequins moved past, or were they listening out for him? *Could* they listen? Obviously they could, or whoever was controlling them could. Suddenly the complete weirdness of his position seemed to overwhelm Bob. He felt sick, his head swam, there was even a trickle of urine in his pants. He groped out with a hand to try and steady himself. It touched something on the table – a tiny box.

Matches.

Why this suddenly gave him hope, he didn't know. He grabbed the box and opened it. A few sticks remained inside. He fingered one out, and then listened again.

There was still no sound.

Unable to stand being blind and deaf any longer, he struck the match. The tiny spurt of flame revealed the room to be something like a caretaker's lock-up. It was small, extremely dirty, and littered with jumble of every sort: step-ladders, tools, buckets, mops, tins of paint, bottles of white spirit – and a few stubs of candles. Bob grabbed one of these and lit it before the match could go out. He screwed it into a niche in the wall, then shoved the matches into his pocket. He moved towards the window. He had to shift the table out of the way to get to it, but there was something underneath preventing this: a large metal canister with a pouring-spout. When he tried to kick it aside, it was too heavy; its contents sloshed and he smelled kerosene. He almost laughed; if the woodwork over the window proved too stubborn, he could always burn it.

Then there was a noise at the door.

Bob whirled around.

It was a soft squeak – the sound you get running a fingertip down polished wood.

He went cold.

A crashing impact followed, and the door burst inwards in a shower of plaster.

The first of them to step through was the tall one wearing the dark uniform and carrying the axe. Bob jumped backwards and fell over the table, completely upending it. Junk cascaded around him as he slid to the floor.

The uniform was that of a Nazi stormtrooper, but crude, homemade. The face above it looked like a demented child's: it was fat-lipped, odd-eyed. Lank, mouse-brown hair hung around it in greasy strands. It was also chillingly familiar. Bob realised that he was facing one of the most horrific killers ever to prowl Britain: Patrick Mackay, the hulking, Hitler-worshiping deviant, who in 1975 confessed to brutally slaughtering three old age pensioners.

"You're …. you're not real," Bob stammered.

But the axe the monster was carrying was real enough. Both hands on the haft, it raised the weapon high above its head. Bob gazed helplessly up. The blow would descend from nine feet at least. It would split him clean in two.

But it never came.

The Mackay thing continued to stare down at him with its bland, demented face. But that was all it did. Several seconds passed, and Bob's heart rate began to slow as he realised that the other figures gathered in the doorway had also frozen into immobility.

Van Ruthers had woken up quickly when Ellen lugged him off the vaulting horse. He now lay wide-eyed as she crouched alongside him, the point of the Ripper's knife at his throat.

"Scared?" she asked. "Perhaps I shouldn't be surprised. You're not in the habit of fighting your own battles."

"Why should I, when I can get others to do it for me?"

"Roll over."

"Checking out my arse, detective?"

"Roll over or I'll slit you open like a fish." She grabbed his t-shirt and yanked him over onto his front.

"Oh dear," he said, now able to see the Ripper effigy, headless and dangling some seven feet up, its arms spread wide, each one tied at the wrist with a climbing-rope. "Now that's a shame. Nice pose though. Makes me feel even more godlike."

She snapped the cuffs on. "Shut up. Get to your feet."

He did so. Then smiled.

"I should kill you for what you've done," she said.

"You should. Seriously, you *really* should. Because it isn't over yet."

"We'll find some way to neutralise this talent of yours."

"I'm sure you will. But in the meantime who's going to save your ex-hubby?"

"You what?"

Van Ruthers smiled all the more. "Admit it, you're still rather fond of him."

"What are you saying?"

"Guess where he's gone? I'll tell you …" And he leaned forwards to whisper into her ear. "Probably the last place in the world you'd want him to be right now."

"You're lying."

"See, I knew you still cared about him."

She brought the knife-tip to his throat again. "You're a lying bastard!"

"Have I lied to you so far?"

Ellen was torn. She didn't want to believe it, but knowing Bob and his unfailing ability to cause her grief, where else would he be at this vital moment? There was a bang at the gym doors; distracted, she saw a couple of uniformed officers on the other side of the glass panel.

"You really had better kill me," Van Ruthers added. "Because all I have to do is close my eyes and concentrate again, and Bobby-boy's a dead man."

There was another impact on the door. By the sound of it, they had a hydraulic ram.

"Go on!" he urged her. "Stick me. It's what you want, isn't it? And it's absolutely necessary to save your ex. What's stopping you? – the security camera's not working, these guys will cover for you." He was now grinning eagerly. "It'll be the perfect ending. It's one hundred percent the way it should be – I deserve to die."

"You do," she agreed. Then she tossed the knife away, and kicked him hard in the groin. "But that isn't how it's going to be."

106

As he collapsed in a gagging heap, the officers outside finally smashed the gym doors open. A couple more had appeared; there was a CID man with them.

"Ma-am?" he said, bewildered.

"*He's* locked up on suspicion of murder," she replied, pointing at Van Ruthers. She indicated the hanging effigy as she pulled her shoes on. "And whatever happens, don't cut that thing down."

And then she was gone, racing along the passage.

Van Ruthers's choked laughter sounded after her. "See if you can save him, DI Blackwood. I hope you can. That'd be even better."

If she'd glanced backwards, she'd have seen him go happily into the custody of the newly arrived officers. She'd also have seen him close his eyes.

Bob's initial thought had been to try and bash out the woodwork that was blocking the window. But this proved difficult: for once, these boards seemed to have been nailed on by professional carpenters. He thus opted, as he'd thought earlier, to use the kerosene to burn his way out.

But then something else had occurred to him: why just burn the window?

How long the effigies would remain immobile, he didn't know. But he now pushed his way out past the figure of Mackay. Those crowded outside were also rigid, lifeless. It was a similar story with the ones dotted down the passage leading to the exhibition hall, though many of these were in attitudes of running or walking. The Sutcliffe and Nilsen effigies were there, alongside the dapper chap with the crazy moustache, who Bob now realised was George Chapman, 'the Lambeth Poisoner'. There were others he recognised: Fred West, Peter Manuel, Gordon Cummins, the John Christie and Neville Heath look-alikes that had figured in the police reports. Gleefully he threw kerosene over them. He threw it over them all. In fact, he didn't just do it to the figures; he splashed it everywhere. With luck the whole place would go up; the floors in this section were timber, there was much pipe-work still covered in rotted lagging.

"You're gonna burn," he said half-deliriously. "You're all gonna burn."

It didn't occur to him that he was working his way deeper and deeper into the museum, until the canister only had a few drops left. Once he'd noticed this, he stumbled hurriedly back, constantly slipping on the now saturated floor. He was half way there when a cat-like claw sunk into his left arm. It happened at the corner where the main passage swerved into the loading area; it was dark there, but not so that he didn't recognise the

Victorian woman from the cellar corridor – Mary Ann Cotton, he now guessed, the original 'Baby-Farmer'.

He swung the canister. The female figure tottered backwards. He lurched desperately on, ducking and weaving as they all came stiffly back to life. The door to the caretaker's lock-up was just ahead, but it was still blocked – by Patrick Mackay.

With no choice, Bob barrelled straight towards the hulking shape, hitting it full in the back. It flew forwards across the room, striking the wall just below the window. Bob stomped in after it, then stomped all over it, kicking its ghastly head as hard as he could. The wax was broken, dinted, knocked out of shape. But already the effigy was scrambling back to its feet, and still it was clasping the axe. Bob flung the canister at it, but it was thrown easily aside. He spun around. Before leaving to soak the premises, he'd made up a pair of Molotov-cocktails by filling bottles with kerosene and stuffing rags into their necks. Both now sat on the shelf. He only had to light one, throw it at the window and he was out of here. He grabbed for the first bottle – and some sixth sense made him jump aside.

With a flash of steel, the axe-blade just missed him and clove the shelf in half. Everything, Molotovs included, went scattering to the floor. One smashed on contact; the other rolled out of his reach. Bob bent down to get it, but the axe caught him in the stomach, this time on the backstroke with its blunted edge. Winded, he staggered sideways. The Mackay thing now threw a punch. It hit Bob's left temple with stunning force. He slumped to the floor, grovelling in wreckage and, worst of all, kerosene – previously he'd avoided splashing any of it in here or on the Mackay figure, but now it was all over the room and himself, and that meant he couldn't use the remaining Molotov to escape. Not that he didn't still want to get hold of it. It continued to roll, and he scrabbled after it – only for a foot to stamp down on his back, pinning him there.

He could sense the axe rising, but then heard a wildly shouting voice: "Bob, Bob!"

"Ellen!" he cried. "Ellen, I'm in here!"

It gave him new strength. He grabbed at the foot and dislodged it. The towering shape fell again. Bob leapt to his feet. As he did, he heard a splintering *crack*; an iron bar had been forced in behind the largest plank on the window and was now prying it loose. Bob joined in, kicking hard – once, twice, three times. With a groan and a *thunk*, the rest of the boarding broke free. Cold air flooded in. He saw Ellen's face over an electric torch.

"Quickly!" she shouted.

"I'm coming," he said. But before he did, he scooped up the remaining Molotov.

It cost him a crucial half-second, and as he clambered for the open casement, a hand caught the waistband of his tracksuit pants. As he was pulled back, he tossed the Molotov through the window, screaming at Ellen to catch it. Then he rounded on his assailant with the ferocity of a tiger goaded to desperate fury. Shrieking, he bore it down with the weight of his body, and beat and tore at it, crushing its face to mangled pulp, ripping out chunks of its waxen flesh, grapping what remained of its head with both hands and slamming it against the floor over and over, smashing it, squashing it like dough.

"Bob!" Ellen screamed.

He glanced up. In the light of her torch, he saw other horrible forms shouldering their way into the small room. He struggled to his feet and sprang onto the window-frame. More flailing hands reached for him, but this time they were too late.

"Believe in Van Ruthers's special powers now?" he stammered.

She made no reply as he half-fell into her arms, but gasped when she saw how filthy and bloodied he was. He snatched the Molotov and fumbled the matches from his pocket, striking three before he could finally light the dangling rags.

"What are you doing?" she asked as he raised it aloft.

"What do you think?" Beneath the grime and congealing blood, he was white-faced, dotted with feverish sweat. His eyes were wild, his lips drawn back in a snarl. "Justice! Biblical style!"

He turned to the window. A misshapen figure had climbed up into it.

"Bastard!" he growled, pushing it backwards.

Then he flung the Molotov after it, right into the midst of the many other shapes now milling about in the caretaker's room. There was a *bang*, a glaring flash, and then Ellen dragged him to the floor as a wave of searing heat engulfed them both.

It was raining again. But that didn't dampen the fire, which now raged in every part of the gutted, roofless ruin. Hoses wove back and forth between the numerous fire-trucks and police vehicles. Firefighters darted here and there. Even civilians had emerged to stand in small, awe-stricken groups.

Bob and Ellen watched from the rear of an ambulance to which, at their request, the doors had been left open. Bob lay on a gurney, beneath a silver-foil blanket. A fresh dressing and clean bandage had been applied to the wound on his right temple. Ellen sat alongside him. Around her shoulders she wore a more conventional woollen blanket.

For a brief time, neither said anything. They were too mesmerised by the scene before them. Flames like red devils cavorted behind the fissures spreading through the brickwork. Windows became larger and larger cavities as the masonry around them crumbled inwards. Of course nothing could be moving in the white-hot heart of the conflagration, but it was difficult not to imagine things.

"You realise you've just burned up the story of a lifetime?" Ellen finally said.

"I thought about that," he replied. "But then … it wasn't really *my* story, was it?"

"No, it was Van Ruthers's. And he'd have revelled in it. It was his whole purpose. But it would still have been *your* scoop. Did you consider that?"

"Sure but, you know, some scoops aren't worth the paper they're written on."

She smiled wryly

"I'm sorry all the same," he said.

She glanced at him. "Why?"

"I should have thought about you … about, well, preserving the evidence maybe."

She looked back to the fire. Its reflection played in liquid patterns over her pale, smoke-stained face. Her smile became grim. "Evidence of what?"

THEIR BONES PICKED CLEAN

Sonny fled through the labyrinthine streets.

He'd grown up in a tough neighbourhood, was trim, athletic, and though he wasn't inclined towards violence, he could handle himself. On this occasion, however, he simply ran. The cobbles beneath his feet were greasy with seagull shit; tufts of thick, spiky grass grew between them, but sheer adrenaline ensured that he kept his footing. He turned corner after corner in the endless, twisting alleyways, occasionally tripping on fallen masonry, but he didn't let this hinder him. He had only one thought – to get away from this place. Not only for the sake of his body, which he knew was imperilled beyond any degree of rational understanding, but for his soul as well. For the thing that stalked him might seek to slake its thirst on *that* too.

It was a remorseless hunter. Though Sonny went pell-mell through the moon-lit maze, stumbling, slipping, but always charging headlong, cutting through the gutted heart of tumbledown houses, backtracking, sidestepping, vaulting broken-down walls like they were hurdles, it always remained close behind; an ungainly, leaping shadow in the spectral half-dark. He'd only seen it full on once, but once had been enough: its humped, misshapen form in a cottage doorway, chuckling its eerie, fluting laugh. And then its snarls had come, and its wild, gambolling pursuit, and the skittering of its iron-hard claws, and the rancid stench of its drool as it slobbered and hungered for him.

Fresh sweat broke on Sonny's brow as he spied a flight of steps leading down to the sea, and at the bottom the tilting shape of the hire-boat. He descended at breakneck pace, his sneakers constantly sliding, but keeping his balance by the walls to either side, his torn, bloodied hands scrabbling down them.

"Yasmin!" he screamed. "Yasmin, start the motor!"

But there was no sound from the boat, and no flash from Yasmin's torch. A horrible chill went through Sonny as he finally got to the waterside. He gazed into the belly of the small craft and saw something there that set his unhinged mind teetering. For a moment he was too distracted to notice the nightmare presence come slinking down the sea-stair and halt directly behind him.

Only slowly did he turn to confront it.

It.

Before he could open his mouth, either to beg for mercy or shriek in fear, there were two vicious swipes, and he was slashed across his face, first downwards and then diagonally, blows that left lacerations in flesh and bone so deep that his eyeballs popped out onto his cheeks.

With horror and agony locked in his throat, Sonny fell stiffly backwards. The world froze around him, and he dropped through an echoing, abyssal dark ...

A blood-red sky stretched from horizon to horizon. Beneath it, the arid plain was broken only by clumps of thorny scrub and the odd twisted tree. There was a pervading stench of carrion. Vultures clustered on carcasses, their dusty wings creaking and flapping as they pecked and stabbed at each other. Ants swarmed in the grit, scorpions clambered over sun-scorched rocks. The heat was intense, furnace-like; it seared the very lungs. And then there was a laugh – a wild, ululating laugh, ghoulish and ghost-like, which rolled and rolled in the hot, still air.

Nick Brooker awoke with a start, but was too fuddled with sleep to make sense of the dream he'd just had.

"It's all change here, sir," the train-manager said with a smile. "Sorry to wake you."

"Er ... it's okay, thanks," Nick replied.

He climbed from the train, and found himself alone on a small country railway-station platform. Above his head, the sign hanging from the old-fashioned canopied roof, read: *Upper St. Beloc.*

He leaned on his stick to regain his strength. He only had a small rucksack with him, containing a few basic toiletries and a single change of clothes, but in his current state of convalescence it had proved heavy and cumbersome on the long journey from Manchester to Cornwall. He took a second or two, before hobbling through the passage to the station forecourt.

Out at the front, he immediately saw the Atlantic: it was a dreamy vista, royal blue with racing ruffles of snow-white foam. He could hear the distant roar of breakers, could smell the salt tang. Closer to hand, a cobbled lane led downhill between green hedgerows and gentle, golden hayfields. Sparrows twittered; the late-August sun was mellow and warm.

"Give you a ride down to the village, sir?" said someone with a strong West Country accent. Nick turned, and saw a taxi parked by the pavement. A plump, elderly man with a pleasant face and fluffy grey curls was standing beside it. "It's only five minutes' walk," the cabbie added, "but ... well, if you're incapacitated."

"A ride would be great. Thanks."

Nick climbed into the vehicle's rear, humping his rucksack onto the seat beside him.

"Where to, sir?" the cabbie wondered.

"It's the ..." and Nick filched a fragment of paper from the breast-pocket of his denim jacket, "it's the Tregarrick Hotel."

"Ahhh, best place in town."

They drove slowly downhill. As the ground levelled out, the farm fields gave way to oak-woods filled with birdsong. They crossed a stream via an arched stone bridge, and passed two picture-postcard Cornish cottages, both whitewashed and thatch-roofed.

"Been to Cornwall before?" the cabbie asked.

"A couple of times."

"If you don't mind me saying, you look like you've been in the wars."

Nick smiled. He was well aware of the scars and bruising on his face; of the ungainly limp where his shattered leg-bones had knitted back together but still hadn't regained their former strength; of the fact that at only thirty-nine years old, his robust, six foot-one frame had shrunk to a crooked shadow of its previous self.

He said: "Got injured at work. Been sent me down here to recover."

"All expenses paid, eh. Better and better."

Nick nodded, liking the cabbie. In his experience this was typical of Cornish folk. They were a laid-back, easygoing breed, who, as a rule, tended to see the bright side of things. The guy could have gone on to ask what kind of 'accident at work' could possibly wreak such havoc on a human body. He could then have expressed amazement that his fare had survived such an ordeal, and milked him for all the sordid details. But he didn't. His original enquiry had been conversational rather than nosy, and now that he had his superficial answer, he was content. Nick had to admit that the Federation's decision to send him here had probably been for the best. Initially, on his release from hospital, he hadn't wanted to go anywhere. But if any place in the British Isles could heal the wounds of the past – the mental as well as the physical – it was Cornwall.

Upper St. Beloc was as picturesque a spot as Nick had ever seen.

Located just to the west of Lizard Point, mainland Britain's most southerly tip, where it caught the cooling Atlantic breeze but also the full force of the Gulf Steam air-current, which meant that it rarely got frosty in winter and, with the exception of the odd thunder-storm, was warm and sunny throughout most of the summer, it sat on a high, broad headland that jutted out a considerable distance into scenic Mount's Bay. The village was a good ninety feet above sea level, hence the inclusion of the world 'Upper' in its official title. There was a Lower St. Beloc too, though this, from what Nick had read in the guidebooks, was long abandoned. Relics of it remained on a small islet about three hundred yards offshore. It had served in the eighteenth century as a fishing-hamlet, when it sat at the end of a long spit of sandy ground, though tides had changed since then, and it was now cut off.

Upper St. Beloc, however, though quiet by the normal standards of Cornwall in August, was all that one would expect it to be. In its centre, booksellers, crafts shops and *olde worlde* pubs were ringed around a cobbled market square, in the middle of which stood a weathered Celtic cross. Its whitewashed housing was exclusively quaint and pretty: all pan-tiled roofs, flower-filled window boxes and straw 'Welcome' mats laid out on well-scrubbed pavements. There was an official 'St. Beloc Beach', but this was only one of several rocky coves that village paths led down to. At high tide, it was said, the sound of the sea as it roared into these natural *zawns* (to use local parlance), could be heard in Upper St. Beloc square. The Tregarrick Hotel was part of the fabric of the town. Of eighteenth century coaching-house origin, it was built from hefty blocks of local granite, and though a trifle gothic in appearance, with spire-topped towers in its four corners and carved griffins on the lintel over the grand front door, it was a focal point for the entire community. Oak-beamed inside and hung with colourful prints of West Country lifestyles now long past, it had two bars – one public, one for residents only – and at the rear a highly-rated restaurant, which opened into a conservatory crowded with exotic plants, and then onto an extensive lawn that backed right to the cliff-top.

Nick checked in at the hotel's reception, and was assisted up the central staircase by a fellow guest. She was a tall, blonde woman, handsome but dressed severely in a dark skirt and jacket and flat-soled shoes.

"Here, let me help you," she said, as he struggled up, walking stick in one hand, rucksack in the other.

"It's okay. I'm fine ... honestly."

"You don't look it," she said, all brusque and businesslike, insisting on taking his rucksack off him even though she already carried a Gladstone bag of her own.

He permitted her to do this out of necessity rather than willingness. He wasn't used to dealing with personal infirmity. It was kind of the woman to offer to help, even if she did it without smiling, but Nick was initially too embarrassed to do more than mumble his thanks. At the top of the stairs she handed him his baggage back.

"That was good of you. I appreciate, it," he said, leaning on the banister to regain his breath. He extended a hand. "Sorry, I'm not used to this yet. Nick Brooker."

She shook the hand, nodding curtly. "Pleased to meet you."

Without introducing herself, she turned and set off down the left-hand passage.

Nick followed her part way along it, though a moment later she turned a corner and vanished. He let himself into his own room, and was pleased to find it small but comfy, with moulded wooden furnishings, a plump double-sized bed, and a huge painting of a clipper-ship negotiating a stormy passage. The window was tall, and slid open on a small veranda, on which there was a white wrought-iron table and chairs. It overlooked the conservatory roof, the hotel lawn, and, beyond that, the wide blue gulf of the Atlantic.

Nick stood out there briefly, before going back indoors and lying down. Even though he'd slept much of the way from Exeter, he now slept again. It was only late afternoon, but his body had been so badly damaged the previous May that it was taking an inordinately lengthy time to repair itself.

"Detective Sergeant Brooker, is it?" someone asked, a minute after Nick had taken his seat in the restaurant.

Nick glanced up and saw a very dapper chap in white, razor-creased flannels and a navy-blue blazer fastened with silver buttons. He was in his late-fifties and white haired, but handsome in a very English, aristocratic sort of way.

"Not while I'm on sick-leave," Nick replied. "What I mean is … you don't have to worry about the 'detective-sergeant' bit."

The newcomer held out a large, gnarled hand. "I'm Ted Tregarrick."

"Oh, right … hi," Nick said, recognising the name of his host.

They shook hands.

"So, how are you feeling?" Tregarrick asked.

"I'm fine."

"How long have you actually been out of hospital?"

"A week or so."

"Well let's hope we can make you as comfortable as possible while you're here."

The guy seemed genuinely concerned for his guest's welfare, which was a pleasant surprise. Tregarrick was only one of several hoteliers dotted around Britain who had a standing-arrangement with the Police Federation to take convalescing officers badly injured on duty. Nine times out of ten, Nick suspected, these fellows did it purely as a source of easy money. After all, in the year 2000 the British police service could provide an inexhaustible supply of wounded men and women in need of rest. But the fact that Tregarrick was interested enough to at least introduce himself and make small-talk was an improvement on what the detective had expected.

"Anything we can do for you at all," the hotelier said, "I mean in addition to the normal things, just give me a shout. I'm always around. Hope you enjoy your meal."

Nick *did* enjoy his meal.

For his first course he ate a lobster and crayfish salad, for his second roasted guinea fowl with limes and an assortment of local vegetables. He also drank a bottle of ice-cold Chablis, though he wasn't really supposed to touch alcohol while he was on his course of ultra-strong painkillers.

Later on, he relaxed in an armchair in the conservatory, watching a whirling overhead fan and listening to the idle chatter of the other guests. These were largely middle-aged or retired folk, with one exception: a strikingly beautiful black girl. She was eighteen at the most, her crimped locks falling in designer wet-look tangles on the shoulders of her glossy PVC jacket. She sat alone in a corner, wearing a truculent expression as she flipped through a dog-eared newspaper. When Nick finally got up and went out to the lawn, he nodded at her and smiled. She regarded him with suspicion before nodding back. But she didn't say anything, and, like the woman on the stairs, she didn't smile either.

It was now mid-evening, and a balmy atmosphere had settled. The grass, though yellowed in patches from the summer heat wave, was freshly cut and smelled sweet. Nick strolled to its farthest end, where a wickerwork bench looked down through palm-filled shrubbery to the sea. To one side was a footpath leading down to the coves. Tregarrick was standing there, chatting with a burly fisherman-type: a rugged-looking bloke in his early thirties with a big body, big arms and a reddish, weathered face; despite the evening warmth, he wore a tatty windjammer and a woollen cap pulled down on his mass of oil-black curls.

"Okay Solomon, no problem," Tregarrick was saying. "Just keep an eye open. Hello again," he added, as he saw Nick easing himself onto the bench.

Nick stared after the fisherman as he stumped away down the steep path. "Solomon, eh? Looks more like an Ike or Barney or ... I dunno, a Davey Jones."

Tregarrick chuckled. "Solomon Jarvis. Bit of a local character. Formerly a bare-knuckle boxer, among other things. Runs a fishing-boat of mine out of Porth Mellin."

"Got your fingers in a few pies, eh?"

116

"I find it pays. Can't rely solely on tourism."

Nick wanted to remark that, from the pristine state of the hotel and the high standards in the restaurant, tourism clearly paid well enough at the present time. But he knew the holiday game was a fickle one at best – as was the fishing industry of course, thanks to rules imposed by the European Union. For all this, Tregarrick was a well-dressed man with a relaxed and lordly air. From what Nick had been told by fellow cops who'd spent time here, he was much more than just the local innkeeper. He was an entrepreneur. A key figure in the local Chamber of Commerce, he'd been mayor of the village at least four times. Not that Nick could imagine things ever got desperately frantic and stressful in a place like this, even for the captains of industry.

He glanced down towards the sea. Barren outcrops denoted the tops of the natural walls jutting out between the coves; gorse and marram grass grew sparsely on them, like tufts of thinning hair. Beyond those, the Atlantic heaved and rolled. The south coast of Cornwall was not as famous for its surfing beaches as the north, but wild water was currently surging into it, fountains of spume hurtling up from its rocks and tooth-like skerries. The island of Lower St. Beloc was practically under siege. From this vantage point, it was an oval hummock of land protruding above the crashing waves by a perilously narrow margin. Even from this distance, Nick could see the roofless shells of ancient cottages crowded on top of it.

"I guess that's your town's deceased twin," he commented.

Tregarrick smiled. "You've heard about that?"

"I read up on the area before I came down here. I like to be in the know."

"Once a detective, eh?"

"Suppose so. Not that I learned *too* much about it."

Tregarrick stuck his hands into his pockets. "To be honest, there isn't much you *can* learn."

"I heard something about all the villagers becoming ill down there?"

Tregarrick mused. "That's the local tradition, but it's hard to unravel reality from myth."

"Wasn't there a story about the fish being contaminated, people getting paralysed?"

Tregarrick glanced at him with new respect. "You *have* been doing your homework, haven't you?"

"As I say, I like to be in the know."

"Well, it's an interesting tale, but it's so long before living-memory that no-one knows what *really* happened. I think the villagers *did* get sick with something. Course, it was never a healthy place in those days, Cornwall. Don't be fooled by all this."

He swept his arm around to indicate the benign environment. "People eked out a miserable living down here a couple of centuries back. It's not good arable land, and fishing the sea can be expensive and dangerous. Mortality rates were high, and if there were major problems, like epidemics or whatever, this place was a long way from somewhere like London, where they could get help."

"Does anyone go out there now?" Nick asked, unsure why the small island was fascinating him so much.

"Well … there's nothing there to see."

"No archaeological interest?"

"Just fishermen's cottages, all ruined."

Nick stared at the distant hump and the relics of housing crammed on it, the husks of lives long extinct. There was always a melancholy feel to places like that, especially if tragedy had afflicted them. He'd definitely seen it mentioned in one of his guidebooks that the village of Lower St. Beloc had been abandoned because the occupants died or became ill, many allegedly found paralysed. Nothing he'd read offered an explanation for that, though one author had theorised that the cause was a toxin in the fish, or something similar. Either way, it had happened back in the eighteenth century, so there was no point pondering it too deeply now.

Yet, just as Nick opted to change the subject, he fancied he saw movement on the island. It was only a flicker in the corner of his eye, but when he looked again he spotted what appeared to be a small, indistinct figure prowling the passages between the gutted houses. He leaned forwards to bring the tiny shape into focus. That was all it was, a shape, though even from this distance it moved at an awkward gambol, and, as he watched it, he felt a cold breath on his neck and a sudden blistering heat on his forehead. An eerie, ululating laugh sounded from some distant place, and with it he heard the crackle of thorns and dry vegetation, and the crunch of desiccated bones. Suddenly there was a smell of carrion and blood, and the next thing Nick Brooker knew, someone was gently tapping his cheek, trying to bring him round.

He opened his eyes, and realised that he'd either been asleep or unconscious.

"Thank the Lord," he heard someone say; it was Tregarrick. "I thought he was a gonner."

Nick glanced around. He was still on the bench overlooking the sea. But he was slumped to one side, and he felt weak and nauseous. A couple of other guests were standing alongside his host with concerned looks on their faces. Crouched right in front of him was the handsome, blonde woman who'd assisted him on his first arrival. She seemed to be checking his pulse. The next thing, she'd dipped into her Gladstone bag, taken out a stethoscope and was listening to his heart.

"This is my daughter, Laura, Mr. Brooker," Tregarrick said. "You'll be glad to know she also happens to be our local GP."

"I see." Nick was still confused. "What's, what's …?"

"Everything appears to be normal," the doctor said. She put her stethoscope away. "Apparently you just passed out."

"I did?" Nick shook his head. "I don't remember."

"What actually happened to you?" she asked. "I mean, originally?"

"Er … last May I was caught in an explosion."

"And what are we talking, multiple injuries?"

"Two broken legs, one broken arm. The rest of it was pretty superficial."

"Head wounds?" she wondered.

He nodded. "A hairline fracture of the skull, but that's cleared up. I can drive again in three weeks."

She dug into her bag, producing a penlight, with which she examined the pupils of his eyes, and an otoscope to look into his ears.

"There was no suggestion you might have suffered wider, perhaps neurological damage?" she asked.

He shook his head. "Never."

"And what medication are you on?"

He produced the packet of painkillers from his pocket.

She assessed them, then gave him a frank stare. "I can smell alcohol on your breath."

"I had a bottle of wine with dinner."

"That wasn't a smart move."

"I'm a copper. I drink."

"Well you mustn't. Not until you've finished these tablets." She stood up and packed her equipment away. "I appreciate that you're probably not used to being an invalid, Sergeant Brooker, but you won't cease to be one as long as you ignore medical advice."

"That's telling him," Tregarrick said, grinning at Nick over her shoulder, though his expression was comradely, as though he too had been on the receiving end of his daughter's curt instructions.

Nick might have responded but now he'd remembered the island, and the curious, ungainly figure he thought he'd seen on it. As the doctor issued one or two final orders, he couldn't help but peer past her down towards the small rock with its clustered ruins, and was baffled and frustrated to see that no-one was present on it now.

119

* * *

There were many things to do in that part of Cornwall.

Land's End was only an hour's drive to the west, while northwards across the peninsula, the popular holiday resort of St. Ives was perhaps half an hour away. Slightly further afield lay the Arthurian coastal fort of Tintagel, the stone circles of Bodmin Moor, and the sailing waters off Falmouth, as well as sundry castles, cathedrals, megaliths, and bird and seal sanctuaries. For this reason, both the Tregarrick Hotel and the town itself were quiet during the day, and Nick contented himself that first morning with an easy stroll around the antiquated shops. He'd slept well the night before, apart from an odd occasion when he'd been disturbed by a curious mumbling sound from somewhere along the passage. He'd got up to investigate, but had found nothing amiss. The sound – which he'd thought of more as a 'mumming' than a mumbling, because he hadn't actually heard any words being spoken – had ceased a couple of minutes later, and he was able to forget it and go back to sleep. As such, he found himself invigorated that morning, so, after he'd browsed among the shops for a while, he took himself down to the shoreline.

The coves were a world apart. The relentless power of the sea had scalloped them out over millennia, creating deep bays between towering granite headlands. There were sandy areas in some of them, but in others masses of shingle, or jagged black rocks projecting into the surf like fingers. It was a rewarding place to wander, even for someone as incapacitated as Nick. Overhead, gannets and guillemots hovered in criss-crossing patterns, while the water-line rocks glittered turquoise in the hot sun and were covered with limpets, mussels and slimy green bladderwrack. The tidal pools were filled with anemones blooming in exotic colours, or crabs lurking beneath sinister, shadowy overhangs.

When he got back to the hotel that noon, though physically tired, Nick felt refreshed and very hungry. He went straight to the hotel bar, where he intended to order himself lunch and probably – assuming that Doctor Laura Tregarrick wasn't anywhere around – a lager or two. There'd be no more bottles of wine; last night's episode had been peculiar but understandable, but he didn't see that a couple of light beers could hurt him. However, he'd no sooner entered the hotel bar than he came face to face with trouble of a different sort. Tregarrick, who was manning the bar-counter, was frowning sternly, while the big fisherman that Nick had seen the evening before, the one called Jarvis, was talking to him loudly and holding by the scruff of her jacket the slim young black girl who'd been in the conservatory. It was a startling scene for such a peaceful environment.

120

"I told you she was trouble," the fisherman spat. "Bitch had it written all over her."

The girl struggled, but the former bare-knuckle fighter had her in a massive paw.

"This is very disappointing, love," Tregarrick replied calmly, though his cheeks had gone purple with anger. "Is this the way you repay our hospitality?"

The first time he'd seen the girl, Nick had been struck by her good looks, but had thought her beautiful in a fierce, tigress sort of way; he'd marked her down as a toughie, probably streetwise and self-reliant. For this reason, he was now surprised to see fear in her face. There was no argument from her, no answering back – which was surely unusual for *any* teenager in this day and age.

"Everything all right?" he said, coming forwards.

Both men glanced round in surprise, and he thought he saw Tregarrick's flushed cheeks pale a little.

"Er ... nothing for you to worry about, sergeant. Just a spot of minor bother."

"Anything I can do?" Nick asked.

"I've not done nothing," the girl pleaded in strong Cockney, only for Jarvis to shove her violently forwards and slam her against the bar.

"Whoa!" Nick said. "What's this about?"

Tregarrick tried to make light of it. "It's all right, sergeant, I assure you. Don't worry about it. Just enjoy your break and leave this to us."

"Well, I'm not sure I can. What exactly is going on here?"

Tregarrick and his henchman glanced at each other uncertainly.

"I caught her trying to break into the Devil's Roundhouse," Jarvis gruffly explained.

"The what?"

"The Devil's Roundhouse," Tregarrick said. "It's a chapel down on the shore. A quaint Cornish thing. For the tourists, you know. It's of no real interest."

"And she was trying to break into it," Jarvis reiterated.

"I wasn't," the girl protested.

"I saw you!"

"I was only trying the door ... I thought it would be unlocked."

"Well, trying the door's trying to break in, in my book, you little slut!" And Jarvis banged her against the bar again.

"Hey, ease off!" Nick said, pointing a warning finger at him. "Just take it easy, okay."

Jarvis gazed at him uncomprehendingly, as if someone standing up to him was so rare that he had no prior experience of it.

121

"If the Devil's Roundhouse is actually for tourists," Nick added, turning back to Tregarrick, "isn't it reasonable that a visitor to the area should try and check it out?"

"There's nothing to check out," Jarvis retorted.

"That's beside the point," Nick said.

"But it's *not*, sergeant," Tregarrick put in. He no longer seemed angry; now he was flustered, as if the situation had got out of hand. "I'm sorry to disagree with you, but this young lady has been causing a bit of annoyance in the last few days. She's curt, she's unfriendly, she's been asking awkward questions …"

"You can't just drag people off the street for that," Nick said.

"But you can for breaking-and-entering, right?"

"Technically, you can't. Breaking-and-entering doesn't exist as a crime any more."

"Since when?" Jarvis scoffed.

"Since new legislation came in to replace it, about twenty years ago," Nick replied. "If I was the officer involved in this case, I'd arrest her for attempted burglary. But, from what you've told me, I'd have a hell of a job proving it."

"Attempted burglary will do," Tregarrick declared.

"No it won't," Nick said, and now he put a hand on the girl's arm to indicate that they weren't taking her anywhere. "I've just told you, it's not that simple. A police officer can arrest purely on suspicion that a crime has been committed. A civilian can't. If you're affecting a citizen's arrest here, Mr. Jarvis, this young lady *must* have committed a crime. If she hasn't done, you're guilty of assaulting her. You call the law now, and it's more likely *you'll* get taken down to the station as a suspect, and she'll be the witness."

He stared at the fisherman's face, waiting for the penny to drop. Jarvis stared back. If he was unnerved by what he'd just heard, he didn't show it, and now, discomfortingly, Nick wondered if perhaps the two men had *not* been planning to contact the law.

"Well, it's a good job we had you on hand to clear things up for us," Tregarrick suddenly said. In a split-second, he'd become the genial host again. "I suppose we'd better let her go."

Nick watched him carefully. "And I think you should apologise to her too, because there's nothing now to stop this young lady going and reporting you both."

"Just a minute!" Jarvis snapped, only for Tregarrick to interrupt him.

"No, no Solomon … Sergeant Brooker's only laying out the facts. The law might be an ass, but it *is* the law, isn't that right, sergeant?"

Nick couldn't help thinking that there was no reason why the law should be described as an ass in this situation, but to diffuse things further he merely nodded. Reluctantly – very reluctantly – Jarvis released the girl, and she pulled free of him.

"I'm sorry for any inconvenience we might have caused you, Miss Campbell," Tregarrick said, all smiles. "If you wish to stay on at the hotel, perhaps we can provide you with dinner tonight free of charge?"

"No thanks," she said, backing away from them all. "I don't want anything from *you*."

And she turned and left.

"See what we're dealing with," Jarvis grunted to Nick. "You saved her bacon there, and not a word of thanks."

"Saved her bacon?" Nick said, bemused.

"Just a turn of phrase, sergeant," Tregarrick laughed.

The Devil's Roundhouse was an unusual attraction.

Nick found it that afternoon with no great difficulty. Local people directed him to it from the village centre, but if that wasn't helpful enough, there was a signpost as well. This pointed to an unmade track that wound down to the sea in an odd circumlocutory route. The track was hemmed in from either side by high banks covered with thistles and clumps of wild sea-campion, and was steep and stony, which made it difficult going for a man with a walking stick. At the bottom, the embankments rolled back and merged with the coastal cliffs. But the track remained visible as a strip of hardened, flattened ground, continuing across thirty yards of sand and shingle, straight into the sea. Before it reached the waterline, it came to the Devil's Roundhouse, which, to Nick's eye, looked as though it had been built *on* the track rather than beside it.

The eccentric building was typical of the Cornish style, being constructed entirely from granite blocks and handsomely whitewashed. It was similar in size to a small garage, and was clearly of religious orientation because of the iron cross at the apex of its thatched roof. But the most surprising feature was that it was entirely circular – hence the nickname 'Roundhouse', he supposed. Nick knew just from skimming the guidebooks that Cornwall's mythology was riddled with stories about the Devil. At one time, Cornish folk had preferred to build circular dwellings so that there'd be no corner behind which His Satanic Majesty could lie in wait for them.

Nick strolled around the small structure. It had no windows, which perhaps was understandable given that occasional spring tides might swamp it. Its front door appeared to be made from oak, but it had a handle and bore no clear sign that it was supposed to be private. It seemed perfectly reasonable that the young black girl had tried to get in. Okay, *why* she'd wanted to get in was perhaps a question that needed to be asked, but given that the Devil's Roundhouse only existed now "for the tourists", the extremely threatening attitude of Tregarrick and Jarvis was hard to understand. Unless they were simple racists, of course, and disliked the girl for that – though there'd been no indication of this in the language they'd used.

He walked around the building a second time. From what he'd been told in the village, the Roundhouse had been built in the eighteenth century for reasons now forgotten. But the place wasn't a ruin, which meant that someone locally was maintaining it. And if it *was* a tourist-attraction now, why wasn't there a plaque on the wall to explain its history? He spotted something else curious. To the right-hand side of it, half-buried in sand, there was a small stump of stone. At first he'd mistaken it for a mooring-pillar or something, but now that he looked closer he could see an inscription. He crouched, scraped away a skin of moss, and saw faded lettering. It read: *Sainte Beloc.*

He stood up and turned towards the sea. Several hundred yards out, slightly to the west and partly concealed by the next headland, was the island of Lower St. Beloc. When cottages were first built out there, he realised, there'd have been no other habitation in the area, certainly not onshore, and the settlement would simply have been known as 'St. Beloc'; there'd have been no need for the additional moniker 'Lower'. This then – Nick regarded the stony track, which ran down into the waves and vanished – was the original road that had led along the causeway to the island. Which meant that *this*, and he glanced at the stone marker, had formerly been the official entrance to the village.

From this low angle, Lower St. Beloc was little more than a row of broken-down walls with surf exploding around them. He wondered about the rush of eerie sensations he'd experienced that previous evening: the bizarre, hump-backed figure that he thought he'd seen gambolling between the ruins, the dry heat, the smell of carrion, and that distant crazy laugh. His head started to spin and he thought he was going to faint again. He backed up a step, almost tripping and falling, but managed to plant his stick firmly in the ground and took several deep lungfuls of air. At last he was able to turn and amble back up the track. Once he'd reached higher ground, he stopped for a rest and glanced over his shoulder. The Devil's Roundhouse was only visible now as a thatched roof with a crucifix in the middle, but Lower St. Beloc had shifted out of sight behind the headland. Strangely relieved by that, he continued on his way.

124

* * *

"I just wanted to say thanks for what you did earlier."

Nick glanced up from his evening paper. He was seated in the hotel bar, where he'd opted for a snack rather than a large dinner. In acknowledgement of Doctor Tregarrick's presence – she was seated in a corner, picking bird-like at a salad while she consulted what looked like a weighty medical textbook – half a lemonade sat on the table in front of him. The person who'd spoken was the black girl. She wore a snazzy white shell-suit, which looked good if garish on her lithe, young form. But she seemed awkward, and was hardly able to meet his gaze.

"Don't thank me," Nick said. "I was just putting them right legally."

"Yeah, well … thanks anyway."

"What's the attraction of the Devil's Roundhouse?" he asked her.

She shrugged unconvincingly. "Like I said, I'm just visiting the area."

"On your own?"

"Yeah, why not?" She turned faintly hostile. "That's what *you're* doing, isn't it?"

Nick couldn't help but smile. "Yeah, I suppose it is."

Duty discharged, she walked off.

Nick finished his lemonade, allowed a few minutes to pass and then followed her out into the hotel gardens. He found her at the far end of the lawn, seated on the bench where he'd passed out. She had several notebooks with her, one of which sat open on her lap and was filled with tightly written script. She wasn't concentrating on this, but on Lower St. Beloc, which she peered down towards with complete fascination. For this reason she didn't at first notice Nick standing beside her. He looked down towards the island as well. The sea had calmed since the previous evening, and now lay serene and streaked with gold from the setting sun.

"Is there a connection between the Devil's Roundhouse and that island?" he finally asked.

The girl whirled around. "Shit, you scared the crap out of me!"

"Sorry."

"What did you say?"

"Is there a connection between the Devil's Roundhouse and Lower St. Beloc? I noticed that it's built on the road that used to lead there. Almost as though it's deliberately blocking the way."

The girl seemed bewildered – probably as much by his interest as by the question he'd asked. Her body language had also changed. It was only slight, but in the space of a second she'd switched to the defensive. "How should I know?"

"A problem shared is a problem halved, as they say."

She seemed even more bewildered. "I'm not going to share my problems with you."

"Any reason?"

"Well, for one, you're a copper."

"Oh, and you don't like coppers."

"It's the other way round. Generally speaking, coppers don't like us."

"Us?"

"You know what I mean."

"And you have personal experience of that, do you?"

"Do I need to have?"

The fact that she was still talking to him was a good sign, he decided. If she really didn't want someone's help, she'd already have moved away or simply refused to engage him in conversation. Of course, she herself might not yet be aware that she needed help, and her cultural antipathy to him as a police officer had to be broken down.

"I suppose not," he said. "Sorry if I'm being nosy, it's just ... well, it struck me as odd that I'd find someone like you down in Cornwall."

"'Someone like me?'"

"Yeah," he said airily. "You know, a black kid. I mean, Cornwall's a kind of swimming and surfing place, isn't it. And black kids don't swim. Everyone knows that."

"What?"

He lowered himself onto the bench. "When I was growing up, I understood there were no black swimming stars because blacks can't swim ... you know, because their bone structure's too heavy, particularly their skulls."

The girl looked more astonished than angered, probably because, given her youth, she'd only infrequently, if at all, been exposed to overt racism of the old-fashioned English sort. "Are you winding me up?"

"Mind you," Nick added, "that was before I learned the truth, namely that black kids tend not to swim because most of them live in poor inner city areas and have no access to public swimming pools." He smiled at her. "And you know what the lesson of that is – *don't believe everything you're told.*"

She ingested his words, and sat back again. Her lip quivered. He thought she was going to cry.

"You're obviously not here on holiday," he said. "In fact, quite the opposite."

"So?"

"So ... I'm a detective, and even though I'm off duty I've been on sick leave for so long that I'm itching to start detecting again. So if there's something I can help you with, I'd very much appreciate the chance."

126

"Are you on the level?"

"Haven't I already proved that?"

She thought about this, then said: "I don't want to talk out here."

"I'd invite you to my room, but that's not really the done thing."

"It wouldn't bother *me*. But if they see me going up there, they'll put two and two together."

"Who's they?"

"I'll tell you later. Can you meet me in one of the village pubs? About ten o'clock?"

Nick nodded.

"You're not messing me around?" Suddenly there was a child-like desperation in her, and he realised that, whatever was going on here, this young woman really *was* in trouble.

"Promise," he said.

"Cross your heart and hope to die?"

Surprised by her intensity, he slowly nodded: "Cross my heart, hope to die."

"My brother Sonny disappeared about seven weeks ago," the girl said.

"What do you mean 'disappeared'?" Nick asked her.

"Just that … he vanished."

"Tell me more."

She took a long moment to compose herself. They were in a village pub called *The White Lion*, and sat facing each other over halves of lemonade. The girl's name was Charlene Campbell, and she'd told Nick that she came from south London. And no, she definitely was *not* in Cornwall on holiday.

"Sonny's involved in some kind of research," she said, "and I think it brought him down here."

"What kind of research?"

She pushed across the table the various notebooks she'd been toying with on the bench up in the hotel's garden.

"These are notes for his thesis," she said. "Sonny's the sort of black guy you coppers would like very much. He doesn't have a criminal record, he doesn't smoke blow, he doesn't even like rap. He's got a job and he's doing a degree with the Open University. He's even engaged to be married, and that isn't because he *has* to be."

Nick glanced down at the first notebook. On its cover, the words *Black Britain* were written in biro, in a neat hand.

"It's part of an Afro-Caribbean Studies course," Charlene explained. "It's the history of blacks in the UK. His thesis was going to be on British social attitudes to the black presence in Britain, past and present."

"And how did that bring him *here*?"

She shrugged. "I don't know. I only came here, myself, because of this last entry." She flipped open the third notebook, which was headed *Early Period: Trans-Atlantic Slave Trade*, worked her way through a couple of text-filled pages, and indicated a footnote, at which Sonny Campbell's written research seemed to come to an abrupt halt. It read: *Check – Countess Abigail – Lower St. Beloc. Devil's Rnd. Field-research req.*

"Lower St. Beloc … Devil's Roundhouse," Nick said.

He glanced back up into the preceding paragraphs, which were also abbreviated and dotted with confusing cross-references. From what he could gather, they dealt largely with the commercial slave trade, in which Britain had been active throughout the seventeenth and eighteenth centuries, but which had eventually been declared illegal by the UK in 1807. The names of a number of African kingdoms who had been willing to do business with British slave-traders were also listed, including Mandinka, Fulani, Susu, Basa, Ibo, Yoruba, Oyo, Dahomey and Ashanti. The final name, 'Ashanti' bore a footnote of its own, which read: *Poss myth link, contact Carlton.*

"Who's Carlton?" Nick asked.

"Carlton Willis," Charlene said. "A friend of Sonny's. He's an *inyanga.*"

"A what?"

"A witch-doctor." She seemed mildly embarrassed by the admission. "Well, he says he is. I know it sounds like a load of crap, but he's into his roots you know, African folklore and all that stuff. He's the one who got Sonny interested in black history in the first place."

"And have you spoken to him about Sonny?"

"Yeah, but he doesn't know anything. He's a typical bloke, he just reckons he'll turn up."

"I don't suppose you've worked out what the reference to 'Countess Abigail' is?"

Charlene shook her head. "I looked on the internet, but apart from a load of old fogies in European royalty, there's nothing."

"Did any of them have connections with Cornwall?"

"Not that I saw."

"You're sure Sonny actually came down here?"

She indicated the cryptic note: "He must have done. The day he made *this* entry … that's the day before he vanished."

"But there's nowhere round here, nothing at all in fact, that's called 'Countess Abigail'? A pub maybe, an inn?"

Again she shook her head. "I've checked everywhere."

Nick considered. "You say he's getting married. What's his fiancée's take on all this?"

"I don't know. Yasmin hasn't been seen since either."

"She's missing too?"

"Yeah. But she was always with him, so it's no surprise."

"Charlene, you *have* reported these disappearances?"

"My mum did, but Sonny's twenty-four and Yasmin's twenty-one. They're not exactly vulnerable persons."

"Whereabouts in south London do you guys live?"

"Peckham."

"Which has got a high crime rate, if I remember rightly."

"So?"

Nick leaned across the table towards her. "So are you absolutely sure Sonny wasn't into anything naughty?"

"Oh, come on …" Charlene's face twisted at the mere thought, but clearly she *hoped* this wasn't the case rather than knew it for certain.

"I'm not saying something bad's happened to him," Nick added, "just that he might have gone on the run for some reason."

"No way. He'd have contacted me."

"And you've told all this to the Met? Because they're the ones who'll be officially investigating."

"They're not investigating anything."

"They *will* be, but it'll be a low priority."

"That doesn't make me feel a whole lot better."

"The point I'm trying to make is, while the Met are handling the London end of the enquiry, me and you might as well handle the Cornish end … assuming there is one."

"I'm sure there is." Again, she stabbed a finger at the notebook reference. "I've been all through the atlas, and there are no other St. Belocs in the whole of the UK. Besides, he mentions the Devil's Roundhouse as well. You can see that, surely!"

"Okay, okay." Nick raised a placating hand. She was getting het-up, which was probably understandable if her brother had been missing for nearly two months. "What's this problem between you and Tregarrick, anyway?"

"What do you think? I'm a black face in a white neighbourhood."

"Yeah, but pardon me for saying … you're a *beautiful* black face, and that makes a difference, even with the most racist bastards. And I don't think Tregarrick is one of those. At least, that's not the impression I get."

She pondered this, barely reacting to the compliment he'd given her.

"I don't know," she finally said. "Maybe I've been asking too many questions. But I've been polite, you know. I mean, I've not gone off on one."

"What sort of questions have you been asking?"

"Well ... 'has anyone seen my brother?' Let's be honest, if he did come down to St. Beloc, he might have stayed in the Tregarrick Hotel. In that bloody place, and they won't even bloody well answer the simplest fucking questions ..."

"All right, relax," Nick said. "Charlene listen, most of the people who go missing turn up safe and sound."

"I wish I believed Sonny was going to." She wiped a tear from her cheek.

It wasn't the first time her street-tough façade had cracked, and again a vulnerable girl was visible underneath. He leaned over and squeezed her hand. "Well you've got *me* to help you now. And I've never had a case yet that I couldn't break."

She swallowed back further tears. "Where do you want to start?"

"The island. Sonny thought there was something out there worth looking at, let's go and see if we can find what it was."

Charlene nodded.

Fifteen minutes later, they'd descended the steep flight of steps from the village centre, and arrived on St. Beloc Beach. Being late-evening, it was now deserted, but a number of rowboats and motorboats lay on the sand, keels turned upwards. The 'for-hire' kiosk was shuttered and padlocked.

"Isn't a bit late to be looking to hire a boat?" Charlene asked.

"We're not going to hire one," Nick said, setting off walking.

She followed him, surprised. "We're going to steal it?"

"No. We'll bring it back when we've used it. We can even leave some cash if you like, but if people round here really *are* suspicious of you, it won't help if they see that me and you have hooked up. So doing it during the day's out of the question."

"You mean we're going out there *now*?"

"Less chance of being seen in the dark."

"Okay." Her enthusiasm grew visibly as the realisation dawned on her that at last she was taking positive action. "Okay, let's do it."

Nick wasn't sure why he was being so proactive on the girl's behalf. She wasn't a friend or relative. Even in his capacity as a police officer, the case of her missing brother had nothing to do with him. Partly, he supposed, it was because he was bored and couldn't face many more days of endless inactivity, but also it was because, in a moment of ill-advised sentiment, he'd rashly promised that he'd get some kind of result for her, so he now felt honour-bound to try and do something.

"Didn't tell me I was going to do all the rowing," Charlene complained from the other end of the boat.

"Didn't I?" he replied. "Sorry. Mind you ... as you've seen, I wouldn't be up to much at present."

She mumbled some less audible complaint and continued at the oars, a dark shape moving steadily back and forth, the timbers creaking in a regular pattern. By her own admission she'd never rowed before, but she was a bright and athletic kid, and had picked it up quickly once he'd shown her how. Of course, that didn't mean it was easy for her. They were now about two hundred yards from shore, and hitting heavier and heavier waves, and she was feeling the strain.

"Shouldn't we have brought a torch with us, or something?" she asked.

"Have you got one?"

"No."

"There you are then. Course, even if you had, it would probably be seen from the shore, which wouldn't be a good thing. Don't worry, it's a moon-lit night."

And that was true: the moon sparkled on the water in a brilliant silver patina, but it didn't make the isle of Lower St. Beloc look any the less eerie as it slowly drew towards them. At first glance it was an amorphous blot on the horizon, but as they approached, the jagged, broken outlines of ruined housing became visible: the triangular shapes of gable-walls, some with window apertures; skeletal spars where roof-beams still remained; the black uprights of freestanding chimney stacks. Once again, Nick was touched by a sense of desolation. Maybe it was to do with his own childhood, which had been spent in the post-industrial wastes of south Lancashire, but abandonment of habitation always struck a deep and ugly chord with him.

"Shit!" Charlene suddenly said. "I've broken a nail."

"Quiet!" he hissed. "Let's not let them know we're coming."

She paused in her rowing. "I thought you said there was no-one there?"

"*I* didn't say there was no-one there."

"So who are you expecting?"

"Keep rowing, eh, or the current will take us off course."

"You've got the tiller."

"Just do as I say."

She bent her back again, but he could now sense her watching him through the darkness. Several minutes passed, and the swell beneath the boat became noticeably stronger. A chill wind whipped spray off the surface, spattering them. Charlene was grunting with effort. Nick found himself hanging onto the tiller with everything he had. The seabed couldn't be too far below them, he reasoned – after all, Lower St. Beloc had been connected to the mainland in relatively recent times – but on night-black water like this it was difficult not to imagine a fathomless, icy gloom down there.

"Suppose we hit rocks, or something?" she said.

"That's why I chose a boat with a shallow draught. But if you feel anything, tell me."

There was probably fifty yards now to go, and the island's north shore had come into view. It was rugged and steep, and there was a repeated backwash from it, which was striking the boat's prow like an underwater sledgehammer.

"We're almost there," Nick said.

"You can ... bloody row back," Charlene gasped. "I don't care how ... bloody incapacitated you are."

Nick watched keenly as they came slowly inshore. Wavelets continued to slap the hull, but the swell lessened and suddenly there was a crunching of shingle along the keel.

"Okay," he said, climbing out, plunging to knee-depth. "Quick and quiet, eh."

Charlene pulled the oars in and followed suite, and a short while later they had the boat upright among steep, slippery rocks.

"Do we leave it here?" she asked.

"I wouldn't advise it." He indicated barnacles and streaked seaweed rising to a point several feet above their heads. "The tide must be due in soon, and if it catches us out, we'll end up swimming back."

They climbed several feet further, dragging the boat with them. It was light but an awkward shape, and it thumped and bumped several times. At last, they were on flatter ground that was dry and sandy. Immediately in front of them, there was a low wall and the stark silhouettes of two ruined cottages. They listened intently, but heard nothing except the breaking of surf and sighing of sea-wind.

"What are we actually looking for?" Charlene asked.

"We'll know when we find it," Nick said. He rose, and started forwards, climbing over the wall and hobbling between the two houses.

The first thing they really noticed about the village of Lower St. Beloc was that many of its street surfaces remained unchanged from when they'd first been laid. In parts they were cracked and split open, and thick with summer vegetation, but on the whole they were evenly cobbled, as they must have been way back in the eighteenth century. The cottages, on the other hand, were little more than moss-covered shells. Their interiors had been scoured out by the elements, and were now deep in weedy undergrowth. Most of the woodwork used in the actual building had perished, though here and there a shutter tapped, a timber creaked.

As they ventured down one narrow street after another, they became acutely aware of countless black apertures on either side.

"Like Lewisham before the Docklands Light Railway opened," Charlene muttered, trying to make a joke but sounding scared.

Nick had sensed from the outset that she was uneasy to be here, and the further in they penetrated the tenser she became. She was unconsciously close to him, not even realising that she'd taken a grip on his arm. Her breathing was short and shallow, probably to compensate for a heart that was beating steadily faster. Inner city kids were never as tough as they thought they were, he reminded himself. He wasn't sure whether she knew about the history of this place – namely that most of its population had sickened and died so inexplicably – but, just in case she didn't, he decided not to mention it. In truth, he was discomforted himself. In his thirty-nine years, he'd experienced quite a lot that was odd and unearthly; he wasn't sure if he believed in ghosts, but he knew there were many unexplained mysteries below the skin of the world, just waiting to leak out through some rent or rip. And Lower St. Beloc was a rent if ever he'd seen one. Tragedy was almost palpable here. The windows in the dwellings were like the eye-sockets in skulls; the interior walls were bone-white in the moon's radiance. He tried to imagine the clacking of clogs, the voices of children, the grating of cartwheels, maybe the calls of tradesmen who'd walked over from the mainland. Every quay around the circumference of this island would once have been jumbled with the rigging of boats. It would have been a lively place, a thriving place – instead of this empty, cadaverous sprawl.

"Look," Charlene suddenly said.

They'd turned a corner and entered a kind of village centre. Like Upper St. Beloc, a Celtic cross sat on a small podium in the middle.

"It's a mirror-image of the other place," she said, as they approached it.

That wasn't completely accurate. Compared to the lovingly cleaned and maintained monument in Upper St. Beloc, this one was broken; one arm of the crossbeam was missing, and those few engravings that remained were hidden under scabrous lichen.

"They're everywhere, these crosses," she added. "Weird place, Cornwall, isn't it?"

There was wonder in her voice, as though the idea had only just occurred to her; sure proof that this mysterious corner of England would not normally be on her network, nor probably on her brother's.

"Yeah," Nick agreed. "It's supposed to be the western end of what they call 'the Great Ley' ... that's a ley-line that allegedly bisects the whole country. There's another thing round here called 'the Penzance Triangle', which is supposedly an epicentre of occult activity. You know, spirits, goblins ... and Lower St. Beloc's right in the middle of it."

"Hardly surprising the locals are scared of coming out here," she said.

"They're scared? Who told you that?"

She shrugged. "No-one. But, you know, I asked around in the village on the mainland, and that was the impression I got."

Nick considered. "If they *are* scared of coming out here, I'm not sure it's the spirits and pixies that are bugging them."

"What do you mean?"

"I don't know. Just a feeling I've got. Whoa ... *hear that?*"

Charlene nodded. She'd gone rigid. From somewhere close by, there'd come a loud *clink* of metal. They pivoted round, scanning the encircling ruins. Another *clink* followed, and then another.

"What the hell *is* that?" Charlene whispered.

"It's coming from over here, I think," Nick said, and he moved towards a cottage that had all but fallen in on itself.

Only two of its walls remained upright. The rest lay in heaps of moss-grown rubble, which extended into what had once been a small garden. He picked his way through, Charlene following, and, on one edge of it, they found a small goat-willow, the only tree they'd so far seen on the island. It was stunted in its growth, probably owing to the paucity of the soil and the constant wind. But of more interest than the tree was what had been hung in it: draped over its lowest branch at roughly head-height were what appeared to be two separate lengths of chain. They *clinked* again in the strengthening breeze. Nick took one down and examined it – it was caked in rust.

"These are old," he said. On the end of the chain, there was a corroded ring like a clamp or manacle. "*Really* old. Most of the links have fused together."

"So?" she asked.

"So I wonder if Sonny put them here?"

"Why would he do that?"

Nick indicated where the chain had been looped over the branch. "If these had been here any length of time, the bark would have grown around them. They've been hung here recently."

"Yeah, but why would *Sonny* do it? I mean, what's it supposed to mean?"

"It doesn't mean anything. He was probably gathering evidence for his research."

"Evidence of what?"

"Of the slave-trade ... and Lower St. Beloc's role in it."

134

Charlene glanced again at the two lengths of chain. Suddenly she looked shocked. "You mean, these are …?"

"Yeah, shackles. Probably from a slave-ship."

"But what are they doing here?"

"Like I said, your brother will have been gathering them. I guess he was rooting all over the island. Probably spent quite some time here. This is the only tree, so it's a good point of reference. He probably dumped the bits and pieces here as he found them."

"Didn't find very much, did he?"

Nick shrugged. "Two centuries have gone. Maybe there wasn't much left. And then again …" he hesitated, as though the thought he was entertaining was too uncomfortable, "… maybe the search was going well and he got interrupted."

"By what?"

As she asked this, a hooting, high-pitched laugh came floating on the sea-air.

Startled, they glanced around. It was a brief sound, and it faded quickly. But then the sound came again, and this time Nick recognised it – from his uncanny dream on the train, from the hallucination he'd had in the hotel garden.

"I think we should get out of here," he said.

"Me too," Charlene agreed.

They turned and began walking quickly, stepping over the broken garden wall and heading along the narrow street in the direction they thought led back the way they'd come. Of course they couldn't be absolutely sure: they'd turned innumerable corners since they'd arrived here, and many of the spectral ruins were identical to each other. Another burst of ghoulish laughter echoed behind them.

"Run!" he said tautly.

"What?"

"Run!"

"What about you?"

"I *can't* run."

Charlene glanced over shoulder, torn by fear but also indecision. And she froze. Her hand locked on Nick's arm, the fingernails almost piercing him through his jacket sleeve.

"Nick, something just ran across the road behind us."

"What do you mean some *thing*?"

"Some*one* then. But hump-backed, like … like, God, I don't know. But Nick, he's following us, he's stalking us!"

"Run!"

"I'm not leaving you."

"You don't even know me."

"No, but I damn well *need* you!"

He cursed under his breath. To either side there were only the rotted hulks of buildings. The island couldn't have been more than a couple of hundred yards across. At some point they had to come to the sea. But which side was the boat on?

"This way!" Charlene said, hauling him down a narrow ginnel that curved away and ended abruptly in front of two gateposts.

They passed between these, and found themselves in another garden, heavily overgrown. The cottage attached to this one was less damaged. Its four walls remained, though it was hollow and roofless.

"Through here," she said, still tugging on Nick's arm.

"You know which way you're going?"

He was struggling for breath. His weakened body was already exhausted; sweat was soaking into his clothes. The reverberations of his stick smacking hard on the cobbles sent judders of pain through him.

"There's a north-westerly wind blowing," she replied, "and we left the boat on the *north* side of the island."

"Good girl," he panted.

"Good girl nothing! You didn't see that thing behind us."

"What do you mean, 'thing'?"

They'd now come out onto another road, but Charlene continued in the same direction. A passage led away between more tumbledown buildings.

"Just what I say, *thing*! And not an animal. It was on two legs, but, like I said, it was hunched and running in a crazy sort of way ... kind of hopping. And it was dark all over. I imagined fur ..."

"Fur?"

"Yeah, or body-hair!" Her voice was turning high-pitched with growing panic. "Jesus Christ, Nick ... what're we facing here?"

"Never mind that now."

They'd come to the top of a flight of steps, which dropped down steeply. At the bottom, waves were foaming on black, weed-covered rocks. They descended. The treads were greasy with sea-spray, and it was an effort not to fall, especially for Nick – and then they heard that sound again, that odd, gibbering laugh, now laced with a bestial anger. It was much closer than before.

"It's sniffing us out," Charlene whimpered.

"Doesn't matter, we're away from here," Nick gasped, lurching along the waterline.

But it wasn't that simple. They blundered over footing that was more precarious than anything they'd yet encountered – shifting shingle, masses of ice-slippery wrack, and nowhere could they see the boat. The tide

136

hadn't risen yet, and, directly across several hundred yards of rolling surf, they could see the shore – its moonlit cliffs and, atop those, the dotted lights of Upper St. Beloc. They knew they were on the right side of the island. But the boat wasn't there.

"Where the hell is it?" Charlene wailed.

"It's got to be somewhere. Keep going."

Nick hurried her along, though of the two of them he was the one tripping and stumbling. The laughter came again, now sounding as though it was somewhere above them. They glanced up. Framed against the stars, they saw the parapet of a low wall that seemed to be running along the village perimeter.

"Is that the wall we saw when we landed?" Charlene asked.

"It sure bloody is," he replied, pushing her on, relieved.

But they hadn't gone another five yards before they discovered a mass of splintered planks and broken pieces of oar.

"Tell me this is driftwood," she said.

Nick shook his head dumbly. It looked too new, too freshly-painted to be driftwood.

It was the perfect cue for another manic laugh, but this time there was no need – for their stalker was upon them. With a single bound it had cleared the wall above, and alighted only a couple of feet away.

Its snarls were ear shattering. The stench it brought with it – of blood and offal, of chewed-up bones, of torn-off hides – was gag inducing.

They could only stand there spellbound. Though the night concealed much, the apparition, which now rose up from its haunches, was twisted and misshapen, but despite this, and despite the hideous hump on its upper back, it was broad as an ox, with a thick, muscle-packed frame and a throat that gurgled as it growled. The eyes it set on them were burning, crimson slits. Nick didn't doubt the frenzied fury with which this horror would attack. So he struck first. It was a mighty, slashing blow, his hickory walking stick arching around and impacting on the creature's upper body with such force that it snapped itself in two.

The monstrosity gave a savage grunt and flinched away; a momentary break in its concentration that Nick was determined to take advantage of. He spun around, grabbed Charlene by the back of her jacket and propelled her towards the waves.

"Swim for it!" he shouted.

She launched herself forwards, diving into the sea regardless that there might be razor-edged boulders just below its surface. Nick flung himself after her, a tumult of black-green water crashing over his head.

* * *

The numbing Atlantic chill was to Nick's advantage for the next two minutes, as it meant that at first he barely felt his numerous aches and pains. However, the effort required just to stay afloat in the swollen coastal waters was immense, never mind the effort needed to swim three hundred yards to the shore.

He struck out as gamely as he could, attempting a steady breaststroke, but he sank repeatedly, the waves booming cacophonously in his ears. The icy darkness both above the surface and below it was a nightmare in its own right. It was difficult to see anything, or even to make out which direction he was travelling in, if indeed he was travelling at all. He was vaguely aware that several yards to his left Charlene was also striking through the water. Initially they were neck and neck, though this didn't last. Weariness dragged on Nick like concrete weights. His strokes became progressively feebler. Brine filled his mouth, poured up his nose. Each time he submerged, he went deeper, and though on the first occasion this seemed to be a good thing because he suddenly felt that he was able to propel himself forwards more easily, the swirling currents of those lower depths quickly took hold of him, turned him around, pushed him sideways. Every time he now re-emerged, he did so desperately, coughing and spluttering.

After ten agonising minutes, the cliffs and lights of the town were still a significant distance away. Nick had never been one to surrender easily, but months in plaster and traction had wasted his musculature, tightened his sinews. The surface of the sea appeared to tilt as he battled to stay above it. Breakers roared, the star-lit sky spun crazily. How much more of this he could endure he didn't know. He barely had control of his limbs. He was floundering, flapping helplessly, going under with greater and greater regularity until at last he was down there for good, squeezed in a turgid, icy embrace, his lungs fit to burst. He could only hope that what they said about drowning was true: that it was painless, that it was just like going to sleep. And then, suddenly, a hand took him by the collar of his jacket, and he was being dragged strongly forwards.

The next thing Nick knew, there were shells and grit under his knees, and then he was crawling through exploding surf, and Charlene was backing up onto the beach, hauling him after her like a piece of essential baggage.

He glanced up at her once before dropping onto his face in the sand. She was barefoot, her white shell-suit plastered revealingly to her form. She stood over him, dripping and glittering with seawater, an ebony mermaid to whom he undoubtedly owed his life.

"Glad?" she said, breathless.

He spat out salty phlegm. "What ... that I ever met you? Not half."

"No. That all that crap about black kids not being able to swim was a load of bigoted bullshit?"

"That goes without saying." He rolled exhaustedly onto his back.

Charlene gazed out towards the island, which was now almost invisible in the dark. "You did well. I didn't think you'd even get half way in your state."

"When there's something demonic at your heels, you'd be surprised what you're capable of."

"Demonic?" Even after everything they'd been through, she looked startled at his use of such a term.

He got slowly to his feet. "What's *your* take on it?"

"I dunno."

"Well whatever it was, there's a reason why it's out there. And it's got something to with the past."

"You think it's because the islanders used to be slave-traders?"

"No. Slave-traders were rich merchants, not impoverished villagers."

"But the shackles we found?"

"I think the islanders were actually worse than slave-traders."

"Worse?"

"I think they were wreckers."

"What?" Clearly she didn't understand the phrase.

"Cornwall was once notorious for wrecking. Gangs of felons would deliberately draw ships onto the rocks with lights in order to loot the wreckage. Survivors, if there were any, were often murdered."

"And you think they wrecked a slave-ship?"

"Maybe by accident, maybe not … slave-ships also carried gold, ivory, diamonds, all sorts of precious goods. Either way, the slaves were chained together and to benches. When the ship went down, they wouldn't have stood a chance."

Charlene said nothing as the reality of the appalling crime sank in.

"There could have been hundreds of them," Nick added

"Hey!" she suddenly said. "The Countess Abigail!"

He nodded. "I bet it was the name of a ship. You know, your brother was really onto something here."

"Yeah, but why? It's two hundred years ago and the local rednecks were a bunch of pain-in-the-arse criminals who didn't care about blacks. What else is new? I mean, why should Sonny get excited about that?"

"It might not be the wreckers whose activities he was looking into. It might be the fact that the crime was never investigated."

"Yeah?"

"Which would be unusual, because slaves would have been a valuable cargo back in those days. Unless, of course … they were also an *illegal* cargo." Nick pondered, the idea growing on him. "According to Sonny's notes, slavery was banned in Britain in 1807. But I seem to remember an earlier date." He racked his brains for the sort of antiquated legal knowledge that only anal-retentive detectives like him managed to accrue. "Something called the Mansfield Judgement was passed in the 1770s, and that started the anti-slavery ball rolling. If that ship had been operating after the 1770s, then it could well have been operating illegally. So if it got wrecked off the coast here, the owners might not have declared it lost."

"Which would just about sum up the attitude of British Empire bosses during the slave-trade era," Charlene said.

"And would give Sonny one hell of an introductory chapter to his thesis."

"Course, this is all guesswork. I mean, we don't actually *know* anything."

"True." Nick mopped seawater from his hair. "Damn, I wish we had access to the Internet. I normally take my lap-top with me everywhere, but not when I'm on sick leave."

"There'll be a cyber café in Falmouth."

"You think?"

"Sure. I can get on-line there. Mind you, I didn't find anything about Countess Abigail last time I went surfing."

"Yeah, but this time you know what you're looking for. Kick off with Lloyds of London. They've been insurers of commercial shipping since the eighteenth century."

"I'm impressed," Charlene said as they trudged back up the beach. "I've been messing around down here for over a week and got nowhere. You turn up and we're already three-quarters of the way home."

"So now is it my turn to ask if *you're* glad?"

In answer, she took his arm to assist him up the steps, and kissed him on the cheek.

The lateness of the hour prevented any lengthy explanations when the drenched pair got back to the Tregarrick Hotel. There was no sign of Tregarrick himself, but one of the night porters admitted them when they knocked.

"Sorry," Nick said with a wry grin. "Boat accident, would you believe."

The night porter asked if they were both okay, and, when they nodded, told them that they'd need to report it to the harbour-master and the coastguard in the morning. Nick said that he would. They went upstairs, halting on the landing.

140

"I'll get off to Falmouth first thing tomorrow," Charlene said.

"Will you need money, or anything?"

"I've got money, and there's a decent bus service."

They bade each other goodnight and went their separate ways. But Nick hadn't let himself into his room before he again heard that curious 'mumming' sound. He paused, key in hand. As before, it was as though someone was mumbling wordlessly. But now that he was wide awake he was better able to locate it. He padded along the corridor. When he reached the first turn, the sound was considerably louder. He looked down the next corridor; it was darkened, though light shone around a single door at the far end. He advanced, so intrigued that he'd forgotten he was still soaking wet. The door bore no number, and the 'mumming' sound was definitely coming from the other side of it; in fact, it was rising to new levels of intensity. Whoever it was, was clearly distressed. Even as Nick watched, he saw shadows flickering in the rectangle of light, denoting flurries of activity. And now he could hear a voice as well. The words were unclear, but were delivered in a firm yet gentle tone, as though whoever it was, was trying to offer consolation.

As he traversed that final stretch of passage, the floorboards squeaked. It was loud enough for the people inside the room to hear, but Nick had already decided that he wouldn't try to conceal his approach. Perhaps it was none of his business, but it sounded as though someone was in trouble, and he was still a police officer. Before he had a chance to knock, the door opened a crack, and he was surprised to see the unsmiling face of Doctor Laura Tregarrick.

"Can I help you, sergeant?"

"Er … maybe. I thought I heard something. Is there anything I can do?"

"There's nothing you can do. Thank you."

"You've got everything under control?" He didn't deliberately make his voice sound doubtful, but the GP's body language was tense; she was using the door as a partial shield, if not for herself, for whoever was in the room behind her.

"Everything's fine," she assured him. "Sorry if we disturbed you. Goodnight."

'We', he thought as he made his way back towards his room. She'd said 'we', as opposed to 'I'. Sorry if 'we' disturbed you. That was interesting. And how come she hadn't noticed that he was dripping wet, or, if she had, how come she hadn't mentioned it? That was surely unusual.

Half an hour later, he'd showered and was in bed with his lamp switched off, but sleep didn't come easily. It wasn't just the doctor's nocturnal activities that were occupying his mind, but the terrifying incident on the island. From his pillow, he peered uneasily around the unlit room. It wasn't difficult to imagine a pair of burning ruby eyes suddenly opening in front of him. He wondered what he'd do if he heard that terrible laugh echoing down the passage outside, or how sick he'd feel if he suddenly smelled carrion.

He turned over, irritated with himself. Ordinary folk might quail at such night terrors, but Nick Brooker was well used to fending things like this off. He'd spent the bulk of the summer – that part of it when he wasn't drugged to his eyeballs – struggling with vague reminiscences of similar horrors from an earlier case. In the May of that year, an almost routine murder enquiry had turned into the investigation of a bizarre witch cult.[1] Nick had brought closure to the matter by using explosives to destroy a circle of standing stones within which a large number of lives had been ruined. He himself had been caught in the blast, and as a result his full recollection of events was fogged. But certain things *had* stood out in his mind all the time he was in hospital: weird phantom shapes that had no right to exist in a sane world, visions of infernal darkness unleashed on Earth.

"Delirium," the counsellors had told him.

"Medication-induced nightmares," the psychoanalysts had said.

"Acute shock," the official report had been worded.

Of course, none of that explained why he hadn't been sacked, or at least suspended, following his wilful annihilation of an ancient monument. Nor why the results of the follow-up enquiries had been kept secret from him, in fact had been kept secret from everyone, and filed away with a zealous resolve that would have done the CIA 'Black Projects' team credit.

As Nick mulled over this, he drifted into a more relaxed state and knew that he'd soon be counting zeds. He already had half an idea that his demons – imaginary or otherwise – would be with him for the rest of his life. So what was one extra fiend on a bleak lump of rock called Lower St. Beloc?

The following morning, Nick met Charlene as she was coming out of the restaurant. Still not wanting to draw attention to their alliance, he made the conversation swift and to the point.

"Do you know what you're doing?"

"Yep," she said.

---

[1] See the novella 'Long Meg And Her Daughters', published in 'Children Of Cthulhu', Del Rey.

"Best of luck then."

"What are you going to do?"

"Poke around down here. They didn't like you asking questions about Sonny going to Lower St. Beloc, and now we know why. Next, I'm going to find out why they didn't like you asking about the Devil's Roundhouse."

He made to move away, but she stopped him. "Nick, about last night?"

He glanced back at her.

"I mean ... what happened?" she said. "Could we have been dreaming it? Did someone put something in our drinks in the pub?"

"Don't get rational on me now, Charlene."

"We've *got* to be. What happened out there? That thing couldn't have been real."

"You never heard it said that the greatest success the Devil ever had is convincing mankind he doesn't exist?"

She shook her head. "You're a strange kind of cop, Nick."

"I'm starting to think that too, but that's something we can discuss later. In the meantime, we've got jobs to do."

He went into the restaurant alone, where he enjoyed a frugal breakfast of toast and marmalade. Afterwards, he made his way on foot through the town and down the coastal track towards the Devil's Roundhouse. Missing his stick, he found it more difficult than he had before, but, as his enthusiasm for the investigation grew, he was feeling stronger and more robust than he had done in ages. Once, he wouldn't have given any credence to the belief that mind could overcome matter, but the way his life was changing, and the way this mystery in particular was panning out, he now found himself questioning a great many of his former viewpoints.

Even so, it was an arduous walk. It was mid-morning, and the sun beat down fiercely as he descended the final hundred yards to the strange, circular structure blocking the path that once led out to Lower St. Beloc.

"I wonder why they built you here?" he said to himself as he idled around it.

The tide was again out, and there were several-dozen yards of shell-strewn sand between the seaward side of the building and the waterline, so he was able to observe the Roundhouse from numerous positions.

"Are you purely symbolic?" he wondered. "Or do you have a more practical purpose? I can see you're a chapel, but you're a chapel no-one uses. So what exactly are you?"

He was looking for any kind of aperture or window, but found none. Eventually he circled back to the door. It was solid oak, but its base had decayed thanks to the occasional high tide. Almost certainly it wasn't as sturdy as it looked.

He cast around in the shingle, finally selecting a large, heavy stone. In his weakened state, he had trouble lifting it, but at last he managed to carry it back to the door and strike the aged wood at roughly the point where a lock mechanism ought to be. Nothing happened. He struck a second blow, and a third, and a fourth, and at last there was a *clunk* as though some rusting metal bar had snapped inside. He dropped the stone and pushed at the door. It creaked open a few inches.

On the other side there was darkness and a cloying, musty stink.

Briefly, Nick wondered if he'd gone too far. Without a search warrant, this could be deemed an illegal entry and therefore criminal damage. In addition, the boat he'd 'borrowed' the night before had been destroyed – not by him, but while it was in his care, and he hadn't even reported it let alone tried to make restitution, so his list of misdemeanours was growing. But something about this place overrode all other considerations. So thinking, he leaned forwards and pushed the door open fully.

Daylight filtered in, and though what it revealed in there made him catch his breath and his hair prickle, it drew him inexorably inside, made the detective within him yearn to know more. A moment later he was standing in the centre of its interior – little more than an alcove, half a square-yard of paved, sand-crusty floor – amid the stacks of macabre objects with which the small building had been packed.

Bones.

Of every type.

And clearly human.

Femurs, fibulas, tibias, clavicles, scapulas, pelvises, vertebrae, skulls, mandibles; every conceivable portion of the human skeleton was represented here, all piled on top of each other and rising in grisly pillars that reached almost as high as the straw-thatched roof. If this wasn't foul enough, each individual fragment was yellowed with extreme age, or hollow like a rotted-out log. The entire collection was sheathed in a single diaphanous shroud of cobweb.

Nick swallowed hard. But he wasn't revolted as much as surprised. This place wasn't a chapel at all – it was an ossuary. One never got used to death, especially when it came at you in a preponderance like this – but suddenly several minor puzzles were solved for him: the lack of windows in the Roundhouse, the fact that it was locked all the time, the fact that visitors were discouraged from trying to enter.

But whose ossuary was it?

Even as he asked this question, he found an answer of sorts.

As his eyes roamed the gruesome jumble, they began to note oddities: a spinal cord in which all the vertebrae had fused together, giving it a branch-like inflexibility; a length of thighbone that was curiously twisted, almost bent, as though it had been folded over.

One by one, he took items down. Many, if not all, were warped and misshaped: an elbow joint had calcified into a solid mass; a skull with its jaws clamped shut – further investigation revealed the two rows of teeth actually stuck together, as though they had somehow grown into each other. There was a skeletal hand, which should by now have come apart like a jigsaw puzzle but was still intact, locked into an unyielding claw. A sternum and ribcage had curved inwards to such a degree that they would surely have crushed the lungs and heart. The various sections of an otherwise normal cranium had opened up like the petals of a flower.

All of these malformations would be understandable, if, for instance, the relics had been exposed to extreme heat. But there was no trace of burning here, no char, no soot. The deformities might have been genetic, but if that *was* the case why should, and in fact how *could*, so many freakish wretches – for there were surely several hundred preserved here – have all been interred together and at the same time?

And now a more frightening idea struck him, and, before he knew what he was doing, he'd spoken it aloud: "They were paralysed. No-one knew why, but they were all struck down with a strange, contagious paralysis. Yet …" and he shook his head, perplexed, "what kind of paralysis does *this*?"

"A very astute question."

Nick spun around. He'd been so absorbed that he hadn't noticed a shadow fall as someone had come and stood in the Roundhouse doorway. It was Tregarrick, as dapper as ever in his blazer and flannels, but now with a frown on his tanned face, and a small, snub-nosed revolver in his fist.

Nick gazed at the weapon, then up at the hotelier's unblinking blue eyes.

"What the hell do you think you're doing?"

Tregarrick ignored the question. "And clearly you're a very astute man. We've had a number of officers down here recuperating from ill health, and, until you, not a single one has shown the slightest interest in this place and the secrets it might contain."

Nick glanced again at the bones. "I thought at first these might be the remnants of a shipload of drowned slaves. But those poor people are at the bottom of the bay, aren't they. These will be the villagers, am I right?" He looked back at Tregarrick. "The ones who died on Lower St. Beloc?"

"That's correct," Tregarrick said. "It was the year 1793, and they died of a paralysing condition that contemporary medicine failed to understand."

"What caused it? Some kind of pollution? Some disease brought from the tropics?"

"Oh no, I'm afraid it was much worse than either of those."

"Tell me about it."

"I doubt you'd believe me even if I could."

"Okay. But why are they all *here*, in this place?"

"Another interesting question, and one, I'm afraid, that you'd have to ask my ancestors. They're the ones who first built the Roundhouse and filled it with these leftovers. I must admit, though, it has a kind of *ritualistic* feel, wouldn't you say? The fact that it's a Christian shrine, and that it blocks the road that once led to Lower St. Beloc. The fact that it provides a gateway."

"A gateway?"

"A closed gateway. Thanks to which, a certain something now can't come ashore."

Nick stared at him blankly.

Tregarrick shrugged. "Don't credit me with some deep, arcane knowledge, sergeant. I'm a modern man. I don't know how it works, but it does. Time's passed, but it still can't come ashore."

"It?"

"You know what I mean, you almost fell foul of it yourself. I call it 'it' because I don't know its true name." Tregarrick gestured at the bones. "But it's undoubtedly the cause of this horror, this blight that twisted living skeletons in a way science even now would fail to understand."

"Is this all the villagers who died?" Nick asked.

"This is *all* the villagers, sergeant. With one or two very fortunate exceptions."

"Don't tell me. Your great-great-great grandparents, or whoever they were?"

Tregarrick smiled. "How else would I be standing here now? Thank God for occasional trips inland, that's all I can say."

"They were wreckers, weren't they? I mean, the *whole* village – they were all wreckers?"

"You wouldn't need to be a genius to have worked that out."

"And this was their punishment?"

"It certainly seems that way."

"But how did it happen?"

Tregarrick sighed. "That's something you'll shortly be seeing for yourself. Unfortunately, at very close quarters."

Nick indicated the revolver. "You realise you're looking at ten years for threatening me with that thing?"

146

"Oh sergeant, I was looking at a lot worse from the very second you started poking your nose into our affairs. But you should *never* have made friends with Miss Campbell. That was an error on your part that I simply couldn't overlook."

"Put the gun down, Tregarrick."

"Oh I will," he said, stepping forwards, raising the weapon and slashing down with it at Nick's head. "I most certainly will."

Charlene didn't expect to get as far as she did so quickly.

It was a glorious August day, and Falmouth, probably west Cornwall's largest resort, was buzzing. Thankfully, however, most of those thronging its narrow streets and browsing its multiple curiosity shops were tourists, so the Internet café she found in a side-alley quite close to the harbour-front, was unoccupied. She rented herself an hour, hooked up to the Net and began to search. Equipped with the new information she and Nick had gleaned from the last couple of days, it wasn't too long before she was able to trace records of a cargo ship named Countess Abigail. Apparently, it had been part of a merchant fleet owned by a London-based company, Telford & Rapley Mercantile, which had ceased to trade in the year 1838.

This information came from an obscure website dealing with the early days of British colonial trade, which seemed to exist purely for the interest of scholars. Mainly it catalogued the names and types of craft that had been used in the trans-Atlantic sea-lanes, and much of it was worded in archaic language. But there was also, rather fortunately, an abbreviated log of voyages made by several of Telford & Rapley's schooner-class vessels, one of which happened to be the Countess Abigail. Charlene noted with interest that the ship had gone out of service in 1793, which tied in neatly with their theory, and before then had spent its forty-year lifespan sailing back and forth between the company's Atlantic trading-posts, making regular stopovers in Kingston, Jamaica, and at a place called Fort James, which, though it sounded American, Charlene had a distinct suspicion would prove to be in west Africa somewhere. Commencing a series of geographical searches, she located Fort James with astonishing ease. It was now called Accra, and it was the capital of modern-day Ghana.

She sat back in her chair, pleased with herself. But the pleasure didn't last. She suddenly wondered if anything she was doing here was actually contributing to the search for Sonny and Yasmin. On the face of it, it didn't seem as though it was, but then she considered Detective Sergeant Brooker and his calm but effective approach to investigation, and she realised that the trail she was currently on was probably the same trail Sonny himself had followed.

She looked again at the screen, at the crude computer-drawn map of colonial West Africa's legendary Gold Coast. Fort James sat right in the middle. What had Sonny done next, she wondered, after he'd reached this stage? She considered some of the other things he'd jotted down: the names of African kingdoms that had occupied that region of the continent: Dahomey, Oyo, Ashanti.

Ashanti – whom he'd underlined as having a "poss myth link".

She commenced a new search, and quickly uncovered further references to these ancient tribal homelands, in particular Ashanti, which had eventually been incorporated into the British Empire. Of course, in educational terms she was flying blind. She'd never really been interested in history, much less the murky history of her ancestors. What she needed more than anything now was an expert on the subject. She took the mobile phone from her pocket, thinking about calling Carlton Willis, the so-called '*Inyanga* of Peckam Rye'. And then another thought struck her.

An *inyanga*.

She wondered if she was going crazy, but she let the idea roll. An *inyanga* might explain an awful lot. In fact, it might explain everything.

Could there have been an *inyanga*, or someone similar, on that ship, the Countess Abigail, when it went down? Unpalatable though it was to admit it, slaves were acquired so easily by European merchants in that long-ago era because African kings, who were trying to get rid of criminals, political rivals and sundry other undesirables, had willingly sold them. And a troublesome *inyanga* could easily have been included in such an ill-fated bunch. More to the point, from what Charlene knew of the old stories, the *inyanga* class were powerful medicine men, magicians who could summon evil spirits by simple prayer ceremonies. Just supposing, as the Countess Abigail went down, wrecked, and the slaves trapped in its hull knew they were going to die, one of them was an *inyanga*, who used his final breath to visit supernatural vengeance on those responsible? Would that explain what had happened to Lower St. Beloc? Wouldn't it explain the horrific presence that still lurked there?

Charlene laid her phone aside and let her fingers play on the keyboard. She typed two words into the enquiry box: A*shanti devils.*

Seconds passed as the computer chittered to itself, racing back and forth through the many options. Then a website appeared on which a list of African-sounding mythological names was prominently displayed. The top one read: *Yandu.*

An explanatory note appeared in a box alongside it.

Charlene's blood ran slowly cold. All at once everything made a harrowing kind of sense. She recalled the humped form in the darkness, the hideous, fluting laugh.

The explanatory note read: *The Hyena Man.*

Nick wasn't sure how long he'd been unconscious, but when he opened his eyes, one of which was so sticky with blood that he had to blink to clear it, he saw the sun low on the horizon. He tried to move, but a bolt of pain shot through his head and knocked him sick. He closed his eyes and lay perfectly still.

And sensed motion around him.

And a creaking of timbers.

And a repeating hollow thump, as water struck what sounded like a wooden hull.

Then he realised there was a motor churning.

He opened his eyes again, and discovered that he was lying against the prow of a small outboard. Tregarrick sat in the stern, one hand resting on the tiller, the other clasping the small revolver, which he still trained on his captive. Nick glanced sideways: foaming water rolled past. They were proceeding at a good rate of knots. He saw a trail of grey smoke veering away behind them towards what looked like the Cornish mainland. His gaze moved back to Tregarrick, who was watching him dispassionately.

"So why the hell," Nick said, "are you risking a long prison sentence to conceal the existence of a ghost?"

Tregarrick shrugged. "It's not so much the ghost. It's what the ghost signifies."

"Oh, I see. A crime was committed in … 1793, I think we said?"

"That's correct."

"So a crime was committed in 1793 … a pretty heinous crime. I'm not saying the wreckers deliberately drowned a shipload of African slaves, but they certainly made no effort to rescue them. But that was in 1793. And even if your ancestors *were* involved, how the hell do you think it makes *you* responsible?"

Tregarrick smiled to himself as if he was dealing with a confused child. "What exactly do you know about the African slave trade, Sergeant Brooker?"

"Not much. Only that it was finally abolished by Britain in 1807."

"Do you also know that there are now moves afoot in certain legal quarters to claim considerable sums of compensation for British families descended from African slaves?"

"I've heard about that, yes."

"And don't you think it's ludicrous?"

"I don't think it's a great deal more ludicrous than those descendents of Holocaust victims seeking compensation from Germany. That doesn't mean to say it isn't a little bit ludicrous. They're not the ones who suffered, so why should *they* be recompensed?"

"At last we agree on something."

"But I can understand the motivation," Nick added. "Horrible crimes were committed, and someone has to pay for them somewhere down the line. Of course, I think the slave families have a lot less chance of succeeding than the Holocaust families. Two whole centuries have elapsed, and there's a growing suspicion that what this is really about is a bunch of greedy lawyers trying to get rich."

Tregarrick beamed. "We agree again. I'm almost regretting what I have to do today."

"But the question stands. Why is this a problem for *you*? These people are going to try and get their compensation from the British Government. No-one else."

"That's undoubtedly true, but the issue may be fully investigated and the wrecking will come to light."

"It's too long ago to matter."

"Is it?" Tregarrick wondered. "Is it really? What would you say if I told you that my family were involved in the wrecking of more than one slave-ship? That, in fact, they were involved in the wrecking of countless. And that these were not accidents, that these slave-ships were deliberately targeted. You see, after 1772, ambushing slave-ships was by far the safest option that wreckers could take."

"1772," Nick said, realising that his earlier guesswork had been alarmingly accurate. "Don't tell me … the Mansfield Judgement?"

"In 1772, Judge Mansfield decided that slavery was unsupportable in law, and that no-one, including blacks brought to Britain as slaves en route to the West Indies, could be forcibly removed from this country against their wishes. That meant that, from 1772, slaves brought to the United Kingdom were automatically freed and could not be re-enslaved. The merchants who traded in human flesh didn't like this. They wanted to make stopovers here en route to the Caribbean, in order to unload their other valuable cargoes. So from this point on, they had to do it secretly."

"And when your family subsequently wrecked their ships, they could hardly complain to the authorities?"

"They couldn't even complain about the loss of their legitimate cargo, because owing to their ships' illegal status, it could only be imported as contraband anyway."

Nick pondered the implications of this. It must have been a lucrative business for the wreckers, but at an appalling cost in human lives. "So how many people were actually drowned as a result of these activities?"

150

"How can I know? There are no written records. It all ended in 1793, but there'd been many by then, and those slave-ships were packed to the gunwales. We could be talking twenty or thirty thousand. As a direct result of which, my people became very, very rich."

"And you're worried they're going to make you give it all back?"

Tregarrick shrugged. "Ordinarily I wouldn't think they'd be able to. But this government of ours is the most rapacious I've ever known, and filled to the brim with expert buck-passers. I wouldn't put it past them to try and get something out of me if this matter became public knowledge."

"I still think too much time has gone," Nick said.

"It may have done. But even if it *has*, the various successful businesses I inherited, and the many others I've built since, are based on collateral handed down from an age of mass murder and gangsterism. It wouldn't do my professional reputation any good if the word got out."

"And you're prepared to kill me just to protect your reputation?"

"I won't be killing you, sergeant. Not at all. I'll be leaving that to someone else. Someone you've already met, albeit fleetingly."

Nick craned his neck to look over the prow. The island was almost upon them. In the fading day, its clutter of roofless cottages was like some neglected necropolis, its sepulchres and mausoleums broken open to the scavenger birds. Dwindling red sunlight lay like blood across its sagging facades.

He spun back round, to feel a tugging pain in his right shin. He glanced down and noticed for the first time that a hefty ball-and-chain – corroded but still of good, solid manufacture – had been clamped on it with an iron brace.

"Oh dear," Tregarrick remarked. "Yet another artefact from that lost age of human bondage."

Nick reached down, only to find that the brace hadn't just been locked into place, it had been *screwed* there. It would take tools to release it. Not that this stopped him trying with his bare fingers.

"Struggle all you want, you won't be able to get it off," Tregarrick said. "This time, you see, there can be no swimming away from Lower St. Beloc."

Paralysis.

Paralysis, Carlton had told her when she'd rung him. That was its prime weapon. Yandu, the Hyena Man – one of the most fearsome of all African mythological demons. It slashed and tore at its victims with filthy, infected claws, and instantly they were paralysed. But not just paralysed: twisted, bent, knotted up like wood.

151

She hurried on along the narrow country lane, mist ebbing across it from the surrounding moor as night slowly fell. Three weeks ago, if you'd told Charlene she'd be facing a foe like this, she'd have laughed in your face. Okay, her family might have come to Britain via the West Indies, having originated in that mysterious 'dark continent', but she'd never believed in *vodoun* or *umbanda* or *quimbanda*, or any of that crap. Charlene was totally westernised. She was interested in shoes, clothes and music. She lived in the heart of London, she got her hair and nails done at weekends, she hung out with her friends down the market, chatted up guys in clubs and wine-bars, read glossy celeb mags, went dancing, occasionally caught a flick. And that was it. Life was short, sweet and simple.

Well, not any more.

Charlene's perspective on things had changed sharply.

Suddenly, the world was a deeper, darker and infinitely scarier place than she'd ever imagined. Suddenly, there were vastly more evil things in it than muggers and dealers and crackheads.

She stumbled on, hoping for the umpteenth time that she was on the right road. She refused to believe that catching the wrong bus from Falmouth had been anything more than an unfortunate accident, though inside she suspected it wasn't. All right, she'd realised her mistake in time to get off at a convenient crossroads, and had been told by the conductor that Upper St. Beloc was only two miles away on foot. But how had it got so dark so early? How had these few skeins of mist turned the verdant moors into a grey and gloomy wilderness?

And who the hell owned those heavy feet that she was sure were now following her?

She turned repeatedly, but never saw anyone. It can't be *him*, she told herself. Or rather, *it*, the hyena-thing. That thing was still stuck on the island; probably something to do with the Devil's Roundhouse blocking the road to it. At least, that had been Carlton's view, though obviously she hadn't been able to tell him too much, so he hadn't been able to give her definite answers. In any case, she hadn't yet heard that terrible gibbering laughter. On this occasion it was purely the sound of boots clumping along, partly muffled – which suggested that whoever it was, was treading on the grassy verge rather than on the road itself.

Charlene hurried on. She'd probably come a mile since the crossroads. That meant she had to see the lights of Upper St. Beloc soon. The outlying farms and cottages would shortly begin to appear, warm and homely, lamplight pouring from their mullioned windows. It was a pleasing thought, but it was rudely shattered. Because, a few seconds later, she heard those pursuing feet start to run.

152

She whirled around, taking a defensive stance. But more mist wafted past, obscuring her vision, and, even when it cleared, the road behind her was empty. That might have been a relief, but at this point there were hedgerows to either side, and now she was wondering if what she'd heard was not someone running behind her, but someone running *alongside* – maybe running on ahead, keeping low so as not to be seen. Even as she thought this, the thudding footfalls seemed to recede again until at last she couldn't hear them.

She turned a full circle, staring in all directions. Cornwall had to be the most rural county in all of England. Its towns were small and scattered sparsely, traffic rarely travelled between them at night, and the majority of its roads were like this – narrow, winding lanes rarely lit by street-lamps.

"Who is it?" she called, deciding that she had to confront, if not her enemy, her personal fears. She wondered if she was turning paranoid, if the whole horror of this bizarre situation was playing mind-tricks on her.

No answer came. She glanced behind her again. More veils of mist rolled across a distant ridge. Wind sighed on the rocks and tors and heathery hilltop tussocks. At that moment, the sense of isolation became almost intolerable. She desperately wanted to call Nick, but as far as she knew he hadn't brought a mobile phone with him. Even if he had, he was in no fit state to come out here and meet her. Besides, from what Carlton had told her, Nick was in at least as great a danger as she was, if not worse. In fact, *she* might be the one who'd have to go and save *him*. So she walked doggedly on. Perhaps it had been her imagination? No-one had overtaken her in the mist. Why would they do that?

She stopped short again, the breath catching in her throat.

Directly ahead, the road dipped into a hollow with gnarled, stunted trees arched over it. She heard the chuckling waters of a brook, but she couldn't see anything because the shadows under those trees, thickened by mist, were virtually opaque.

At once it became glaringly apparent why someone might have wanted to overtake her – because they knew the lie of this land, and had figured out the best place for an ambush.

It was against all logic to go down there. Even if she was imagining things and no-one had been following her, it would be utterly foolish to walk freely into such a menacing situation. She glanced sideways, and saw that the hedgerow had become a rock wall. What's more, there was a stile in the middle of it, which meant there'd be a footpath on the other side, probably leading away across the moor. It would be risky in the dark, no doubt stony and rutted and slippery. But there was no question which was the safer route in Charlene's mind.

She hurried to the stile and climbed onto it. As she did, she heard what sounded like a muffled grunt, and a renewed thudding of feet. And this time they were coming up from the hollow. Someone *had* been waiting down there. They'd seen what she was doing, had given up any pretence of secrecy and were running after her.

She jumped down the other side of the stile and fled for her life.

"Get out," the hotelier said, gesturing with his revolver.

"Tregarrick," Nick replied, "you're a bloody lunatic."

"Get out."

They were on the west side of the island, bobbing at the foot of the green and slimy stair that Nick and Charlene had run down before. A wind had picked up, and the tide was swelling. With the gun trained on him, Nick had no option but to stand up, though it was difficult with the heavy ball linked to his ankle.

Tregarrick watched him intently. "I told you to get out. I won't tell you again."

Nick glanced over the side. With night upon them, the water was black as ink. The first dry step was at least four feet away. "If I get out here, I'll drown."

"We're right over the top of the stair. You'll be able to stand up."

"Can't we at least get a bit closer?"

"Forget it. The thing that lives here has a habit of smashing up any boats it finds beached. It likes nothing better than to trap its prey on the island and then go hunting."

"That doesn't exactly encourage me to go ashore."

"Don't try my patience, Brooker. At the end of the day, it doesn't matter to me how you die. I'm giving you a fighting chance here, but if you prefer it, I can just as easily shoot the kneecaps off you and pitch you over the side."

Nick bent down and stuck his unfettered foot into the water. Leaning further, he took the gunwale in his free hand and tried to slide over it, dragging the ball-and-chain behind him. Needless to say, the encumbrance unbalanced him and he fell into the sloshing waves. Thankfully, as he'd been promised, it wasn't deep at this point. Two feet down, his body hit the lower treads of the sea-stair, and though the shock of the icy water knocked the breath from him, and the weight of the iron ball threatened to drag him down deeper, he managed to gain a purchase and clamber upwards until he'd reached dry concrete. He was briefly dizzy, his enfeebled body drenched, his head still spinning from the brutal blow it had received earlier.

He glanced backwards, to where Tregarrick had started the motor again. The bastard was still pointing the gun at him, even though the small craft was now chugging away.

"I suppose it's only fair to tell you at this stage," Nick shouted. "Charlene knows most of what I know."

"Charlene's being taken care of too," came the response. "Goodbye sergeant. Sorry it had to end this way."

The boat and its passenger were now a shapeless hump on the darkened sea. Nick's throat tightened. Very quickly, it seemed, his only chance of escape from this place was out of sight altogether. There was a blast of wind, and he had to cling to the steps. As he did, he released the heavy ball, which landed on the tread next to him, but rolled down to the next one, dragging painfully on his leg. He had to scramble after it. It was astonishingly heavy for its size. It was perhaps half the mass of a soccer ball, but it gave him no end of trouble as he hugged it to his breast and tried to re-ascend. The wind blew all the harder. Whitecaps were now rushing in on every side. Freezing spray washed over him.

It would be easier inland, where he could find shelter. But of course, with the growl of Tregarrick's outboard now a distant memory, Nick's ears were already attuning for that demonic, fluting laugh. And no sooner had he achieved level ground than he heard it. It was some distance away, but the island was only a couple of hundred yards square in its entirety. What was it the crazed hotelier had just said – that this thing liked nothing better than to hunt?

There was another insane gibber. It was closer already. The shadow-black denizen of this hideous, haunted isle was coming for Nick again.

Charlene raced down a flinty track, constantly sliding in her sneakers. She fell several times, but always rolled forwards, jumped up and continued to run. The person pursuing her had more affinity with an ape than a human. She was plunging headlong through near-total darkness, but she frequently glanced over her shoulder, and, in the vague shimmer of moonlight, glimpsed a heavy male outline with a squat frame and big shoulders.

She'd already given up on screaming and shouting; she now sought to conserve every inch of breath so that she might use it for running. She could get away from him, she told herself. She was lithe, youthful, and, as the ground evened off again she lengthened her stride, accelerating purposefully. The sweat streamed off her. Her heart was so fuelled with adrenaline that it thudded relentlessly, actually hurting the inside of her chest. But she knew she could make it. Spectres of mist still drifted across the path, but now they were driven on a strengthening sea breeze, which gave her hope. She was running downhill, she was running into the wind. That meant she had to be approaching the coast, and on the coast was Upper St. Beloc. But ahead of her the folded land was still concealed by night. Farm-walls came at her out of the blackness, and she had to vault over them. Bushes would tangle her legs and tear at her jeans. And nowhere – nowhere on the expanse of open moor – could she spy the lights of a township or even an isolated house. Behind her, meanwhile: the mighty impacts of booted feet managed to keep up.

As she ran, she filched her mobile from her pocket. She tried to tap out 999, but in the darkness that was impossible. More than anything, of course, she didn't want to risk losing the phone – it was more vital now than ever before – so she shoved it back into her pocket and pushed it down as far as she could.

"Gonna get you, girlie," she heard a male voice stammer. "Gonna get you good. Gonna put you where they'll never find you."

Charlene couldn't believe it. All her life she'd grown up in an inner urban district, where gun-crime was rife and almost everyone out after dark was up to no good. Like any animal coming of age in a jungle, she'd got used to it. Her instincts had become well honed: she was a fighter, a born survivor. Neither the grim alleys and rubble-strewn lots of south-east London, nor the many predators who roamed them held terror for her, because she was part of that world herself. But this was Cornwall: the land of grass and sky, granite coast and golden beach; it was a hunting ground for those in pursuit of a gentle holiday or a slower pace of life. How could something like this have befallen her *here*?

She was now descending steep ground again. It was trickier still because it was wet with dew, and the inevitable soon happened: she slipped, and went tumbling head-over-heels, bouncing on stones, crashing through stands of prickly gorse. Finally, with a pile-driving *thump*, she landed on tarmac.

It was another road.

Groggy with pain, she struggled to stand up. Moonlight reflected from the road's smooth surface, but still, as she turned dazedly around, she saw nothing to show that safety was at hand. And now she was lame as well as exhausted. She'd twisted her left knee as she'd fallen: she put weight on it and an agony of fire lanced up her thigh.

"Oh God," she whimpered. "Please help me …"

"God ain't gonna help the likes o' you," came a low, coarse voice.

Charlene turned and saw that the stalker had now descended the slope and was standing by the edge of the road. He was still only an outline, but his shoulders were hunched, his hands clawed. She could smell his rank sweat.

156

"Who are you?" she screamed. "What do you want with me?"

He made no answer.

"I've got a friend," she warned him. "He's a copper. *He'll kick your arse!*"

The stalker only snickered, and immediately Charlene recognised that repulsive sound. "It's you!" she blurted.

It was Solomon Jarvis, or whatever his ridiculous name was. The big, burly fisherman who worked for Tregarrick; the guy who'd grabbed her before with his dirty, grubby paws, and dragged her all the way through the town to the hotel.

He came quickly towards her.

"You owe me big time, girlie. And I'm gonna take everything ..."

But just as he jumped at her, there was a blinding glare of light. Charlene saw his face: blanched with the effort of running, moist with sweat, his eyes bulging like marbles, his tongue hanging out – and then there was a howling *squeeeal* of brakes.

The vehicle that had come surging around the corner turned side-on as it skidded, yet it still slammed into Jarvis with such massive force that all eighteen stones of him was catapulted across the road. He cart wheeled through the air, only to rebound from the trunk of a roadside yew and come to rest in a crumpled, lifeless heap.

Charlene flicked her gaze from the body of fisherman to the car, and back again. A series of hollow clicks sounded from the vehicle's engine as it cooled. There was an aroma of melted rubber. Then, with a *bang*, the driver's door burst open and someone jumped out. Charlene wondered dully what new threat this might be – and was hugely relieved to see that the driver was a woman; tall, dressed in a dark skirt and jacket, her silky blonde hair cut square at the shoulder.

"What on Earth ... ?" the woman began. Her eyes alighted on Charlene, and in the same instant they recognised each other, though the visiting London girl had not yet got to know Doctor Laura Tregarrick personally.

"I've ... I've seen you at the hotel," Charlene stuttered.

"I've seen you. But, what on Earth's been ..."

"He was chasing me. He was trying to attack me ... I don't know why."

"I'm afraid I do," Laura Tregarrick finally said. She walked over and knelt beside the fallen fisherman to check his vital signs. It wasn't encouraging that a trickle of dark, oily fluid was snaking across the tarmac from his head.

"Is he alive?" Charlene asked.

"Just about."

Charlene felt slightly relieved at that, though she didn't know why she should be. "So ... so, what do you mean you know why he was after me?"

The doctor stood up, took a mobile from her jacket pocket and tapped out a quick number. "I'm calling an ambulance. If you wait here, I'll give you a ride into Upper St. Beloc."

"You think I'll go with *you*?"

"I think you've got no choice. This madness has gone on long enough."

Nick's first thought was to try to free himself of his burden. He smashed the chain as hard as he could between two chunks of brick. But all he succeeded in doing was wearing himself out. Shackles like these had not been designed to be broken. When he got back to his feet, he again heard that chilling laugh. It was even closer.

Determined not to panic, he looked around for a weapon. Last time he'd hit the monster with his walking stick, and, though he doubted he'd injured it, he'd bought himself a vital half-second in which to escape. But this time there was nothing lying around. Flight was the only option. He grabbed up the ball-and-chain and hobbled through the ruins. Might there be a chapel on the island, and, if so, could it provide a kind of sanctuary? Even wrecker communities would have had ministers to tend to them on Sundays. They might have been murderers by trade, but, like all career-felons, they'd have somehow managed to convince themselves that they only did what was necessary for their survival and that it wasn't really their fault.

Not that Nick was certain a chapel would help. If there was one, it might have been deconsecrated. And indeed, a couple of minutes later, he found a roofless structure that had probably served as a place of worship: it was a squat, granite building with a cruciform slit-window in its gable wall. Its front entrance was arched but lacking a door, and its interior deep in grass and broken timber.

The laugh came again, chillingly close.

Nick retreated into the church-shaped interior. At the far end of it was a narrow doorway that led into a passage. He stumbled down it, but it brought him out into another tiny garden, again filled with rubble, and edging onto the ocean. He peered over the seaward wall; it fell to the foaming waters in a sheer drop.

When he heard the laugh this time, it was *inside* the chapel: a tumult of noise followed, as though someone was throwing the broken timbers around.

Nick felt fear of a type he'd never known before. It was so overwhelming that he almost started shouting hysterically for help.

Instead, he got a grip on himself and sidled through a gateway, hurrying up a ginnel. Fifty yards later, he emerged in the village centre again. He recognised the weathered cross, and on the other side of the square, the fragments of fetters still hanging from the tree. It was tempting to rush over there and grab the chain to use as a weapon, but Nick felt too weary to put up a fight. So he kept moving, veering left and right, taking avenues at random.

His lungs wheezed. Every joint ached; his right leg was turning numb.

"When I get out of this and arrest you, Mr. Ted Tregarrick," he said under his spittle-filled breath, "remind me to give you the 'Salford caution' first[2]."

He'd now worked his way to the far end of the island. Soon he saw shingle sloping down into the waves. But not before hearing another frenzied ululation close behind, and the skittering of what were almost certainly claws. Frantic, he lumbered along the shingle in what he thought was a southerly direction, deliberately splashing through the wavelets; if nothing else, his spoor might be concealed. But then his path was blocked by the rotted remnant of a water-break. It slanted down across the narrow beach, and, though it was only five feet high, he couldn't climb over it in his current state. He followed it back up to solid ground, and found himself among more ruined buildings. And still the thing was close. The next gibbering laugh sounded as though it was *above* him.

Nick glanced upwards, spying a dark shape perched on the apex of a gable wall. He tried to dart away, but he was so exhausted that the iron ball slipped from his grasp, hit the floor and stopped him like an anchor. He fell face-first, banging his chin on the cobbles. With a guttural snarl – the sound a dog makes when fighting to the death – the thing landed several yards to his right. Nick didn't look, but grabbed the iron ball, hauled himself to his feet and, with his last vestige of strength, tottered towards the nearest building.

He ducked under its lintel. This particular house had retained its upper floor. The moonlight spilling through its window-frame showed a dusty hearth with a piece of netting hung over it, and beside that a spiral stone stair leading upwards. Nick lunged towards this, but, even as he did, the light in that tiny room was blotted out by something jumping onto the windowsill.

Sweat-soaked, scarcely able to breathe, Nick climbed the stair. He was half-minded to stop part way and try to defend the position. But some sixth sense told him that in no circumstance must he grapple with this abomination. He felt certain those claws would rake the flesh from his

---

[2] Greater Manchester Police vernacular for a good, hard head-butt in the face.

159

bones, but even if they didn't, just to be scratched by them might prove fatal. So he went all the way to the top. Only rib-like spars remained of the roof. The flooring was uneven, flimsy, consisting of broken, mildewed planks. There was a single window, but it was too small for someone of Nick's size to climb out through. And now the monster was coming up the stair after him.

This was it, he realised. He was finally trapped.

He backed away, eyes riveted on the top of the stairwell. The blood thundered in his ears. His beating heart was so loud that he never heard the incoming *whine* of a motorboat just beyond the cottage walls. He cast around for a weapon – any weapon, but there was nothing to hand. And now, at last, a shadowy form was rising into view.

At first Nick could make out no detail, but it was dark all over and hunched forwards, its neck and shoulders huge with sinew. Nick's mouth went dry as it lurched towards him, following a predatory zigzag path. Its feet padded soft and stealthy, its curved bone claws clicking on the rubble. As it slid through a patch of moonlight, he saw an immense, wedge-shaped torso covered by a thick pelt of glistening hair matted with rancid sweat and quivering with hungry excitement. Its skull was flat and anvil-shaped, its ears spiked. Its eyes were ember-red, and centred around black pinpoint pupils, which rolled crazily and gave it a kind of demented glee. They held him in a hypnotic embrace, those eyes. They were pits of flame, pools of burning oil. He gazed helplessly at them, appalled but also fascinated. As it approached, its heat enveloped him: a seething, raging heat; the heat of wasted, sun-blistered savannah. And then its breath fell over him – foul, nauseating, with a stench like blood, bones and maggoty, bird-pecked carrion.

Nick barely even noticed when his legs buckled and he fell backwards.

The horror was now standing directly over him, its teeth bared and clamped like rows of interlocked knives, and yet he remained powerless, petrified. The purring growl that began in its famished belly, and rose and rose until the entire building reverberated with it, was as gruesome and ferocious as anything he'd ever heard. With fiendish slowness, it reached a twisted talon down towards his face, the razor hooks on the ends of its crooked fingers dangling with threads of torn, diseased flesh.

"Nick!" came a wild voice. "Nick, where are you?" It was Charlene. And it sounded as though she was outside in the street.

It tore the cop from his reverie.

"Charlene, get away from here!" he shouted.

The monster was distracted. It turned towards the stairwell, strings of glutinous drool hanging from its lupine jaws.

"Nick, I'm coming up!"

160

"Get away from here now!"

The only response was the sound of her feet as she ascended the spiral stair. The monster swung round to face her. But when she came into view at the top, she didn't seem half as shocked or frightened as Nick had expected. Instead, she had something in her hand, which she now held up in the air. She pressed a button, and light shone from it. Nick still didn't know what was happening. And then he heard a voice; it was small and tinny, like a tape-recording on playback. Instantly he realised what it was.

Charlene's mobile phone.

She was playing a message that had been sent to her: a message in a language so foreign that Nick couldn't recognise it let alone understand it, but which sounded distinctly like a chant or prayer. Had he been closer, he'd have seen that the light shining from the phone's tiny screen was the moving image of a young black man clad in colourful but ornate robes, and wearing a small, circular hat bearing African designs. He was standing at a table wreathed in candle-smoke. As he chanted, he was in the process of hacking off a sparrow's head with a bone-handled knife.

Now it was the monster's turn to be fixated.

It was staring at the intruder and the small device she held as though it could hardly believe what it was seeing and hearing.

Nick took advantage. He grabbed up his ball-and-chain, and scrambled around the thing on all fours, making sure to give it wide berth. Charlene reached down with her free hand, and pulled him towards her protectively. And still she held the phone, and the chanting voice rolled on, and the tiny AVI played out relentlessly in the crimson eyes of the hyena horror, which, even while they watched it, seemed to shrivel in shape and stature. Its molten gaze visibly faded. An attempted snarl dwindled to a meek, dog-like whimper. And then – *it came apart.*

As simply as that.

Like a cinematic special effect, a solid, living being, a mass of muscle, fur, teeth and bone, exploding into a swirling cloud of black, feather-sized flakes, which disintegrated further, one piece after another puffing out of existence until there was nothing there at all except a vortex of twirling dust, the energy of which was rapidly draining.

The chanting voice abruptly ceased, and the AVI switched itself off.

An ear-pummelling silence filled the roofless room.

The dust continued to settle, but with unnatural speed. Within moments, its numberless grains had blended with the detritus that already strewed the floor. A faint fragrance of sweat, and maybe blood, lingered on the air, but very soon that too was gone. All they could smell was the strong salt-breeze.

Neither said anything for several minutes. It was Nick who managed to mutter the first few words: "This ... this is some convalescence."

When dawn broke, Charlene was sitting on the bench at the end of the Tregarrick Hotel's extensive rear garden. She was vaguely aware of police activity going on in the building behind her, but was totally focussed on Lower St. Beloc, the ruins of which were tinted gold in the rising sun. West of the island, close to the foot of the sea-stair, she could see that the Devon & Cornwall Police launch was still moored. Divers from the underwater-recovery team were going over its side one after another.

A short while passed before she realised that Nick had come from the hotel and was standing alongside her. They were both bedraggled, sallow-faced from lack of sleep. Blankets hung around their shoulders.

"He's dead, isn't he?" she said.

"Sounds like he fell into the water after he was attacked," Nick replied. "Under the circumstances, he almost certainly drowned. I'm sorry, Charlene."

"I suppose I expected him to be dead after all this time." She glanced up. "Yasmin?"

"Still improving. From last night, it seems she started making a remarkable recovery."

"And they kept her in that back room all this time?"

He nodded. "Same floor as *my* room, would you believe. From what I can gather, that fisherman character, Jarvis, found her adrift in a boat about seven weeks ago. She was totally paralysed."

"And instead of taking her to hospital, they kept her here?"

"Tregarrick was determined to protect the secrets of this place. Mind you, she wasn't being looked after too badly. Sounds like the scheming old sod talked his daughter into doing what she could for her, though it got tougher each day. Poor lass should've been in ICU." He paused to think. "I suppose it's a *good* thing really. Because that's the only serious crime we're going to be able to charge him with – unlawful imprisonment. That and a couple of extra bits and pieces, like assaulting me, illegal possession of firearms and so on. Should still be good for fifteen years."

Charlene was unimpressed. "And what justice will there be for Sonny?"

"What justice can there be? Tregarrick didn't kill him. Tregarrick didn't even know he'd come out here. When you first showed up, Tregarrick assumed you were Yasmin's sister."

She looked back to the island. "And that place is safe now, is it? I mean, *really* safe?"

Nick stared at the island as well, seeing more frogmen go over the side of the police launch. "Looks like it. That little trick you pulled off appears to have done the business."

"Thank God for email, huh."

"Thank God for *inyangas*."

"Carlton came through for us, that's for sure. He wasn't even certain the ritual would work. Thought it might backfire and sweep him away to the land of demons."

"Lucky for us it didn't."

She sighed. Even though Charlene had experienced all this for herself, the rational side of her mind was already trying to convince her that it wasn't really possible, that many of the things she thought she'd seen had probably been optical illusions.

"Carlton reckoned it could never come ashore because certain kinds of evil spirits can't cross moving water," she finally said.

"Yeah, I've heard that." He sat down beside her.

"He reckons that Devil's Roundhouse thing was built when the causeway was still above the surface, to stop the thing crossing over that way. He wasn't sure but he said there must be some kind of relic inside it."

Nick thought about the heaped bones that had once been heaped corpses.

"According to Ashanti tradition," she added, "one sure way to stop the Hyena Man is to present him with a carrion feast. He'll never be able to pass that by, especially if it's a feast he can't get at, perhaps because it's inside a holy casket or something similar."

"Treasure this guy Carlton, Charlene. Sounds like he knows what he's talking about."

"And back in the real world," she said, "what's the *official* line going to be? I mean, how are you going to write it up?"

"I'm not going to write it up at all. I'm on sick leave, remember."

"They'll have to say that *something* paralysed these people."

"No doubt they'll think up a convincing lie. That's what government bodies usually do when they're totally baffled. Last time they said it was a toxin in the fish. This time they'll probably call it a chemical spill, or a gas leak, or something."

If it was possible, her expression saddened further, and he knew why – more truths that would be buried along with her brother.

"I'm sorry about Sonny, Charlene. Honestly, I am."

"I'm just sorry he died before he was able to expose what happened here."

"I understand how you feel. But, when all said and done, it was two centuries ago. The interest in it would have been purely academic."

She glanced around. "But Tregarrick's family got rich on blood and murder."

"Yes, over a period of generations. It's difficult to see how a single one of them could be held accountable now."

"It stinks, Nick."

"I know."

"Just thinking about it is ... well, unbearable."

"In that case don't." He shrugged glumly, ineffectually. "Always works for me."

THE BALEFUL DEAD

You could easily be forgiven for thinking that, with a name like Troy Tooley, he was a rock star. But, though he'd spent all his working life in the music industry, you'd be wrong. You could also assume that it wasn't his real name. But again, you'd be way off.

To answer the second question first, he came from blue-collar origins in Dartford, his mother a checkout girl, his father a diesel fitter, though both were fanatical movie fans and from the outset they'd been determined to give their children exotic and glamorous-sounding names. On the subject of his long-term showbiz involvement, Troy wasn't a performer (though I suppose you could argue that point when he took the floor in front of a lounge filled with record company execs), he was a professional manager. He might have had a string of successes to his name – from his days as a columnist for various 1960s music-press publications, to his emergence as chief UK talent-scout for Atlantic – but essentially his skills were of the cold, Philistine variety. He was accountant, agent and lawyer all rolled into one. A rare and valuable combination to be sure, even if he didn't have a musical bone in his entire body. In truth, he didn't even *look* like he was involved in the rock business, being thin and gawky, with lank, unfashionable hair and having a penchant for narrow ties, cheap suits and large round glasses; looking, in fact, rather 'dweebish', a plastikit Woody Allen if you like, minus the wit. But who were we to complain? Because Troy Tooley made us.

And when I say that, I mean it. He had literally *made* us.

And now he intended to make us all over again.

1

"Course, I'm not saying you'll all be capable of going the distance," Troy said over his G&T. "Putting an album like this together requires a lot of effort and discipline. Normally it would take years, but we've only got months. Which means it's going to be intense. Like *really* intense."

Rob sniffed. He'd been the least willing to attend this so-called reunion, and was so far proving the hardest to sell the new project to. "No-one here's actually broke, Troy. What makes you think we *want* to go the distance?"

Troy smiled and leaned back against the coach window. Blossoming hedgerows sped by outside. "Never knew you to turn down a challenge, Rob."

"Who's talking about me?" Rob replied, before nodding across the aisle to where Luke was slumped in a foetal bundle, snoring loudly.

Troy smiled again. "Let Luke be for the moment. It's not as if we're going to need any lyrics about orcs and ringwraiths, is it."

"Amen to that," Charlie said, going back to his copy of *The Times*. "At least some things about the industry have grown up."

We said nothing else for several minutes, just gazed through the windows at the passing countryside. The South Downs are very scenic in late spring: a rolling succession of long, green uplands, interspersed with dry coombes and lush low valleys where myriad freshly-bloomed flowers sparkle in the cottage gardens. I hadn't been in this part of the country for five years at least, but then I hadn't been with the rest of the guys – not all at the same time – for several years longer than that. In fact, the truth is that I couldn't remember the last time we'd had a full get-together like this. Okay, Wolfbane – the band, *our* band – had never officially broken up. We were 'inert', I suppose would be one way to describe us. Part of that ageing bunch of formerly mega-sized hard rock outfits, now perceived as dinosaurs, who had gradually drifted to the wings as musical tastes changed, and then, when they thought nobody was looking, made a quick, relieved exit. Most of us, to be honest, preferred it that way. Better to gradually ease your way out of the public consciousness than to publicly crash and burn, the way so many others had.

Not that this latest meet-up was anything to do with producing a hard rock album, though Troy was hoping that we'd be able to draw on the influence of one; namely *Eagle Road* – an LP we'd released way back in 1975, which had instantly gone stratospheric though, oddly, possibly because it was so 'non-rock' in many of its lengthy compositions, which had just as quickly vanished from the charts and now was remembered by no-one.

With the single exception, apparently, of Mike Broderick, Executive Music Producer for Century Films.

"What I don't get, Troy," Joe said from the bar, where he was inexpertly mixing himself a cocktail, "is why, if this movie is about Julius Caesar, it's got anything to do with a stately home in Hampshire."

"Ah …" Troy winked. "You will."

Joe sipped at his drink, then promptly pulled a disgusted face and shoved it to one side.

Our budget didn't seemingly stretch to having our own on-board barkeep, though, as it was, we were riding a forty-seat, fully air-conditioned long-haul cruiser, complete with bar facilities (so long as you were prepared to pour your own), reclining seats and VCR. We were currently speeding through the leafy byways of southern England, having agreed – with no small reluctance (the whole thing was testimony to Troy's powers of persuasion) – to spend a whole week at a seventeenth century pad called Brebbington Chase, and to mull over a potential new project that our manager was dead keen for us to work on. Aside from that, none of us knew too much about it.

"Just accept it as a nice holiday, and the chance to make a quick few hundred-thou while you're at it," Troy added. "If not a whole lot more."

Joe grunted. "I was already on holiday."

"Suppose you were about to make a few hundred-thou as well?" Charlie asked, glancing over the top of his broadsheet.

Joe looked hurt at that. "You never know."

But of course we *did* know. All of us.

Joe Lee's career as a professional showbiz pundit wasn't exactly catapulting him across the firmament like a meteor; I don't think he'd been asked for his opinion on a new release by any radio station that mattered for eight years or more. The truth was that we'd, none of us, really done well since we'd stopped recording. We all had plenty of money, it would be churlish to deny that, but a string of failed business ventures lay in our collective wake, not to mention the odd disastrous book or solo project. Joe, our lead guitar, had done his share of session work, but he'd always been first and foremost an 'axe-grinder', lacking the true finesse of a Clapton or a Brian May, and even that door had eventually closed on him.

In fact, to look at any one of us now, you'd never believe that we'd once filled countless football stadia or sold over sixty million records. To begin with we were all in our early fifties, in terms both of age *and* waistline. Charlie Smollet, our drummer and elder statesman, tended to wear sweaters, slacks and sensible shoes, and today resembled someone from middle management out on a team-building break, rather than a one-time rock and roll hell-raiser. Rob Ricketson, our keyboards and percussion wizard – and probably the genius behind our most ground-breaking work – still sported the shaggy mane and untrimmed 'tash that he'd had all those years ago, but it was now generously streaked with grey. Joe, who'd used to come swaggering on stage in full biker regalia, with a ciggie hanging from his lips and a menacing sneer on his truculent, boyish face, these days opted for nothing more outlandish than a t-shirt and tracksuit pants, not at all concerned to conceal his hefty beer-paunch. Then there was me, Rick Bailey: I'd always suffered from that archetypical bass-player's affliction – anonymity, though these days,

167

possibly because I worked out and lived in Tenerife, and was thus reasonably tanned and fit, I tended to get pushed to the front if there was an interview to be given. Not that I ever enjoyed this. With my bronzed looks and iron-grey curls, I always felt like some latter-day George Hamilton. And finally, there was Luke Hennessey, our lead vocalist, who would always basically – be Luke.

2

I don't think we'd ever set out with the express intention of becoming metal-heads.

We formed Wolfbane in April '71, in Blackburn, Lancashire, with a simple plan to play high-energy rock and roll. We'd only had long hair and sideburns and wore greasy, stonewashed denims because everybody else did. Troy Tooley had seen something in us, however ... some inner wrath or turmoil, some frenzied but creative *tour de force* that simply had to be unleashed. And of course, as always, he'd had his finger right on the pulse, because in 1971 all that violent, vitriolic stuff was just about to become very, very hip.

We were doing the clubs at the time; small, sweaty, smoky venues, whose volatile atmosphere had ideally encapsulated what we were about. But it wasn't all anger and aggression. Thanks to the recently-deceased 'acid era', rock was still about the weird and wonderful: mysticism, fantasy, dream-like states in which ideal, 'Elvish' modes of existence vied with darker powers often represented in the unsophisticated but instantly understandable forms of goblins and evil sorcerers. Our first album was *Swords of Chaos*, and it contained tracks like *Knight's Vigil* and *Woe to the Conquered*. Our second, *Firestorm*, featured a fifteen minute epic called *Iliad*, which at one point was cut with battle noises – pounding hooves, clashing blades and screams of rage – unofficially pillaged from various 'sword and sandal' movie soundtracks. And all of this, of course, was served up with spasms of searing guitar-work, ear-splitting vocals, state-of-the-art synth effects and thunderous, bludgeoning drum rhythms. At the time, the only bands in the UK doing anything similar to us were Black Sabbath, Led Zeppelin and Deep Purple. Not bad company to be in, if you know your music, though we didn't just feed off *their* publicity. We were able to riff with the best of them, and while our songs weren't perhaps so memorable, our onstage performances were, frankly, explosive. Audiences were still lulled by the peace-loving late-'60s, many exponents of which were by then drifting out of flower-power and into the

168

even more gentle and melodic folk and country scene. We must have hit them like a steel fist. I remember certain reviews at the time. *Rolling Stone* said we were "rock's new power-punchers". *Oz* called us "a shock even to *our* system!"

And yet here we were, a blink of an eye later (at least, that's the way it seemed) wandering around a gravelled car park, straightening out cricks in our backs, rubbing our stiff necks and generally grumbling like aged codgers as we tried to get the circulation going after only a couple of hours on a coach. We didn't even have a bunch of glamorous, sleazy women to help us out with it.

In fact, only one member of the fair sex was present, and that was Barbara, Charlie's wife, who was now as much a part of Wolfbane history as screaming guitars, tasselled leather jackets or phantasmagoric album sleeves. She'd started out, like so many, as a groupie, an ex-biker chick in fact, but once she'd got her hooks into our drum maestro she'd never let him go. Not that he'd wanted her to. Bleached blonde but with a pretty face and incredible, torpedo-like bosoms, and good company to boot – a riot at dinner parties, and able to argue intellectualisms with the best of them (but never a power-seeker, and thus no threat to the band's unity) – she had clearly been the soul-mate that God had always intended for him, and we'd been happy to take her along. They'd married in 1978, and had been inseparable ever since. These days she was a less sultry presence, being grey-haired (short and spiked up – it suited her) and running voluptuous-to-overweight, but she was as witty and intelligent as ever, and now so familiar to us that I think we regarded her as a sort of surrogate mother rather than a mate's tantalizing bit of fluff.

The rest of us were currently without female company. Joe, though he'd waded through rivers of prostrate women in his rampant youth, had never married; in fact he'd never even had a regular girlfriend, which I think he now bitterly regretted. Rob *had* got married, back in the early '70s, to a childhood sweetheart, but it hadn't lasted. His new girlfriend, Sheena – who was about twenty years his junior, and something big in the fashion industry – was presently in Paris at a show. My wife, Andrea, who I'd only hooked up with in the early '90s, and who was also my business-partner, had not been able to come over as it was now May, and the season was just warming up down in the Canaries. We ran three bars and two nightclubs in Los Cristianos, so there was no way we could both be absent at this time of year. In fact, I'd scarcely been off my mobile to her since I'd arrived back in England, which had probably got on everyone else's nerves.

But my loyalty to Andrea, like Charlie's loyalty to Barbara and Rob's loyalty to Sheena, did not stop us all suddenly ceasing our feeble

169

perambulations and gazing in open admiration at the woman who Troy was now bringing across the car park towards us.

If you can imagine Gwyneth Paltrow in riding-boots, jodhpurs and a smart tweed jacket, you'd be somewhere close to the mark. This lady was thirty at the most, I reckoned, but tall, statuesque and wore her long, darkly golden hair twisted into a neat pony-tail, which hung over her right shoulder. In addition to this she was devilishly handsome, with glittering green eyes and very full lips. Before we could compliment her, however, she complimented *us*.

"Wow!" she said, with an excited smile. "The original Wolfbane."

We glanced at each other nervously. There was a hurried clearing of throats.

Charlie ambled forwards, hands behind his back. "You look impressed, Miss ...?"

"Ryder-Howe," she said, still beaming.

"Miss Ryder-Howe." Then he shook his head with deep regret. "Unfortunately, that's a sure sign you can't remember us."

Miss Ryder-Howe laughed. "I remember you all right. I saw you at Reading in '83"

Charlie shook his head all the more. "That's a shame."

"Oh?"

Joe – on stage the genuinely aggressive face of the band, but off it always shy and tongue-tied – shuffled from one foot to the other. "He means you didn't catch us at our best," he said helpfully. "We were starting to get old."

"Well it didn't show," Miss Ryder-Howe replied. "I loved that record you did about the Trojan War."

Joe smiled. "*Iliad.*"

"*Iliad*, yes."

"I think that one got slagged off for being pretentious even at the time," Charlie said.

"Well I liked it," she asserted.

"Because you have exquisite taste," Troy put in. "Folks, come over here. I'd like to introduce you to Lucille properly."

We shuffled forwards, still awkward, desperately trying to mind our manners. And that would be *us* – Wolfbane, who'd once been as famous for our bar room brawls, police busts and round-the-world shagging exploits as the Royal Navy ever were. One by one, we nodded and smiled as Troy introduced us, stepping up and shaking Miss Ryder-Howe's hand. I swear, it was all we could do not to tug our forelocks and apologise for living. This was probably a combination of our hostess's effortless upper-class grace, and the low self-esteem, which, after so many years of

170

watching ourselves fade from the music-buying public's memory, now afflicted us like a daily dose of the clap (one Radio One DJ had recently played a rap cover-version of our classic number, *Dog's Moon*, and afterwards asked if anyone knew who the credited song-writers, Hennessey, Lee and Ricketson were). Not that Miss Ryder-Howe was in any way snooty or superior, even though she was clearly a fully paid-up member of the landed gentry and we were working-class oiks born and bred.

"Lucille is the proud owner of Brebbington Chase," Troy said, turning and presenting the house and its expansive grounds to us. "Where you'll be spending the next week, entirely at her generous expense."

It was hard not to be impressed by the house. We'd all spotted it immediately on arrival here, but now that we had the owner in our company, and the cricks and stiffness of the coach-trip were wearing off, we could appreciate it properly. It wasn't gigantically vast, but of a sufficient size to dominate the surrounding parkland, and built in an economic, rectangular style with marble and white stone. I'm no expert on architecture, but a brochure I'd already read had informed me that the house's 'Classical' design dated from the Restoration period of the 1660s, and that its many elegant adornments included "hipped roofs, pediments, dornier windows and cornices". At a guess, I'd expect it to go for five or six million (the rolling acres of formal gardens included, of course). The long, gravel drive swept up to its palatial front doors between two lawns that were more like green velvet.

"People still own these places?" Joe said wonderingly. "I thought they were all in the hands of the National Trust, or something?"

"It's been in my family a long time," Miss Ryder-Howe replied. "And I intend to keep it that way."

"Well … if we can strike the album deal that we're hoping for, the spin-offs for you will be terrific," Troy said.

Charlie snorted. "*If* we can strike the deal." He turned his gloomy face on our hostess again. "You know what the necromancer's apprentice said to his boss when they tried to revive the Bronze Age warrior they found in the nearby peat bog? … Long time dead, man, long time dead."

Troy waved him away. "Ignore these pessimistic bastards, Lucille. They never thought they were any good even when *A King Will Come* went to Number One in the UK and Number Three in the States. The deal's practically done."

And then, *it* came. The inevitable first expletive of the day, delivered in hoarse, screeching tones: "Oh, baby … *oh, fucking hell, baby!*"

And that was Luke's first contribution to the weekend.

Reluctant as I am to get onto the subject, my hands are tied. I *have* to talk about Luke Hennessey, our 'throat-guy' as he'd always liked to introduce himself, our 'lead vocalist' in normal parlance. I'd prefer not to mention him at all, but I simply have to. He's too integral to the tale. And to the biography of Wolfbane, if the truth be told.

What a waste, though. What a sad waste of an excellent front-man.

Luke had been a founder member of the band; in fact, we'd all been founder members – the line-up had never changed, but it's important to remember that Luke had been there at the outset because he was so rarely *there* later on. Formerly a church choirboy, but now with an incredible adult range – he could reach three octaves, can you believe that! – he had thrown himself into the birth of the band with such gusto that for the first few years he *was* the band. A natural performer in the Mick Jagger mold, he didn't just sing up a storm on vinyl, but was so charismatic on stage that he had girls throwing their knickers at him long before Tom Jones had ever heard of such lewd antics. He also wrote. Boy, did he write – soaring, extravagant lyrics, which drew on all the familiar mythologies and Tolkienesque fantasies of the era, but which were so politicised, so scathing, so riddled with angst and violence that they took the traditional, empty-headed hippie dreaming onto an entirely new plane. In appearance too, he was right on the nail. I mean, Luke cut a dash even in the age of Glam. He'd come on stage in skin-tight spandex pants, billowing silk shirts, reams of beads and gothic jewellery, leather doublets, thigh-length boots. His lacquered jet-black tresses flowed around him; mascara stained his pallid cheeks. At the time, such in-yer-face flamboyance was more than sexy; it was dark, decadent, dangerously transgressive.

And this, I think, is where the problems start. Because all these years later – and yes, he still dressed in exactly the same way – with his once-formidable physique shrunken through years of abuse, his limbs like pipe-stems, his hair dyed and thinning, his face a wrinkled parchment, and personal hygiene his lowest priority, it was all rather – well, skuzzy.

You see, Luke had spent the best part of his career doing the many risky things that rock stars are supposed to do, but which those who really want to make a success of themselves, actually don't: partying 'til dawn every night of the week, getting arrested, endlessly bingeing, not just on wild and willing girls, but on drugs and booze, and potentially lethal mixtures of both – to such an extent, in fact, that entire tours had had to be cancelled because he simply wasn't up to the job. He'd twice had to be resuscitated in hospital intensive-care units after unintentionally OD'ing.

He was more of an apparition now than an actual presence, and as he came stumbling off the bus that warm May evening, still yawning, his unwashed hair sticking every which way, a pair of purple-tinted shades protecting his fragile eyes, he made a very unpleasant apparition indeed. As he homed steadily in on Miss Ryder-Howe, she regarded him with something close to undisguised horror.

"You must know Luke Hennessey?" Troy said, stepping nimbly between them.

"Er ... how could I not?" she replied.

"Used to be our vocalist," Troy added.

Luke glanced round at him. "*Used* to be?"

"Slip of the tongue. Sorry." Troy turned back to Miss Ryder-Howe. "Well ... shall we go in? I believe there're some staff who can come and collect our bags, yes?"

She beamed. "Of course. This way everyone."

We followed her at a leisurely pace, trying, I think, to take it all in our stride, to make out that we were used to such lavish environs.

"We're here, bud," Joe said, taking Luke by the arm and trying to draw him back to reality.

"Er ... yeah," Luke replied, tottering alongside him. "Where's here, man?"

I brought up the rear, enjoying the tranquility of the evening. And it was only then, as I strolled casually along, that I first noticed the trees. Don't misunderstand me. To get to the manor house, we'd driven for ten minutes through its grounds, and as I said, they were all superbly landscaped and included stands of trees everywhere, but this particular bunch of trees looked different from the rest. They were densely packed together, and, while everything else we'd seen had been pruned and snipped and trimmed, these seemed to have been allowed to grow with wild abandon. They were located to the left-hand side of the main drive, just beyond the nearest lawn, which was about thirty yards from where we were now. Every type of species was visible – chestnut, holly, hazel, sallow, hornbeam, sycamore, yew, silver birch – in a long, largely unbroken rampart. I realised I was seeing the outer fringe of an actual wood, though even by English woodland standards, there was very little space in there, and even less daylight. How far back it went was anyone's guess. Sunlight dappled the outer trunks, but beyond those I saw nothing except leaf and shadow.

And – very fleetingly – a hint of movement.

At least, I *thought* I did. I looked again, straining my eyes to penetrate the wood's fathomless murk, but nothing was visible. I carried on walking, writing it off as a fox or deer or some such thing. It was easily possible. This country estate was so at peace with itself that I could imagine anything living here in complete seclusion and secrecy.

3

Century Film had put the cash up for a period blockbuster called *I, Caesar*. From what we'd heard, it was going to be a fictionalised biopic of the great general, taking in all his major battles and love affairs, and ending with his famous murder in the forum at Rome. A host of historical celebs were expected to make appearances: Cleopatra, Mark Anthony, Spartacus, Calpurnia, Brutus, Pompey and Augustus, to name but a few – offering juicy roles indeed for Hollywood's great and good, who, by all accounts, were champing at the bit to get involved.

That's about as much as we really knew, along with the fact that the producers were seriously interested in utilising certain key themes that we'd written for our seminal album of 1975. *Eagle Road* had been something of an oddity even back then when 'progressive' and 'concept' were buzzwords in rock. It had charted the rise and fall of the Roman Empire in the west, and, while track titles like *Cross Of Blood*, *Roman Wolf* and *Attila's Pride* probably didn't promise much to historical sophisticates, we'd really gone out (when I say 'we', I mean Rob mainly, one of whose greatest inspirations was always the composer Miklos Rozsa) to create the authentic sound of that lost age by using combinations of oriental, Greek and Jewish music. Of course, it would be untrue to say that there hadn't been considerable head-banging material in there as well – I mean, that was our staple diet. But on the whole we'd created an ancient, arcane sound, which Century Film wanted to use at least part of for the background music on their new production.

I suppose this made it all the more confusing that we were now in an English country house dating back to Charles II, in order to discuss it. Don't get me wrong – many rock bands, particularly from our era, were often pretentious enough to retreat to scenic and isolated abodes, where they could 'take song-writing inspiration from their surroundings' (and probably take a lot of drugs as well, only this time in complete privacy), but we weren't even at the song-writing stage yet. This was nothing more than a get-together to discuss the potential of the project, and, if we were all in agreement, to perhaps lay down some ground-rules as to what we could plunder from the original album and how we might update it. But it was hard to see why we had to do it here and not in some London hotel.

Mind you, there was no denying that this was a very pleasant place to be. The interior of the Chase was as lovely as the exterior, the rooms all on a grand scale and filled with artworks and fine old furniture. At first we were assembled in 'the parlour', another huge, spacious chamber. Its high ceiling was covered with ornate plasterwork, but its walls were oak-panelled and hung with Cromwellian armour and weapons. A long banquet-table ran down one side, and on this, the housekeeper – a Mrs. Hacket – had laid out brandy and champagne cocktails for us. Mrs. Hacket could have been made to match the environment, being trim, elegant, and looking very prim (and somewhat sexy) in her tight flower-print dress. She was in her mid-forties, and wore her ash-blonde hair cut severely short, but she was undeniably handsome and possessed of a delightful smile. A huge but youngish bloke, who I learned was her son, Lionel, was also on hand, hurrying to take away any trays of empties, and, if necessary, to bring in new bottles from the kitchen. By his dusty overalls, I judged him to be the caretaker here, which was no real surprise. With his hulking physique, carroty red hair and odd, vacant-eyed smile, I couldn't imagine that his normal duties lay on the domestic side.

"Anyway," Troy said loudly, drawing us all to attention. He raised his glass. "To our new venture together, and the hostess who is making this all possible."

We mumbled in agreement, before taking sips of the fiery aperitif. Luke didn't sip his, of course. He drank it down in one, and then lurched back to the table to get another.

"The plan's fairly simply, folks," Troy added. "Tonight we're just going to relax. You've all been allocated rooms, which I think you'll like. Lionel will take the bags up. All we have to do this evening is enjoy ourselves. You might want to know a bit more about the place, though, and if you do, well ..." he turned to Miss Ryder-Howe, "Lucille's your man. Ridiculous as that may sound."

Our hostess smiled. "I'd like you all to take a leaf out of Troy's book and call me Lucille while you're here. Please, treat this place as your own. Refill at the bar, help yourself to snacks from the pantry. We've got tennis courts and a croquet lawn. There are even private fishing rights on our stretch of the Beaulieu. Feel free to wander round wherever it takes your fancy. Everything's on the house."

"Sounds good," Joe said.

"Your rooms are ready and Mrs. Hacket will take you up whenever you want to go," Troy added. "Any questions at all?"

"Yeah," Rob said. He was standing alone and to one side. "*How* is Lucille making it possible?"

Troy glanced at him, puzzled. "Sorry?"

"How, in what way, is Lucille making it possible?" Rob shrugged. "It's very kind of her letting us stay here and all, but what's this place got to do with *Eagle Road*? I don't get it."

Troy considered this, then stepped back. "Lucille, perhaps you'd like to explain?"

If our hostess was in any way offended by Rob's rather curt question, she didn't show it. "Well, really ... it was your manager's idea," she said. "But I think it's a good one. We're on the scene of a famous battle here at Brebbington Chase, and ..."

"What battle?" Rob asked. "I've never heard of the battle of Brebbington Chase."

"If you'd let Lucille explain, Rob," Troy put in, "I think you'll understand in a sec."

Miss Ryder-Howe continued: "The exact location of the battlefield is unknown, but lots of archaeological artifacts have been found around here, in the grounds. Basically, in 43 AD, several cohorts of the Roman Second Legion were destroyed in a savage fight with local tribesmen."

She paused, but we were still listening – even Luke, who leaned on the table as he refreshed his cocktail with yet more brandy.

She added: "I don't know too much about it, but it seems that in that year the emperor Claudius sent a massive invasion force to Britain to try and conquer the entire island. His armies fought battles all along the South Coast, as far west as Maiden Castle. Somewhere around here, a Roman force encountered the Dumnonii tribe, who were reputedly very fierce. In the battle that followed, the Romans were massacred. It meant, at least temporarily, that a halt was called to the Roman march west."

She paused, and then smiled again – rather hopefully, I thought.

Rob nodded. "Okay, so that's the history lesson over. Now perhaps you could answer my question. Like, what we're doing here?"

Joe turned to him. "Come on, man ..."

But Rob ignored him, regarding our hostess stonily.

She cleared her throat awkwardly. "Well, I think Troy sort of hoped you'd be inspired to write something wonderful and Roman."

"You've got a museum here then, have you?" he asked. "Full of Roman art, that sort of thing?"

Now there was a flush to her cheek. "No."

"Any ruins?"

"Just the battlefield."

"Which we don't even know is definitely here?"

"It's definitely here," she replied. "But, well," and she smiled again, looking round at the rest of us, "the main thing is, I think, the ambience of the place."

We nodded warmly, as embarrassed by Rob's attitude as she was.

"Oh, so there's a Roman *ambience*," Rob said. "Sorry, it's just that ... well, I didn't notice it."

"You *will* Rob, I'm sure," Troy interjected, not exactly glaring at him but clearly irritated. "Once you get your imagination in gear. After all, that's what you're being paid for, isn't it."

Rob looked like he was about to argue further, and knowing some of the ding-dongs that he and Troy had had in the past, I decided it was time to intervene.

I spoke up quickly: "So, what's the story behind the actual house, Miss Ryder ...?"

"Lucille, please," she said, turning to me.

"Er ... Lucille."

"Well ..." She took a breath, as though about to give a pre-prepared spiel, "Brebbington Chase was built shortly after the English Civil War by Alexander Brebbington, a loyalist nobleman who only returned to England when Charles II had been restored to the throne. Apparently there had been a manor house here for centuries before then, but it was in a bad state of repair. Brebbington rebuilt it with money he'd made from investments in the American colonies. I don't know whether there was any evidence of the Roman battlefield then, but the story that it was built on the sight of the battle was well known. Later on, in 1804, the estate passed into the hands of *my* family. A great-great-great-grandfather, or something or other, Thomas Ryder-Howe, was Marquis of Westbourne. He was also an antiquary, and fascinated by the ancient history of Britain. He allegedly bought the place purely because Roman relics were being ploughed up in the fields nearby. In 1805, he even built a folly because of it."

Joe looked nonplussed. "A folly?"

"A pointless, expensive building," Charlie explained. "Rather like that new mayoral bubble on the South Bank."

Joe glanced at him. "Come again?"

Charlie sighed. "A meaningless structure. Usually quite fancy, but with no real purpose. Nineteenth century types were always building them."

Miss Ryder-Howe laughed. "That's right. Ours was called 'the Lamuratum'. It took the shape of a small Doric temple. My ancestor built it in honour of the Roman soldiers who fell here."

Considering the reason we'd been brought to the estate, *this* was starting to sound interesting.

"Does it still exist?" I wondered.

"Er ... it does," Miss Ryder-Howe replied, though with brief hesitation. "Only I wouldn't ... well, I suppose there's no reason why you can't go and look at it. But it's pretty shabby now, possibly dangerous. It's a shadow of what it used to be."

"Whereabouts is it?" I asked her, thinking that I wouldn't mind checking it out.

She gave me an odd gaze, which suggested that she really *was* uncomfortable with this line of enquiry. "It's in 'the Plantation'," she finally said. "That's the wood you'll have passed on your way up the drive. On the left."

"Oh yeah, right." I'd *known* there'd been something peculiar about that wood.

She seemed to read my mind. "Yes, it's a bit unsightly, the Plantation. But ... well, I'm not really in a position to make extensive changes to the place at the moment. My ancestor had it planted deliberately to sort of ... well, to encircle the Lamuratum. To give it some privacy."

That confused me. Follies were surely constructed so that visitors could stand in awe of them? She saw the question in my face.

"It became a curiosity, I suppose," she explained. "For local people. Probably for vandals as well. Most folk don't even know it's there now."

"How deep is this Plantation?" I asked.

"Extensive. Covers a good three or four square-miles. The Lamuratum's right in the middle somewhere. To be honest, *I* couldn't lead you to it." Then, remembering that she was our hostess here and that nothing was supposed to be out-of-bounds to us, she added: "Lionel works as groundsman and gardener as well as caretaker. *He* knows the way to it and could probably show you. There's a path, I think, but it's almost certainly overgrown."

"Sounds kind of spooky," Barbara said.

We glanced around at her. As always, she was right. She'd hit the nail on the head in a single, short sentence.

Miss Ryder-Howe tried to laugh that off. "Yes ... well, it's acquired something of a reputation over the years, I admit. But I don't know why. I mean, it's just a folly, isn't it."

"And it would be sheer folly for us to continue nattering in here when we've got such a lovely evening to explore the grounds," Troy said, deliberately changing the subject. "So, are we going to hang around in the reception hall all night, or are we going to get this show on the road?"

4

The bedrooms at Brebbington Chase were as sumptuously furnished as the rooms downstairs. Mine had a four-poster bed, a large fireplace and two luxurious armchairs, and its wide window looked down on the manicured lawns and front drive.

And on the enigmatic 'Plantation', which from this position lay to the right, a dense coppice, twisting, leafy and filled with greenish shadow.

I'd now changed into a t-shirt and jeans, and stood and took in the view. An eventual glance at my watch told me it was nearly six o'clock, which still gave us two hours to kill. Shortly before we'd all ascended to our rooms, Mrs. Hacket had announced that dinner would be served at eight.

I stepped out of the room into the corridor, which, in keeping with everywhere else in the house, was more like a passage in an art gallery. At least one antique ornament or original painting was situated every five yards or so. Apparently the floor above us was being refurbished, and at present consisted of sheets, trestle tables and buckets of paste, but that wasn't the case down here. The walls were smoothly papered, the carpet a rich, maroon pile. I turned to close my door and noticed the picture hanging alongside it. It depicted what I assumed was the Lamuratum.

It was one of those Regency landscapes, done in watercolours that always look more watery than they need to be. Clearly it had been painted before the Plantation had grown, for though there were trees in evidence, the Lamuratum stood in open ground. It was a circle of marble pillars with a series of lintels connecting them together. A plume of brackish, foul-looking smoke appeared to be rising from the middle of it, though what was causing this I couldn't see. I stared at the picture for a couple of minutes, then heard a sound and looked around. Rob had emerged from his bedroom. He nodded when he saw me.

"You gave her a hard time down there," I said. "What's the problem?"

He shook his head. "I don't know. Are you buying all this?"

"What do you mean?"

"All this! Brebbington bloody Chase. Doesn't it all seem a bit OTT?"

I still wasn't sure what he meant. We started walking.

"I mean," he said, "if Troy wanted us to get wired up to ancient Rome and all that, wouldn't he have taken us to somewhere like Pompeii, or, well … Rome?"

"Perhaps he couldn't afford it."

He gave a snort of contempt, which was exactly the sort of response so foolish a suggestion merited.

"What exactly are you thinking, Rob?" I asked him.

"You know Troy. He's got more angles than an octahedron."

"I know he wouldn't fuck us over, if that's what you're worried about."

Rob didn't seem convinced. "Times have changed, Rick. We're not hot stuff any more. What's to be gained by trying to bring us back?"

"We own the rights to *Eagle Road*, that's what."

We'd now reached the top of the grand staircase and he stopped, gazing at me hard. "You reckon that's all it is? I mean, genuinely?"

I gave this some thought as I set off down. Rob followed.

"I've seen the paperwork from Century," I said. "*They* approached him. He's not pulling a fast one."

"Well, I suppose it wouldn't be beyond him to try and get one last payday out of us before we're consigned to the rock and roll graveyard."

Rob had always been the introspective one, but this level of despondency was a new low.

"Look, I said. "If all we've got to do is rework a few themes from an album we wrote twenty-eight years ago, maybe run out a new song to go with it, I'm up for it. I need the cash."

The lobby came into view below. We descended towards it.

"We never had a Hollywood hit, did we?" Rob said.

I knew what he meant. It would have been nice, but it wasn't the sort of thing that you did back in our heyday. Of course there'd been some classic ones since. I remember envying Guns'n'Roses for the publicity they got on the strength of the number they released to accompany *Terminator 2*, while Aerosmith did very nicely from the piece they knocked out for *Armageddon*.

"We left the scene too early, that's all," I said.

Rob snorted again. When he felt contempt, he rarely tried to conceal it.

"What is it with you?" I asked. "Why do you underrate your work so much?"

"Bloody hell, Rick!" We were now at the bottom of the stairs and he rounded on me. "*Eagle Road* was nothing to do with real Roman stuff. It's not like I did any research or anything. I pulled most of those tunes out of my head."

"So what? You got the right sound."

"It's just so dated."

And that, I had to admit, was probably true. Concept albums really *were* old hat now. Though – and this was the thing I was hanging onto – old-fashioned stuff can come back in, often when it's least expected. *Eagle Road* had been filled with mysterious, ancient world-type themes, all produced on contemporary instruments – as had the music for the recent movie *Gladiator*, which had also ploughed an allegedly outdated furrow. Despite studio doubts, that picture had then gone on to rocket at the box-office, and to prove the catalyst for a whole new generation of historical epics. And if we could do for *I, Caesar* what Hans Zimmer and

180

Lisa Gerrard had done for *Gladiator*, then maybe we too could be looking at a major comeback. And thanks to *Eagle Road*, the blueprint already existed. In short, I didn't see how we could fail – unless we seriously screwed things up at the writing end, though evidently this wasn't what was bugging Rob.

I was about to speak again when Barbara appeared, planting a plump, be-ringed hand on each of our shoulders.

"And what are you two cooking up?" she asked.

Rob gave her a weak smile. "Just discussing the project."

She shook her head "Working already. Well, me and Charlie are going for a boat trip."

"Boat trip?" I said.

Charlie had now appeared as well, his jacket draped over his shoulder. "Apparently there's an ornamental lake five minutes walk that way." He pointed in a vaguely westerly direction, then raised a sardonic eyebrow. "We've been given permission to take a boat out on it."

"How sedate," I said.

"Hey!" Charlie snapped, ushering his wife away. "We *are* sedate."

A moment later they'd gone. Rob turned back to me as though all his previous suspicions had now been confirmed. "See what I mean? Sedate, for Christ's sake! *We're fucking sedate!"*

We strode on towards the front doors, on the way passing the entrance to what Miss Ryder-Howe had called 'the bar'. It was basically another reception room, with its own bar-counter to one side. Not surprisingly, Luke was already perched on one of the stools. Nobody was at the bar serving, though its shelves were well stocked and he seemed to have acquired a full bottle of Jack Daniels from one of them.

When he saw us, he grinned and raised the bottle in toast. "To the old fucking Romans, eh? Long may they reign!"

"I don't believe that guy," Rob said as we moved on.

"Just shows," I replied, "there's always someone worse off than you."

No-one had actually voiced it yet, but I think there was already an assumption that we wouldn't be needing any vocalisations for this project. And if we did, we'd probably hire session singers to do them.

We wandered outside onto the front steps, and peered over the sweeping grounds. Even jaded appetites like ours were enthused by the pastoral scene. There was no sign of anybody else. Charlie and Barbara had already vanished from sight, and, apart from Luke, I wasn't sure where the others were. Joe would almost certainly be catching some sack-time, and I had the feeling that Troy was with Miss Ryder-Howe, doing what I couldn't imagine. Well – to tell the truth, I *could* imagine, but it didn't seem likely. The two of them were very matey. They'd probably hooked up in some hip Chelsea wine-bar, but I didn't think it possible there was more to it than that. I'd always assumed (though never known for sure) that Troy was gay, while Miss Ryder-Howe was apparently engaged to some chinless wonder from the City. Either way, there was no sign of them at present.

"Where are we going, anyway?" Rob asked. "Fancy a game of croquet, Rick?"

I sniggered at the thought. And it broke the ice a little.

"No," I finally said. "I'm checking out the Lamuratum."

I don't know where that idea came from. Earlier on, I'd anticipated a languid evening spent drifting aimlessly; now I suddenly had a definite goal, and, for some reason, a vaguely ominous one. Rob's smile faltered a little. But he pursed his lips, and nodded.

Within a few minutes, we'd crossed the drive and the expansive right-hand lawn, and had come upon the first line of trees earmarking the Plantation. Despite what we'd been told, we only scouted for about fifty yards along the boundary of the wood before a pathway opened in front of us. I thought about Miss Ryder-Howe's earlier advice, and wondered if she genuinely *didn't* know the layout of her own land, or had simply been trying to put us off coming here. Of course, no answer was to be gained from dawdling, so we threw all caution to the wind and pushed on.

Once inside it, the Plantation wasn't nearly as sinister as one might have expected. This was no nightmare forest of twisted shapes and naked, claw-like branches. The trees were close together, but the golden sunlight of early evening now shafted between them, casting violet shadows – a striking effect that any cinematographer would have been proud of. Undeniably, there was an odd quiet. A 'listening quiet', you might call it. It *did* give you the impression that you weren't entirely alone. As we ventured along the winding trail – which was grassy and rooty but fairly well trampled considering that no-one was supposed to come here any more – we scanned the avenues of trunks to either side. Nothing moved between them.

I glanced at Rob. He'd always been a big guy, perhaps six feet three inches tall and burly to go with it; on stage he'd been a hulking presence. A lot of that had now run to fat, but he wasn't grossly overweight, and anyway, I'd never known him be intimidated by anything, even the hell's angels who'd muscled up to the front of the stage at the Freewheel Festival in 1973 (Rob had personally thrown one back into the crowd, who'd climbed up alongside us 'to get a better view'). But already, not five minutes into the Plantation, his brow was beaded with sweat.

"What's up?" I teased him. "Not used to the exercise?"

182

He grinned unconvincingly, and mopped the sweat away with his denim sleeve.

That was when we heard the first noise: the simple *snap* of a twig.

It sounds like such a cliché, that; in fact, worse yet, it sounds like exactly the sort of thing you'd expect to hear in a wood, so why the heck should you be alarmed by it? But Lord – in reality, the snap of a twig, when there isn't supposed to be anyone else there, is so loaded with menace that I can't adequately explain how quickly it brought us to a halt.

We stared around. Still nothing moved. Beyond the first cover of the trees, only more trees were visible: gnarled, mossy stanchions, their lower boughs heavy with bright new leaves. Here and there, masses of rhododendrons had risen up between them, great profusions of glossy, tangled vegetation, which blotted out all vision.

A shiver of unease passed down my spine.

"Are we going back?" Rob wondered.

"No," I said defiantly.

Don't get me wrong. I'm no hero, but I'm fifty-one years old and I've been around. I've seen and done things, both good and bad, that the average man couldn't even dream of – I wasn't going to be spooked by the eerie hush of an English woodland.

So we pressed on. And eventually we came to the Lamuratum.

It emerged through the trees ahead of us in steady, unspectacular fashion.

The Grecian pillars, each one about nine feet tall, were made from marble and arranged in a neat circle. As the picture I'd seen earlier had illustrated, small lintels or roofs connected them. Initially it must have been quite startling; a gleaming white edifice amid all this lush, natural greenery. But over the decades it had accumulated considerable filth: leaf-mould, watermarks, streaks of bird-droppings. The tall stones were now mottled a yukky grey-green and filmed with lichen. I think its phoniness – the fact that it wasn't really ancient, that it wasn't in fact a totem from some long-forgotten era – made it all the more repugnant. It was like a modern building gone to rack and ruin through neglect.

We approached it reluctantly. I'd expected the structure to be half-buried in undergrowth, but that wasn't the case at all. The open space surrounding it was bare earth, largely beaten flat as though trodden by countless feet. Its interior was equally accessible. No fence or barrier had been put around it. All we needed to do was walk in between the pillars and there we were. The ground inside was also firm and bare. In the very centre, there was a low marble plinth, squarish, about three feet wide by three, and standing to knee height. Its upper surface was slightly concave and coated with a greasy, black residue that was odious just to look at.

"I'm liking this place less and less," Rob said.

"We *were* warned not to come here."

"No ... I mean this whole place. Brebbington Chase."

I didn't bother answering that. I still didn't share Rob's misgivings about why we were here. In fact, I couldn't understand them. Not that this particular part of the estate was very wholesome. It was strange, I thought, that I couldn't hear any birds singing here. When I glanced directly upwards, I saw the sky; it was a pleasant pebble-blue in colour, but framed by branches, and it looked a long way away. Suddenly *everything* felt a long way away; the house, the coach, the rest of the band. The encircling ranks of forest could have been colossal, could have covered hundreds of square-miles and I wouldn't have felt more cut off.

"Is that writing on there?" Rob suddenly said.

He'd spotted something beneath the black, sticky mess on the plinth. At first glance I hadn't noticed it, but, now that I leaned forwards to look, I saw an inscription carved into the marble surface. Rob picked up a stick, which he used to scrape away as much of the scum as he could. Soon the inscription was visible. Part of it had been erased, probably by the passage of time, but the rest of it was legible. It read:

ELIGAT A – PROFICIS TVA

"Latin," he said.

I mumbled agreement. As former grammar school boys we'd both studied Latin, but only briefly. I scarcely remembered a word of it, but I could identify it when I saw it. Then I noticed that Rob had taken a notebook from his back pocket and was jotting something down with a stub of pencil.

"What are you doing?" I asked.

I was surprised, but pleased. My first thought was that he'd suddenly started gaining inspiration from his surroundings. For as long as I'd known him, it had been Rob's habit to carry a pad wherever he went – even when we were on tour, or on holiday – so that if some new idea came to him he could write it down. His answer, however, soured my mood.

"This might mean something. I'm copying it."

"It's probably gibberish. Put there to make the thing *look* authentic."

"Whatever," he said. But he continued writing.

I turned, assessing the rest of this so-called Lamuratum. There was a silliness to it, I now realised. It was rather sad, even pathetic, that some bloke who had more money than sense was so into his pet historical period that he could go off and rebuild a small portion of it for no other

184

reason than to be able to say that he'd done it. No wonder these things were called 'follies'. Then I noticed something about the pillars that I hadn't noticed before. From this angle – the inside of the circle – they were all covered with large, brackish stains. I mean, they were as sullied on the inside as they were on the out, but this was something extra. This staining was darker, more ingrained into the stone. It was also extensive – and I instantly thought again of the picture I'd seen, and how great plumes of sooty smoke had been spilling upwards from the middle of the little temple. I looked sharply back at the blackened plinth.

Then I heard an alarming sound: a slithering, a crackling, a creeping in the undergrowth.

I froze. There was no mistake.

Somewhere beyond the pillars, there was stealthy movement amid the trees and bushes.

Rob made to speak again, but I held up a hand for silence.

He clamped his mouth shut. We both listened intently.

There it was again. A rustling, as of leaves being brushed aside, interspersed with the occasional snap or crack of twigs.

"Charlie!" I said aloud. "That you?"

Instantly there was dead silence. All movement abruptly ceased.

Rob and I looked at each other. Sweat spangled both our brows.

"Oh, this is fucked!" Rob suddenly said, turning and striding out between the two nearest pillars. *"Who the fuck's farting around?"*

I hurried out with him, but quickly came to a halt once we were outside. Rob had stopped too. The profanities had died on his lips. The encircling woods now looked dimmer, cooler. The long violet shadows had turned purple. Here and there, a twist of ground-mist had arisen. But there was no sign of anybody.

"I think maybe we should go back," Rob said.

I didn't bother with a verbal reply, just started walking.

But now it struck us that we didn't know the way.

Inside the Lamuratum we'd turned ourselves around several times. As such, we were faced by an unbroken wall of trees and bushes. There was no trace of the path.

"Must be round the other side," Rob said.

I went with him, all the time scanning the undergrowth. Briefly, I thought I caught a glimpse of something – a glint of metal perhaps, but dull, tarnished metal. However, the speed with which we were moving precluded any further investigation.

"Must be around here," Rob said, with urgency in his voice that I'd never heard before.

From somewhere behind us, there came a long, low creak – like old leather, or an aged bough being bent against its will.

Neither of us looked back. We just walked faster, much faster.

And now, at last, the pathway hove into view ahead, but it wound off into a Plantation that we no longer recognised. Suddenly the woods were bathed in spectral twilight. Gone were the shafts of sunlight, the dappled shadows in the verdant glades.

"We've been in here longer than we thought," I said.

Again from somewhere to our rear, perhaps inside the Lamuratum, there was a curious sound. This time it was a short, sharp *clatter*, like the collision of metal on stone. It rang after us in a series of *clanking* echoes. There was something else too; I didn't risk a glance sideways, but to my left I'd just spotted movement – awkward, capering movement, like something crippled or deformed, keeping a steady pace with us.

"Rob, we've got to get out of here," I said tautly.

He grunted. Then ducked – almost spasmodically, as though in direct nervous response. I didn't bother to ask him if something had just been thrown at us. Neither did I stop to look around to see what it was.

I just ran.

We both ran.

And now there definitely *was* movement in the surrounding trees.

Vegetation tore as it was rent aside. Another clash of metal on stone rang loudly to our rear. More twigs broke. And about thirty yards ahead, a shape limbered out in front of us.

And that was when we diverted from the path.

It was an automatic response. We veered sharply to the left, oblivious of the undergrowth tangling our feet, of the thorns catching our clothes, of the foliage whipping our faces. We drove through it all frantically, already gasping for breath but urging each other on. We only had eyes for the route ahead, confused though that route remained. Huge trunks swept at us, and we had to sidestep around them, tripping on roots, often slipping in mulch. Low tree-limbs threatened to shatter our skulls. We had to crouch to get under them, and, in some cases, hurdle to get over. But it came to us naturally, for we were now past our second wind and the adrenalin rush prevented us feeling our already numerous cuts and scrapes.

The ordeal ended, however, almost as quickly and inexplicably as it had begun.

One minute we were tearing through a cramped jungle of half-lit flora – and then, in the space of a second, we were out of it, in the fresh air again, a sward of neatly mown turf lying in front of us.

We came to an abrupt and tottering standstill.

186

Evening had not yet relapsed into night. The sky was still blue, the sunset throwing a ruddy hue over the frontal façade of the house, which stood perhaps fifty yards to the left of us; we were much closer to it now than we had been when we'd first penetrated the Plantation. The rotund figure of Joe, standing on the front step in a fresh t-shirt and jeans, smoking a cigarette, was hugely reassuring.

He spotted us and raised a finger in acknowledgement. He wasn't close enough to see the lacerations on our hands or the sweat on our florid faces. Though, even if he had been, it's unlikely he'd have commented. Joe wasn't the sort of intrusive, instantly suspicious person who'd automatically assume you'd been up to no good. He just stood there and smoked as we strolled shakily across the lawn towards him. By his continued lack of reaction, I assumed that nothing obvious was going on in the trees behind us. But at that moment neither Rob nor I were in the mood to look back and check.

5

It's a difficult thing to bring off in the hard rock business, to reach middle age with your health and credibility intact, but at the same time to have grown old so disgracefully that you're still able to sell thousands of records to hordes of hardened, cynical youngsters. Ozzy Osbourne and Alice Cooper managed it, but legions of others didn't. And Luke Hennessey was one of the latter. He was raw talent through and through, but had never had anything like the necessary levels of discipline and professionalism to keep it all together for longer than a few years.

That evening, at dinner, he made another sad spectacle of himself.

All the way through the first course he told dirty jokes – and I mean *really* dirty ones – and as he did, he waved his brimming whisky glass around with a long, bony hand that didn't look as though it had been washed in several weeks. He'd also been smoking something – probably up in his bedroom – because his eyes were glazed and rolling and he stank of cannabis; for once it was stronger than his usual combined body-odour of sweat and patchouli oil. He was just about to give us another predictable punch-line, which no doubt would be riddled with terms like 'cunt', 'shit' and 'arsehole', when he suddenly collapsed.

Just like that.

Like a marionette with its strings cut.

187

His eyes snapped shut and he slumped forwards over what remained of his meal – which was quite a lot, as he hardly ever ate anything – and started snoring.

The embarrassed silence that followed weighed heavily on the portraits of the great men gazing down on us, on the extensive silver tea-service laid out on the oak sideboard at our rear, on the heavy tapestries and rich, Italianate woodwork. We'd met for dinner in the baronial banquet hall, which really was the last word in first-class dining. An eighteen-foot long mahogany table ran down the centre. Wonderful chairs were arranged along either side of it, all high-backed, medieval affairs but astonishingly comfortable; they were actually leather canopies fixed loosely on carved frames (wherever your butt wanted to go, these chairs could effortlessly accommodate it). The food Mrs. Hacket had prepared was exquisite. For the first course, we'd had asparagus tips steeped in sugar and melted butter, and, after that, a choice between roast quail in orange sauce or eggplant parmigiana with parmesan.

And now Luke was slumped at centre-table, the ratty, greasy mop of his hair spread out over his half-full plate, making noises that would have shamed a pregnant walrus.

Charlie gave our hostess a solemn stare. "You must think we're a bunch of complete wasters, Miss Ryder-Howe."

She smiled. She was the only one who'd dressed for dinner, and now wore a delightful pink silk evening gown, which seemed to meld itself around her graceful form.

"Not at all," she said. "And it's Lucille … how many times must I remind you?" She glanced back across the table towards Luke. Her expression was almost fond. "Everyone's entitled to find their lifestyle too much for them now and then."

"Trouble is," Joe said, "he never knows that that's what it is. He'll be awake again in half an hour and back at it. Won't remember a thing."

"The memory's the first bit that goes," Barbara put in. "Do you know, Lucille … at Christmas '88, which is the last time this lot were on the road, I found him in the dressing-room writing a card to his mother. When she'd already been dead for six years."

Miss Ryder-Howe looked horrified.

"It's a miracle he hasn't already joined her," I said.

Joe nodded. "It's a miracle he lived out the '70s."

"Oh!" Charlie threw his hands up in mock-despair. "Don't talk about that halcyon age. I can't believe it's gone."

We chuckled and sipped our wine. Mrs. Hacket meanwhile, politely and unobtrusively, began to clear away our dishes.

"It was back in the '70s when I first heard about you guys," Miss Ryder-Howe said. "I was in infant school at the time."

Charlie almost fell off his chair. "I'm glad someone admits to remembering us from way back then."

I agreed. "It always bugs me how so many people only recall the '70s for disco and punk. It's almost like the long-haired, guitar subculture never existed. And it isn't just head-bangers, like us, who get overlooked. What about Genesis under Gabriel, what about Pink Floyd, ELP?"

"Never mind *them*!" Joe blurted. "What about Uriah Heep, Nazereth? We'd only been news half a year when they hit the scene." He rounded on Miss Ryder-Howe. "And they hit it big, I'm telling you. But you never hear them mentioned either."

We all lapsed into thoughtful silence. I recollected that glorious first decade. At the time, it had seemed that we'd go on forever. After *Grease*, disco fizzled out almost as quickly as the first part of John Travolta's career, and while punk soon fell victim to the very excesses it had set out to parody, we hard rockers just kept on going, cutting a steady if unfashionable swathe through the entire music business. TV pop shows and mainstream radio stations might have ignored us, but we made a fortune and filled houses everywhere we went. Wolfbane had helped set a trend in motion that by the mid-1970s was bringing some stupendous bands into the public arena. Judas Priest and UFO came shortly after us. But there were foreign outfits who could really hack it, too: AC/DC, Rush, Van Halen.

"And of course," Joe added, "the 'New Wave of British Heavy Metal' was only just around the corner. We nodded in sage agreement. He was about to comment further on this – the NWBHM was a pet-subject of his – when Rob suddenly looked up and radically changed the subject.

"Anyone here speak Latin?" he asked.

There was a momentary silence. Perplexed glances were exchanged. Only I knew what he was driving at, but I kept my mouth shut.

"It's just that we went out to the Lamuratum earlier," he said.

"Oh ..." Miss Ryder-Howe's buoyant mood seemed to flag a little.

"We found it no trouble at all," Rob added, looking at her in a way that implied she'd been lying to us earlier on. Then he turned to Troy, who was seated at the head of the table, watching him carefully. "Well, I mean, it's the most Roman thing here, isn't it. Even if it *was* built in 1805. We thought we ought to check it out. There's an inscription on it. Eligata Proficis ... something or other. Here ..." and he produced several slips of paper, which he commenced to pass around the table. "I've written it down. Anyone know what it means?"

There were murmurs in the negative. Troy, I noticed, didn't even bother to glance down at the piece of paper that was placed in front of him. "Is it really essential you possess this information?" he asked.

Rob sat back. "Not essential. Thought it might be interesting. You want us to get into this project, don't you?"

Troy considered, and then made a vague, dismissive gesture. Rob was still in a belligerent mood, but, thanks to all the wine and good food, Troy had clearly mellowed out. He didn't want a confrontation.

"There's an Anglo-Latin dictionary, if that would help," Miss Ryder-Howe said. "In the sitting-room. Which is where we'll have our after-dinner coffee, if that's okay with everyone?"

We all mumbled that it was, though she looked for specific approval from Rob, who, now that he'd had his bluff called, seemed to lose interest in the subject. He simply shrugged. But later on, when we were all relaxing in the sitting room, I noticed that he took the Anglo-Latin dictionary from a shelf and leafed through it.

The most interesting thing that *I* found in the sitting room was a huge oil-painting of a very impressive Regency man. A caption below it revealed that he was the famed Thomas Ryder-Howe. The portrait dominated the entire room, which was actually smaller and cosier than most other rooms in the house, but teak-panelled and lined with shelves of books, and in that respect very elegant. The furnishings were primarily sofas and armchairs, though there was also a central coffee table against which Barbara was already kneeling, playing herself at patience. The rest of us were lolling around, chatting idly or smoking. Rob was in a chair in the corner, working his way studiously through the Latin dictionary, though it didn't take him long to lay it aside and lift another book from the shelf. For my part, I was fascinated by the huge painting. I sensed Miss Ryder-Howe come up alongside me.

"So this is the man?" I said.

She nodded. "This is indeed *the man*."

"He looks very pleased with himself."

She giggled. "So he ought to. He was the making of my family. Oh, we had a title and all, but we were very much the poor relations. Not after this chap had got done with us, though."

I considered what I knew about him, namely that he was a fanatical antiquarian. Not that he looked like an antiquarian. At least, he wasn't how *I'd* imagined an antiquarian to look. At first I'd expected a Dr Johnson type; a portly gentleman in a white wig, with jovial apple-cheeks and a soft smile. This real version was smiling, but not so attractively. If anything, he was rather rakish. He had sharp, aquiline features with high, prominent cheekbones. His hair was jet-black, almost slick, and aside

190

from his two sideburns, which were diamond-shaped, it was cropped very short. He was clad as a period dandy in a dark green smoking jacket, the frilly cuffs of his shirt showing at the ends of its sleeves. A chain with a pendant was visible around his neck, and his black-gloved hands were steepled in front of him. As I said before, he wore an inscrutable, somewhat self-satisfied smile. It wasn't massively endearing.

"Will that be all for tonight, ma-am?" someone asked.

I glanced sideways and saw Mrs. Hacket, who'd served us all coffee and cigars, and had then opened a drinks cabinet in which several quality malts and brandies were contained. She was now standing with her coat on and a handbag over her arm. Her son Lionel was hovering close behind her, as though eager to be given *his* marching orders as well.

Miss Ryder-Howe nodded. "Yes, Francine. I'll see you and Lionel tomorrow."

Without another word, Mrs. Hacket and her son withdrew from the room. The double-doors closed quietly behind them.

"They don't actually live on the estate?" I asked.

Miss Ryder-Howe shook her head. "They live in town, in Lyndhurst."

Joe had ambled up alongside us, a fat King Edward dangling from his lips. "Like in that horror film," he said with a snigger. "What was it? ... *The Haunting* ... 'if you're all alone in the dark, we'll be in town'." He raised his arms phantom-like, pulled a ghastly face. " 'There'll be no-one any nearer than that. No-one will come nearer than that. Not at night. In the dark'. Wooo-ooo ..."

"Unfortunately it's not quite so melodramatic," Miss Ryder-Howe said with a smile. "Mrs. Hacket has a husband and a young daughter, who both need looking after."

"I need looking after," Luke wailed from a nearby armchair. Again he'd taken possession of a bottle of Jack Daniels, but apparently even this wasn't enough. Eyes half-closed, drool on his chin, he gestured weakly around with the bottle. "Codeine, someone get me codeine."

More out of habit than annoyance, we ignored him.

"Is anyone else living on the estate?" Barbara asked as she laid rows of cards on the table.

Miss Ryder-Howe glanced round at her. "No. No-one."

"Oh." Barbara seemed confused. "It's just that, well ... when me and Charlie were out on the lake, earlier, we could've sworn we saw a woman walking on the far shore."

"A woman?" Miss Ryder-Howe looked genuinely bewildered.

"Yeah ... well, looked like a woman. Whoever it was, they had a long purple dress on."

Miss Ryder-Howe could only shake her head, nonplussed.

"People must wander onto the estate all the time, mustn't they," Troy said from the open French window.

Our hostess gave this some thought. "I suppose so. There's nothing really to stop them."

Barbara continued: "She looked very at home, the way she was just strolling along."

"How close were you to her?" Troy wondered.

"It was a fair distance. A hundred yards maybe."

"Oh well, you're probably mistaken."

Barbara glanced up at him. "No, Troy. I'm not. I definitely saw someone."

Charlie, who'd been slumped by the empty hearth, contemplating the room through his glass of Glenfiddich, looked up and nodded. "There *was* someone, yeah."

Troy shrugged. "Whatever you say. There'll be a perfectly good reason for it, though."

Miss Ryder-Howe and I were still standing in front of the portrait, and now Rob came and joined us. He still had the second book in his hand. It was backed with faded green leather, and, up close, I saw its title:

RELIGIO ROMANA
Being a list of holidays and festivals of the Greeks and Romans

However, he already seemed to have lost interest in it. He gazed at the painting. "This the bloke you were on about? Thomas what's his name."

"That's him," Miss Ryder-Howe confirmed. "My great-great-great grandfather, or whatever he was."

"Ever tried to communicate with him?" Rob asked.

She looked bemused. "I'm sorry?"

"Have a séance, like?"

"Er … no. No, I haven't."

I looked at Rob quizzically, but he seemed perfectly serious.

"It'd be a gas," he added. "Gramps here could probably tell you what you want to know about the Roman history of this place. If you're that bothered."

Miss Ryder-Howe looked as though she didn't know how to take this. "That's silly, isn't it? I mean, do séances work?"

"Ask Barbara," Rob said. "She's the expert."

Barbara glanced up at us.

"You'd know what you were doing if we had one?" Miss Ryder-Howe asked her.

"Well, I'm no medium," Barbara said, "but I've done it a few times."

192

Miss Ryder-Howe turned back to Rob and I. I thought she was going to burst out laughing. "You seriously think we could contact him …?"

I was uncertain, and said so. Now that he'd been put on the spot, Rob also looked unsure. A split-second later, Joe made the decision for us.

"Can't do any harm to try, can it!" he said with a laugh, swiping the table clean of cards and moving the tray of coffee-things to a sideboard. "Too early to go to bed yet, anyway."

We were soon kneeling around the table in a circle, an upside-down whiskey tumbler placed in the middle of a ring of cut-out letters and numbers. As Luke was still panned out in the armchair, there were seven of us in total. Barbara assured us that this was a good number, as seven had many connotations in esoteric lore. Besides, it also meant there was just enough room for us all to get a fingertip on the bottom of the upturned glass. To improve the atmosphere, Miss Ryder-Howe had turned the lights down and lit several fat candles, which she'd now placed at strategic locations around the room. They burned brightly, but with the dark teak panelling and mainly red and ochre-brown décor, much of their illumination was leeched away, leaving a sombre, smoky dimness.

Our hostess was starting to look nervous, as though she was unsure what exactly she was buying into here, whereas for the rest of us it was more commonplace. We'd held countless séances before, often as the result of being drunk or stoned, and invariably these occasions had been punctuated with tomfoolery, hoaxes and much ribald humourising. Several times we'd tried to contact the 'metal gods' as we called them; those giants of the field who'd gone on before us. In '76 it was Paul Kossoff, in '80 Bon Scott, in '86 Phil Lynott. Needless to say, we'd never had much success, except for on one occasion, when we'd got really ambitious and had gone after Hendrix, only for some wag to hit us mid-way through with an unexpected, multi-decibel blast of *Purple Haze* from a hidden speaker. After we'd recovered from our momentary but very real shock, that one had gone down a hoot. This time, oddly – considering that we'd been well fed, had had a good drink and were now chilling out in the cordial surroundings of a grand country house – the atmosphere was strained and rather serious.

"Hello?" Barbara said, after her customary opening minute of contemplative silence. "We're gathered here in the hope that we might be able to speak to someone."

There was a pause.

"A spirit perhaps?" she asked in a quavering voice, which I hadn't heard from her before.

The glass remained resolutely still.

"A specific spirit, in fact. The spirit of …"

She stopped mid-sentence, very abruptly.

Wondering why, I glanced down at the glass, speculating as to whether it had moved or not. In truth, though we'd only been at it a short while, it had never before taken us this long to get some reaction, though on most occasions – as I said – it had been someone cheating.

Then I realised what it was. A curious smell was suddenly in the room with us.

At first I saw Barbara's nostrils twitching – only slightly, but clearly twitching. Then I smelled it, myself. It was faint, only a whiff, but I knew what it was: rot, decay. Not of flesh, but of vegetation, like leaves and forest mould. There was an underlying freshness to it as well, like dew.

"What the heck is tha ..." Joe was half way through saying, when a glare of light drew all our attention to the far corner.

The candle-flame had suddenly reared to unusual height, maybe six or seven inches. A split-second later, it receded. Shortly after that, another one – this one on the mantelpiece – did exactly the same thing. And now the woodland scent was growing stronger. There was a chill in the air too, a dankness. Still the tumbler remained motionless, but there was no-one in that room who was now in any doubt that we'd contacted someone – or something.

Rob turned to Barbara. "Ask it something, anything ... *Barbara?*"

We all looked, and received a horrible shock.

Barbara was kneeling upright, as she had been before, but was now rigid as a board. There was a glazed look on her ashen face. Her eyes bulged, as though they were about to pop out of her head, but there was no sight in them. And then she spoke.

"Eligatu," she said slowly, in a deep, harsh tone that was clearly not her own. If anything, it was the guttural tone of a man. "Eligatua ... eligatua proficiscatua ..."

There was a stunned silence. I can't speak for the others, but my hair was prickling. Goose pimples ran along my arms. All of a sudden, I was absolutely certain – for the first time in my life – that I was in the presence of the supernatural. Across the table from me, Charlie was gawking at his wife in something like fascination rather than fear, but I could see the worry and doubt growing in his face.

"Barb ...?" he said slowly.

"Eligatua proficiscatua!" she proclaimed, but this time it was a bark – a loud, aggressive bark.

And somewhere behind us the candles flared again, and the whole room was now rank.

194

"Eligatua proficiscatua!" Her eyes remained blank, her features rigid. Her frothed lips drew back, as though for a final furious roar: *"ELIGATUA PROFICIS ..."*

"Oh that's enough!" Miss Ryder-Howe shouted, pulling away from the circle and hurrying for the nearest light-switch, which she slapped hard.

As soon as the electric light came on, the spell seemed to break.

There were gasps of relief all round. I think every one of us fell backwards, as though invisible supports had been withdrawn. Barbara, with a hiss-like exhalation of breath, slumped down onto her side, narrowly missing the corner of the table with her head.

I climbed quickly to my feet and sniffed at the air.

Nothing – the smoke from the cigars; the sizzled wax of the candles. But nothing else.

Despite her innate politeness, Miss Ryder-Howe was unapologetic and to the point.

"I have to live here, remember!" she stated emotionally. "When you lot have gone, I don't want to find that some ... *entity* has been invited in!"

Charlie had now scrambled over to his wife. He lifted her gently into an armchair, and checked her vital signs, something you learn to do promptly and proficiently after living for three decades in a world where drugs-overdoses are common. Barbara looked to be okay, though. The colour was returning to her cheeks, and she was mumbling.

"Is she all right?" Miss Ryder-Howe asked, suddenly sounding worried, as though it had only now occurred to her that there might be more at risk here than her own peace of mind.

"She's okay," Charlie replied, patting his wife's cheek to bring her round. "She's only fainted. Can someone get her a drink?"

I hurried to assist. Before she'd gone out, Mrs. Hacket had left us a pitcher of iced water on the drinks cabinet. I handed it over, and Charlie took the glass we'd been using for the séance, filled it and put it to Barbara's lips.

"Did you hear what he was saying?" a voice whispered in my ear.

I turned to find Rob there, his eyes wide.

"What do you mean *he*?" I asked.

"That voice! You heard what it was saying. It's that phrase from the temple."

"No way."

"It is, man, I'm telling you."

"Crap!" I retorted, though I knew it wasn't.

"Eligatua, proficiscatua," someone else then said, in grand Shakespearean fashion.

Rob and I turned and looked in disbelief at Luke, who was still slumped in the armchair, the half-full JD bottle resting in his lap. The others were all so concerned with Barbara that we two were the only ones who'd noticed. Luke's eyes were lidded, but he was smirking like a happy schoolboy. It was clear that he was now at least half awake.

"Say that again," Rob said slowly.

"Eligatua, proficiscatua," Luke repeated. "One is chosen, one will go forth."

"One is chosen, one will ..." Rob looked at me, then back at Luke again. "You're not telling us that *you* speak Latin?"

Now Luke opened his eyes fully and sat up, hitching himself against the backrest. He yawned and rolled his shoulders. "Nah, but I was a choirboy. Remember?"

It was very hard to remember, looking at the physical wreck that he'd become. *I* certainly couldn't picture him wearing a surplice and a cherubic smile.

"I did most of my voice-training with Brother Aelfric," he added. "Big one for his medieval Latin, he was. Had us singing all sorts of stuff. Psalms, bits of the Mass ... you name it."

For a moment we were tongue-tied. I think, initially, it was just the shock that Luke was awake enough to converse; that in itself was a rarity. I wondered fleetingly if the grass he'd been smoking and the alcohol he'd so copiously imbibed had somehow worked to counteract each other. I'm not even aware that such a thing is possible, but you never knew what miracles of science could occur in Luke's overly polluted system. All that would have been bewildering enough. But add this sudden outpouring of theological knowledge, and you had a *real* event on your hands.

Rob was having more difficulty with it than me. He still sounded highly doubtful. "You're saying that ... Eligat," he faltered, "that eligatua ... profic- ..."

"Eligatua, proficiscatua," Luke corrected him.

"Eligatua proficiscatua ... that comes from the Latin Mass?"

"Nah." Luke shook his head. Then, ludicrously – considering that he'd just defied all the laws of chemistry and biology by sobering up so quickly and painlessly – he unscrewed the cap to the JD bottle and took another long swig. "Nah ... I've never heard that actual phrase, but it's easy enough to translate."

There didn't seem any point in arguing with him. What the hell did *we* know?

"And it means what again?" Rob asked him.

"One is chosen ..." Luke broke off to give a loud hiccough, " ... one will go forth."

6

That night, I dreamt that it was 1978 all over again, and that we were performing at the Free Trade Hall in Manchester. I was aware that it was a dream from the beginning, but I dug in straight away to enjoy it because the Free Trade Hall in '78, the third UK venue in our 'Conquest of the Earth' tour, had probably seen us – not just Wolfbane, the band, but each one of us as individual musicians – at the apex of our powers. It was, quite simply, our greatest ever night.

We used all the familiar on-stage effects – trees, mist, chanting monks – and then, later on, a groundbreaking thunder and lightning storm, which many people I spoke to said was almost identical to the real thing. But it was the music that counted. I don't think we were ever better, before or since, and the audience responded in kind. They went crazy, contributing to an atmosphere that was almost pagan in its idolatry. The heat, the sweat, the hysteria all around us, it was almost indescribable, and yet, in our quieter, more melodic moments that night, this uncanny, all-enveloping hush fell on the house, and a forest of lighter-flames would spring up before us.

Your sodden hair prickled at something like that. Even in eighty degrees of heat, the chills ran down your spine.

Of course, Luke did more to stoke up that atmosphere than anyone else. His performance that night was incredible, his vocalisations ranging from breathless purrs, which had the girls in the front row going into conniptions, to a whiskey-soaked battle roar that was enough to send anyone running for cover even without the accompanying barrage of drums and guitars. And of course, he never stood still, but gyrated from one side of the stage to the next, barely stopping to take a breath, always just out of reach of the clawing, clasping hands, though finally – and this really was the defining event of the gig – collapsing full-length into the crowd, to then be lifted up and carried like some decadent, reclining god to his altar of sacrifice. None of it was planned, none of it was rehearsed, but we were so carried away with events that we just kept on playing, jamming, improvising, going in and out of frenetic solos, not in the least concerned for Luke's safety. Afterwards, Troy, who'd been watching from the wings, mesmerised by the power of the show, said of that incident that he felt his stomach constrict, and that he wondered what would happen if the raving mob, who by this time had totally overwhelmed Manchester's infamously strong-armed bouncers, had carried him right down the hall and out through the building's front doors. Though Luke had later insisted that never once, even during the height of the frenzy, were things out of control. It was a frenzy of adulation, he'd assured us – of worship, of "blistering, uncontrollable love".

But then, whatever Luke says, there *was* something else.

And I've often wondered about this.

Something about that Free Trade Hall gig was a little darker than most. Maybe the Free Trade Hall itself.

It was an old building, constructed in the Dickensian era, and it had always had something of a reputation. It's long gone now of course, demolished and built-over, but other bands I've conversed with over the years also reported odd sensations in the Free Trade Hall, Manchester; mainly backstage and in the dank rabbit warrens that served as its dressing rooms, but sometimes out in the auditorium as well. Dylan faced astonishing and unexpected hostility there in '66, while in '76, the then-unknown Sex Pistols had a similar experience to us, a single concert projecting them to satanic superstardom after scenes of mayhem and wild sexual abandon overtook the entire theatre.

We'd only played there the once, and, as I said, it had been a sensation. But then – *had it?*

What if Luke hadn't been as much in control during those chaotic moments as he liked to think? What if that mania we'd felt from the audience hadn't been "blistering, uncontrollable love"?

The building itself had risen out of violence. In 1819, on St. Peter's Field, a huge meeting of Lancashire cotton folk, who had assembled to hear speeches condemning the injustices of the Corn Laws, was broken up by mounted redcoats, who slaughtered eleven and left four-hundred severely wounded. The 'Peterloo Massacre', as it became known, caused a national scandal, and the Free Trade Hall was raised on the same spot during the 1840s partly in commemoration of the event. But other, earlier massacres had also occurred on this site. The Free Trade Hall stood quite close to Castlefield, an area of inner Manchester once occupied by the Roman fort, Mamuciam, which was built by Julius Agricola as part of his northern British campaign. This bastion was an outpost on the Roman road between Chester and Carlisle, and saw off frequent attacks by the Brigantes tribe (so unrelenting were they in their raids that the word 'brigand' would later derive from them). The same fortress later became a town, but was burned down and saw its population annihilated, first by heathen Saxons in 429, and later by the Vikings in 870. The Manchester district of Reddish first appears around the time of this second incident, having drawn its name from references to fields and ditches that were literally red with blood.

You may wonder where all this is leading to. Why reminiscences of a rock gig in the long-ago 1970s, and a social and political history lesson from even earlier ages, may have any relevance to a story about a quiet stately home at the opposite end of the country.

Well, the truth is that I don't offer these anecdotes as sure-fire proof that terrible events can stir dark forces. But I *do* wonder about that. I mean, it was nothing unusual that I awoke that second day at Brebbington Chase having dreamed about our performance at the Free Trade Hall; I regularly relived our greatest moments in my dreams, probably because these days there were so few of them during waking hours. But isn't it at least a little bit strange that Luke Hennessey should also wake up, having experienced exactly the same dream, at exactly the same time?

I was on my way down to breakfast when I first found out about this. I felt refreshed and was starting to convince myself that the unusual events of the previous day had been nothing more than feats of an over-excited imagination. That was when I met Luke. He was at the top of the stairs, staring out through a large casement. The very fact that he was up and about at nine-thirty in the morning was remarkable. Less so was his glazed, almost hypnotised expression. He was peering through the window as though seeing something there that really thrilled him. For a second, he wasn't even aware that I was with him.

I looked out too, but saw only blue sky and the rolling greenery of the manor grounds. The ponderous shape of Lionel went chugging past on a quad-bike, drawing behind him a wheelbarrow filled with compost. Luke didn't seem to see this either.

"Hey," I finally said. "You with us, or what?"

And only now did he turn to me, and I was startled. At how good he looked. Well – at how *fleetingly* good he looked. Don't get me wrong; he was still wearing the same clothes from the previous night, and now, as he'd probably slept in them as well, they were even rattier than before. The combined aroma of sweat, cannabis and alcohol still hung over him, his hair was greasy and unkempt, his thin face unshaved and cheesy-white. But for once his eyes were clear and he was smiling beatifically.

"Oh man," he said. "Remember that gig we played up in Manchester?"

Ice went through me. The way things had been going I should have expected something like this, but ice still went through me. Like a spear.

"We played Manchester lots of times, Luke," I reminded him.

"Yeah ... but only once in that big old building. The one with the three-tiered seating."

"The ... the Free Trade Hall," I said, struggling to get the words out.

His eyes were virtually shining. It was as though he was seeing me, but seeing something beyond me at the same time.

"Remember that gig, man?"

I nodded.

199

"Was that the moment, or what?"

Again I nodded. "It was a good night."

"I was there again," he said, "*last* night."

"Yeah?"

He shook his head. "Aw, it was only a dream of course, but what a dream. I woke up thinking it had only just happened. I could feel it here," and he thumped his chest. "I mean, right *here!*"

And before I could say anything else, he'd gone off downstairs, still talking, only now talking to himself.

I tried to rationalise what I'd just seen and heard.

Okay, our experiences hadn't been *exactly* the same. I'd just remembered the Free Trade Hall gig as a performance to be proud of, while, by the looks of him, Luke had *re-experienced* it – the whole thing, drawing every possible feeling of euphoria from it. By the same token, I'd woken up unnerved, as though looking back on that famous concert and now, with the wisdom of age and experience, thinking that something had been amiss – for the first time wondering *why* it had apparently gone so well, and even *if* it had gone so well. Luke, on the other hand, was living for the moment all over again; like a junkie, I guess, who's spent his entire addiction seeking the same joy he felt from his first fix, and suddenly, by sheer good fortune, stumbling across it one last time. I suppose he was just too primal a creature to react any other way than to revel in such a thing. Or maybe *I* was the one at fault – maybe I was being too negative, had become too much of a cynic to assume that pleasure could come without a price, that something good didn't always have to have a sinister flipside.

Of course, it was very early in the day for such complex ruminations, so I hurried on downstairs, trying to shake the whole thing from my head, but feeling spooked nevertheless. No, our experiences hadn't been exactly the same, but they'd been so similar as to rule out simple coincidence. And that thought, after everything else that had been going on, was seriously bugging me. As such, the last thing I wanted over breakfast was yet more weirdness.

Our *petit-dejeuner* was served in the same majestic room where we'd enjoyed our supper the night before, and consisted of rolls and croissants, eggs, bacon, black puddings and kidneys, all of which were arranged along the sideboard on silver dishes. Mrs. Hacket, now resplendent in a pearl blouse and tight black skirt, was on hand to serve. She was in the process of dishing up eggs and toast for Luke, but advised me to take a seat at the table as she'd get round to me very soon. I sat, and, aside from Luke, found myself in company with Joe, Rob, who was still reading the book he'd pilfered from the sitting room, and Troy. There was no sign of

200

Charlie or Barbara. I mentioned this, and was surprised to be told that they'd called a taxi and had gone into Lyndurst for the day.

I was puzzled. "For the whole day?"

Troy nodded matter-of-factly. "I told them to take as long as they want. The weather's still holding. I think you should all enjoy yourselves today. Relax."

I glanced around, confused. Luke was now eating, in unusually hearty fashion – which I suppose had to be a good thing – while Rob was absorbed in his book. Mrs. Hacket appeared at my shoulder. I ordered 'the full English', and then turned back to Troy.

"But what about the project?"

He shrugged. "It'll wait."

"How long for? I mean, how long are we actually going to be here?"

"We all agreed to see the week through."

"Yeah, but shouldn't we at least be putting some thought into it by now?"

Again, he shrugged. "Who says we aren't? You're soaking this place up, aren't you? Getting as much inspiration as you can handle."

And now, at last, I let it get to me. All the oddities we'd come across, all the unexplained incidents, and, more than anything else, all of Troy's strange, furtive, secretive behaviour.

"What *is* all this inspiration crap, Troy?" I snapped. "We wrote the fucking album in 1975!"

He glanced apprehensively towards Mrs. Hacket, embarrassed by my use of profanity. If the housekeeper took offence, she didn't show it; in fact she didn't even flinch, but I'd briefly forgotten that she was there, and I wasn't boorish enough to do the same thing again. At least, not until she'd gone. She finished serving my breakfast, and then strode briskly from the room.

"We wrote *Eagle Road* in 1975," I repeated. "Why don't we just pick over that first?"

"We *will* do," Troy assured me.

"Have we even got a copy of it here?"

"Of course."

"Have we got a sound system to play it on? Any of the original music that we wrote for it?"

"It's all in hand," Troy said in a patient voice. "But like I said, today you've got the day off."

"Suits me, man," Luke said, waving an egg-stained paw (which was a bit of a laugh actually, as Luke hadn't had a day *on* in the last decade).

"Well, I'm happy just to poke around," Rob added, closing the book and sitting back. "It's an interesting enough place."

I couldn't help feeling a little mystified by that. Up until last night, Rob had been the prime instigator of revolt, and now, suddenly, he was content to go with the flow?

Troy nodded, as if this was a perfectly good plan. "Fill the day any way you want."

"I might do a bit of writing," Joe said. He was trying to pen yet another book about his life in the rock business. Even now, I was sure that some publisher would probably snap his hand off – if only he could get more down on paper than 'Chapter One'.

Troy looked round at me as if waiting to hear *my* plans.

"I haven't decided what I'm doing yet," I replied tersely. "In the absence of anything else, I'll probably go for a walk."

I hadn't planned to do that, but I was so surprised by the fact we *still* weren't doing any work, that I blurted out the first thing that came into my head. The second thing that came into it, I kept to myself – it was a reminder that, however much spare time I had today, I was not going anywhere near the Lamuratum.

After breakfast, I made a point of speaking privately to Rob. He was out in the passage when I caught up with him, and moving away fast. I had to hurry and grab him by the arm.

"I thought you were the suspicious one?" I said.

He pondered this. "*Imaginative* might be a better word."

"Oh. So you've slept on it and now everything's okay?"

"No, but ...well, I've been reading, and well ... sometimes I get carried away."

"*What* have you been reading?"

He became defensive. If he hadn't already got the book tucked into the front pocket of his jeans, I'm sure he'd have put it behind his back. "It's nothing. Just a load of rubbish."

"This is why you're going to spend the day finishing it off, is it? Because it's such a load of rubbish that you need to check it out in full?"

"Rick ..." he sighed, "I don't trust people as a matter of principle. You know that. Not even our own manager. And quite often I've been right not to. I've helped get us better deals, helped make sure we weren't being ripped off."

"So?"

"So that's it, basically."

"That's it?"

"I've got a nose for mischief. And it's done a job for us. I'd like to leave it at that. Because when you start going off into the realms of fantasy, you wonder if you're beginning to lose it."

I stared at him. "What are you talking about, Rob?"

202

He set off down the corridor. "Just go and have your walk. I'll speak to you later."

"The 'realms of fantasy'?" I called after him.

Rob walked away. "See you later, Rick."

7

Whatever my first impressions of Lionel, the big, hulking caretaker, I had to admit that he was a more than capable groundsman. The gardens surrounding Brebbington Chase were immaculately kept, vast though they were.

I deliberately walked in the opposite direction from the Plantation, but even ignoring that region entirely I still found extensive acres to view, all exquisitely pleasing to the eye. The entire park had been laid out in roughly geometric patterns, but it comprised all manner of classical features, from terraced walks, to topiary, to hedge-lined avenues. Here and there I encountered sculptures or fishponds, stone-built grottoes, arbours and benches arranged so as to enjoy scenic vistas; and of course rows of bedding-plants, at this time of year bursting out in their full preponderance of colour. I came across the ornamental lake where Charlie and Barbara had spent a sedate hour or two, and beyond that a row of greenhouses filled with what looked like orchids. Behind these there was stream. Again, this appeared to be man-made, chiefly because the water was clean and gurgled over a bed of chalk-white pebbles. At this point, however, the estate's formal artistry seemed to end. A wooden footbridge led over the stream and, on the far side of it, a narrow path wound off into dense stands of trees.

I opted to cross over and continue exploring. Likely the path was nothing more than a short cut for the grounds-keeper. Possibly it led to the edge of the estate and provided quick and easy access out to the main road. But one never knew unless one looked, and in this case one had a considerable amount of time to fill.

I was still thinking about the events of breakfast as I set off. Rob's apparent change of tune was not difficult to understand. He quite often 'went off on one', as he liked to call it, but usually, after a brief period, he would rein himself in and try to see things rationally. It didn't mean that he wouldn't come to the same conclusion later on, but at this moment he was trying to work out exactly what it was that was bothering him about this place. That left *me* to do the worrying, which was usually the case. Even in our greatest days, when nothing we did was wrong, I was always the band's worrier. I've been a born worrier as long as I can remember. On most occasions, of course, there actually *was* something to worry about – be it record sales, tour schedules, personal issues, you name it – whereas here there was just this vague feeling of unease. A feeling not diminished in any way by the object that the overgrown path suddenly brought me to.

It was a church. Or rather a chapel.

At first it took me completely by surprise. It nestled deep amid the trees and bushes, and seemed to spring out on me like a large animal that had been lying in ambush.

I looked it over, and briefly took it to be another folly – a stone frontage with an arched doorway, and what looked like a heavy bronze door set into it, firmly closed – but then I saw the two tall windows, one on each side, neither of which contained glass but both of which were frilled around their inner rims with fragments of ancient leading, suggesting that stained-glass images had once been held there. I glanced upwards. A stone crucifix stood at the peak of the facade, with two crossed sceptres in front of it. At either side of this, at roughly the point where the sloping ends of the roof came down to the eaves, two figurines abutted outwards, both angels blowing on trumpets, both now sorely eroded. This was no folly. A crumbled ruin, yes, but reduced to this state through venerable age rather than indifference or neglect.

I approached it warily, trying to remember what I knew about the relatively recent history of this place. The Brebbingtons had been Catholics who'd fled abroad during Cromwell's period of power. They'd returned under Charles II, when their religion was tolerated again, so it wasn't beyond the bounds of possibility that the chapel dated from that era. That it had fallen into disrepair was odd, given that so much else here that was historical had been preserved, but it was possibly explainable if the modern-day owners had no religion, which they didn't appear to.

However, that certainly did not provide a reason for the extensive *claw-marks*.

For that is the only way I can describe them.

Of course, they weren't claw-marks really. They couldn't have been. But they looked like claw-marks. The entire front of the aged building had been slashed and scarred all over, as though some party of hooligans had attacked it with a variety of edged implements. There was no rhyme or reason to the damage, and no damage that was actually more than skin-deep, though it was clearly deliberately inflicted. Every portion of the structure had been assailed. Slashes and gouges were visible on all parts of it, like pockmarks on a diseased face.

I was fascinated but also baffled. It occurred to me that maybe this vandalism dated from *before* the Restoration. Maybe Cromwell's puritanical hordes, who would have preferred the austere meeting house to a miniature basilica like this, had come and taken out their self-righteous wrath on it. But if that had been the case, why hadn't the destruction been completed? They'd had powder at their disposal, horses, ropes, demolition skills; they could easily have razed the small building to the ground. The question lingered, and I was just about to lean in through one of the windows to investigate further, when I heard feet approaching. I turned sharply, imagining that I'd done something wrong by coming here.

But when Miss Ryder-Howe emerged from the path, she was smiling, as if delighted to see me.

"Hello," she said. "I hope you don't mind me following you. I saw you coming this way from the house, and wondered if you wanted some company?"

Looking at her then, it was difficult to imagine any red-blooded man *not* wanting her company. She was stunning, though she'd dressed down considerably from the night before. She'd loosened her blonde hair over her shoulders and wore a sleeveless pink t-shirt, a short denim skirt and white sneakers, which did the world for her sleek, brown legs.

She watched me hesitantly. "You don't mind?"

"No … of course not."

She shrugged. "I didn't fancy hanging around the house all day."

"No, of course."

"I usually spend the weekends up in London, you see. I've a flat in Chelsea."

"I, er … I thought you probably would have. Something like that, I mean."

We smiled at each other awkwardly.

"You were the bass player, weren't you?" she finally said.

I couldn't help laughing, which surprised her.

"Sorry," I replied, "sorry … I'm not laughing at you. It's just, well that's the sort of thing I get a lot of. Some industry big-shot would come up to us after a gig, and say: 'You're Luke Hennessey, you're Joe Lee, you're Rob Ricketson, you're Charlie Smollet, and you're, er … *you're* the bass player'."

She looked worried, as if she'd upset me. "I didn't mean anything by it."

"I know. Don't fret. It goes with the territory."

There was another uncomfortable silence.

"I was just examining your chapel," I eventually said.

"Oh yes." She glanced up at it with the sort of wide-eyed interest I'd normally associate with someone seeing something for the first time.

I ran my hand along one of the gouge-marks. "Looks like someone's been over it with ... I don't know, a blade of some sort. It's almost like a deliberate desecration."

"It may be. We're in the New Forest, after all. A lot of weird stuff goes on here."

I'd heard that, myself. The New Forest is only one of many places in modern England where the old witch religions are alleged to be secretly re-establishing themselves; even by current 'New Age' standards, it's reputedly a hotbed of activity.

"Don't suppose that's anything new to you, of course," Miss Ryder-Howe said. She was now standing quite close to me. Her lips glinted and the sun made a fine golden mist of her hair. "You being an ex-heavy metaller and all."

I laughed again and shook my head. "Don't get me on that one. All that Satanist bullshit is what cost me my enthusiasm for the industry in the first place."

"How do you mean?"

I shrugged, and stepped up to the bronze door. When I leaned against it, it gave slightly. I pushed harder. The hinges squealed and the door grated on the old flagstones.

"We used to get slagged off for it back in the old days, when all we were writing about was elves and wizards," I said. "But thanks to that thrash, speed-metal crap that came later ... say 'heavy metal' now and it instantly means devil-worship."

She seemed surprised. "It's just an act, though, isn't it? All pretence?"

"I dunno." I kept pushing. The door was now half way open. "Some of this modern lot don't seem to think so. As soon as all that rubbish started, we decided to get out. We were old fogies by then, anyway. No-one wanted Wolfbane when they could have Celtic Frost."

The door was now open sufficiently for me to step around it and enter. So I did.

The interior of the chapel was even more devastated than the exterior, though this was mainly due to time and decay. Almost nothing was left of the building as it had once been. The roof had long ago fallen in, and only blackened oak ribs remained. The pews were reduced to moss-covered stumps, while the altar area was buried in brambles. The internal walls, which once must have been plastered and probably bore all manner of religious frescoes, had crumbled to the bare lathing.

206

I wasn't quite sure what I'd expected, but was disappointed that all I'd found was bog-standard dereliction. I didn't hear our hostess come in behind me.

"I wouldn't say you were old fogies," she said quietly.

"Well, that's kind of you. But we're not under any illusions about who and what we are."

"I'm not saying it to be kind. I'm saying it because I mean it."

There was a subtle change in the tone of her voice, and I turned to face her.

It was no great surprise to see that she was smiling in rather wanton fashion. But the fact that, while my back was turned, she'd removed her lace panties and now had them looped over her forefinger was a bit more than I'd expected. This sort of thing hadn't happened to me for several years at least.

"And what's this?" I asked.

"Well ..." and she glanced around at the rotted walls encircling us, "I'd call it a nice bit of privacy."

"This is a joke, right?"

"Oh yeah. I always take my knickers off for guys I've just met. Mind you, normally I don't have any on. I only put *these* on so I could take them off for you."

And there was something naughty and saucy, and undeniably horny about that.

"And you want to do it here?" I said. "Like ... now?"

Almost casually, she tossed the undergarments at me. Once I might have caught them, maybe been bold and sniffed them. Not now. I let them strike me on the chest and drop to the floor. One advantage of being, or having been, a rock star, is that you get more than your share of willing girls. Eventually, even the most undiscerning among you learn to separate the wheat from the chaff. Not that Miss Ryder-Howe wasn't sexy and gorgeous, and moneyed to boot – which under normal circumstances might make her a very fetching catch indeed – but she wasn't anything I hadn't encountered before; an upper-class wild child, so rich that she didn't have anything else to do but slum it for a day with some burnt-out pop relic.

"I think you might have made a mistake," I told her.

She shook her head confidently. "You're easily the most fanciable of your lot."

"That wouldn't be hard."

"I like your sun tan then. Come here ..."

She took a step towards me, but I backed off.

"I'm married," I reminded her.

She gave me a puzzled look. "So what? I'm engaged."

And to emphasise the point, she ripped the engagement ring from her finger, and flung it – diamond centre-stone and all – off into the undergrowth. I continued to retreat, until the hulk of an old pew came up behind me and stopped my progress.

"Look, I'm not some rock and roll mattress-jockey any more," I said. "I'm old enough to be your dad."

She halted, apparently baffled.

"What exactly are we talking about here?" she said. Then she raised the front of her denim skirt. "We're talking about *this*. And how much it needs you right now."

I stared down at her exposed vulva. It was shaved smooth and very plump. Moistness glistened down its central cleft.

From the moment I'd realised what she was up to, I'd been determined to resist. I loved Andrea. It was that simple. She was my wife and my best friend. Okay, we'd only been married ten years, and before that I'd played the field like there was no tomorrow, but I now considered that I'd grown-up, that I'd finally found my soul-mate and was happy to remain with her for the rest of my life. Call me old-fashioned, I don't care; I'd been modern and free-spirited for two decades, and it had never brought me anything comparable. Of course, I'm heterosexual as well, and, owing to me being here and Andrea still being in Tenerife, I hadn't made love for several days, so there was no denying that I was stimulated. In fact, I was *more* than stimulated. Because Miss Ryder-Howe *was* beautiful and statuesque, and this approach was so unashamedly explicit and lewd and in-yer-face that my resolve was seriously undermined by it. I felt sweat on my neck and the inevitable stiffening in the front of my jeans. And the next thing I knew, I was in her arms.

Our open mouths clashed forcefully, our tongues entwining like two voracious snakes. Her pubis was still naked and available to me, and now she guided one of my hands down and pressed it home, and suddenly I felt my fingertips penetrate her hot, drenched cavity.

And that was when the failsafe kicked in.

When the alarm bells started to sound.

It was like we'd reached the point of no-return too quickly. Like, if I took one single step more, everything I'd so painstakingly built over the last few years would fall apart. And for what – a few seconds of sensual pleasure?

Thank God for maturity.

I stepped sharply backwards, disentangling us. "No … I'm sorry. I'm sorry, but this is crap. I'm a married man now. I've done all this shagging around bit … and frankly, it's overrated."

208

At first she seemed shocked. Very quickly, though, that shock turned to simmering anger. She made no effort to come after me again, but stood there gazing, her green eyes suddenly slitted and cat-like.

"God, you really *are* finished, you lot, aren't you. Without Troy, you'd be on your way to the knacker's yard without a chance of looking back."

There was such vitriol in her voice that I was taken aback. I've known beautiful women get angry when blokes turn them down before. It's because they're confused, because rejection is something unknown to them. But on this occasion more than pride appeared to have been hurt. Her eyes blazed as she snatched her knickers up and climbed back into them. Her once-lovely lips now curled into a feral snarl, and, without warning, she launched herself forwards and dealt me a furious, stinging slap on the cheek.

"Well, don't let me bother you any more!" she snapped. She backed off, breathing hoarsely. She'd literally gone white with rage. "Jesus H. Christ ... go back to your wife's wrinkled old cunt, if that's what you want! Or is it some underage rent-boy's arsehole!"

I stood there stunned, my head still spinning from the blow.

She stormed towards the half-open door, but looked back before she got there. "You'd better get your fucking act together though! You're going to need it!"

"Wh ... what?" I said.

"You're not here for a holiday, Mr. noble fucking bass-player, whatever your name is! You're here to deliver. And you'd better, or there'll be real trouble!"

"Trouble? From who?"

"You don't want to know." And she almost laughed at the thought. "Believe me, you really don't want to know."

And then she was gone.

And I was alone in that gutted, decayed shell of a church, surrounded only by weeds and thorns and the moulding remnants of a faith that seemed, from appearances, to have fled this part of the country many, many years before.

8

It was a little while before I could actually bring myself to go out of that chapel again.

It wasn't that I was frightened that the girl might be hanging around in the bushes, waiting for me, though it did cross my mind (I'm no coward, but the look of hatred on her face when she'd fired her parting shots had been amazing). I was more concerned that one of the others might spot me coming out of the old building shortly after her, and draw the wrong conclusion. If that happened, it was a near-certainty the word would get back to Andrea, and then the one source of solace I could draw from the nasty incident – namely, that I'd gallantly resisted a very tempting offer – would be wasted.

But there was something else as well.

I was shaken up. I mean, *seriously* shaken-up. Up until five minutes before, Miss Ryder-Howe had been all peaches and cream – pleasant, polite, wholesome, pretty as an English summer morning. And now she was a venomous harpy, who – by her own words, at least – would be quite happy to see harm done to us. Such a swift and complete a turnaround had been shocking and inexplicable, and again made me wonder why we were even here.

When I finally did emerge, it was slowly and stealthily, and I carefully scanned the surrounding foliage before coming fully out into the open. Once I realised I was alone, I set off back at a hurried pace, but I didn't head straight towards the house. I didn't think I could manage that just yet. The others would only need to take one look at me and they'd know something was wrong. And then there was our hostess. I didn't have a clue how I was going to face her again.

Instead, I went back to the main drive, then down it towards the car park, where the bus still waited. The driver, by prior arrangement, had been dismissed to a hotel in nearby Lyndhurst, with a fat cheque in his pocket and orders to return in five days' time. I wasn't sure whether, in his absence, the bus would even be open or not, but I'd left the charger for my mobile in there, and now sought to retrieve it so that I could power the phone up and call Andrea. Not only did I suddenly have a desperate yearning to hear my beloved's dulcet tones, but I also thought I'd tell her what had just happened – before someone else gave her a more imaginative version. Other items of luggage would still be on the coach as well. Not quite sure what we'd be doing while we were here, we'd brought along several bits and pieces of gear which we hadn't yet unloaded. With this in mind, it was perhaps odd that I finally reached the bus, and saw that not only were the sliding doors open, but that the luggage compartment was open too.

I came to a halt, wondering if we'd been robbed. Then I heard a voice coming from the other side of the vehicle. It was low and intense, and seemed to be speaking in verse, or some kind of chant.

I didn't think anything else could surprise me that day, but I was wrong.

I circled around the vehicle, and on the other side found Troy. But Troy as I'd never seen him before.

At first his back was turned and he was oblivious to me. Some property of ours – a selection of our instruments, by the looks of it – had been laid out on the grass beside the bus and Troy was walking slowly around it. He was carrying a small paper bag; at first I thought it was full of sweets, because he kept on picking into it, then popping items into his mouth. After that though, he would spit them out again. And each time he did this, he intoned the following mantra: "With these beans, I redeem me and mine."

Yes that's right, "beans".

I even checked. I walked slowly behind him and picked one of them up. It was indeed a bean – a hard black bean, like a coffee bean.

I was still gazing down at it when he turned round and spotted me. His eyes shot open behind his thick glasses, he dropped his paper-bag, went rigid.

"Shit!" he finally said, and then he laughed. But it was feigned – I could tell that at once. "Shit, you scared the crud out of me."

"What are you doing?"

He shrugged, then swooped down, scooped up the bag and stuffed it into his jacket pocket. "Nothing."

"Nothing?"

His good humour faded a little. "*Nothing.*"

"I see." I glanced over the assembled items. One of my battered bass guitars was there, alongside Joe's old flying-V, a pair of Charlie's sticks and Rob's Yamaha keyboard, which, in one of his most inventive moments, he'd had fitted with a shoulder-strap so that he could play it like a guitar. "So all this is on a need-to-know basis as well, is it?"

Now Troy's smile faded completely. He realised that he hadn't fooled me. He started picking the instruments up and crossing the gravel to the coach, where he shoved them unceremoniously into the open trunk.

"Don't talk like you're Rob, Rick," he said over his shoulder. "It's not convincing."

"Meaning what exactly?"

He gave me a glance that was somewhere between uncertainty and contempt. "You're no conspiracy theorist, so stop trying to pretend you are."

I watched him as he piled the rest of the stuff onto the bus. The bag of beans remained deep in his pocket.

"Our hostess is something of a headcase," I eventually said.

"No. She's just short of cash."

"Do you want to run that by me again?"

Troy rolled his eyes. "Rick ... try not to show your lino-filled council house roots too much, will you. This isn't the 1920s. These aristocratic bluebloods are all skint. The cost of living's gone up for them, too. Fifty times more than it has for us. And most of them haven't even got jobs. Lucille Ryder-Howe's just one of a whole bunch who are now seriously in the red."

"She should admit people to her house, then," I suggested. "Make it into a stately home, or something."

"She can't even afford to run it as a private home. Seen the top floor?"

"She could charge for entry."

"What ... you think charging people to look around her house would finance the playgirl lifestyle that *she* thinks she's entitled too?"

"So that's why she's trying to get her hooks into the rock business?"

"What do you think?"

Now it was my turn to sound contemptuous. "And she actually believed you when you told her that letting us camp out here while we wrote the new album would secure that for her?"

Troy noticed the enflamed mark on my cheek. He stepped forwards to examine it. "Apparently not."

"I was starting to think we were here purely because *you* had designs on her," I said.

He shook his head. "Nope. It'd take more cash than she's got to get me near a bird."

"I was thinking all this Roman inspiration stuff was a con-job just for *your* benefit."

He slammed the trunk closed. "You know me better than that, surely?"

"I thought I did," I said to his back.

He laughed.

"I'll tell you, Troy," I added, "I may pull out of this venture."

Now, when he turned to look at me, he wore a questioning frown.

I shrugged. "It just ... doesn't feel right."

"You'll be making a mistake, Rick. A big one."

I didn't say anything else, just walked away. Not back towards the house, but down the lengthy drive in the direction of the main gates. I half-expected him to call me back, but he didn't – and that was so like Troy. Even if he feared that he was going to lose out, he rarely got flustered enough to make quick or ill considered moves. He tended to think first, to consider all options.

I glanced back over my shoulder when I was about a hundred yards away, and he was still beside the coach, watching me. He didn't beckon or hail me back. So I kept on going. Ten minutes later, I was off the estate on a road that I assumed was the B3056. I followed it, and about half a mile

212

later came to a pub, an archetypical wayside inn called *The Cocked Hat*. On the outside it was all whitewashed brick, black beams and hanging baskets full of flowers, and inside a traditional mix of smoke-stained wood panels, horse brasses and hunt trophies.

I sat at the bar for a couple of hours, though in that time I drank only three pints of locally-brewed ale. I'd seen too many of Luke's calamities to imagine that drowning myself in alcohol would actually make things better. Not that I entirely wasted my time while I was there. Various locals came and went, mostly farm-workers, and I spoke with a couple of them, wondering if the phrases "with these beans, I redeem me and mine", or "one is chosen, one will go forth", meant anything to them. Mainly, I received only blank looks. Later on, the landlord appeared – a portly, white-haired gent in tweeds and a smart waistcoat – and I asked him if they'd ever had any trouble around here with occultists and the like – damage to churches, desecrations, that sort of thing. Again, I got no satisfactory answer. Apparently, oddballs did pass through now and then – "travellers, tinkers, that sort", and the mystical Rufus Stone, which was only about ten miles to the north-west, had "more than its fair share of eccentrics visiting it". But there were no real problems that he knew of. Eventually, sensing that my presence at the bar was now being tolerated rather than enjoyed, I retreated to a corner of the snug, where I ordered a ploughman's lunch and one last pint.

It must have close on four o'clock by the time I headed back towards the estate. It could have been my imagination, but just before I passed out through the pub door, I sensed a gaggle of locals muttering darkly among themselves and casting relieved glances in my wake. Briefly, I wondered if it wasn't just the fact that I was a stranger who'd asked a lot of silly questions that had made me unwelcome there.

9

"So when did this become part of the plan?" Rob was in the process of asking.

I'd just entered the main hall, and immediately found myself in the midst of a heated debate. Rob and Troy were not exactly squaring up to each other, but by Rob's expression they weren't about to get cosy either. No-one else appeared to have taken sides; at least, not yet. Joe, Charlie and Barbara were all watching with interest. There was no sign of Luke or Miss Ryder-Howe.

"Look … Rob," Troy was saying, "you agreed to go along with anything I had planned for this week."

Rob shook his head, seemingly lost for words.

"I haven't camped out anywhere for ages," Joe finally said, clearly feeling it was time that *he* chipped in.

"Me neither," Charlie agreed.

"I did it when I was a girl-guide," Barbara said in a lighter tone.

Joe glanced round at her. "I bet that was a sight to be seen … you in a guide's uniform."

She winked at him. "You wouldn't have believed your eyes, love."

"I'll bet I wouldn't."

"Look," Rob cut in, "can we just talk about serious things for a moment." He turned to Troy again. "Just tell me this … *why?*"

Troy shrugged as if it was the most obvious thing in the world. "The Lamuratum is the reason we're here."

"I've already seen it," Rob replied. "I don't need to go and sleep next to it."

"Whoa!" I exclaimed, shouldering my way in among them. "What's all this?"

Sleeping out at the Lamuratum? They had to be kidding – but then I saw the heaped camping gear at the bottom of the stairs: the tent-poles, sleeping-bags and bundles of rope and canvas.

Rob fixed Troy with another irritated glare. "*You* tell him, Troy. It's your bloody idea." And he turned and walked away.

Troy, attempting to make light of it, slapped me on the shoulder. "Hope you've got your warm undies with you, Rick. We're camping out for the night at the Lamuratum."

"Forget it," I said.

"No stomach for it, eh?" someone asked.

I glanced up, and saw our hostess coming down the stairs towards us. She'd changed her mini-skirt and vest for khaki pants and a sweat-top. Her hair still hung past her shoulders in glorious golden waves, but I couldn't see her as anything more now than a scheming upper-class strumpet. She returned my gaze with scornful amusement.

"I was joking about the undies by the way," Troy told me. "It's not *really* going to be cold. It's May, for Christ's sake."

I looked back at him. "It's not the last word in comfort, though, is it."

"I don't mind too much," Barbara put in. She at least seemed to be in a jovial mood. "We can get a fire going. Sing a few songs. Roast a few potatoes."

"It'll certainly be different," Joe admitted.

"Going to play hell with my sciatica," Charlie grumbled.

214

"Ohhh ..." Barbara rubbed at the base of his spine. "A night in nature's bosom? Moss for a mattress, leaves for a quilt?"

Charlie pulled a disgusted face, but didn't argue.

"So it's agreed then?" Troy said. "Great. We'll meet back here at six. Lionel will show us the way out there."

"You mean before he dashes off home?" I asked. "Before it gets dark."

Troy patted me on the shoulder again – yet another of his infuriatingly disingenuous 'hail-fellow-well-met' moments – then trotted away up the stairs. Soon everyone else had drifted off as well, including Miss Ryder-Howe. Which left just Rob and I.

"Where's Luke?" I asked him.

He grunted, deep in thought. "In his bedroom. Off his head."

"He wasn't too bad this morning."

"He's had several hours to make up for it since then, hasn't he."

I surveyed the camping-gear. It was old-fashioned stock, but, by the looks of it, in good condition. Not that this was any consolation.

"So what do you think of this?" I asked.

Rob still seemed preoccupied. "This camping trip? It's novel, I'll give him that."

"He's up to something."

"I know."

"What?"

Rob shrugged, which vexed me.

"Come on!" I blurted out. "You've been looking into something since last night. What've you discovered?"

"I don't know." He set off upstairs. "But you've got to balance apparently legitimate concerns against the prospect of appearing a complete dipstick. And it isn't easy."

"Rob ...?" I said.

"Later, Rick."

I could only stare after him until he'd vanished from sight. To anyone who didn't know Rob, his attitude would be flummoxing. But I'd seen it before, many times. Normally such vagueness signified that he'd reached a key stage in a composition but was struggling to progress it any further. In *these* circumstances, it suggested that he was almost onto something but not quite able to nail it down. Or not quite willing.

At that moment, Luke's recommended solution to all ills – namely, to get staggeringly pissed – seemed entirely sensible. Before I knew what I was doing, I'd wandered along the passage to the sitting room where the well-stocked drinks cabinet was located. No trace of the previous evening's séance remained, but Mrs. Hacket was present, now resplendent in a blue silk dress and scarf, and blue high-heeled shoes, and engaged in an energetic spot of housekeeping. She didn't notice me in the doorway, and I watched with admiration as she went around the room like a whirlwind, plumping up cushions, straightening the upholstery.

"Hello," I eventually said.

She looked sharply round. There was a pause, then she gave me a brusque nod. Hers was a refined, mature beauty, though there was a touch of the feline about it. And a distinct wintriness.

"Can I help you with anything, sir?"

I wandered in, making a beeline for the still-open drinks cabinet. "It's Mrs. Hacket, isn't it?"

"It is. Can I help you with anything?"

Her tone was polite but curt, implying, I suspect, that she was quite busy and that if I *did* want something, could I please be quick about it and then go out again. This wasn't a side of her that we'd seen so far, so it also occurred to me that she was possibly one of those servants who are very close and very loyal to their master, or in this case mistress, and are privy to all plots and schemes, no matter how distasteful they might be.

"Maybe you can tell me a bit about Brebbington Chase?" I said, as I poured myself brandy from a decanter. "The house, the grounds, that sort of thing."

"I'm sorry, sir. Miss Ryder-Howe would be the one to speak to."

"Really?" I gave her a surprised smile. "I got the impression you'd been here quite a while."

She eyed me coolly. "Is there anything else I can help you with, sir?"

"No."

She collected a pile of linens from the coffee table and turned to leave.

"Oh ... there is one thing," I said.

She stopped and glanced back.

"I was just wondering who your mistress's fiancé might be?"

And how her face fell. How pale her cheek suddenly went. How quickly the haughtiness was replaced by confusion, uncertainty.

"I ... I really can't say," she replied.

"You can't say?" I maintained a pleasant if disbelieving tone. "Your mistress is to be married, and you don't know who to?"

"Miss Ryder-Howe is my employer, not my mistress."

"I stand corrected. Nevertheless, that isn't the question I asked you."

Mrs. Hacket watched me carefully. She said nothing.

"I meet a lot of people, you see," I added. "Particularly when I'm up in London. It would be a marvellous thing if I ran into the lucky man somewhere. I'd be able to tell him how superbly his wife-to-be had catered to our every need."

"Will that be all, sir?"

216

"Yes. I think that'll be quite enough."

And when she left the room, I poured myself another generous tot of brandy, though I wasn't drinking to get drunk; I was drinking in celebration of one small but very satisfying victory.

I revelled in it for another quarter of an hour, then went upstairs to get my anorak and to see if I could raise Luke. His room was two doors along from mine, and I entered it without knocking, as it was unlikely he'd hear me anyway. Inside, it was much like mine in terms of layout and décor, and thus far even Luke hadn't had enough time to transform it into the sort of pit that he was normally to be found in. He hadn't unpacked yet, so there were no items of clothing strewn all over the floor, while the empties on view were still so few that they only managed to clutter up the table-tops. The bed was certainly messy and crumpled, especially as Luke was currently sprawled out on it, and there was a strong, sour odour – a typical post-party smell, like a combination of stale booze, ciggie smoke, sweat and maybe a faint hint of pot, though so far there was only one half-smoked roach in the ashtray. In fact, when I yanked the curtains open and had a proper look around the room, there was very little evidence of major bingeing; a few beer tins, and a Jack Daniels bottle still with at least a quarter of its contents remaining.

None of this explained the state he was now in. I bent over him to look. He was semi-delirious, drifting in and out of a tortured sleep, froth on his lips, an ashen pallor in his cheeks. I knew that he'd used both heroin and cocaine in the past, but again, on looking around, I saw no evidence that he'd been shooting up or chasing the dragon. It occurred to me that he might have been pill-popping. In fact that was probably what he *had* been doing. I remembered that he'd been calling for codeine the night before. This was very much the thing with Luke; his appetites were so wide-ranging that if he couldn't get his hands on illegal drugs, prescription drugs would do just as well.

"Luke!" I said, leaning over him, tapping his cheek, "come on, mate, snap out of it."

He woke at once, and gazed up through eyes that were like glazed pools. At first he didn't recognise me, but then seemed to focus and a smile cracked open amid his bristles. "Hey … Rick, man."

His breath was indescribably foul.

"What've you been taking to get into this condition?" I asked him.

"Er … no," he mumbled. "Had a clean day, today, mate."

And he tumbled off into sleep again. Suddenly I was alarmed. I'd seen all manner of narcosis over the years, but this was something new.

"Hey!" I shook him hard. "How can you have had a clean day? Look at the state of you."

217

I continued to shake him until at last his eyes flickered open. There was now a yellow tinge to their whites, and his pupils had shrunk to pinpoints. I was just wondering if it might be advisable to call an ambulance, when he began to talk again.

"Need to walk," he blathered, pawing at my arm. "Get ... get some air."

"Couldn't agree more," I said. "Come on."

But he couldn't walk. I managed to get him upright and stand him against me, but, as soon as we set off across the bedroom, he slumped down and it was all I could do to drop him into an armchair before he fell to the floor. Thankfully, at that moment, Joe sloped past the open door, a denim jacket draped over his shoulder.

He spotted us and stopped. "You lot ready?"

I shook my head and indicated Luke. "He's totally out of it."

"Leave him then."

"Uh-uh. I don't like leaving him in the house all night. Not if there's no-one else here."

Joe considered this, then, deciding that it made sense, put his jacket on and came in to help.

"Really surpassed himself this time, hasn't he," he said, as we hefted our former stage-strutter between us and half-carried him out into the passage, then along to the top of the stairs. "He's been like this all sodding day, you know."

Getting Luke down to the hall was more difficult than I'd expected. For all that he'd withered over the years, he was still heavy, and on at least two occasions we almost collapsed in a heap. When we finally reached the ground floor, nobody else had arrived, so we manhandled him across the hall and plunked him down in one of several sofas ranged along the facing wall. By the time the rest of the gang started to gather, he was asleep again, snoring loudly.

Charlie and Barbara turned up at the same time as Troy, all now equipped for a night in the open air – carrying waterproofs, windbreakers, and plastic bags filled with booze and food – and shortly after that Miss Ryder-Howe appeared, clad in a cagoule. She joined the others without once glancing at me, so it was hard to tell whether or not my indirect threat had already been passed on via her snooty employee; but the scornful smirk of before was notable by its absence.

Then, quite unexpectedly, a long-handled croquet mallet was pressed into my hands. I peered down at it, puzzled, then looked up again. Rob was alongside me. He too was armed with a croquet mallet, holding it over his shoulder like a woodsman's axe.

"What's this?" I asked.

"Just a precaution," he said.

"Against what?"

But we weren't able to discuss it because everybody else was ready, and Troy seemed particularly eager to be off. I pointed out the state that Luke was in, but Troy had prepared for this beforehand.

"If you can get him to the front doors, it's all sorted," he said.

We did, Joe and I again hauling the sozzled singer between us. Outside, just at the bottom of the steps, Lionel was waiting on his quad-bike, its engine turning over noisily. As earlier, he'd improvised a trailer by attaching the wheelbarrow to the back of it. The various items of camping gear had already been stowed inside this, but there was room for more. On seeing us, Lionel dismounted and lumbered up the steps to help with Luke.

"Put him on the barrow, Lionel," Troy said.

I pulled a face. "It's not very dignified."

Troy gave me a pitying look, as if wondering – probably with some justification – when it was that I'd suddenly started caring about Luke Hennessey's personal dignity. Besides, there was evidently no other way that we were going to get him out into the Plantation.

Troy nodded to Lionel, who proceeded to pick Luke up in a mammoth bear hug and lay him down in the barrow, on top of the camping gear, where, typically for Luke, he promptly curled up and actually seemed to get comfortable.

It was only then that Troy noticed the coquet mallets that Rob and I were carrying. "What the hell are those for?"

"Self-defence," Rob told him.

Troy frowned. "Against who?"

"Against *what*, don't you mean?" Rob replied. "The New Forest's full of wild boar. You knew that, didn't you, Troy?"

Generally speaking, Troy was difficult to ruffle. But not on this occasion. Clearly he hadn't known about the wild boar, and neither, I must admit, had I, and if the colour drained from our manager's face like ink down a drain, then I'm pretty sure that it did the same with mine.

"Jesus Christ," Troy breathed. "Wild boar?"

"Having second thoughts, are we?" Rob wondered.

Fleetingly, it looked as though Troy might be, but then he shook his head and pushed his glasses back up his nose. "Er ... no. Course not. Why should I?"

"I dunno," Rob replied. "But he who turns and runs away ... "

And with that merry thought, he drifted off in pursuit of Charlie, Barbara and Miss Ryder-Howe, who were now ambling towards the lawn and the dark wall of trees that marked the edge of the Plantation. We set off walking too, in a straggling procession. Lionel had got back on his quad-bike, and chugged up to the front, Luke slumped in oblivion in the carriage behind him.

If Troy had genuinely been unnerved by Rob's comment about boar, it didn't last for long. We were just onto the grass when he reverted back to his glib, chatty self.

"Listen Rick," he said conspiratorially. "Sorry about earlier. That row we had near the coach."

"Wasn't really a row, was it," I replied.

"No. But ... I mean, you weren't serious about pulling out of the project, were you?"

"Not sure yet. We don't seem to be doing much about it, Troy. I mean, nothing creative. We're not even discussing it."

"We will, we will," he tried to assure me. "You know, Rick ... this film score. If you lot put something together that works, well ... it might be a way back into the big time for you."

I glanced sidelong at him. "What, you mean the band? *As* the band?"

"Why not?"

"Why not? Because the sort of heavy rock we used to play doesn't cut it any more."

"Really?" He chuckled. "Heard The Darkness? Heard Queens Of The Stone Age?"

And I had to admit he *did* have a point there. To some extent, quite unexpectedly, hard-edged but melodic rock was regaining some of its old popularity, while the stuff that had finally killed off our interest in the '90s – the thrash-speed genre, and then the wailing, bearded, grunge vintage – had now died its own death. There was one key problem still remaining, of course.

"The trouble is, Troy," I said, "we're all old blokes."

"So what? So's Keith Richards ... and look at the fucking renaissance *he's* going through."

The Plantation now loomed before us. Ash-grey shadows lurked beyond its bulwark of trunks and leafy boughs.

"Rick," Troy added, "... these fucking manufactured acts they've got out there now. They're trash. And everyone knows it. These boy bands, these girl bands, these airbrushed pop idols ... sure, they're news now, but they haven't got the depth to leave a real mark in this business. At the best, they're fucking lounge-singers. They'd never fill Madison Square Garden like you buggers did, I'll tell you that."

"And the world's really waiting for Wolfbane to make a comeback?"

"Listen ... you imprint yourselves on this movie, and they'll certainly give you a chance." Troy was now in full flow, in classic manipulation

220

mode. "Look, Rick ... you've seen the marketing crap that surrounds these box office slammers. The publicity machine will have your faces on billboards, on buses, you name it. If the film's a real hit, you'll never be off the radio. Then there'll be CDs ... DVDs ... 'making of the soundtrack' documentaries. What more do you want?"

I glanced at him again. "You're really serious about this, aren't you?"

"Bloody right I am, pal. The wolf'll howl again, you'll see."

He pointed a determined finger at me. And then, quite suddenly, as though our conversation was over, scampered off to join Joe, who was just about to follow the others into the Plantation.

At first when he'd hooked up with me on that march across the lawn, I'd assumed that Troy had been there to apologise for his odd behaviour. But clearly it hadn't been that at all. If anything, he'd just given me a pep talk. Like a coach would give a player before a crucial match. And, after me, he'd moved on to Joe, and it looked as though he was doing exactly the same thing with him.

10

The trees of the Plantation closed around us like a pair of dusty, green curtains.

That must sound like a very over-the-top description of an English coppice on a warm spring evening, and I can't really deny it. Of course, my previous night's experience had left me prejudiced, though twenty-four hours later, even I, who had run for my life, or so I'd thought, was becoming detached from that experience. It didn't seem as though it had ever happened; it was as if it had been a dream or an active imagination working overtime. To look at the Plantation now, as we wound our way through it, nothing even vaguely sinister came to view. It wasn't as thick and entangled as I remembered. We passed countless open dells, many knee-deep in bluebells and dog's mercury, and all aglow with the setting sun. Somewhere out amid the avenues of trunks, a cuckoo called, and, above our heads, breaks in the canopy revealed a lilac-tinted sky.

Even when we reached the Lamuratum itself, there was a solemnity and grandeur about the standing stones that I hadn't noticed before. The deep, lush stillness in the surrounding woods seem to compliment it rather than render it frightening or mysterious.

Barbara strode forwards, fascinated. "To think that something so fine has been buried at the end of someone's garden all this time."

"It's only a folly, remember," Charlie advised her.

221

"It's impressive, though."

I glanced at Rob. He was regarding the circle of monoliths with dislike and visible trepidation. Their upper portions were flame-red where they caught rays from the setting sun. I imagined evening shadows slowly clustering in the woods around us. Lionel abruptly turned off the engine of his quad-bike, and a heady silence exploded. Momentarily, there wasn't even a twitter of birdsong.

"Something about this place creeped you out yesterday, uh?" Joe said, coming up alongside me. He too was staring at the monument. Blue smoke spiralled from the end of his cig.

"Something about it, yeah," I confessed, still loathe to admit to the phantom shapes that we'd imagined we'd seen.

"Pagan, you see," Joe replied.

I glanced sidelong at him. "Pagan?"

"Yeah ... pre-Christian."

"And that automatically makes it bad?"

"No. But it makes it scary."

And I don't suppose he was too far wrong about that. Britain is planted thick with the relics of lost cultures: barrows, dykes, hill-forts, stone circles and the like, and though all of them attract a high degree of superficial saturnalia, many have a genuinely menacing aura, especially when you see them deserted or at twilight. Their very ancientness commands an awe and respect that most other tourist attractions can only dream about.

"It's only a folly!" Charlie reminded us again, with rather more force than was necessary.

I gazed at him, startled, wondering who he'd been trying to convince the most; Joe and I, or himself.

We unloaded our gear after that, with more speed and precision than our combined lack of experience merited. Luke, who really *was* out for the count by now, was left on a bed of sponge-like moss under the low boughs of a holly tree, while the rest of us unpacked everything. Troy told us there were four tents in all, and paced out an area directly in front of the Lamuratum where he felt we could set them up and get a good campfire going. Lionel assisted in the unloading, but once we had everything we needed, he seemed eager to be off. He hadn't said a word to us – but then I hadn't heard him say a word since we'd arrived here. He hurriedly re-straddled the quad-bike, only for Rob to step into his path.

"Er ... just leave the quad-bike, eh," Rob said. "There's a good lad."

The burly gardener stared at him with a brutish lack of understanding, but made no effort to climb off the bike.

"Does anyone have a problem with that?" Rob asked, turning to look at the rest of us. "I mean, someone may want to nip back to the house for something during the night."

And that *did* seem to make at least a modicum of sense.

Lionel glanced at his mistress, who gave an almost imperceptible nod.

Doggedly, he climbed from the vehicle, and set off along the path at a trudge.

"Lionel," Rob said, "it's no good without the key, mate."

Lionel glanced back, then, rather disconsolately, walked over to Rob and handed him the key. A second later, he was sloping away along the path. I watched his huge back as it retreated through the spreading gloom. Almost certainly he'd set off with the key because he was a big, cumbersome ox who probably made oversights like that all the time. On the other hand, he was the only gardener here, and he was clearly good at it, so perhaps he wasn't quite as muddled as he seemed. And that wasn't an encouraging thought.

"Well," Troy said. "First croquet, now quad-bike riding. You planning a sports evening, Rob?"

Rob turned and looked at him. "Why are you sweating, Troy?"

Troy touched his brow, which was indeed damp with sweat. That seemed to surprise him, and he dabbed at it with a handkerchief. "Lack of exercise. Quite a walk to get here."

"You're not nervous about anything, are you?" Rob wondered.

"*You're* making me nervous," Troy said.

"I'll tell you what." Rob offered him the key, dangling it temptingly by its metal ring. "Why don't I give this to you?"

Troy stared at it. New beads of sweat had already replaced those he'd just wiped away. "What for?"

"A quick getaway, maybe."

"And why would I want to make a quick getaway?"

"You're saying you don't want it?"

Irritably, Troy snatched the key. "I'll hold it, if I must!"

When Rob turned round to me, there was a knowing look on his face, which unnerved me. It seemed to imply that Troy had just failed a very important test.

11

The four tents were each designed to hold two occupants. Barbara and Charlie were obviously going to go into one, while Troy and Miss Ryder-

Howe had bagged another. This meant that either Joe, Rob or me was going to have to share with Luke. Joe volunteered before it became embarrassing. He didn't think it was such a bad idea, he said. Yeah, Luke stank, but he was so stoned that it wouldn't be difficult to shove him over into a corner and get most of the room. This meant that Rob and I would take the final tent, which ordinarily wouldn't be much fun, Rob being so massive and all, though on this occasion I felt it was a good idea.

By nine o'clock that night, with darkness now surrounding us, we were all packaged against a gathering chill and seated around the campfire. As well as sandwiches, pies, cold chicken drumsticks and several flasks of rum-laced coffee, Mrs. Hacket had provided us with jacket-potatoes wrapped in foil, which we were now baking on the ends of sticks. It wasn't the sort of thing any of us had done recently, so the novelty lasted longer than it might normally have. As we did it, Barbara, with a mischievous twinkle in her eye, regaled us with tales of the Girl Guides camping holiday she'd been on up in the wilds of Scotland. Apparently, they'd pitched for one weekend in a pinewood belonging to a remote monastery. It hadn't taken long for some of the monks – and not just the younger ones – to work out that several of the older, more buxom lasses in the party – Barbara in particular, I imagined – knew a bit more about the ways of the world than they should have done; apparently, several 'educational sessions' (educational for the monks, that is) were being held behind a shed in the monastery herb-garden. Joe, less subtle by far, then chipped in with his reminiscences of hippy festivals in the late-'60s, before we'd formed our own band. Once the sun went down, you only had to walk out among the sleeping-bags, and apparently "there was shagging for England, going on".

"Sex under the stars, eh," Charlie said, giving a luxurious stretch. "Dreamy stuff."

Joe unwrapped his potato and started picking at it with a plastic picnic fork. "Don't suppose there'll be much opportunity for that tonight?"

"Speak for yourself," Barbara retorted, putting an arm around Charlie's shoulders.

I glanced across the flames to Miss Ryder-Howe. She was watching me with interest but no longer the predatory anger of earlier. When she realised I was looking at her, she shifted sideways, closing the gap between herself and Troy – as though to hint that I'd missed my chance and that he was next in line for her affections. Troy, for his part, didn't seem to notice. He was peering into the fire, preoccupied and frowning.

"So what exactly are we supposed to gain from this night, Troy?" I asked.

He glanced up. "What? Oh ... atmosphere. Enthusiasm. Spiritual enlightenment."

"Spiritual what?" Joe said, his lips flecked with potato fragments.

Troy prodded at his own sizzling, foil-wrapped orb. "Today's a special day."

I eyed him with interest. Was this it then? Now that we were out here, was he finally going to come clean?

"Go on," I urged him.

He looked up again, the flames reflecting brightly in the lenses of his glasses. "Don't know your classics, I see. Well ... today is May 13th, otherwise known as the Ides of May. It's a very old Roman festival."

There was a brief silence, broken only by the spitting of the flames.

"I've heard of the Ides of March," Charlie said, "but ..."

Troy shook his head. "Every month has its Ides. March is only famous because Julius Caesar got killed on that day. But that was coincidence. The Ides of the month is a benign festival, a good luck thing, even though it always falls on the 13th."

There was thoughtful quiet. The fire continued to snap as we baked and then ate our potatoes. We'd, all of us, looked the Lamuratum over thoroughly on our arrival, and the others had been quite impressed by the Latin characters under the sticky black mess on its central plinth. I'd even brought the dog-eared Anglo-Latin dictionary along with me, in case we found any other inscriptions. But none had come to our attention before, and none did now, even when Rob, Barbara and I, all equipped – somewhat melodramatically – with burning torches, went back and looked inside the thing again.

"Now this really *does* seem spooky," Barbara said.

With the darkness and the fire, and the dancing shadows caused by the encircling monoliths, the interior of the little temple seemed tighter, more confined. There was a strong odour of charcoal. Above us, framed between the flickering orange branches, the night sky was like an awning of black silk.

"You could be right back there with the Romans, couldn't you," she went on. "It makes you wonder even more why the old bloke ... what's his name?"

"Thomas Ryder-Howe," Rob said.

"Thomas Ryder-Howe," Barbara added. "Why he kept it hidden, doesn't it?"

"There are quite a few things you could wonder about where Thomas Ryder-Howe was concerned," Rob replied.

She glanced sidelong at him. "Do tell."

I got the impression that Rob was about to, when there came a sudden, rude interruption.

"Barbara!" It was Charlie, shouting from over where the tents were. Yet again, he sounded uncharacteristically terse and flustered. "Barbara, I can't get this sodding zip on the sleeping-bag down! Give us a hand, will you!"

Barbara rolled her eyes. "Duty calls, I'm afraid. See you in a minute."

She turned and walked out of the Lamuratum. We watched her go. The reflections of our torches flowed rose-red up and down the inner facades of the aged stones.

"So?" I said.

Rob glanced at me. "So what?"

"So what about Thomas Ryder-Howe?"

"Oh that, yeah." He looked guilty, like a schoolboy caught doing something disgusting behind the bike sheds. "Well ... I might as well tell you I suppose. I've done quite a bit of reading today. There are a few good books on those shelves in that room where we had the séance. There're wills, deeds, all that sort of stuff. To do with the estate, you know."

"Sounds like prying?"

He nodded. "It *was* prying. And I'm not ashamed to admit it. Why should I be when our lives might be in danger?"

I looked at him. By his expression, he was perfectly serious.

"Come on Rob, *our lives*?" I didn't want to sound incredulous, but even after everything else that had happened that seemed excessive.

"Just hear me out, Rick. Thomas Ryder-Howe ... remember, he was the bloke who first bought this place from the Brebbingtons. Well, get this ... he was broke. He was a gambler, a ne'er do well. He bought Brebbington Chase entirely on credit."

"Credit? But a place like this would have cost a fortune even then."

"Yet he'd paid all his debts within a year. Including the mortgage on this property."

I couldn't say anything. I didn't have the facts at my fingertips, but it sounded so unlikely as to be almost nonsensical. Drunks and gamblers – even *good* gamblers – do not just conjure up vast fortunes. And they certainly don't see it coming from several months beforehand.

"He was no antiquarian either," Rob added. "Judging by some of the stuff I've been reading, he was more of an occultist."

"Am I missing something here? That book you were absorbed in was all about the Romans."

"No. It was about Roman rituals. Roman religious observances, Roman folklore."

226

He was about to say more when a long low ululation, like the yowl of a wounded animal, interrupted us. It broke off abruptly, and then was followed by another similar sound, this one longer, more drawn-out. And it was this second one that we recognised.

We slipped back out between the pillars into the camp, where Joe and Charlie were half carrying Luke across the clearing towards the tent that he'd been allocated. He'd revived sufficiently to start grinning inanely, and then to throw his head back and howl like a wolf. At least, it was *supposed* to be a howl, though in actual fact it was deliberately a very human sound. On *Boys Who Run With The Pack*, the opening track on our *Eagle Road* album, we'd felt it essential, in order to capture the essence of Romulus and Remus, the twins who would later found Rome, but who at birth had been abandoned in the wild and reared by wolves, that all the animal sounds must issue from human throats – and Luke had obliged us most impressively.

It struck me as he howled again – this time gleefully – that he'd assailed the crowd in similar fashion back at the Free Trade Hall in '78, when they'd picked him up and carried him over their heads.

"He's really overdone it this time," Barbara said.

Luke overdoing it wasn't exactly a new thing in our lives, and Barbara had been present at some of his most spectacular moments, but even she seemed surprised at the mindless level he'd apparently descended to.

"I just don't see how he could have got into this state," I replied.

On the face of it that was a ridiculous comment, because Luke was a past master at getting into any sort of state. But all I could think about was the relatively clean condition of his bedroom, and how little evidence there was that he'd been drinking or doing gear to any greater extent than the rest of us.

For all his continued yipping and yowling, it only took a minute or so to install Luke in his tent, and after that we were able to relax again. We sat around the fire, chatted some more and shared the alcoholic coffee. We covered a variety of subjects, but mainly the old days, past acquaintances, and things we'd each been doing in the meantime. We studiously avoided the subject of the new project. I don't know why this was, but I still don't think that any of us believed it was really going to happen. For the most part, since our glory days had ended, we'd failed in our attempts to remain millionaires. Oh, we were all comfortable, there was no problem there, but once people had stopped buying our music, we'd lacked the wherewithal to generate the vast incomes we were used to by any other means. This movie project could be the solution to all our problems, yet it seemed too good to be true, and I don't think anyone wanted to raise the subject properly until Troy finally sat us down and laid out a properly costed business plan.

We were also getting tired. It wasn't even midnight yet, but despite the fact that we were all time-served ravers, the events of the day – we'd all of us risen relatively early, had put ourselves around and perhaps had taken in more fresh, vital, country air than we were used to – were taking a toll. One by one, we declared ourselves ready for bed. And it was only then, I suppose, that the reality of what we'd let ourselves in for dawned on us. No soft sheets, no plump pillows, no sumptuously furnished bedrooms awaited us; just sleeping-bags, hard ground and tents, the interiors of which have always smelled damp and mildewed to me.

"So, Troy," I said, as we stood up, stretching and yawning, "how exactly is this ordeal you've arranged going to inspire us to write about the Romans?"

He smiled. "Think of yourselves as legionaries on campaign, bivouacking somewhere in Cisalpine Gaul."

"Eh?" Joe said.

"Or here," Troy amended. "Claudius's troops, newly arrived and about to press north into the barbarous interior of the mysterious island that is Britain. And remember that back in 43 AD, that's exactly what *was* happening. Right on this spot."

"Or somewhere near to it," Charlie corrected him.

"Somewhere near to it," Troy agreed.

"Doesn't really work for me, Troy," Rob said dourly.

But Troy made no reply to that. And I noticed that Miss Ryder-Howe, who'd been quiet all night – which was understandable, as she had nothing in common with us, and no past that she could share – was standing inordinately close to him. She was even holding his hand. Fleetingly, I felt contempt for her, that she should be so open and unashamed about her motives. But then I began to think that maybe I was wrong. And the clue seemed to be in her taut body language. There was nothing erotic there, or even vaguely suggestive. Gone was the panting, sensual vamp of earlier; gone the mannered, delightful hostess. If anything, she looked like a frightened little girl. Her posture was stiff, yet she moved uneasily from one foot to the other. A smile was still plastered to her pretty face, as it had been all evening, but it was a phoney smile; it didn't reach her eyes, which seemed to gleam as they were so wide, so visibly frightened.

I didn't comment on this. Not even to Rob, shortly afterwards, when we clambered into our dark, dank tent, thrust our croquet mallets to one side and wormed into our sleeping-bags. I simply pondered it. Was she just unnerved by the proposition of camping out in the middle of a wood when she was no doubt used to greater comfort and security, or was it something else? Did she actually know more about this place than she was letting on?

Rob announced his intention to read for a while, and switched on an electric torch. I didn't object. I'd only removed my trainers, and though it's hardly ideal to try and sleep fully clothed, I was soon snug and relatively warm, and oblivion began to steal up on me. I was probably half way gone when Rob suddenly sat bolt-upright and hissed sharply: "That bloody little bastard!"

"What?" I mumbled, glancing up.

Rob was still staring into his open book. "That bastard Troy was lying to us? About the Ides of May?"

"What about it?"

He shook his head. "This isn't the Ides of May."

For some reason, I woke up fully when he said this. I propped myself on my elbow. "Today, you mean?"

"Yeah. The Ides falls on the 13th of every month with the exception of March, July, October and *May* ... when it falls on the 15th." Now he sat up. "And Troy knew that. He must have."

I sat up too. It didn't take a genius to work out that something was afoot. Troy had specifically brought us out here on this night to bask in the ambience of a Roman festival, the Ides of May, which it actually wasn't.

"So what's today?" I asked. "I mean, what occasion *is* May 13th?"

Rob kicked his way out of his sleeping-bag. "Good bloody question."

"Wait ... what're you doing?" I asked, but he was already climbing down the length of the tent, where he turned awkwardly and began to drag on his boots. A moment later he'd unzipped the flap and started to crawl outside, hauling his croquet mallet behind him. "Rob?"

"I'm going back to the house to check some stuff."

By now he was outside, so I had to crawl out after him. "At this hour?"

He was now standing beside the tent, and glancing around at the fire-lit woods. "It's only ten minutes' walk."

"It's after midnight," I told him.

But he was already on his way, in such haste that he'd forgotten to take the quad-bike, or maybe had *decided* not to as its engine would almost certainly have woken up the others. I gazed after him while he strode off, the mallet over his shoulder, the torchlight bobbing along in front of him. I was unsure what to do. It felt vaguely disloyal not to go along with him, but I'd just got warm and comfortable, and besides, he'd given no indication that he'd expected my company. On top of that, of course, I really didn't fancy traversing that winding path back through the silent, black tangles of the Plantation. I turned and surveyed the encampment. No-one else had been disturbed, and the only sound was the popping and hissing of the fire as it died down into a heap of glowing embers.

Reluctantly, I crawled back into the tent. But when I got in there, I saw Rob's book lying on top of his sleeping-bag. I picked it up. It was open on a page dedicated to the month of *Maius*. With growing interest, I scanned down it. Snippets of scholarly text were attached to many of the dates there listed. As Rob had said, the 15th was indeed the official Ides of the month, but others of note were also mentioned. The 1st and 2nd were named *Floralia*, and deemed sacred to the goddess Flora, patroness of the spring. May 21st was *Agonalia*, and as well as being used to honour Vediovis, was a passage of right for young Roman males, who would receive their first adult toga on this day. May 25th was called *Fortunis*, and was the day on which the goddess of fate and fortune was worshipped. Other dates, however, had no written explanation beside them, and one of these was May 13th, which was simply listed as *Lemuria*.

Which struck me cold.

Because however you look at it, *Lemuria* and Lamuratum don't sound worlds apart from each other.

I flicked through a few additional pages, but found nothing else. Then something occurred to me. It was a long shot, but why not give it a try? I fished into my anorak pocket and produced the dog-eared Anglo-Latin dictionary. It was a small, compact piece of work, and, even as I raced through it, I assumed it would do no more than skim the surface of the Latin language, let alone go into detail about practices and traditions. And I was right. It didn't even mention the word *Lemuria*.

But it did mention the word *lemures*.

Which sounded uncannily similar.

With an odd creeping of my spine, I checked it out.

It read:

Lemures *n. pl.* – the baleful dead

That was all it said. Nothing further was given, no insights offered.

Somewhere in the back of my head, a voice was shouting: "It doesn't mean anything. It's nothing more than an entry in an old, probably discredited book."

But that book fell from my hands all the same. I felt sweat on my face and under my clothes.

May 13th – the Feast of the Baleful Dead.

No, it might not mean anything. It might be entirely a coincidence.

But it didn't bloody sound like one.

230

I pulled my trainers on without even bothering to tie the laces, then scrambled for the entrance, stopping only to grab up my croquet mallet. The next thing I knew, I was crossing the camp, then following Rob along the footpath. He'd be a good ten minutes ahead of me by now; he might already be at the house. The temptation to shout was strong, but I didn't dare. On one hand, I didn't want to alert any of the others – it was still possible that I was foolishly overreacting. But on the other, I didn't want to alert *anybody else*.

I know that must sound ridiculous, but suddenly I was in pitch darkness with deep stretches of woodland on all sides of me, stumbling along a path that I could barely see. In fact, once I'd got a few yards from what remained of our fire, I couldn't see it at all. I frequently veered off it and found myself kicking through undergrowth. On one occasion, I blundered into a tree-trunk. And always there was my memory of the night before, and the gnawing sense that I wasn't alone, that in the distant reaches of this wretched wood someone was listening, just waiting for the first sign that I'd ventured away from the safety of the others. And all the while, that phrase continued to go through my head:

Lemures ... the baleful dead, the baleful dead....

If it had just said 'the dead', or even 'ghosts', I perhaps could have stomached it better. But 'the baleful dead'. Jesus!

Maybe because I was so preoccupied, and also, I don't doubt, because I was refusing to glance either right or left, I emerged from the path onto the lawn with my sanity intact. I glanced around. Only starlight illuminated the open spread of gardens and driveway. There was no sign of Rob. I looked towards the house. Much of the building stood in darkness, but the front door was open and light spilled out. I dashed forwards across the grass, at last feeling brave enough to call out.

"Rob! Rob ... hold up! I've just found something!"

There was no reply, which didn't really surprise me. He was probably in the sitting room, going through the rest of the books. I hurried through the front door into the great hall, where all the lights had been turned on. I'd have made a beeline for the passage leading down to the sitting room if something hadn't stopped me in my tracks.

A gargled choke, which was abruptly cut off.

12

I could not believe what I was seeing.

I *would* not believe it. I simply refused to accept it. And I think that would have been any normal person's response. Forget what you've read in books, or seen at the cinema. When you're actually, in real life, confronted with homicidal violence, especially when it's directed against you or a loved one, you do not go into a heroic action-man routine. In fact, you don't do anything. You are rooted down with shock and horror.

And that was what I felt as I stood there in the doorway to the kitchen at Brebbington Chase. I'd followed the choking sounds to this particular room. It hadn't been hard to find, as it was huge and located just to the rear of the stately dining room. Like everywhere else here, it was spacious and airy and, though equipped with modern fittings, still retained its *olde worlde* charm. The floor was stone-flagged, the ceiling beamed, the walls wainscoted and hung with pots and pans, while the central table was a good fifteen feet in length and made from solid oak.

None of this mattered, however.

All that mattered was the sight of Rob being throttled.

I felt myself go weak at the knees, almost had to lean against the doorframe. But it was happening. It was really happening. And right before my eyes.

Rob was in the process of making a call on the kitchen telephone. Or he'd been *about* to make that call, because, though he still had the receiver in his right hand, Lionel – the gargantuan gardener – had approached him from behind and launched what could only be described as a ferocious attack. Rob was a big fellow, but Lionel was all that and more. He literally dwarfed our former keyboards and percussion man. What was more, he had clearly attacked unseen, for he'd thrust his left arm around Rob's neck from behind, tightened it over the throat and was now yanking Rob's head backwards, exerting a strength and power that was difficult to resist.

As a rule, I don't fight. Why should I? In the latter part of my life I've hardly ever needed to. But that wasn't always the case. When we first formed Wolfbane, we'd all of us shared the same working class background and ethos. More to the point, we'd made a pact that we wouldn't take any shit. Don't get me wrong, we weren't like Zeppelin, whose mean reputation was already known far and wide, but we swore that in tight spots we'd look after each other. And in the very first moment of our very first gig, that vow got put to the test. We were on Tyneside, in one of the roughest nightspots I've ever seen. A minute after we came on stage, a thrown bottle hit Charlie in the face and broke his nose. Joe spotted the miscreant responsible, hurled down his guitar and went into the crowd like a Viking berserker. We all followed and, through sheer defensive anger, we cleaned up the front row yobbos – then, later on, feeding off the same fuel, we cleaned up the club with a blistering set. Of course, in those days we'd been lean and hungry, and since then I'd grown lax, soft. I might still have been trim because I worked out. I might have looked good because I lived in a healthier climate than Great Britain's. But I hadn't thrown a punch or kicked an ass in as long as I could remember. Even so, the fact was that Rob was being murdered right in front of my eyes. The bear-like Lionel was apparently intent on snapping his neck.

I advanced towards them slowly, unwillingly, all the while wishing that this wasn't happening. And Rob was the one who saw me first. The eyes were straining like cue balls in his sockets, already crimsoned with broken blood vessels. There was spew and froth all over his mouth. I needed no further invitation.

I threw the croquet mallet over my shoulder like a battle-axe, and made a furious charge.

If I'd really been an old-fashioned warrior, I'd have struck hard and true without giving my opponent any warning. However, the semblance of a civilised man remained. I wanted him to desist, to back off, to surrender before we even engaged. So I shouted, in fact roared, letting him know that I was coming. The giant looked sharply round. But the eyes, which earlier on I'd seen glazed with apparent docility, were now feral. The carroty red 'village idiot' hair was matted across his florid brow with licks of sweat. He knew exactly what he was doing, and he wasn't going to stop it now. All the same, he had to respond to my threat.

I swung the croquet mallet down in a full overhead arch, but he moved with amazing agility for a man of his size, and threw up his left forearm to deflect it. The next thing I knew, he'd released Rob, dropping him face-first onto the kitchen table, and was aiming a blow at me with his massive right fist. I ducked it, and drove my mallet upwards into his ribs. It impacted solidly, but there was no great power behind it, and this time he managed to grab hold of it, which left him free to punch me again. He drew his ham-fist back, but forgetting about Rob had been a mistake. Rob was still conscious: his face was slathered with spittle, his eyes leaking blood, but his mouth had twisted with rage. Because he didn't have any other weapon to hand, he struck hard with the telephone receiver.

Lionel didn't see it coming. It smashed across the side of his head and burst apart with the impact. Even then though, aside from knocking the giant sideways, it had no discernible effect. Lionel hadn't uttered a sound during the entire fight, and he didn't do now. He just responded to this new assault with a huge, well-aimed left hook, which connected cleanly with Rob's jaw and slammed him backwards onto the table.

With Rob out for the count, the giant turned back to me, but I was ready for him. I'd hauled the croquet mallet from his grasp, and now

233

swept it around in a wide circle. It whacked him full in the side of the face. The *crack* was deafening. A broken, bloody tooth flitted from his scrunched-up mouth. He went staggering leftwards, caromed off the cast-iron cooking range, and fell chest-first to the floor.

This time, his eyes had rolled white even before his face smacked onto the flagstones.

I stood there breathless, racked with pain even though I hadn't taken a single blow. Then I scrambled to the table to check on Rob. Once again, my makeshift medical expertise came into play. He was out cold but breathing; his heart rate seemed steady. There wasn't much more I could do, other than check around his neck to ensure there was no obvious damage there, then roll him over into the recovery position. After that, I stepped back and scanned the wreckage of the room, trying to piece together what had happened. A book lay on the table top. By the looks of it, Rob had gone back into the sitting room and found something. Whatever it was, it had prompted him to come straight in here and make a phone-call, almost certainly to the police. Lionel, probably acting under orders, had been lying in wait, and had viciously intervened.

I looked at the telephone receiver. It was shattered; just sharp fragments of plastic and a nest of twisted wires. I had my mobile, but if I rang someone for help, what was I supposed to tell them?

I snatched up the book. This one was titled *Ancient Feasts and Ceremonies*. It was already open on the page I sought:

LEMURIA: Day of the Baleful Dead

Eight paragraphs of detailed text followed.

I read them with trepidation, and fairly soon my blood was running cold. I didn't want to believe what I was seeing. I wanted to scoff, to wave it all aside as superstitious mumbo-jumbo. Yet it all fell so perfectly and horribly into place.

I dropped the book and glanced sideways to where Rob still lay unconscious. He might be out for ages yet. It left me no choice, I realised. I had to go back to the camp alone, and I had to go quickly. It was imperative that I get them all out of there and back to the safety of the house. If safety could be found on such an occasion as this.

I blundered down the main hall towards the still-open front door. Outside, I cut across the drive and then the lawn, making towards the wall of black and silent trees. So panic-stricken was I that I hadn't even thought to bring the electric torch, which must have been lying around in the kitchen somewhere. Having a source of light with me would have been more than useful, but my mind was too filled with other things, namely the passages I'd just read in that book – the passages that described the *lemures* in such hideous detail.

The *lemures*.

The 'baleful dead'.

In more specific parlance: those unquietly or ruthlessly slain, those murdered or massacred, those for whom there was no memorial or justice. Most often, it had referred to Roman soldiers killed in battle, particularly if that battle had been a defeat, because then no sacred offerings would have been made at the end of it.

I followed the path like a madman, sweat stinging my eyes, blinded by the dark yet weaving my way among the groping trees with unerring accuracy.

I didn't believe it, I told myself. I didn't believe *any* of it.

Yet could it really be coincidence? That we were here on this day – the day of the *lemures*, on this very spot, the ancient battlefield where several cohorts of the Second Legion were annihilated? Or that we were beside the Lamuratum, which, it was now clear to me, Thomas Ryder-Howe had erected as a glorification of those who fell! (For had it not also been written in that book that the *lemures*, if suitably honoured, would grant boons from the afterlife? And in the case of Thomas Ryder-Howe, hadn't those boons been spectacular indeed?)

"Troy … you can not be doing this!" I jabbered as I ran. "You can't! You mustn't!"

Don't get me wrong. I was born a Christian, but I've never lived a Christian life. The only god who ever mattered to me was Mammon. At one time, I'd happily have knelt at a heathen shrine if it meant a fabulous reward. But this wasn't so simple. Not according to the book I'd just read. For the 'baleful dead' were not called *baleful* for nothing. Doffing your cap, muttering a few prayers, even raising a circle of standing stones would never quite be enough for them. No, to win their favour, a greater, more terrible restitution was first required.

I came stumbling to the edge of the camp, then stood there on the rim of the firelight, glancing around. Nothing appeared to be moving. All of the tents, with the exception of our own, were zipped up, closed off against the night.

The sweat poured off me. My heart was thumping. But in truth I wasn't entirely sure *what* I'd been expecting to find: perhaps Troy behaving like some maniac, creeping around with God knows what implement in his hand? It was all nonsense, I told myself. It *had* to be. Yet, a few moments ago, the horrors inscribed in that book had seemed so real that they'd prompted Rob to make a phone-call to the police, and had caused me to come dashing back out here.

235

I stood there helpless, surveying the scene. Clearly no-one had been disturbed. The silence I could hear was the silence of sleep. In which case, would they thank me if I woke them on a whim, and an apparently nonsensical whim at that?

I deliberately held myself back, my palms slick on the haft of the croquet mallet.

Then I heard something.

A faint rustle in the undergrowth.

My nerves went taut as cello strings; I'd attuned myself to react to the slightest sound. I spun around and stalked across the camp to the far side, from which direction the sound had come. It was only Dutch courage of course, a bravery inspired by the fight-or-flight mechanism. And even then it didn't extend so far as to make me risk a glance at the Lamuratum, which stood ominously to my right. By the time I entered the bushes, fresh sweat bathed my brow. My hair was now a sodden mop. My belly flopped over and over. I pressed on, thrusting my mallet through every mass of vegetation that came in front of me, ready to swing it like a sledgehammer at the first sign of danger. And because I was so wired, I barely noticed when a figure came casually up through the dimness behind and stood alongside me. A second passed before I realised he was there.

I turned wildly, a scream stuck in my throat.

But it was only Joe. He gazed at me, puzzled, over the red tip of his cigarette.

"What are you doing?" he asked.

"What am *I* doing?" I wanted to sit down. In fact, I *needed* to. I overbalanced and had to support myself on a tree. The croquet mallet slid from my grasp. "I could ask the same bloody thing of you."

He took his cig out. "I'm having a stroll."

"A stroll?"

"Yeah … just making a quick recce."

I shook my head. "You've been out here all this time?"

"A few minutes, yeah."

"Jesus Christ!" I almost laughed. "You're telling me it's you I've just heard?"

Joe frowned. "I don't get you."

"I thought I heard someone prowling around. That's what *I'm* here for. To see who it is."

"Well that's why *I* came out here?"

"Eh?"

"I thought *I* heard something."

"Well it can't have been me," I replied. "I've only just arrived."

236

He pondered this, then took another drag on his cig. "Well, it's all right. It's probably nothing."

It didn't seem likely that it was *nothing*, but at that moment I was too relieved about finding Joe there to give it any thought. Even a split-second later, when we both heard the almost infinitesimal *snap* of a twig, we dismissed it. In fact, after briefly scanning the surrounding darkness, we looked at each other and grinned.

And that was when the javelin came hurtling through the moonlight.

It flew silent and deadly. The first I knew of it, a fleeting blur of steel had passed my eye-line, then I heard a heavy, sickening *thud* as it struck home – as it hit Joe in the left shoulder, driving him backwards and pinning him bodily to the trunk of a tree.

13

At first Joe was too stunned to react. Then he gave a hoarse scream, which rose rapidly to a shockingly shrill crescendo.

I grabbed hold of the javelin with both hands and tried to yank it free. Joe writhed in agony, but remained firmly spitted. I ended up having to plant my left foot against the trunk, and lean backwards with all my weight, to try and get the missile to dislodge. When it finally did, there was a loud *thunk* and an even more intense shriek from Joe. I fell backwards onto my arse. Joe hunched forwards. His screams broke down into a series of gasps and pants.

I clambered back up, gazing at the weapon. It comprised a trimmed wooden shaft with a weighted metal head now slick with gore. But there was no time to examine it properly. Joe glanced up and, even in the half-light, I saw the eyes bulge in his tortured face. A strangled shout burst from his lips.

I turned, still holding the javelin.

The smell was perhaps the first thing I noticed, a mingled aroma of earth and forest-mould. But then I *saw* them too.

They had emerged in silence from the foliage and were now spreading out to encircle us with clumsy, awkward movements. They were spindly, stiff, scarecrow-like, and there were vast numbers of them. I couldn't make a head-count, but even as I watched, more and more came hobbling through the trees to crowd around us.

I heard Joe whimper.

Then they attacked.

Again I was ready for fight-or-flight. It wasn't a matter of courage. It was a simple chemical reaction inside me, and it virtually exploded.

As the first one came lunging in, I drove the javelin point-first at its chest, entirely running it through and shoving it backwards. But as I did, I saw things that I'll never forget: limbs that were little more than bones wrapped in shrivelled flesh; tarnished metal plating; bare ribs showing through rotted leather.

Then I'd grabbed up the croquet mallet and was whirling it around my head.

I landed blow after blow – massive, cranium-shattering impacts – and figures went down left and right. There were dry *crunches*, hollow *cracks*, and bell-like *clatters* as the wooden hammerhead impacted on aged iron helms; but each time the ghastly things were back on their feet and closing to attack again. Even the one I'd impaled was unhindered. It lurched back towards me and struck with an edged weapon, which sheared clean through the haft of the mallet, leaving me unarmed. I twirled around, took Joe under his armpit and tried to steer him away.

We stumbled rather than ran and, all the way, clawing, twig-like hands raked at our faces. Directly in our path, an upright, convex shield appeared, hung all over with rotted, stinking hide. It was thrust straight at us, and, behind it, I fleetingly saw a face that was more like a mask cut in parchment. So wild was our flight, however, that we buffeted it aside. Spears were driven at us, there was more clawing, more scrabbling. We responded in kind, kicking, pushing. Even Joe, wounded as he was, snarled and spat and lashed out with his good arm. And now the camp was ahead, looming through the pillars of the trees, and there was movement there. Our screams and shouts had sounded the alert.

It was total confusion as we scrambled in among the tents. Charlie and Barbara, dishevelled but awake, had risen first. They'd quickly piled fresh fuel on the fire to give us light.

"What's going on?" Charlie demanded.

"Hurry!" I panted. "For Christ's sake, we've got to get out of here now … *right now!*"

And one proper look at the state of us – for Joe was staggering, his t-shirt and denims running with blood, while I had blanched white with terror – was enough to show them how deadly serious we were.

"We've got to wake the others," Barbara said.

Frankly, I couldn't believe they hadn't already woken. I pushed Joe into Charlie's arms and dashed to the nearest closed tent. I dropped to my knees and yanked the zip down. But what I saw inside that tent made me recoil in shock even under *these* circumstances.

Troy and Miss Ryder-Howe were already awake and fully dressed. Troy was kneeling upright, our hostess cowering behind him. The eyes were gigantic behind the lenses of his glasses; his brow was furrowed and beaded with sweat. What really shook me, though, was that he was fending me off with what looked distinctly like a Luger pistol.

It only took a split-second for the full penny to drop.

"You son of a bitch!" I roared. "You knew this would happen! You even came armed!"

He cocked the pistol. "Get back, Rick. You don't know what you're saying."

"You fucking son of a bitch!"

"Get back!" he said again, now shooing me out as he crawled forwards.

I retreated, to afford him room. "It's you who'd better get back," I said. "Back to that God-damned house. Those things are all over the sodding Plantation. You bastard ..."

"What the hell is going on?" Charlie demanded. He was clinging hard onto Joe, who looked ready to faint. Barbara was assisting as best she could. Blood dabbled all their clothes.

"Don't ask." I ushered them all across the camp. "Just get back to the house now."

"Joe's mumbling something about Halloween costumes," Barbara said.

"Hah ... I wish!"

I'd have liked to tell her more, but other things were now distracting me: Troy for one, frantic-eyed, soaked with sweat, and wafting the Luger around as though ready to shoot everyone; and a renewed thrashing in the undergrowth from all sides of us.

We turned, each one in a different direction, and each one sighting something different yet equally indescribable – some nightmare form encroaching from the leafy shadows, something black or green, ungainly and bent, clad in filth-caked rags, mottled plate-armour and hanging leather bindings. Troy and I looked towards the Lamuratum, where all manner of movement was visible beyond the rib-like monoliths, where all types of scrapes and shuffles issued from the hidden depths. Troy didn't wait to see any more. He pointed the Luger and fired a single shot, which *crashed* and *crashed* in the clearing, and an instant later ricocheted with a scream as the bullet rebounded from one of the pillars. And then he was off, zigzagging across the camp, abandoning us almost as callously as he'd brought us here, aiming straight for the quad-bike, which was standing alone behind one of the tents. Without a backwards glance, he leaped upon it, dug the key from his pocket and jammed it into the ignition. The machine thundered to life and Troy was away, leaning forwards over the bars yet handling the machine deftly, so deftly that I thought he must have been practising, which might well have been the case, the traitorous bastard.

He skidded across the clearing, taking one of the tents down, fishtailed on the dewy grass, and then accelerated headlong into the black throat that was the path. In an instant it was over. He'd gone, and we were alone, hemmed in by the rustlings and the cracklings and the repeated *slithering* of steel as it was drawn from a hundred ancient scabbards.

The most startled among us was Miss Ryder-Howe. Clearly she and Troy had cooked up this scheme together, yet now, at the critical moment, she was being left behind. I couldn't help but think: "Welcome to the rock world, love".

She began screaming hysterically. So much so that I dashed at her and slapped her across the face. Not that the rest of us remained cool and level headed. We turned en masse, and scrambled off along that benighted trail in a disorganised scrummage, knocking into one another, tripping, cursing, egging each other on – not just verbally, but with pushes and shoves. And all the while I sensed the pursuit in the surrounding undergrowth. Horrific images still spun in my mind's eye: bare ribs under ragged mail, yawning sockets emptied of eyes. My head felt ready to burst. I wanted to screech. But the thought of getting even with Troy kept me focussed. Somewhere ahead in the darkness, I could still hear the whining of the quad-bike as he negotiated every twist and turn. It spurred me to run all the harder.

It's astonishing how when you're *really* fleeing for your life, it's genuinely a case of every man and woman for themselves. I wasn't aware whether anybody was assisting Joe, and he'd lost so much blood that he surely needed assistance. But *I* wasn't doing it, and in my panic I made no effort to look for him to check. We just shunted each other along, jostling, shouting, not stopping to help anyone who fell. And then, suddenly, directly ahead, there was a dull glimmer of star-lit sward. The lawn. We broke for it, charging pell-mell out into that open space, where Troy was waiting for us, still saddled on the quad-bike. He'd made a wide circle, and was now bearing uncertainly back towards us, the engine revving, the headlamp playing over our wet, chalk-white faces.

"You bastard!" Miss Ryder-Howe shrieked, running at him. "You left me!"

He wove the bike around her, pulling it up alongside the rest of us. "Everyone here? Okay, quick … we've got to get back indoors?"

There was a demented gabble of voices, furious demands for explanations and further agonised groans from Joe. I shoved my way into the middle. "Everyone shut the fuck up! I've got to make a head-count."

240

It didn't take long to work out that we were one short.

"Shit!" I hissed. "Oh shit! Oh fucking shit ... Luke! *Are you fucking dipsticks telling me no-one thought to bring Luke?*"

There was a stunned silence. Everyone gazed accusingly at everyone else.

I rounded on Troy. "Gimme the bike!"

I swear I saw the whites of his eyes as he stared back at me. "Are you crazy?"

"Gimme the bike!" I held out a shaking hand. "And the gun!"

Troy shook his head. "Rick, he's gone, man ... leave him."

"You son of a bitch!" And I stuck my fist under his chin.

He flew backwards, landing hard on the grass, his glasses dislodged. I heard the air *whoosh* out of him, then wild and angry exclamations from the others. But I ignored them all. A moment later I was astride the vehicle, which still throbbed with life, and the Luger was in my pocket.

I hadn't ridden any kind of motorised bike for several years, but even if I say so myself, at first I handled that four-wheeled hog like a past master. I tore along the wooded path at breakneck speed, taking deadly curves, leaping over ruts, swerving and skidding through the mud patches, but always maintaining a direct course. Again though, I was acting on pure instinct. If I'd actually been *thinking*, I'd probably have been headed the other way. Not that a sense of horror and dread wasn't slowly overwhelming me. The deeper into the Plantation I rode, the more I saw grotesque figures darting back and forth ahead of me.

I kept going, hammering the throttle, the sweat streaming cold on my face. Also ahead, dancing in glimpses between the trees, I could see firelight – *our* firelight, though figures now seemed to be milling around in it.

I wanted to shout: "Luke! Hang on buddy, I'm almost there!"

But Luke shouted first.

Or rather *howled*, like a wolf – that long, low, semi-delirious ululation that was so familiar.

A bolt of ice went through me. Tears blurred my eyes as I saw him again, in the midst of the mayhem, being carried head-high by the frenzied crowd at the Free Trade Hall.

And now I *did* scream: *"Luke! Luke ... wake up man!"*

But it was too late. Because now they were onto me, ragged hordes of black and twisted things suddenly swarming out from either side of the path. I shrieked for them to get out of my way, then ploughed right into them, *crunched* headlong into their midst as though driving through a cluster of saplings. There was a furious grinding of metal, a tearing and snapping of fibrous limbs, and then bodies were being hurled aside or

241

going down flailing beneath my wheels. The next thing, the world turned upside-down: the quad-bike flipped over and I was flung hard onto the verge. I took the brunt of it on the right shoulder and the right-hand side of my head. It knocked me senseless, and for some time I lay there grovelling in the leaf-rubble and what I assumed was a pool of my own vomit. But even groggy, I knew that I wasn't alone. With agonised dizziness, I was able to look up.

The crash had put out the headlight, so I wasn't quite sure what I beheld, but they stood all around me – those that were still capable of standing, for I had mown a good number of them down – and I had the distinct impression that, beneath their dented plate and mildewed leather, they were more bones and filth than actual flesh. Further proof came in their stench. Perhaps because several among them had now been smashed and mutilated by the collision, torn through to whatever corrupted innards they still possessed, a foetid stink of death filled the air. But it was only when they finally closed in around me, when their twig-like fingers began to grope through my hair and over my face, that I saw them for what they truly were; that my eyes attuned sufficiently to focus on the grinning, yellowed teeth beneath their visors, on the bony juts of jaw to which strands of hair and scabrous threads of skin still clung.

I shouted in delirious horror, struggled madly to resist – but I was still in a daze, one half of my body numbed, my head spinning. And the blows I struck were weak, futile. As they took hold of me with their cold, dead talons, I spotted one who stood back from the others and seemed simply to watch. And bizarrely, I found myself gesturing to him, beseeching him for mercy, for forgiveness for whatever transgression I'd committed. There was no glint of life in the cavernous hollows of his eyes, yet I knew he could help if he had a mind to, for I felt the command and power in his posture, in the remnants of the purple robes draped over his kite-like torso, in the circlet of laurel leaves clasped on his desiccated skull. Still though, he watched, unmoved, and now I glimpsed the aged rusting weapons – the short swords, the daggers, the falchions – rising slowly around me. Hysterically, I knocked their withered claws away and scrabbled about for the Luger, which I'd dropped when thrown from the bike. My hand closed upon it and, with a triumphant yell, I swept it up – only to feel it wrenched from my grasp before I could even fire it. And then they'd seized me again, by the throat, by the hair, by the chin, craning my neck back so that I could see my death as it descended.

I choked and spat, swore, screamed hoarsely, stared bug-eyed at the storm of downwards-pointed blades, the firelight glinting wickedly on their corroded tips.

The firelight – *which suddenly was magnified a hundred-fold.*

242

Despite everything else, I ripped myself free of their grasp and looked around, astonished. Shafts of glaring light now flooded through the meshwork of branches. A wave of heat came with it, and immediately I knew what had happened. A bonfire of immense proportions had suddenly roared up into the night. As I strained my eyes to penetrate the thickets, I could *see* it, sparks shooting into the air from a mighty surge of flame.

And in that moment, I was transfixed – not just with surprise, but with despair.

For I knew what it signified.

Then I was flung carelessly aside. My head struck the ground again, and unknown seconds passed before I could look up once more.

I'd been abandoned, alive but unimportant, beside the crushed wreckage of the quad-bike.

Not that my ambushers weren't still visible. From the corner of my eye, I spied their hideous shadows cavorting off through the trees like a flock of silent bats. They weren't fleeing, however. Quite the opposite. If there'd been tongues in their empty throats, I'd have heard them cheering, roaring, baying with wild adulation. And if I hadn't been on the verge of complete mental collapse, I'd have seen them more clearly – capering joyously back towards the exact location of the roaring fire.

Towards the Lamuratum.

14

The plan – the very loose and makeshift plan – was to call at hospital in Southampton, to ensure first that Rob's dizzy spells were nothing more than concussion, and then to get Joe's dressing changed and check that he wasn't suffering from blood-poisoning. Though, as he said himself, if he *was* he'd probably know about it by now. And that was true. Because over twelve hours had elapsed since he'd received the wound, and, though he was stiff and ashen-faced with pain, he sat on the coach in otherwise stoic silence.

We all did. We *all* sat that way on the coach, gazing out at the rolling green lawns and the magnificent white-stone manor house, again basking in the mellow sunlight of another delightful May afternoon. Dusk was fast approaching, however, and we were anxious to be off.

At length, Troy came aboard. He too was a little pale around the gills. One side of his jaw was visibly swollen and discoloured, but he'd produced a new set of glasses from somewhere and had spent the best part of the day straightening out his crumpled suit.

He made his way down the aisle towards us warily, but still managing to force a smile. First off, he stopped beside Joe. "How's the shoulder?" Joe shrugged sullenly. "Don't worry ... it's only the left one. I'll still be able to play."

There was an awkward silence. Troy turned, sensing that the rest of us were watching him. He made a vague gesture. "I promise, you'll all thank me for this in a few months' time."

"Apart from Luke," I said.

Troy shook his head with feigned regret. "I already told you, Luke was finished. There was no role for him in this new project."

Just at that moment, with uncannily perfect timing, Lionel came marching past outside. He too bore the scars of last night's battle, but he also had recovered. He now lumbered along, shoving the wheelbarrow. He'd come from the direction of the Plantation and was no doubt bound for some hidden compost heap in a forgotten corner of the grounds. His mother, the ice-cold Mrs. Hacket, who, among other things, I now realised with disgust, had prepared Luke's breakfast on the fatal morning, strode along behind him. Normally, I imagined she left all the outdoors work to her ox-like son, though on this occasion – and probably *only* on this occasion – she felt it necessary to keep her beady eye on him throughout.

I didn't need to look down through the window to know what his wheelbarrow's contents would be: great dismembered hunks of butchered, sticky char.

My gorge threatened to rise, and inwardly, for about the twentieth time, I cursed myself. Cursed myself for being so ineffective, for not seeing it coming before I did, for having to have the entire thing thrust down my throat before I took action, for needing to read about it in that final book, for needing to actually see on the printed page that the only certain way to appease the *lemures* was to offer them a captured chieftain or something very similar: a defeated leader, a broken hero, a fallen prince.

I didn't say anything else to Troy after that. Not even when he made his way down the bus and asked me if *I* was okay. Like Rob, I kept my trap shut. It was surely apparent to anyone with eyes that I wasn't okay. I was sorely bruised from my crash on the quad-bike, and, despite the long shower I'd taken that morning after being found sprawled and raving on the Plantation path, livid claw-marks were still visible all over my face, neck and arms. It was the inside of me, though, that had *really* been wounded. To be made party to such an atrocity, even without my knowledge, was more than I could bear to contemplate.

And when Troy tried to allay our dismay, he only made things worse.

244

"He'll not be found, or even missed," he explained. "Look ... the guy had alienated himself from just about everyone. He was living in a squat in Wandsworth when I found him. I doubt anyone even knew he was there."

We still said nothing, just sat in stony silence.

A short while later, Miss Ryder-Howe came on board. She was dressed brightly, as though for a holiday, and was wearing mirrored, wraparound shades. The driver, who'd returned to the mansion mid-morning, helped her carry on a couple of bulging suitcases. Troy hastened to assist. It seemed that she'd already forgiven his betrayal of the night before. She was clearly determined to do as well out of this project as it was possible to, and I think that stuck in my craw more than anything else. You'll notice that I've steadfastly refused to refer to Lucille Ryder-Howe by her first name alone. That's because I can't. It's because calling someone by their first name implies at least a modicum of warmth or companionship. Lucille Ryder-Howe was none of these things to us. Granted, she hadn't been the instigator of the plot, but she'd gone along with it, and her prime intent had been to get rich on the back of it. Or should I say, rich*er*. Because she was already very rich. I mean, she might have pleaded poverty to us because she couldn't afford the full upkeep of her stately inheritance, but she could just as easily have sold Brebbington Chase, bought a luxury five-bedroom detached in the suburbs and lived out the remainder of her life in the sort of comfort and security that ninety per cent of the British population are denied. To kill in order to get rich is bad enough, but I don't think there's a lower creature on Earth than he or she who kills to get rich*er*.

I'm being hypocritical, of course.

Despite my disapproval now, and my apparent rejection of Troy Tooley and all that he stands for, I strongly suspect that I'll play bass on the new soundtrack, and that I'll take my cut as willingly as all the rest. In fact, if I'm true, I've already started to make excuses to myself about this: it's because of the ordeal we went through – who wouldn't endure such horror and not want compensation for it? And, if nothing else, it'll be a memorial for Luke; he paid the ultimate price, so the least the rest of us can do is get the whole thing moving – he'll still be credited, because he was instrumental in writing the original *Eagle Road* album.

Yeah, right.

So here we are, all set to drive away from Brebbington Chase, after several days that never happened, towards an unknown but undeniably promising future. The blockbuster movie *will* be made, and we *will* get our shot at writing the score. And for all my disgust and fury, it goes against every instinct I have to turn my back on the potential rewards of such an endeavour. I can only hope and pray – if I *dare* pray – that in due course, when *I, Caesar* is in the can, and the music for it has won a succession of Oscars, and we're all millionaires again, that the events played out here at Brebbington Chase will become nothing more than a blip in time, a footnote of history that will quickly dwindle to insignificance, just like the slaughter of those men of the Second Legion on this very same spot nearly two millennia ago.

Of course, it's never that simple.

I'm not a literary man, but I can't help remembering a quote from Shakespeare's *Titus Andronicus*, at the point in the play where the victorious Roman general addresses the beaten barbarian queen, and draws her attention to his dead soldiers:

> *'Religiously they ask a sacrifice:*
> *To this your son is marked, and die he must,*
> *To appease their groaning shadows that are gone.'*

Eloquently put, as always.

And deeply distressing.

Because, for all the wealth and glory that awaits us, in *my* mind at least, there is one lonely shadow who now will groan for evermore.

Gray Friar Press

Check out these other great titles at the GFP website . . .

- Poe's Progeny – 30 great new horror stories
- Bernie Herrmann's Manic Sextet – six dark novelettes
- Dark Corners – short stories by 'Afterlife' creator Stephen Volk
- The Faculty of Terror – John Probert's portmanteau horror novel
- Stains – novellas and short stories from Paul Finch
- Dirty Prayers – short stories by Gary McMahon
- Rain – a devastating novella by Conrad Williams
- Hard Roads – two novellas from Steve Vernon
- The Appetite – a novella by Nicholas Royle
- Passport to Purgatory – short stories by Tony Richards
- The Impelled and Other Head Trips – short stories by Gary Fry
- Mindful of Phantoms – a new collection by Gary Fry
- Pictures of the Dark – short stories by Simon Bestwick

www.grayfriarpress.com

Printed in the United Kingdom by
Lightning Source UK Ltd., Milton Keynes
141139UK00001B/28/P